MW00816761

RUTHLESS ENFORCER

by Lucy Monroe

1st Printing 2023

COPYRIGHT © 2023 LUCY MONROE

ALL RIGHTS RESERVED

No part of this book may be reproduced, scanned, or distributed in any printed or electronic form without express, written permission from the author Lucy Monroe who can be contacted off her website http://lucymonroe.com.

This is a work of fiction. Names, characters, places, and incidents either are the product of the author's imagination or are used fictitiously, and any resemblance to actual persons, living or dead, business establishments, events, or locales is entirely coincidental.

RUTHLESS ENFORCER

LUCY MONROE

LUCY MONROE LLC

DEDICATION

We are all broken. That is how the light gets in. – Ernest Hemingway

Writing about broken and imperfect people finding love and acceptance is one of my favorite things. A perfect vessel doesn't allow anything in. Not light. Not moisture. Not sustenance. It is completely self-contained, but that is not how human beings survive. We are in this thing called life together.

This book is for all of the imperfect people who enrich my life and accept me for the less than perfect person that I am. Especially my husband, Tom and my oldest and dearest friends, Mona, Myra & Carolyn.

*Greek Mafia Hierarchy**

***Ádis Adelfótita* | Hades Brotherhood**

Territory: West Coast & Parts of Western Canada

***Nonós tis Nýchtas* | Godfather of the Night**

Constantin Petros

***Kai* | Second-in-Command**

Tobias Nikolaides

***Eidikós* | Specialist: Lawyer**

Vasileos Rokos

***Anax* | Head of the Local Territory**

Zeus Rokos

***Kai* | Second-in-Command**

Orion Rokos (Lawyer)

***Eidikós* | Specialist**

Enforcer & Assassin

Atlas Rokos

***Eidikós* | Specialist**

BookkeeperHelios Nikolaides

***Eidikós* | Specialist**

Smuggling & Weapons

Zephyr Nikolaides

* While the criminal syndicates found in this book are loosely based on known hierarchies within Greek mafia and Russian bratva organizations, they are fictional. They do not represent any actual mafia or bratva family. Nor are their hierarchies meant to be an exact replica, but rather inspired by research.

PROLOGUE

LUCIA

5 Years Ago

Porca miseria!

The left side of my head throbs. There is a faint tang of copper in my nose and on my tongue.

Opening my eyes, I groan. The sunlight coming in through the open curtains is too bright. I am on the floor of my father-in-law's office.

I sit up, shifting so I can lean against the side of the desk. Trying to remember how I got here, I reach up to my forehead. It hurts. I touch something wet and sticky and look at my fingers. I blink. They are smeared with red. Blood.

Memory comes back in disjointed flashes.

Leo screaming at me. Trying to shove me at the safe. Shaking me so my head snaps back and forth on my neck. Me falling.

Terror makes my heart pound erratically in my chest. I jerk up onto my knees so I can see the gun safe. It's still closed.

Grazie a Dio. Thank God.

Relief washes over me. I didn't open it for him.

Leo needs professional help. However, my husband, Tino, and his father insist I figure out how to care for Leo on my own. We don't go outside the family for help.

Only, there is no one in the Detroit Cosa Nostra trained to deal with a man who suffered traumatic brain injury at the age of twelve. Leo is now 20, only three years younger than me, but he still responds like the twelve-year-old he was when he took a shot to the head while out learning the business with his father.

Only now he's the same six feet tall as his brother and equally as strong. However, while Tino would never hurt me, Leo has. Not on purpose, but that doesn't change the outcome. This is only the second time he's gotten this bad.

My mind shies away from memories of the first episode like this and what it cost me.

I don't know how long I've been knocked out, or where Leo has gone. I can't expect help from Tino or my father-in-law. They are doing their weekly inspection of the nightclubs they run for the Cosa Nostra and will not be home much before dawn.

Leo didn't get into the gun safe though, and for that I have to be grateful. He is obsessed with the idea of becoming a made man like his father and brother.

The prospect of the unpredictable man with a mind of a child carrying a gun and thinking it is okay to kill people sends chills down my spine.

My phone rings and I pull it from the back pocket of my jeans.

My father-in-law prefers me in dresses, but during the day while he and Tino are gone, I wear casual clothes and tennis shoes. Keeping up with Leo requires flexibility of movement and the ability to run, even on the marble floors that cover so much of the first floor of the mansion.

The phone keeps ringing and I see that it is Tino. I tap to answer. "Hi, Tino."

"Listen, *amore mio*, there's paperwork in the safe that has the information you need to access my accounts in the Caymans. Get it and then you and Leo have to get out of there."

"Tino—"

He cuts me off. "Go to the cabin and wait for me to call you there."

I don't waste time trying again to ask why, or what's going on. Tino's voice is tight with tension and an emotion I don't think I've ever heard in it before. Fear.

"Okay. I'll get Leo and we'll go."

"*Ti amo.*" In the three years we've been married, Tino has only told me he loves me three times.

When I told him I was pregnant. The day I lost the baby and now.

Dio mio, this is serious.

"Be careful," I say.

I don't know if he hears me before he cuts the call. Something bad is happening and I've got to find my brother-in-law and get us both out of Detroit.

I get Leo to the cabin and we settle in. My texts to Tino go unanswered, but I don't contact anyone else. That is the protocol.

Protocol doesn't stop me from checking the online news outlets for information. I am horrified by what I find.

Two, possibly three, gangs are waging war in Detroit. The initial violence erupted in one of our clubs.

Reading between the lines from who is quoted as saying what, I realize the Irish mob and Russian bratva have teamed up to take over Cosa Nostra territory in Detroit. And everything is being played off as a war between rival gangs.

It's warfare all right, but the main players aren't street gangs. They are organized crime syndicates vying for territory.

Rumors of bystanders shot dead abound, but by the next day, twenty deaths are confirmed. The vise around my heart tells me that one of those people is Tino.

He still hasn't answered my texts. The one call I made to him in the middle of the night, breaking protocol, went straight to voicemail.

Hoping against hope, I read the news obsessively over the next two days, sleeping very little and only eating when Leo gets hungry. I gasp as I read the headline to a breaking story. My home has been fire bombed. Leonardo and Lucia Revello are presumed dead, burned to ash with our home in the chemically enhanced fire.

My stomach cramps.

Reading about the tragedy of our *entire* family being killed on the same night sends me running to the bathroom before I vomit bile all over the cabin floor.

Tino is dead. Agustino Sr. is dead. Leo and I are presumed dead.

Tino and Agustino are considered collateral damage to the gang warfare. The death toll has risen to nearly forty people. Authorities are baffled as to why our home was bombed. Right now, the two incidents are being treated as unrelated.

They aren't. I am Tino's legal heir. The Irish and the Russians don't want me around to be able to fight their possession of the nightclubs on a legal front.

Not that I would be the one doing the fighting, but my standing as owner to the properties would give my don legal leverage in this war.

The same don who allowed the mounting tension between the bratva and our mafia to continue. Don Russo took the path of least resistance too many times and now my husband, father-in-law and more than two dozen other Cosa Nostra men are dead.

From the names listed of the victims, it seems only nine are Russian or Irish. No names are given for the supposed gang members engaged in the conflict.

Returning to the city would be signing my own death warrant. Leo's too.

Just as important is the promise I made to Tino when we got back from our honeymoon. He and Agustino Sr. told me that I would be responsible for Leo's care. Tino made me promise him that if anything ever happened to him and his dad, I would take care of Leo as if he was my own brother.

I look over to where Leo is playing a video game on the cabin's big screen television.

Tino would expect me to take Leo back to Detroit, to his grandfather, the Revello patriarch. But my promise was to take care of Leo as if he were

Rocco. If Leo were Rocco, I would make sure he got the medical treatment denied to him since his accident.

Family takes care of family.

Well, me taking care of Leo means doing what is best for him, not what is best for *la famiglia*.

When I discover that the papers Tino wanted me to get show me how to gain access to several accounts in both our names in the Cayman Islands, I know I can do that. It means letting my family continue to believe I am dead.

My heart hurts at the thought of never seeing my parents or brother again, but if I go back to Detroit, chances are both Leo and I end up dead for real. And maybe my family with us. Our enemies bombed one house. What's to stop them from bombing another?

It is better for everyone if me and Leo stay dead as far as the Detroit Cosa Nostra and their enemies are concerned.

CHAPTER 1

ATLAS

Present Day

The pounding bass of the club's music thrums through my body. Swirling lights play above the gyrating bodies on the dance floor.

A woman on the edge smiles and crooks her finger at me. I pretend not to notice.

Instead of wearing my usual dark suit, I'm dressed to blend in. My black dress shirt is a snug fit and open at the neck. No tie. My slacks are clubwear not the bottom half of my usual designer suit. Nothing about me screams enforcer for a Greek mafia family.

Ádis Adelfótita, the Hades Brotherhood, is my family and my life. Tonight my job is to gather intel on potential business tithes for our protection racket before anyone realizes we're claiming territory here.

It's nine o'clock and Nuovi Inizi is already half full. People are dancing and drinking.

I take note of the bar to my left, staffed with three bartenders. I count four waitstaff serving customers on the floor. I bet that number increases once the club gets busier. Very promising.

This place is doing well even though it's in a suburb of Portland and not downtown. Whoever did the décor, knows how to draw in people who want to party in a trendy setting. I bet the drinks are expensive and the booze to make them is cheap.

I make my way to the bar and order a Scotch, neat. I'm right that the price is at the high end. Exactly one shot is served in a rock glass by a smiling bartender. I toss it back and am surprised. The Scotch is a higher quality than I expect. It's not top shelf, but it's not bought for profit margins alone.

That could be good, or bad. Higher quality liquor might bring in more customers to the club, but overall the profit margins are going to be lower.

The percentage we require for tithe once we take over protecting an area can go up or down depending on the profit margin for the business. We can't expect 10% of net out of a restaurant when their profit margin is only 7%. Doesn't leave enough money to put back into the business. A bankrupt business doesn't make us any money.

A nightclub like this should be able to support ten though. The owner might need some advice on how to increase their liquor margins, but that's an easy fix.

A feminine voice interrupts my calculations. "*Ciao, bella*. Give me a cranberry juice and soda would you?"

The husky tone of the woman's voice sends an arrow of desire zinging straight to my cock. I have to control my body's instinct to spin and face her and force only my head to turn. And I stare.

She is beautiful. No more than five-foot-four, her red heels give her an extra three inches. She still only comes up to my shoulder. I want to reach out and touch the silky waves of her chestnut brown hair. My hand starts to lift and I have to press it into my side.

Pretty dark eyes observe me from her heart shaped face. One sculpted brow raised in silent question.

I'm too busy looking my fill to answer.

Encased in a red dress that barely brushes the top of her knees, her body is all curves. The sleeves are long; the neckline does not plunge and it's still the sexiest damn thing I have ever seen. Her generous tits are lovingly accentuated by the red silk clinging to them. The skirt fits her luscious hips like a second skin. If I could see her ass, it would be a perfect, juicy peach.

I *need* to get my hands on it. *Gamó*. What is happening?

I'm never like this when I'm on the job. I would like to blame this reaction on how long it has been since I got laid, but I got my rocks off last night.

My cock is hard as steel, wanting *this* woman. Women are interchangeable to me. A pussy is a pussy. But not this one. This one I crave.

I will have her.

This job just got a whole lot more interesting.

A practiced smile curves lips I want to crush under mine. "Are you enjoying yourself?"

I am now.

Even if I can tell she is not hitting on me. She's asking like someone who works here, even though she's not dressed like one of the servers. A manager maybe?

Not only a woman to fuck, but someone who will have good information for me if I ask the right questions.

"It's a bangin' club," I say.

Pride shines in her chocolate brown eyes. "Thank you."

"Do you work here?"

Her laughter is a sexy trill that hardens my cock further. This time her smile is genuine. "It's worse than that, I own the place."

I am not often surprised, but I am now. She seems young to own the club. I'd assumed the L. Esposito behind the LLC was older and probably a man. She's neither and my dick is thrilled.

"That means you're not on the clock." I shift my body closer to hers.

She doesn't move away, but takes a sip of her cranberry juice and looks up at me through her lashes. "Or I'm always on the clock. It depends on how you look at it."

"Dance with me."

She's opening her mouth to turn me down.

I can tell, but I'm already taking her drink from her hand and putting it on the bar. "Watch it for her," I instruct the bartender.

The woman nods, her eyes wide, like she's never seen anyone pick up her gorgeous boss before. Good. That means I don't have anyone I have to incapacitate to claim all of this woman's attention. And that is what I plan to do for the foreseeable future.

Sliding my arm around her, I settle my hand onto the curve of her hip and guide us to the dance floor. She gasps, but she doesn't try to pull away.

When we reach the dance floor, I turn her body into mine. I lift her left hand and put it on my neck and place her right hand over my heart. Then, pressing her against me, we grind. Her red painted lips are parted, her eyes filled with the same sexual need crashing through me.

LUCIA

What am I doing? I don't dance with customers. I haven't danced with anyone in more than five years.

I don't even know this man's name, but his hard thigh is between mine and our bodies are moving together like we've been doing this for years, not seconds. One of his hands is pressed against the top of my ass, holding my body close to him. The other is on my nape.

It's a possessive, dominant hold and my ovaries are exploding.

It's wild. Unbelievable. And irresistible.

Since Tino, I don't date. I don't let men get close.

Suddenly, my body is telling me how starved it is for touch. My inner sex kitten that has been hiding my whole darn life comes out to play. *Dio mio.* She wants to rub against his thigh and push my breasts against the hard plains of his torso.

He reads my mind and his leg shifts so he's making my dress ride up my thighs. If I don't get a hold of myself soon, I'm going to be dancing with my thong exposed and the round globes of my butt along with it.

I can't get that inner sex kitten to care. She wants this. She craves it.

He leans down and nips at my earlobe. "Tell me you have a storage room we can go to."

"I..." I try to shake my head to clear it, but he's kissing a spot under my ear that has my vagina clamoring for more.

Somehow, I find myself leading him through the club and to the right of the bar, down the hall and to a nondescript door. I press the unlock code into the keypad and the heavy steel door clicks open. He reaches around me and yanks it so he can push me through.

The lights go on, revealing the stairs. He picks me up and throws me over his shoulder, taking the stairs two at a time.

I laugh breathlessly and push myself up so my soft stomach isn't bouncing on his hard muscles with every step. "Take a right at the top."

These rooms were used for storage, but I renovated the area into a small, one-bedroom apartment when I started Nuovi Inizi.

Living here makes sense financially, but right now all I care about is that my bed is only two doorways away.

He stops in front of the entrance to my place and lets my body slide to the floor in front of him. "Get us in, *ílios mou*."

"My name is Lucia."

"You burn hot like the sun. You are my *ílios*."

His sun? Isn't it enough he has a body to die for and his voice sounds like sex? Does he have to be charming as well?

"What language is that?"

"Greek, like my family," he growls in a deep, sexy tone that goes straight to my core.

My fingers slip and it takes two tries to get the code into the keypad and my apartment door unlocked. I don't remember ever being this hot. Desire runs through my veins like lava.

Is it because it's been so long since I had sex? I'm not like this though. My vagina keeps clenching and it feels empty.

Sex is fun, but it's not necessary.

At least that's what I've told myself for the past five years. It's how I thought of it before my husband was killed in the war over territory in Detroit. I don't want to think about Tino right now, or my life before I came to Oregon.

I am a new woman and apparently my body got the memo. Because I want this man who uses Greek endearments and makes my heart race in my chest. Enough to leave the club in the hands of my employees and bring him into my personal sanctuary.

I don't bring strange men home. I don't bring men home at all. I don't even invite my friends over, but this man? I want him here. In my bed.

Is it because I'm finally realizing my dreams? Have my body and mind slipped the tight leash of relentless work and effort of the last five years?

He shoves the door open and pushes me inside. His roughness doesn't make me nervous. It turns me on. But then I was once married to a mafia soldier. Normal men don't scare me.

This one though. He is something else. He wouldn't even be intimidated by the don.

Kicking the door shut behind him, he starts unbuttoning his shirt. "Do you like that dress?"

"Yes."

"Then take it off before I rip it from your body." There is no teasing in his blue gaze, merely intent.

I'm so freakin' aroused right now. My panties are soaked, and I can feel slick wetness where my thighs rub together.

Reaching behind me, I undo the zip and then pull the dress off, leaving me in the red lace panties and matching bra I never expected anyone else to ever see. Lingerie has been a private indulgence since I ran from Michigan with my brother-in-law. The single reminder that I am still a woman, not just a nightclub owner earning money to support the last living member of my family.

Those blue eyes heat, burning over my body like a physical touch. "You are fucking beautiful."

I feel beautiful with his gaze on me. Sexy.

"Your turn."

His shirt is unbuttoned, giving me a glimpse of his sculpted chest, but that's as far as he's gotten. Shrugging out of his shirt, he reveals the rest of the chiseled perfection of his arms and chest. He has tattoos. Lots and lots of tattoos.

His right arm has a full sleeve of monochromatic images inked into his skin. A snarling three headed dog guards his heart. Under it is something written in Greek letters.

I had no idea I found body art such a turn on. Does he have ink on his back?

Wanting to know, I ask, "Can I see your back?"

He gives me a smoldering glance and then turns around. His entire back is covered with a tattoo so detailed, it looks real. A Spartan warrior stands victorious over a dead bear with a sword sticking out of it and rivulets of blood running from the wound.

The blood looks wet; the warrior's muscles almost ripple.

Unable to stop myself, I step forward, my hand outstretched to touch.

Something about the Spartan feels familiar.

The only facial features showing behind the Corinthian helmet are the warrior's eyes, mouth and chin. The eyes are the same blue as the man on whose back I'm ogling. The lips and jaw are the same shape too.

"It's you," I say.

"Yes."

My fingertips trace the tattoo, and I discover small ridges under the colorful ink. Scars?

What caused them? Are they why he got such a huge piece of artwork on his back? What does the bear symbolize? I'm pretty sure these questions are too intimate to ask a one-night stand. So, I don't.

But I wonder.

The man I am practically drooling over bends to take off his boots, giving me a delicious view of his perfect backside. Okay, there's nothing *practically* about it. I swipe moisture from my lips with the back of my hand, greedy to see it all.

I wait with bated breath while he undoes his trousers and shoves them, right along with the black knit boxers clinging to his muscular buttocks, down his legs. He turns back around, and I finally suck in air that almost chokes me.

Fully aroused, his penis juts out and upward with impressive length and girth. He's huge.

If I'm going to jump off the bridge of celibacy, there could be no better specimen of masculinity to do it with.

He crosses the space between us so fast, I barely realize he's moved. Wrapping his hand around my hair, he holds it like a ponytail, keeping my head in place. He dips down so our lips touch. Just that. A simple touch.

I make a needy sound and I push up toward him, wanting a deeper kiss.

He gives it to me, suddenly devouring my mouth and I respond with an alien, wild passion. His big hands are on my back, touching and pressing me closer. Then he undoes the clasp of my bra and pulls it from me.

My soaked panties are next, but when I go to step out of my heels, he says, "Don't. Leave them on."

With an arm under my bottom, he picks me up and carries me across the room until I feel the wall at my back. Then he lifts my body like it's nothing and drapes me over his shoulders. My sex is right in front of his face. He breathes against my most intimate flesh and I shudder in response.

Inhaling like he's savoring my scent, he nuzzles forward. My own head thunks back against the wall, my hands digging into his hair of their own accord.

How is he holding me up like this? I'm not tall, but I'm by no means tiny. I don't wear a size two, in fact I shop in the plus size department when I have time to look for new clothes. My boobs and butt are what is referred to as curvy. I have thighs that will never be referred to as pencils; my tummy is not flat, much less concave.

Yet, he shows no strain from this position. That is so freaking hot.

His tongue flicks out to taste me, laving my folds and then pressing against my clitoris. Already so hot, I am gasping on the verge of orgasm. How did he get me here so fast?

Uncaring, my body responds to his teeth and tongue with unabashed delight. He eats me out like he's enjoying himself, not like he's chasing my climax so he can get his rocks off. His tongue is all over my vulva, but then he thrusts it inside my vagina and I cry out.

I haven't had anything but my own finger in there in five years. I touch myself to get off to relieve stress. It never feels like this.

Rubbing his nose up my labia and over my clit, he sends jolts of pleasure sparking along my nerve endings. When his mouth settles against my swollen nub, he nips it with his teeth.

"Oh!" I gasp out.

Then he sucks on my clitoris and ecstasy radiates out from my core.

I scream when I come, squeezing his head with my thighs, shoving myself forward to press against his willing mouth. He's not done though, and he keeps eating me until a second climax hits with even more ferocity than the first.

Then I'm begging. "*Basta!* Stop. It's too much. *Per favore*...please..."

I'm American, but in the Detroit Cosa Nostra, Italian is the first language we teach our children and it falls from my mouth too easily when I experience deep emotion. Or incredible sexual pleasure.

I don't even know this man's name and I don't care. Not right now. I'm begging him to stop, but my thighs aren't relaxing so he can move his head back, are they?

How am I twenty-eight years old and only now realizing I can feel like *this*?

When my leg muscles finally give and they nearly slip off his shoulders, he does a little jog with his shoulders and I slide back. He doesn't let me fall. He doesn't even let my feet hit the floor. He puts his arms around me and unerringly carries me to the bedroom.

I would say it's instinct for a sexual master like this man, but really, there is only one door. The bathroom is through the bedroom.

He lays me on the bed before turning to go.

No way did he just give me multiple orgasms with his mouth only to leave without getting off himself. Right? Before I can fret too much about it, he's back, a small foil packet in his hand. He rips it open and rolls the condom down his length.

Then he joins me on the bed, positioned between my legs.

Before he can put that monster inside me, I say, "Wait."

He does and something inside me cracks. This man.

"What is your name?"

His smile is sexy as hell. "Atlas."

"I'm Lucia. When I say it's a pleasure to meet you, I mean it."

He's still smiling when he lifts my legs and pushes my thighs wide so he can press the head of his big dick against the entrance to my body.

"The pleasure is mine." He thrusts forward, hard.

A string of Italian curses explode out of my mouth.

Sliding into my wet heat, he stretches my vaginal walls until I'm sure I can't take another millimeter. But do I want him to stop?

No. And he does not.

He keeps thrusting in and out, going deeper with each thrust until he's hitting my cervix. A different kind of pleasure explodes in my core. Tinged with erotic pain, it's so intense it radiates outward, devastating every nerve ending in its path.

He pistons in my body, dragging his thick penis along the hypersensitive tissue of my inner walls.

And all I want is more.

Then he discovers my breasts. Or at least that's what it feels like. Because he stops moving to play with his new toys and as frustrated as I am, I'm also experiencing an overload of sensation. Every tweak of my nipples results in a burst of pleasure in the flesh clinging so tightly to his hardon.

It's a feedback loop that I never want to stop.

I cant my pelvis, taking him deeper and suddenly he's moving his hips again, but his hands are still on my fleshy mounds. His fingers playing a catch and release game with my nipples.

He grows impossibly big inside me and then he shouts his release so loud my ears ring. It takes me over the edge again and I scream too. His name.

"Atlas!"

When he comes back from taking care of the condom, he doesn't get dressed, but joins me again on the bed. His hands explore my body, running over already sensitive skin and dipping between my legs with intent.

"Again?" I ask.

"I am nowhere near done with this gorgeous body." Delivered in that deep, masculine tone, it is both a sensual promise and a threat.

At some point, I slip into exhausted slumber only to wake sometime later with his rock-hard erection rubbing up and down my labia. My overworked clit is swollen and super sensitive, and I can't help wanting him all over again.

"More?" I ask with sleepy disbelief.

Does this man ever go soft?

"As often as you'll let me."

My body thrills to his words and I say, "As often as you like."

He likes hearing that and shifts so his bulbous head is pressing against my entrance. "You might regret that offer," he warns.

"Never." I'll drown in the pleasure I find in his body tonight and do so willingly.

His growl is the only warning I get before he surges inside me and takes me on another wild ride that leads to yet another screaming orgasm.

It doesn't surprise me when he makes good on his promise and wakes me twice more in the night. The man is a machine.

However, when I wake up in the early morning hours and his big body is still curled around mine? That shocks me.

I expected him to sneak off during the night. I have no personal experience with morning-afters and only know what I hear around the club. The one man I had sex with before this was my husband. Our first morning-after was after our wedding.

Will Atlas expect me to make him breakfast? The idea doesn't bother me. In fact, I like the thought of feeding him and fall back to sleep planning the perfect morning-after menu in my head.

CHAPTER 2

ATLAS

I wake with Lucia pressed close to my body and my cock already throbbing with the need for another round inside her tight pussy.

I've never had sex with a virgin, but I swear her pussy is tight enough to be one. There was no blood though. Even though she must be at least in her mid-twenties, I checked when I took care of the condom the first time. She is that tight.

Maybe it's been a while for her. She responds like a dream, but I would swear there were times when the pleasure she felt was a surprise to her.

She's too beautiful not to have men in her life though. My muscles bunch with the need to hurt any other man who dares to touch her. The urge to kill those faceless bastards who already have rides me hard.

I let my hand slide along her generous curves. I will fuck all memory of other lovers from her mind and her body. I will ruin her for anyone else.

This possessiveness is new.

Sharing women with my brothers has never been an issue. In the past.

If one of my brothers or cousins makes a move on Lucia, I'll beat him into next week. It's a new thought, but I don't question the rightness of it.

This woman is mine.

She makes a soft sound when my fingertip circles her nipple, but she doesn't wake. I wore her out last night.

Let's see what I can do with her this morning.

Reveling in the feel of her satin smooth skin under my hands, I touch her slowly and gently. The idea of keeping her asleep a little while longer as I rev up her body turns me on. I've never done anything like this before.

Never been interested in exciting a woman who wasn't offering anything back to me.

When I brush two fingers over her mons, sliding over her lips without dipping between them, Lucia moans and rolls onto her back, unconsciously giving me better access.

I'm hungry for her pussy, but I want to taste all of her. I start with the join of her neck and shoulder, kissing her there. Goosebumps form on her skin, revealing this is an erogenous spot for her. I slide my tongue up her neck and tug her earlobe gently with my teeth.

She shifts restlessly but doesn't open her eyes.

Is she pretending to be asleep?

Her breathing is still that shallow, even inhalation and exhalation of sleep though. Her heartrate remains steady, even though I can smell her arousal on her skin.

Gamó. My heart is pounding wildly in my chest.

My hands shake with need and excitement as I touch her body. Her body's instinctive response calls to something primal in me. That her subconscious trusts me enough to allow her such deep sleep when I am in the bed with her? It makes me want to beat my chest and stake my claim.

I don't sleep with women. When the sex is over, I leave. Or they do. The only people who I can sleep in the same room with are my brothers and cousins. Even with them, I sleep lightly, atavistically alert for any danger.

No one shares my bed.

Last night I shared hers though and I slept deeply and well.

I sip at her lips and even in sleep, her mouth clings to mine as I pull my head away. But I'm on a mission. And when I am on a mission, I am hyper focused. Right now, I'm determined to kiss and taste every inch of her skin.

I learn the spot below her ribs makes her shiver. She kicks her legs restlessly when I kiss the bottoms of her feet, but her thighs part invitingly when I sample the skin behind her knees.

Seeing the glistening folds of her pussy, my mouth waters and my focus shifts to waking her with pleasure.

LUCIA

I wake from the most amazing sex dream of my life, only to discover that it's real. Atlas has his head buried between my thighs, his tongue thrusting inside me.

Tino didn't do this. He always said real men got their wives off with their dicks. Which was probably why my climaxes were few and far between with him.

I've had more orgasms in one night with Atlas than I had during my first year of marriage. Maybe *all* the years of my marriage.

All thoughts of Tino and his limited view of sex fly out of my head as Atlas shifts his tongue up to my clitoris and thrusts a finger inside my swollen core. I grab his head, holding him in place and thrust my hips upward toward his talented mouth.

He hums in approval and the sound vibrates through my sensitive, intimate flesh adding to the blissful sensations.

My body is buzzing with ecstasy, like we've been at this for hours, not minutes. My muscles contract and I go rigid as it coalesces inside me before exploding, sending ricochets of pleasure outward.

I scream his name and I'm still chanting, "*Bene...bene...bene...*" when he surges up my body and slams inside me, hitting my cervix and causing another climax to overlap the first one.

He pistons through my orgasm, never letting me come down completely and I grab his ears, tugging his head down so our mouths meet in a passionate kiss. I taste myself on him, the proof of how he pleasured me increasing my excitement.

I meet his thrusts, my body aching in the best way possible from a surfeit of sex. My vaginal walls cling to his demanding penis each time he pulls back, but give way again with every thrust forward. He grinds his pelvis into my overworked nub of pleasure, twisting his hips and forcing my body to surge toward cataclysmic release again.

This time when I come, he comes too, his erection buried as deeply inside me as it will go. He wraps his arms around me, pressing our bodies together as we ride out the waves of ecstasy together.

He kisses me over and over again until my panting breaths settle into a normal rhythm and my body goes lax under his.

Then he lifts his head. "You sleep really deeply, *ílios mou*."

"I don't," I deny. Though I slept better last night than I have since the early months of my marriage.

"I'm a light sleeper." Have been ever since I lost my baby. My body and subconscious mind are always on alert for danger. Even though the danger is gone, happily living in a beautiful facility in another state. "I guess you exhausted me last night."

Or I felt safe with him in my bed like I haven't in a very long time.

He tugs at my earlobe with his teeth and huffs a breath of warm air, sending pleasurable shivers down my neck. "You are so responsive. I could stay inside you all day."

My stomach snarls. His rumbles right after and I laugh. He joins me and I have another revelation. Laughing while a man is still inside my body is wonderful.

"I think I need to feed us before anymore bedroom gymnastics."

"You want to feed me?" he asks, smiling.

"Yes. I already planned out the perfect breakfast, but you're going to have to let me up to make it."

"You planned it?"

My face heats, but I nod. "I woke up earlier, around dawn, and you were still here. I thought—"

"That you would feed me. I like that *ílios mou*, almost as much as I like being inside you."

"Glad to see you have your priorities straight," I tease. But when his stomach growls again, I shove at his chest. "Up. Time to eat."

"I've already eaten." His blue gaze traps mine. "And it was delicious."

"Your libido may be satisfied, but your stomach isn't. Neither is mine. We need sustenance if we're going to keep this up." I blush again, realizing I may have put my foot in it.

Why should I expect that he'll want to stick around for more? We'd barely shared first names before having sex. I don't have experience with one-night stands, but I'm pretty sure that's an indication of one.

"If you are promising me both food and further access to your body, who am I to deny you?" he asks, like he didn't get the memo on the one-night stand thing either.

Was this wild, amazing, unexpected and terrifically intense sex the start of something more?

CHAPTER 3

ATLAS

I disengage from Lucia's body, wanting nothing more than to go for another round, but she's hungry too. So, she must be fed.

As I stand, I look down at my still semi-erect cock and the sight of my seed mixed with her juices gives me a primal sense of satisfaction. I've claimed my woman.

And she enjoyed it, chanting how good it was in Italian. Like me, her American English has no accent, but Italian slips in when she's excited. I like it.

It's sexy.

In a flash, what I'm seeing on my cock registers on a whole different level. *My seed mixed with her juices*. Oh, Fuck.

"I forgot the condom." Shock nearly strangles me. I don't fuck women without gloving up. Ever.

Not one time since I started having sex have I forgotten that layer of protection. Not even when I was a teenager discovering the joys of dick in pussy.

She's up on her knees, staring at me, horror etched in her beautiful features. "You didn't use a condom? *Dio mio*, tell me your clean."

"I am clean."

"Can I believe you? I met you last night."

"You can believe." I cross the room and dig my phone out of my slacks. With a few taps I have my most recent test results on the screen. I show her. "Clean."

She grabs the phone and reads carefully, but then she grabs her throat. "This was taken three months ago. How many women have you had sex with since then?"

"None without a rubber."

"But..."

"I have never had sex without one." I'm glad her primary concern seems to be about STDs.

She must be on birth control. A beautiful, sensual woman like her would need to be. I'm sure I'm not the first man she's brought up here from the club.

My mind throws up images of other men standing where I am. The beast inside me roars. I'll need a list of names.

Any man who has known her sweet pussy needs to die and who better to kill them than me? Called Dímios, the executioner, because I am *Ádis Adelfótita's* most brutal assassin.

Her chocolate brown eyes search mine, like she's looking for the truth in their depths. I will never lie to her about something important like this, so I let her look her fill.

"I'm clean too," she says, "But we should probably both get tested."

"If you want our second date to be a trip to the clinic, I'll indulge you," I tease.

I never tease women. Sometimes I give my brothers or cousins shit, but this lighthearted man? He isn't me.

Only he is with Lucia apparently.

"I'd call it our third date. Breakfast will be our second," she sasses back with a grin.

A grin that goes straight to my cock, which fills with blood until I'm once again fully erect. I have a strong sex drive. It is a Rokos family trait, but this is next level. I am insatiable for this woman.

Her gaze slides down my naked body, only increasing my desire to rejoin her on the bed.

When she sees how ready I am, her eyes widen. "It's only been a few minutes. How..."

"Last night didn't clue you in to how fast I recover around you?"

"Around me?" she asks.

I decide to answer her with my body rather than words. Breakfast is put off for another hour, but this time she reminds me about the condom. And for the first time in my life, I resent gloving up.

I don't want barriers between us.

LUCIA

While Atlas showers, I put together the breakfast I planned in the early hours.

I can't wait to have a full-size kitchen again. Not that the kitchen in the modest house I'm buying is big, but it will be a huge improvement over this kitchenette.

Even if I had something bigger than a toaster oven, there's no space in here to do any real baking. I'm only able to cook frittatas because I have a special pan for making them on top of the stove. It makes single serving sized frittatas, which is all I've needed up until now. Because I'm only cooking two eggs at a time, it has the added benefit of cooking them faster as well, so I wait to pour the egg mixture in until I hear the shower shut off.

Imagining him drying off his naked body in my tiny bathroom has my mouth going dry. I've been fighting the temptation to join him since I told him if he didn't shower alone, we'd be eating breakfast for dinner. Because I didn't like our chances of being naked together under water and not having sex again.

I've never been this *horny* in all my life.

I was married to a husband I loved for three years and even our honeymoon sex wasn't this good. Is it my age? I'm not thirty yet, but my ovaries want to explode every time I look at Atlas.

The shock of the forgotten condom didn't diminish my desire for the sexy, tattooed man one iota. Right now, I want to go into the bathroom and explore every single one of those tattoos with my tongue.

Instead, I put the croissants in the toaster oven to heat up and pour the egg mixture into the frittata pan. I set my kitchen timer for two and half minutes before putting the jam in the center of my bistro style table. Small and round, it's the only table that would fit in the efficiency maximized space of my apartment.

The timer goes off and I flip my frittata pan, setting it again for a minute. I've prepared two cappuccinos and I'm starting the second pesto frittata when Atlas walks into the room. He's wearing black knit boxer shorts that form to his muscular body. No shirt, no slacks. His gorgeous body is on display for my enjoyment.

And I do enjoy it. I fan myself. "Do you usually eat breakfast in your underwear?"

"I wouldn't want you to feel underdressed, considering you aren't wearing any." He pulls me in for a kiss, his big hands sliding under the silk of my robe to grope my naked flesh.

The timer goes off for the second frittata and I force myself to pull away from his mouth and his touch.

I put the food on the table, and he smiles when he sees it. "You went to a lot of trouble. Thank you."

I shrug. "I like to cook, and frittatas are easy."

"If you say so." He hums appreciatively when he takes his first bite.

It's so surreal to have a nearly naked man sitting at my table, I almost forget to eat, but then my stomach growls and reminds me the last food I had was sometime around lunch yesterday. I reach for a croissant and slather some raspberry jam on it.

I have a sweet tooth. So, sue me.

We eat in comfortable silence until he's polished off his eggs and I've managed to drink most of my cappuccino.

"Were you having a nice dream this morning?" he asks me, his blue eyes filled with sensual heat.

I choke on my last sip of coffee and start coughing. He gets up and hands me my glass of water, encouraging me to drink.

"You know I was," I tell him.

He winks. "You must have been. You took a long time to wake up."

Mortified, I gulp down more water rather than answer.

He squats down beside me, his hamstrings bulging. "It was sexy as hell."

"You liked doing that while I was sleeping?"

"Tasting you gives me pleasure, but bringing you to the point of climax while your body slept? That was fucking hot."

"You want to do it again?" I ask.

"Absolutely. The question is: do *you* want me to do it again?"

Atlas is a complicated man, one who has shown he'll take what he wants. However, I sense that he won't take more than I want to give. Hence his question.

"Yes. I do." I'm not going to play coy.

I want all the pleasure this man wants to lavish on me because it's beyond anything I've ever experienced. And we've only had one night and morning together.

"Good." He leans forward, putting his face into my neck. "You smell like me. Like sex. It's fucking addictive."

"I like being addictive, but I'm still going to shower after breakfast."

He inhales deeply, kisses my neck and then stands and returns to his chair. "I'd prefer you didn't."

"I have things I have to do today, and I can't do them reeking of sex."

"You don't reek. You smell good." He takes a croissant and starts to eat it without any jam.

Warmed by his blatant sexual approval, I take a bite of my frittata. I make my own pesto and the eggs are yummy if I do say so myself.

"What do you have to do today? Besides go to the clinic with me?" he asks.

To get tested. Right.

I am not a slut for sleeping with a man I met last night. I am free. Sexy. Things I haven't been in a long time. "We can go there first thing so you can get back to your day."

"I plan on spending my day with you. What are we doing?"

He doesn't ask if I mind. And that turns me on instead of irritating me. Which is all kinds of wrong, I'm sure, but no one else is inside my head to judge me.

Not anymore.

No longer a mafia princess, I am Lucia Esposito, nightclub owner and newly discovered sex kitten.

I stand up and start clearing the table. "I need to pick up packing boxes."

"You're moving?"

"I'm buying a house." My voice holds all the delight and pride I feel at that reality.

I've worked hard to get to a place where I can take care of Lenny and have a home of my own. The one thing I've missed since leaving my family behind that I can actually do something about.

Atlas grabs the rest of the things off the table. "I'll do the dishes while you shower."

Surprised, I put the plate I'm holding down and stare. "You're going to wash my dishes?"

"You cooked. It's only fair."

"But I don't have a dishwasher." No room in the kitchenette.

He gives me an odd look. "I can wash a few dishes and pans by hand. I'm not helpless."

"Okay."

Why does the thought of him doing dishes in my kitchen make me wet?

Ignoring my body's response, I hightail it to the bedroom and grab a short floral dress I usually pair with dark leggings. Fall has been warmer than usual this year, but it's nearly the end of October and there's a nip in the air despite the bright blue sky.

The dress hits me a few inches above the knee but I don't put on my usual leggings. Instead, I toss a pair of thigh-highs on the bed beside the dress. They have elastic at the top to hold them in place and I won't have to wear a garter belt.

The scooped bodice of the dress shows off my cleavage while the stretchy fabric clings to my curves. The a-line skirt drapes flatteringly over my ample bottom and hips.

I would normally wear yoga pants and a sweater to run errands. After leaving Detroit, I stopped dressing up to leave the house. I'm no longer a capo's daughter-in-law, constantly under scrutiny.

Here, I am simply me. A woman who doesn't have to impress anybody when I'm out and about. That doesn't mean I'm wearing my yoga pants to hang out with Atlas though. I guess I still have some vanity.

I put my long hair up so it won't get wet, before stepping into the shower. Washing quickly, but thoroughly, I'm finished and drying off less than fifteen minutes later.

While I'd love to luxuriate in my own body right now, I'd rather be with the man who made me feel so decadent to begin with.

Besides there really is no luxuriating in my small shower cubicle.

That doesn't mean I rush through getting ready.

Apparently, my inner sex kitten wants to look her best for the man who gives such copious and amazing orgasms.

CHAPTER 4

LUCIA

Atlas offers to drive and I let him. I'd planned to run my errands using the MAX and taking a rideshare home once I picked up the boxes.

He presses the button on his key fob to unlock the doors on a shiny black metallic BMW X7.

Opening the door for me, he gives me a hand up so I can slide into the leather passenger seat of an SUV nicer than the don's. I'm surprised Atlas felt comfortable leaving this vehicle parked in the unsecure lot overnight.

Put the luxury SUV together with Atlas's designer clothes and shoes, and that spells serious money. His own? Or his family's?

It doesn't matter to me. I'm not looking for a sugar-daddy. Or even a boyfriend. Heck, until last night, I didn't think I was looking for a sex partner either. I might change my mind about the boyfriend thing. We'll see how this goes. For the first time in years, I have breathing room and can consider the possibility.

The fact that I want to? I blame on my ovaries.

Maybe a little on his amazing sex skills too.

Pulling into traffic, he says, "Tell me about your house."

"It's a ranch style house built in 1957, but the kitchen is fully updated."

"What about the wiring and plumbing?"

"Oh, that too, but it still has its original charm. The carpet someone used to cover the floors in the 1970s has been pulled up and it has hardwood throughout. There's an extra half bath and a laundry room."

I have a stackable washer and dryer in my place, but it's in a closet with no space to hang things up when I pull them out of the dryer. It's funny the things you learn to miss that you've taken for granted your whole life.

I don't miss having a maid, or bodyguards, but a place to bake? That I can't wait to have again.

"The garage has been converted into a family room too."

"Where will you park your car?" he asks, like he doesn't see that as a bonus.

"Well, if I had one, I could park it in the driveway."

"You don't have a car?"

"No."

"How will you get to and from the club?"

"Both the house and Nuovi Inizi are within walking distance to a MAX stop." It's one of the reasons I was so happy when my offer on the house got accepted. "Would you like to see it?"

Hearing the words come out of my mouth startles me. I haven't invited anyone to see the house. I'm still trying to decide if I want to have a housewarming and have my employees over after I move in.

He doesn't hesitate. "Yes."

"I'll text the realtor." The house doesn't have anyone living in it, so it should be no problem.

While I'm texting back and forth with my realtor, Atlas drives to a private clinic near Portland's downtown.

Once we get there, he guides me into the discreetly elegant building with a hand against my lower back.

It feels nice. Not like the actions of a one-night-stand. Though can it be called a one-nighter if he stayed for more in the morning and breakfast after?

I have very little experience with this kind of thing, but it feels like the beginning of something and not a casual hookup.

Which scares me a little, but I'm in a better place to start a relationship than I have been since Tino's death.

Atlas and I go separately to get our blood drawn for the tests.

The nurse asks me the usual screening questions.

"Is the day after sex too early to take a pregnancy test?" I ask her when she's done.

"Ten to fourteen days is preferred," she replies without judgment. "Do you need the morning after pill?"

That gives me pause. It should be a no-brainer. Getting pregnant with a man I met so recently would be foolhardy, to say the least.

But the prospect of pregnancy tastes sweet to my soul in a way it hasn't since I lost my baby. Not that there's much chance of it happening. I never went on birth control after my miscarriage. Once Tino and I started having sex again, I never got pregnant.

Still, if there is a chance, I want to take it. I *can* take it. A year ago, I wouldn't have been able to, but the club is making enough profit now to cover Lenny's care and my own living expenses. Including paying the mortgage on a house that could easily accommodate another person.

I shake my head. "No, thank you."

"Are you sure?" the nurse asks, this time with a tiny bit of judgment.

Or is that me judging myself and blaming her?

Whichever it is, I say, "Yes, I'm sure."

After I am done giving my urine and blood samples, I find Atlas waiting for me in the reception area.

He looks big and forbidding until he sees me and then he smiles. "Ready?"

I nod.

He guides me out to the car. "Some of the tests will be ready later today, but a couple require time to culture and won't be available for a few days."

"You asked?" I shouldn't be surprised.

Atlas hasn't shown any reticence asking for what he wants so far.

"You didn't?"

I laugh. "I didn't have to. The nurse offered the information."

"My nurse wasn't nearly as helpful." There's something in his voice.

"Why not?"

"She was too busy trying to give me her phone number."

Unreasonable anger surges through me.

It's not as if Atlas and I are a *thing*. But I am hoping we might become one.

"That's very unprofessional." But then, so is a nightclub owner having sex all night with one of the patrons.

"I told her I am seeing someone."

"You did? You are?" I stop before getting into his SUV. "You'd better mean me."

If he's in a committed relationship with someone else and I spent all night and morning naked with him, I'm going to feel like crap. I didn't even think to ask.

The look he gives me could sear concrete. "Who else but you, *ílios mou?*"

"Okay, good. Just so we are clear, I'm not seeing anyone either."

"If you were, you wouldn't be any longer."

"Sure, caveman." I roll my eyes and climb up into the truck.

Atlas pulls the seatbelt across me and hooks it and while he's still leaning over me, presses his lips firmly to mine.

"No one else touches you." He closes my door.

I wait for him to come around and get into the driver's seat before I say, "I don't share either."

He smirks and starts the engine.

The smile I give him is filled with the delight coursing through me. We *are* starting something and neither of us wants to see anyone else while we see where this thing goes.

I give him the address for the house I'm buying and he puts it into the GPS.

It takes twenty-five minutes to get there and we talk the whole way. Atlas tells me he's only moved to the Portland Metro area recently.

"What brought you here?" I ask.

"Business and family."

The same reasons I settled in Oregon. To start a business that could support me and Lenny's care and to get away from what was left of our families. I doubt Atlas is trying to get away from his family though.

"Where did you move from?"

"San Francisco. Our parents still live there, but my brothers and I wanted to build our own business."

"That's admirable." So different from the mafia culture I was raised in.

Sons in the Russo Famiglia followed in their fathers' footsteps to become made men, never straying from the same zip code. Unless it was for an alliance.

Atlas reaches for my hand and puts it on his thigh while he drives. "Does your family live here?"

It takes me a second to answer. The gesture feels so intimate, like we are a couple already. "I don't have any family."

It's why I use Esposito as my surname now. It's common in Italy to give it to children without family. For all intents and purposes, mine is gone.

"I am sorry."

"Don't be. Life happens to us all." And it is my choice to live without any connection to mine.

It is the price I pay to keep both me and Lenny safe.

"How long have you lived here?"

"So sure I wasn't born in Oregon?"

"Besides your slips into Italian? I hear some Michigan in your voice. Maybe Detroit."

Ice washes through my vein, momentarily freezing my vocal cords. "How?"

"I notice things."

I wish he hadn't noticed that. It makes me feel exposed, and I'm not about to confirm or deny it. "I moved here five years ago to open Nuovi Inizi."

"Why a nightclub?"

Memories of another life in another place assail me. "I started the night-club because that's what I knew."

After I lost the baby, Tino thought keeping me busy would help me get past the grief. It worked to an extent, but losing a baby isn't something you get over quickly.

Tino and his dad ran the Cosa Nostra clubs in Detroit. He asked me to take over doing the books for the clubs. I discovered an aptitude for bookkeeping, both balancing the real income and expenses and for ways to launder money.

I liked my new job. It was a respite from babysitting my adult brother-in-law and it gave me a chance to spend more time with my husband. Every aspect of running a club goes through the books in one way, or another. Hungry for knowledge of any kind, I ate it up.

What I didn't learn about running a club from doing the books, I learned from listening to Tino. Once I started working for the clubs, he never hesitated to talk business in front of me. Not that he was ever interested in my opinion about running them.

However, back then? I thought he was a modern thinking man because he let me listen in. Other mafia wives I knew weren't allowed to work and their husbands never talked shop in front of them.

I never got used to the noise and the crush of people at the clubs though. Mostly Tino made sure I spent time in them during the day.

I could have suggested he bring the paperwork to me and I do the books at home, but I never did. Because I didn't trust my husband not to expect me to watch over Lenny and do my work at the same time. So, I put up with the sounds and smells of the clubs. Something I still struggle with at Nuovi Inizi.

My favorite part of owning the nightclub is the administrative stuff that happens during the day, when the club is closed.

"I'm good at it," I add, realizing I've been silent too long while lost in my memories.

"You are. Nightclubs fail at a rate of 75%," Atlas says. "That you made Nuovi Inizi a success shows you're savvier than most."

I'm surprised he knows that. "Are you a trivia geek as well as an accent savant?"

Why did I say that? It implies he's right about where I'm originally from. Not that he'd find my family looking for Lucia Esposito.

"It's not trivia to me," he dismisses. "My family owns a few clubs in San Francisco and LA."

Woah. Okay. Seriously rich family.

"What would you do, if you didn't own the nightclub?" Atlas asks me.

"That's not an option." Lenny's care will always require a level of income I can't make anywhere else. "I'm not a dreamer I'm a doer."

Although the profit margins for Nuovi Inizi are good, they will just cover Lenny's care, my new mortgage and putting aside the money monthly that will be necessary for expansion.

Once I have enough saved, we will open up the second floor to private parties and install a VIP area for patrons willing to pay what will be hefty membership fees.

"Why here? Why the suburbs and not downtown?"

I answer his second question because answering the first would reveal too much. Unless I lie. And for some reason, even though I've spent the last five years lying about myself to pretty much everyone, I don't want to outright lie to him if I don't have to.

"A combination of factors. Rents and property are less expensive in the suburbs and there are more options available. Onsite parking is a huge bonus, but not something I could have offered in a downtown nightclub." Not with what I had for starter money.

Maybe, not even if I'd had twice as much to work with. Getting space in a building with a parking garage in downtown Portland can take a year, or longer, on a waiting list.

Properties that have their own parking lots are real estate unicorns and I've never believed in magic.

"It was busy last night." He brushes the top of my hand with his thumb.

Pleasure travels up my arm and zings along no well-traveled nerve endings to my nipples and core.

This man.

"Yes. The customers that would have gone downtown for the latest boutique bar are happy to find something closer to home that offers the same sense of urban sophistication." I work hard to make sure the ambiance and music feel of the moment.

It requires subtle updates to décor, which I assess monthly. Sometimes, it's a simple matter of removing some tables and rearranging others. Other times, it requires paying a graffiti artist to repaint the wall outside or a muralist to do one inside.

I bring in new DJs weekly. When they hit, I have them back. Bringing in popular guest DJs from bigger cities is also important.

"I'm exploring the possibility of doing live music once a week," I tell Atlas. "Portland's music scene is vibrant and popular local bands can bring in their own clientele with them."

"You're a savvy businesswoman, Lucia."

My cheeks warm, I smile. He has no idea how much the compliment means to me. To be recognized for my brain and not only my body. Born a mafia princess, I was considered good for two things by my family:

1. The potential to make a good marriage alliance, which I did.

2. Having babies. Which I didn't.

But that last one wasn't my fault. I got pregnant like I was supposed to. What happened after, well that wasn't on me.

CHAPTER 5

LUCIA

Atlas pulls his SUV into the driveway of the house that is going to be mine in less than three weeks. The pale-yellow ranch style home with its partial brick façade gleams brightly in the autumn sunshine.

Crimson mums fill the brick flowerbox that runs under the picture window in the front of the house.

It's not a big lot, but there's a fenced-in back yard and well-maintained flower beds in the front. Most importantly, it will be mine. My sanctuary. My home.

Elaine, my realtor, is waiting by the front door.

She eyes Atlas with interest before turning to me. "Lock the door from the inside on your way out. I'll leave you to it."

"You don't have to stay to see us out?" Atlas asks, his eyes narrowed.

"No." Elaine smiles at him. "Practically speaking, Lucia is the homeowner."

"If that is the case, then you should install a deadbolt. A lock on the door handle won't keep an intruder out."

"Oh, is he your security consultant?" Elaine asks me.

"No." But apparently, he's very security conscious.

I don't tell Elaine who Atlas *is* because I don't have a label for him.

Hookup? Embarrassing.

Boyfriend? Not quite ready to use that label, despite our discussion about exclusivity.

"Right, well. Once you take possession, you can install all new locks. I always suggest doing that to all my clients."

"I intended to," I tell her.

"If you don't need anything? I've got a showing in half an hour. I need to hop to it."

"Thanks for letting me in," I say, waving her off.

I turn to find Atlas glaring dourly at the door. "How does she know no one else is inside?" he asks.

"Why would they be?"

"I can think of at least five reasons and none of them good."

Laughing, I grab his arm and pull him inside. "No one is waiting inside to rob us, I promise."

Atlas comes in, but an air of watchfulness surrounds him now. His muscles seem bunched, ready to spring into action while his gaze darts around the living-slash-dining area as if someone is going to jump out at us.

"You really do have a thing for security," I say wryly.

He looks down at me. "Whereas I would say, you do not show enough concern for your own wellbeing."

"What do you mean?"

"You are standing in an empty house with a man you met only last night. I could do anything I wanted to you and the only person who even knows I was here with you is that dippy realtor. You didn't even tell her my name."

"You did what you wanted with me last night. And this morning," I remind him with a teasing smile, trying to keep things light.

"You are safe with me," he says, no humor lightening *his* features. "But if you had allowed another man up to your apartment last night, or gone with him in his car this morning, you might not be."

"If another man had wanted to go up to my apartment, I wouldn't have let him. Do you think you're the only guy to hit on me in the last five years?" I ask, irritation starting to take over my delight in being in my soon-to-be new home.

"Did you at least get the names of the others before you took them up?" he asks, almost snarling.

What the heck does he have to be mad about?

"There were no others. I've been too busy building up the club to date anyone." And why did I admit that?

My dating life, or lack thereof, is none of Atlas's business.

He goes to grab me, stops himself, makes an honest to goodness growling sound and stalks off. He does a quick but thorough walkthrough of the house before coming back to where I'm still standing, fuming in the living room.

"The house is clear."

"What are you, a cop, or something?" I demand.

"I am not a cop," he says with such disgust, there's no doubt Atlas is no fan of law enforcement.

I cross my arms over my chest and cock my hip. "So, why are you acting like one?"

"I am acting like a man who cares about your safety."

"Oh, I thought you were just a guy who got off on insulting the woman he had sex with. It goes both ways you know? I could have been a serial killer and you followed me up to my apartment like a lamb."

The look he gives me questions my sanity. "I can take care of myself."

"So can I."

"Your code for the downstairs door and your apartment are the same. Anyone could get inside."

I can't believe he noticed that. Or that I let him. He might have a teensy-tiny point about my lack of caution with him.

"No one else knows them," I say defensively.

"I know them."

"You watched me type them in?" He must have to know they are the same.

I'm appalled at myself. I never let anyone close enough to see me enter the code. Not even the employees that have been with me since the beginning. But he didn't merely see me enter it and notice the two doors have the same code. He remembers that code.

I'll have to change it when I get back. On both doors.

"Yes."

"That's rude."

"Most criminals are not polite," he grits out.

All belligerence, I ask. "Are you a criminal?"

"That is not the point." He glares down at me.

"I didn't think so," I say with narrowed eyes. "The point seems to be you trying to make me feel like I'm not very smart."

"What the hell are you talking about?" His glacial blue eyes spear me with ire.

"This was a mistake. *Uscire*." Realizing he's not going to understand me telling him to get out in Italian, I say, "You need to go."

Why did I think I could build something with a one-night stand?

He's right. I treated him like I could trust him without any reason to do so. I blame it on lust. That's better than thinking of myself as desperately lonely.

I hate that word. *Desperate*. I am not desperate and I'm not lonely. I'm not.

I have my friends...well, my employees.

My brain stops there. Because there is no one else. Not a single person would miss me if I were gone. Not really. When I ran from the Detroit Cosa Nostra, I left behind family and friends.

And I haven't replaced any of them in five years.

I didn't want to. Letting people in puts me at risk of being found out. Which is a paranoid way to look at relationships, but I was raised in the mafia. Paranoia keeps you alive.

Only it didn't keep Tino breathing. Or his dad, or the dozens of other made men that died that day when the Irish mob and the bratva joined forces to take over Cosa Nostra territory.

"I'm not going anywhere." Atlas runs his hand along my arms, the back of his fingers brushing my breasts.

I should jerk away from his touch, but I stand there, staring up at him. What is wrong with me?

A second ago, I was furious with him. Now, I want to know where else those fingers of his are going to go.

He pulls me closer to him until my chest presses against his warm body. "You are safe with me."

"I believe you, but I shouldn't." I really, really shouldn't.

I am an intelligent and usually cautious woman. But with this man, I throw caution to the wind and run almost entirely on instinct.

"You should because it is true. I will protect you, *ílios mou*. I need you to protect yourself when you are not with me."

"I do. I'm only like this with you." And I hate admitting it. Even to myself. "None of my employees know the code to get upstairs at the club."

His expression is skeptical.

"I don't let people close enough to see over my shoulder and I always, always block it with my body."

"Except with me." He sounds confused by that, but his expression? It's 100% male satisfaction.

I step back, away from his touch. "We should leave."

CHAPTER 6

ATLAS

At least she is saying *we* should leave now, not trying to get rid of me.

Telling me to get out in Italian. Should I tell her that I'm fluent in the language? The *Ádis Adelfótita* has a close relationship to the Camorra in California and men of rank in the *Ádis Adelfótita* are required to learn a language of either our allies, or our enemies.

I learned two. Italian and Russian.

Being able to understand my little sun when she is angry, not to mention passionate, will give me an edge. I decide not to reveal that edge yet.

She is so irritated I pointed out her deficiency in security that her generous tits are heaving. She frowns when she notices me looking at the mouthwatering cleavage on display.

I shrug. What does she expect? My cock might feel like it's been chiseled out of granite when I'm around my beauty, but I'm not made of stone.

"You were going to show me around," I remind her.

She rolls her eyes at me. "You already took your own tour."

"No. That was me confirming no one else was here." Lucia coming here alone when someone could break in so easily gives me an unfamiliar sick feeling in my gut.

Ilios mou needs to be more cautious.

I will kill anyone who hurts her, but that won't undo the harm already done.

She frowns and shakes her head. "And I thought I was paranoid."

I shrug. It's not paranoia, but knowledge. The world is a dangerous place. My family contributes to that danger, so I should know.

But I will keep any risk away from my woman.

"You seriously want me to show you the house?" she asks, her voice dripping with disbelief.

"Being able to see it how you do is why I came with you." I don't care about the house, only what it means to her. "Tell me what it will be like when you live here."

She sucks in a breath. "How can you have me so angry one minute and say the most perfect thing the next?"

I don't answer because I don't know. I don't know why me wanting her to stay safe made her mad or why telling her the truth about why I'm here made her happy.

Giving me a tentative smile, she waves her hand around her. "This is the living area. It's not huge, but the way the living and dining room flow together in the L shape makes it feel bigger. I'm going to put a sofa facing the fireplace. I don't have a lot of other furniture for in here, but it will come."

She takes my hand and walks me through the rest of the house, telling me her plans for now and for later when she can buy more furniture and make more updates.

Her whole house would fit in my suite in our family mansion, but I like how happy this space makes her.

She shines like the sun I call her. Her parents named her Lucia. Light. I call her *ílios mou*. My sun. For a Greek man it is the same. I could call her *astéri mou*. My star. Both fit her. She is beauty and brightness. But she is not *a* star. She is *my* sun.

Warmth, illumination and beauty for my world.

Her voice goes dreamy talking about her plans, turning me on.

When we reach the master bedroom, I have some ideas for how to christen it. There is no furniture, but that's not a problem. Images of taking her against the wall play an arousing montage in my head.

I've been sporting a semi this whole tour, but now my cock grows hard as a pike.

I like sex. It's a good way to blow off steam. Not a necessity though. I never think about the woman after I leave her. I don't go back for seconds.

With Lucia, having repeated and prolonged access to her sexy body is fucking necessary. It's a good thing I need to spend so much time with her over the next couple of weeks.

I am so insatiable for her pussy, my hands cramp with the need to grab her tits.

She pulls her hand from mine and shakes it out. "Is something wrong, Atlas?"

"No." I grab her hand again and rub her palm until she relaxes. "Better?"

She nods and turns to leave the room. "Come on. There are only two rooms left to see."

I'm not interested in those rooms. I want to stay here and put the master bedroom to its intended use.

Reaching out, I clasp her shoulders and I pull her to a stop. "Come here."

Lucia's eyes widen, her beautiful face filled with confusion. When I yank her body flush with mine, she gets it.

Her soft lips part and her breath stutters, but she shakes her head. "We can't. The house isn't mine yet."

I don't bother arguing. She's a firecracker in bed, but innocent in ways I'm not sure I ever was.

I slam my mouth down on hers, staking a claim on her berry red lips. She tastes so damn sweet, but she has plump and juicy lips between her legs that are even sweeter. Getting her to let me eat her out here, in a room with no curtains on the windows, is going to take some doing though.

Lucky for me, backing down from a challenge is not in my skillset. I kiss Lucia until she stops fighting my hold, spearing her mouth with my tongue like I want to spear her silky, warm pussy.

She moans and wraps her arms around my neck, making her own effort to close any distance between our bodies. Taking two handfuls of the delectable ass under the skirt of her flirty dress, I lift her, moving until her back is against the wall. She lifts her legs and locks her ankles behind my back.

She's wearing thigh-highs, not tights.

Fuck. Me.

Lucia writhes against me, trying to increase the friction, her thin panties and my slacks no barrier between her soft pussy lips and my hard cock.

That's right. Let it go, *ílios mou*. Let me have what is mine.

Her movements grow erratic, telling me she's nearly there. Not ready for her to come, I move back. Breaking the hold of her thighs on my torso, I lower her to the floor and let go of her ass.

"No," she mewls. "I was so close."

My smile is diabolical as I slide my thumbs under both sides of her dress's neckline and slip them under her bra straps.

She's too lost in her passion for self-preservation or to worry about who might see us. Exactly how I want her.

I yank the stretchy fabric of her bodice down her arms along with her bra straps until her large tits bounce free.

Puckered and rosy with blood, her nipples call to my mouth. Leaning down, I take one between my lips and suck. Hard. Lashing it with my tongue, I cup her other breast in my hand and start to play. When I pinch the tender peak between my thumb and forefinger, she moans, her body straining toward me.

Her nipples are so fucking sensitive. Can I make her come from stimulating her beautiful tits alone?

I bite softly on her tender flesh, eliciting another long, high-pitched moan.

"Basta!" she cries.

No way is it enough. And with her arms trapped in her dress there's nothing she can do but take the pleasure I give her.

"Oh, Atlas, *bene*," she breathes.

It is better than good. She is perfect and so is her response to my touch.

"Don't stop. *Per favore*, don't stop."

Her pleading words act like kerosene on the fire of my libido.

Kneading her fleshy mounds, I suck and bite on her nipples until she's breathing so harshly it sounds like she's sobbing. She's close to coming, but my patience is gone.

I reach under her dress and tear her panties right off her. The sound of silk rending draws another long moan out of Lucia.

I lay her on the floor, glad the carpet that was removed in the rest of the house was replaced in here instead. Shoving her skirt up her thighs, I push her legs apart and upward so she is open to my gaze.

Her thigh-highs frame her pretty pussy. The dark pink flesh is swollen and glistening. My mouth waters and then I dive in.

Her sweet honey bursts onto my taste buds. She's so wet, her juices slide across my tongue. A litany of pleas and demands in a mixture of Italian and English falling from her lips, Lucia bucks up against my mouth, trying to get what she needs to climax.

Not yet, beauty.

Her little pearl is hard and protruding from her hood. I suck on it and she screams, but I pull back.

She starts swearing.

I grin and then lick around her tight little asshole. I haven't taken her here yet, but I will. For at least the next couple of weeks, this woman is mine. Every sexy inch of her.

Sucking one plump nether lip into my mouth, I sweep my tongue side to side along the engorged flesh.

She's still fighting to get her arms out of the dress. "*Porca miseria*, Atlas, help me."

But I like her the way she is. As good as trussed up for my pleasure.

I give her other lip the same treatment until she's moaning, begging me to put a finger inside her. I'm a generous man. I give her two.

Her pussy walls suck at my fingers as her hips buck. She's trying to ride herself to completion, but that's not happening. Not until I'm ready.

And I'm not ready. I'm having too much fun.

LUCIA

I don't know how many times Atlas brings me to brink of orgasm before backing off, but I'm sobbing and cursing. And yes, *begging*. When I realize I'm doing it in Italian, I switch to English. Not that it makes any difference to the sadist torturing me with pleasure.

My arms are trapped in my dress. As much as I fight it, a secret part of me thrills to the knowledge I can't get free.

He has me exactly where he wants me, my over stimulated breasts on display and my thighs spread wide in lewd invitation.

He lifts his handsome head. His eyes should glow demonic red with the look in them, but they are still blue.

"Please, Atlas," I beg again. "Let me come."

He stands and I whimper. He can't leave me like this. He strips out of his clothes, leaving them in a heap on the carpet. He's not going anywhere.

Dark with blood and aggressive with need, his heavy erection bobs upward.

Kneeling beside me, he helps me out of my dress and bra with surprisingly gentle hands. I don't wait. I'm too far gone. I shove him on his back and mount that oversized steel pipe between his legs like a trick pony.

But the only trick is how swollen my inner flesh is. Despite my gushing wetness, I have to keep rocking to get his big dick inside me.

He grips my hips with his inhumanly strong fingers and guides me up and down on his shaft. A galaxy of stars exploding inside me, ecstasy pounds through my blood with every beat of my heart as my muscles seize with the ultimate pleasure.

I scream so loud the neighbors probably hear me.

I don't care. I have never come so hard. My soul is tethered to my body by the hard flesh filling me and stretching my inner walls.

Flipping us, Atlas starts to pound into me, bringing another earth shattering climax piggybacking onto my last one. This is no aftershock. My womb clenches with extravagant need. My muscles contract and I cry out, incoherent words, demands...but one word resounds around us.

His name. *Atlas*. I scream it, over and over again.

He keeps thrusting into me, grinding down with his pelvis and keeping me on the edge of bliss, before toppling me over again and again. It's too much. Too good. Too intense.

I start to hyperventilate.

He cups my breasts and caresses them in what is probably meant to be a soothing manner, but I'm so over sensitized, it only adds to the overload of sensation. My vision goes black around the edges.

I am going to pass out and I can't get the breath to tell him so. My body bucks and writhes, but he meets me thrust for thrust, forcing layer after layer of pleasure into my system.

It's too much.

I gasp out his name, but it's barely more than a whisper. "Atlas." Then everything goes black.

I don't know how long it is before I wake up, but I'm straddling his lap while he leans against the wall. My head rests over the Cerberus tattoo. The sound of his steady heartbeat against my ear comforts me.

My vaginal walls contract around him. His still hard erection is deep inside me. Although the copious amount of fluid leaking out of my vagina tells me he came too.

He's petting my back and whispering things to me in Greek that make goosebumps break out on my flesh even though I don't know what they mean.

I nuzzle into his neck. "We did it again."

"What?"

I yawn. "No condom."

I could nap right here. Even with him inside me. Maybe especially because he's inside me. I am safe. Protected. Connected to another human being in a way I've never experienced.

"The tests are for your peace of mind, *ílios mou*. I am clean. You are clean."

"I could get pregnant." Yes, I decided to take the risk and not use the morning after pill, but he deserves to know it *is* a risk.

If he has reasons for not wanting to father a child, I will take the pill. I'm still well within the window of effectiveness. Regardless, it only decreases the chance of pregnancy by 75%. Odds improved by my lack of ability to get pregnant the last two years of my marriage.

Atlas goes still, his hand halting midway down my back. "You're not on birth control?"

"No."

"Why not?"

Here it is. The moment of truth.

"I haven't had sex with a partner in five years." I've masturbated, but there's no risk to pregnancy with that.

His penis grows impossibly bigger inside of me, stretching well used flesh in a silent claim to my most intimate flesh.

Cupping my shoulders, he pushes me back far enough so he can see my face.

His is an emotionless, impenetrable mask.

A chill goes down my spine and I shudder. It's like the man sitting under me, still buried deep inside me, is not the same man I've been with since last night.

This man is a dangerous stranger.

And then he smiles and the fear sending icicles along my nerve endings evaporates like the mist.

"You could be pregnant with my baby." He doesn't sound angry, or even worried.

If I didn't know it to be impossible, I would say he sounds pleased by the prospect.

"You're not upset about that?"

"I am not."

"Most men would be." I think. Not like I have a ton of experience dating.

He shrugs. "I am not most men."

"I guess I'm not most women either."

"What does that mean?"

"I'm not upset by the idea of having a baby, even though I'm not in a committed relationship and I've only recently managed to get my life to a place where I have breathing room." I've always wanted to be a mom.

But I thought that dream died with my husband. Now, I realize I can fight for it, like I fight daily for my independence and the ability to take care of Lenny.

"I'm not looking for you to play daddy, or anything. If you hate the idea of your progeny out in the world, I'll take Plan B." Now that I know what I want, I can save up for a trip to the sperm bank.

Why not?

"No," he says forcefully. "No morning after pill. If you carry my child, we will work it out together. Family means everything to me, my brothers and cousins."

"Not your parents?" I ask.

"No." His tone doesn't invite further discussion.

I can't help wondering why his parents are excluded. This thing between us is too new to press for answers though.

Regardless of how much of his family he included in the sentiment, it is not a foreign concept to me. It is a familiar refrain in the mafia. I guess it's not so surprising that normal people feel that way too.

So, I nod. "Okay. We'll work it out together."

It's not a promise of a future together, but an understanding that we are both responsible for the life that could be growing inside me. We're both culpable for forgoing the condom and we have both agreed that I won't take the morning after pill.

Against all odds, and knowing what a long shot it truly is, I can't help hoping I'm pregnant.

CHAPTER 7

ATLAS

After dropping Lucia off at Nuovi Inizi, I drive home.

I need fresh clothes and Zeus wants an update. After showering and dressing in my usual suit, I find him in his office.

"What did the computer do to you?" I ask.

Zeus shifts his glare from the laptop screen to me. "Nice of you to finally show up."

"I wasn't aware I was expected, *anax*." I emphasize his title.

The head of *Ádis Adelfótita* here in Portland, Zeus is my oldest brother. I respect him, but I'm nobody's lapdog. The ability to bend knee was tortured out of me when I was ten years old, and the Golubev Bratva kidnapped me.

Zeus leans back in his chair. "You never spend the night with women."

I shrug. It is true, but Lucia is different. "I slept."

Zeus's eyes widen. "You slept, as in went somnolent beside another human being? A *woman*?"

My brothers and I don't trust people in general, but we are particularly wary of women. Our mother lied to my brothers when I was taken and told them I had been sent away to school. Our nanny colluded with the Golubevs.

Both women betrayed us for their own comfort and security.

The bratva wanted part of my grandfather's territory in Los Angeles. They believed I was the leverage to get it. I believed my grandfather, who was the *Nonós tis Nýchtas* (the Godfather of the Night for the *Ádis Adelfótita*) would rescue me.

We were both wrong.

The Golubevs tortured me, sending videos of my abuse to my grandfather as incentive. He was unmoved and by the time I returned to my family, I no longer allowed emotion to move me either.

"There was a hell of a lot of sex too." The memory has my cock wanting to surge in my slacks.

"Didn't need that bit of information."

"Maybe she wore me out." It would explain why I was able to sleep next to Lucia.

I don't feel worn out though. After burying myself in her body and eating her pussy so many times, I am ready to take on a whole nest of enemies.

Too bad we're lying low right now.

"Maybe." Zeus doesn't look any more convinced than I am. "Should I be worried?"

"About me getting a lot of phenomenal sex?"

"About you being compromised." The *dipshit* goes unsaid, but I hear it anyway.

"My loyalty to you will never be compromised."

My grandfather didn't rescue me nineteen years ago. His men, including my father, did not rescue me.

Constantin, who is my uncle and the current *Nonós tis Nýchtas*, defied his father and came into Golubev territory to get me. He brought my older brothers along, who were twelve and thirteen at the time. Constantin was only seventeen himself.

Nearly a whole generation younger than my mom, he rules over the *Ádis Adelfótita* very differently than my grandfather did. He'll order the death of an entire family without blinking an eye, but his loyalty to his men and his family is absolute.

That started nineteen years ago when he, Zeus and Orion breached enemy territory to save me. We all became made men that night, killing all my captors staying at the compound. Three, and the most brutal, of those kills were mine.

After a year of torture, I had a lot of rage. The beast the Golubev bastards woke inside me had his first taste of retribution that night. It has had many tastes since. I have killed so many Golubev bratva soldiers, they have a permanent bounty on my head.

I'm not worried. Their bratva is a shadow of what it once was because of me. One day, I will make sure the Golubevs cease to exist altogether.

"You've got that look in your eye," Zeus says.

"What look?" But I know.

"You're thinking about them."

The Golubevs. He doesn't have to say their name. We both know.

My destiny as an enforcer and assassin is carved into every scar they put on my back.

Constantin gave me the nickname *Dímios* when I killed my captors so brutally the night my uncle and brothers rescued me. In an ironic twist of fate, the bratva call me *palach* and whisper about me like the bogeyman. Like the Greek word *dímios*, it is Russian for executioner.

"Other than getting lucky, how did it go last night?" Zeus asks sourly.

We all have our damage from that night.

To survive the torture, I built a wall between me and any of my soft emotions. Ruthlessly killing my captors only put a layer of cement over that wall.

Zeus drowned the nightmares in sex. He was a manwhore until the girl he was promised to was murdered by the bratva. Now he's so celibate, we call him The Monk.

Orion seems the most normal of all of us, but that's only because he hides his damage behind humor and charm. It's there. Every bit as ugly and remorseless as mine and Zeus's.

"Luck didn't come into it." Lucia is as hot for me as I am for her. "Like I thought, the Nuovi Inizi is solid. With the other businesses in the area, our yearly take on protection will be eight figures easy."

Laundering money through some of those businesses will only sweeten the deal.

"How many businesses did you recon last night?"

"One."

"One?" Zeus does not look impressed.

It's a good thing, I don't worry about impressing my brother, or anyone else.

"One," I repeat. "I met the proprietor. She researched the area before building her club and keeps tabs on it to keep Nuovi Inizi running successfully."

"You're cultivating her as an asset." It's not a question.

So, I don't answer. "Has Zephyr locked down our dock access?" I ask.

"He's working on it."

Establishing a new territory is never easy. We'll succeed, whatever palms we have to grease and blood we have to spill.

We plan a controlled start though. Recruitment, the port and marking the boundaries of our protection territory are top priority.

Later, we buy our own clubs. The plan is to own at least two strip joints and one nightclub within a year. Lucia's knowledge will help with the latter. Maybe the former too.

Zeus closes his laptop and studies me. "Tell me about the owner of Nuovi Inizi."

"Her name is Lucia Esposito." I found her last name on one of the escrow documents for her new house when I searched her apartment while she showered.

There is nothing in her purse with her full name on it. No driver's license. No library card. Her credit cards are for Nuovi Inizi.

"She's in her mid-twenties. Young to own a club, especially as a sole proprietor," I add.

"You're sure she's alone? No backers?" Zeus sounds skeptical.

"I'll do more digging, but it doesn't look like it." She talked about building her life by herself and didn't mention anyone else when talking about choosing the club's location. "No close family by the look of it either."

My sexy little nightclub owner puts up a friendly front, but she's a loner. The LLC is a dummy corporation for one L. Esposito. Now that I know her last name, I know that is her. No other names are included in the articles of incorporation.

If she has silent business partners, she's done a damn good job of hiding it.

"Married?"

"No." Fury at the thought of another man touching her erupts inside me.

I put a lid on the volcano, like I always do. Unless I need to use my rage to serve me in my role as *Dímios*.

The look on my brother's face says he noticed my reaction. And he's surprised by it.

Not sure why. I'm not incapable of feeling emotions. It's my choice not to let them rule me. Most of my emotions are locked down so tight, they are atrophied.

Anger is a useful emotion though. As long as it is controlled. Anger feeds the beast that kills for our family without remorse.

Lust is also a useful emotion, but I will never let a woman lead me around by the dick. Last night, I chose to give into the carnal hunger Lucia arouses so easily in me. And I plan on feeding that sexual fire until it burns out.

"You think I would fuck a married woman?"

"No. Make her a widow so you could fuck her without remorse? Yes."

If she had a husband, would I off him? Memories of how many times and how many ways I fucked Lucia flip through my brain. Would I get rid of anyone in the way of me having her? Yes, and I would enjoy doing it.

"The fuck is that look on your face?" my cousin, Helios, demands as he plops down into the other chair facing my brother's desk. He looks to Zeus. "Is he smiling?"

Zeus and Helios both stare at me.

"What's going on?" Zephyr asks from the doorway.

We live together in the compound. My family lives in the main house, described as a mansion by the realtor who sold the property to us. The soldiers we brought up from California live in a separate building.

Security is tighter with us all in one compound, but it has its drawbacks. The chief one being my brothers and cousins all under the same roof with me, getting in my business.

The only one missing right now is Orion, my middle brother. A lawyer, with a practice in the city, he takes on clients that can build our network of contacts.

"Atlas was smiling," Helios tells his brother.

"What the hell?" Zephyr demands. "I don't believe you."

Zeus gives me a look. "He's banging the target."

"She's not a target," I deny. "She's a resource."

Zeus shrugs. "Who you plan to collect protection money from."

"You went to the club for the first time last night and you're already bumping uglies?" Zephyr asks. "What's this chick's name and where do I find her? If she put a smile on Atlas's face, she's got a magic pussy and I want me some."

I'm on my feet and Zephyr is flying across the office before I'm even conscious of standing. My cousin shatters the glass on the watercolor Mom painted for Zeus before we left LA and lands with a loud thump on the floor below it.

"What the hell?" Zephyr jumps to his feet.

My lungs bellowing like an enraged bull, my hands fist tightly at my sides so I don't reach out for him again. "Lucia is off limits."

Zephyr's hands go up, palms out. "Whatever you say, cousin. There's plenty of pussy if you don't want to share this one."

"Brother?" Zeus asks.

My gaze locks with his. "What?" I snarl.

"Something you want to tell us?"

"She's different," I grind out.

"How?"

"I want her." She's mine.

"You've screwed plenty of women. You've never been possessive of any of them."

I don't have an answer for that, so I speak my truth. "If anyone touches her, they die."

"Shit," Helios breathes.

"Do the rest of the men going to her club know that?" Zephyr asks, sounding too damn amused.

"She doesn't fuck the customers."

My brother and my cousins all look at me like I'm not making sense.

Finally, Zeus points out, "She had sex with you."

"Enough sex to keep you with her all night and part of today," Helios says.

"You keeping tabs on me, cousin?" I ask, wondering if I need to remind him to keep his trap shut like his brother.

Maybe use my knife. I won't kill him. Just cut him a little. Shooting him would be overkill.

"I want to live to see another day," he says.

I take that as a *no*.

"It's not a secret you didn't come home last night," Zeus says.

I acknowledge his words with a slight dip of my chin, my body still in battle ready mode.

"You going to keep seeing her?" my brother asks.

"As long as it takes."

He doesn't ask, *As long as it takes to what?* He thinks he knows what I mean. That I will fuck Lucia until I get her out of my system.

But that's not what I'm talking about. I mean until I get her pregnant, which is fucking news to me. Since when do I want to have a kid with somebody?

She might be pregnant already though and the thought of using a condom with her again makes my skin itch. So, a pregnancy is more likely than not.

If it happens, there will be no letting her go. Ever.

Something inside me, in the dark depths of the soul I'm pretty sure atrophied along with my more tender emotions, is deeply satisfied at that possibility.

Lucia will be mine forever, not a few weeks.

We could raise a child separately, but why would we?

She and our child will be safer with me there to protect them. Besides, Lucia runs a nightclub. She doesn't need the stress of raising a child on her own. I'll be good for her.

It's a strange concept. Me being good for someone as something other than a stone-cold killer. I like it though.

I'm thirty years old and I've never known another *magic pussy* as my cousin calls it. Lucia's is the only one I want to lock down and keep for myself.

It's not merely her banging body though. It's her quick mind and the way she makes me laugh. And smile.

"That's creepy as hell," Zephyr says.

"Right?" his brother agrees.

"You're smiling again, brother." Zeus's eyes narrow. "Are you thinking about her?"

"It would be hard not to since we are talking about her."

My brother nods, but there's something in his eyes. Like worry. It must be a trick of light. No way is Zeus worried about me. I'm the last person Zeus needs to worry about. I left the weak little boy behind the night I made my first kills. And he knows it.

I am *Dímios*, the executioner. I can take care of myself.

And I will take care of Lucia too.

CHAPTER 8

ATLAS

I change into street clothes and pack a duffle before returning to Nuovi Inizi. I don't plan to return to the house tonight. Maybe not tomorrow either.

The service door is open when I arrive, and I can hear Lucia's soft tones talking with someone.

Someone who sounds like a man.

The presence of a delivery van near the back door does nothing to dampen the instant rage flooding my system.

Shoving the door all the way open, I step inside the club, but she's not in the hallway.

Her laughter sounds from an open doorway about ten feet along the corridor. My long legs eat up the distance in a couple of seconds.

This door smacks against the wall when I push it open.

Huh. Might have hit it a little hard.

Lucia jumps and spins to face me. "Atlas! I didn't know you were coming."

"I told you I would be back." I'm talking to her, but my eyes are fixed on the man who is standing way too close to my woman.

He takes a hasty step away from her and toward me, thinks better of that and shuffles to her other side. "I didn't know you were seeing someone."

"Is there a reason you thought she would tell you?" I ask in a tone I usually reserve for interrogating our enemies.

"What? No. We're friends, that's all." The guy swallows nervously.

Wonder what is stressing him out? Is it his imminent death he sees in my eyes?

"Are you friends? Or are you an inventory supplier for her club?"

He flinches at my tone. Huh. He's a pretty perceptive guy. He knows when he is in trouble. Too bad he's not as good at staying out of it to begin with.

Lucia lays a hand on my arm. "I thought you'd text before coming."

That small touch brings all my focus onto her. Big brown eyes blink up at me in confusion.

"Didn't think I needed to."

Her brows furrow and her pretty lips tilt down. "It's polite behavior to warn a friend before dropping in on them."

"You are not my friend," I bark.

She snatches her hand away and steps back, hurt darkening her eyes. "Fine. We aren't friends. You still could have texted to say you were on your way. I might have been gone."

I don't like the distance she's put between us, so I close it and pull her close. "You are not my friend. I don't fuck friends."

She gasps. "Atlas!"

She doesn't want Mr. Invading Her Personal Space to know we're lovers? Too bad.

"You are *mine.*" I flick a glance to the other man to see if he gets the message.

He is looking at Lucia, not me. I revise my estimation of his smarts.

"Possessive much?" she teases, letting her body relax against mine.

What is her first clue? "Yes."

"There's no need to be jealous. I'm taking a delivery. That's all." She licks her lips and that seals it.

I pull her body up at the same time I crash my mouth down on hers.

She tries to shove at my chest, but I'm not budging. She might not see the supplier as anything but a business connection, but he looks at *ílios mou* like a starving man in front of an all-you-can-eat buffet.

The only man allowed to feast on her voluptuous curves is me.

Sliding my forearm under her ass, I lift her higher, so I don't have to bend to kiss her. Her feet leave the floor, and she makes a startled sound, wrapping her arms tightly around my neck.

Determined to remind her who she belongs to, I eat her lips and press my tongue against the seam of her mouth, demanding access to the sweet heat within.

She keeps her lips tightly sealed for a heartbeat and then she sighs, melting into me. Her lips part and I don't hesitate to slide my tongue inside. She tastes like no other woman ever has.

Like mine.

Hell, I don't kiss. I fuck. But with Lucia, I want it all.

The sound of a throat clearing and rubber soles squeaking on the floor reminds me we are not alone. Unfortunately, it reminds *ílios mou* too because she tears her mouth from mine.

"*Basta!* Stop! Let me down, Atlas." She pounds on my shoulder with one of her small fists. "I have work to do."

Letting her body slide down mine, I glare at the man interrupting my hello kiss with Lucia. I guess he has a death wish.

"If you'll sign for the delivery, I'll get out of your hair," he says to Lucia, doing his best to ignore me.

It won't work. He and I need to set some ground rules. Like if he touches Lucia, I will break every bone in his hand.

When *ílios mou* pushes away from me, I let her this time.

"Thanks for personally making the delivery, Shawn. Customers wouldn't have been happy if we tried to get through the weekend without your ale." She uses her finger to sign the digital receipt on his tablet.

He smiles at her, showing his sense of self-preservation is much worse than I thought. "You should think about increasing your order."

"Maybe. It's not fair to you to keep asking you to make these emergency drop-offs between our scheduled deliveries." The look on her face tells me she doesn't want to though.

Why not? I'll ask her after I have a little talk with the beer supplier.

"Leave the crates there. I'll help you with them after I walk your *friend* out," I tell Lucia.

Settling her fists on her hips, she gives me the stink eye. It might have the effect she intends if her posture did not make her generous tits stick out in a way that has my mouth salivating for a taste and my hands itching to touch.

The beer supplier notices too, and any possibility our little talk would only be a verbal one explodes on the impact of his gaze on my woman's breasts.

I grab Shawn's arm and hustle him out of the temperature-controlled storage room. Lucia is a hell of a businesswoman. Nothing in this club is below par, not even the storage facility for her alcohol.

"No need to see me out. I know the way." Shawn tries to pull away from my hold.

Good luck with that.

I don't say anything until we are outside. Then, I let my fist make the first conversational salvo and punch him in the stomach.

He gasps and doubles over, his arms windmilling to keep him upright.

"She is mine. Get within two feet of her again and I'll break both your arms."

"Who are you?" he wheezes, trying to stand up straight.

"Her man."

He sucks in air and then manages to pull himself together enough to stand. Neither of my brothers or my cousins would have taken that hit without retaliation.

"You think she's going to thank you for losing her account with us?" he sneers.

I crack my knuckles. "I think you're smart enough not to inconvenience her like that."

"I'm going to the cops. I'll press charges," he says, all bravado.

Some guys need an extra lesson to really learn. I give it to him. This time kicking him in the side of the knee. Not hard enough to break bone, but he goes down.

"Go to the cops," I dare him. "Five men will say I never left the house."

He's crying and holding onto his knee, showing enough smarts not to get up. "But Lucia saw you. She's not going to lie to the cops for you."

"She won't have to. You make a nuisance of yourself and I'll take care of it. It's my specialty."

"Are you threatening me?"

"If you need to ask, you're not paying attention."

"You can't do that."

I roll my eyes. "You'll keep supplying Lucia's club with as much of your product as she wants. You will not call the cops, or tell your Uncle Harry—"

"I don't have an Uncle Harry."

"Are you really this dense?"

"No." He shakes his head and wipes snot and tears from his face with the back of his hand. "I understand what you are saying."

"How close are you going to stand to Lucia?"

"Two feet." His answer is immediate.

He's finally getting it.

"Are you going to tell anyone about our discussion?"

"No."

"Good. Lucia's customers like your beer. It would be a shame if you weren't around to make it for them anymore."

To show what a reasonable guy I am, I help him to his delivery van. If I drag him so he has to hustle on his sore leg, well, what can he expect?

I don't have time to mollycoddle the man. Lucia is waiting for me.

CHAPTER 9

LUCIA

There's something wrong with me. When Atlas comes in acting like Cro-Magnon man, I soak my panties. I should feel badly for Shawn. Atlas clearly intimidates him.

Only, the ale distiller has always been flirty, and lately he's gotten a little aggressive with it. I've turned him down no less than four times for dates, but he never gives up.

Maybe now he will.

Atlas comes back into the storage room as I'm setting one of the crates of ale on the shelf.

"I told you to leave that for me," he growls.

His voice goes through me like an electric current. My heart races. My thighs clench in an involuntary spasm.

But I finish what I'm doing before turning to face him. "Who do you think does it when you're not around?"

There's something wild in his eyes. Intent, like a predator.

An atavistic shiver goes through me.

He grabs the last two crates and brings them over, stacking them neatly in the spaces left empty by my dwindling supply.

"I am here now." Sliding his hand under my hair, he grips my nape. "Do you need anything else before?"

"Before what?"

His eyes smolder at me. "Going upstairs and using your bed instead of bending you over these boxes."

He waves toward my whiskey inventory, which happens to be stacked three boxes wide and waist high. My waist.

The wetness between my legs becomes a veritable flood.

There's still lots to do before opening the club tonight, but my body isn't listening to my brain. My core clenches and releases over and over again, wanting to be filled. My nipples tighten, aching for his mouth. I lick my lips, not because they are dry, but because they crave stimulation.

"If I bend over here, how fast can you get me off?" I challenge.

Unable to believe the words that came out of my mouth, I barely breathe as I wait for his reply.

He yanks me toward him and mashes his lips to mine, kissing me until I'm rubbing against him like a cat in heat.

His mouth breaks away from mine to find that spot on my neck that sends me into the stratosphere. "Here it is then."

Wanting bare skin, I tug his black t-shirt up his rock solid abs. He helps by grabbing the back of the neck and yanking it off over his head.

I rub up his torso with both hands, mapping his bulging muscles and then tunneling my fingers in his silky chest hair.

"I love that you don't shave this," I tell him.

"Why would I?" he asks.

"I don't know, but some men do."

"Who?" he asks in that gravelly voice that makes my ovaries want to explode. "Who have you seen without his shirt?"

I should roll my eyes, but my body is going haywire again. His possessiveness should not turn me on, but it does. So, so much.

"Men take off their shirts to dance." I don't mention my dead husband.

I never understood why Tino waxed his chest. I guess he thought it was sexy. He never asked me what I thought. He was too macho to need my opinion. About anything.

I loved him, but if he'd lived, I'm not sure I still would. I am a different woman at twenty-eight than I was at twenty-three. Even without losing him and going into self-imposed exile, the years would have changed me. Matured me.

The truth is, that those last two years of my marriage, the cord tethering my love to him had grown pretty taught.

"Not anymore, they don't."

"It's cute that you think you can stop them." I sound sarcastic, but my vagina is yelling, *gimme, gimme, gimme.*

He doesn't reply, but shoves up my shirt and unhooks my bra, tugging it up too so my breasts spill out.

He steps back and looks down. "I could look at your naked body all day."

"I'd rather you touched it."

His expression is filled with male confidence. "That's right. We're on a timer."

He spins me around to face the boxes, bending me only far enough that I can stay upright with my hands on the top of the boxes for stability. Then he shoves my leggings and underwear down together, exposing my wet folds to his gaze.

"Perfect," he breaths as he reaches around to massage my already sensitive clitoris.

He shifts behind me. There is the sound of a zipper. His blunt head presses into my dripping opening and I arch back, wanting more.

He gives it to me, thrusting forward powerfully to fill me with his engorged penis. For a second, it feels like he's splitting me in two and then my inner walls give way and he surges forward even more.

I can feel the bite of his open zipper against my bottom and the rough denim of his jeans against my thighs. I don't know how he's maintaining the squat he needs to keep himself inside me, but his show of strength makes my lady bits swoon.

All thought flees my brain as he sets a pounding rhythm, driving me toward climax.

"You're so fucking tight." Both of his hands grip my hips as he pounds in and out of me.

Releasing my arms, I bend over the boxes, my breasts hanging over the edge, my belly pressing into the cardboard. He shifts his body further over me, reaching around with one hand to pinch my nipple.

Pleasure shoots straight from my nipple to my core and I moan.

"Touch yourself," he grits into my ear.

The angle is tricky, but I get my arm in front of my thigh and manage to press my middle finger against my clit. That's all I need before my body detonates in wild ecstasy.

Atlas isn't finished and he keeps pounding into me. I let my hand drop away and float on the feeling of being taken by this powerful man.

"I didn't say to stop touching yourself." He grabs my hand and puts it back where he wants it, so I'm once again massaging my clitoris with every thrust of his hips.

My body jolts with sensation after sensation. "It's too much."

"No, it isn't." He nips my earlobe. "We're not done."

Porca miseria! No way is he going to get another orgasm out of me right now. I shift my fingers off the over sensitized bundle of nerves, but don't move my hand away.

He knows immediately about my disobedience and makes an animalistic sound. Pulling out of me, he steps away.

Despite having got off already, my whole body rebels at the loss of him inside me.

Oh, crap. We forgot the condom again. He's going to come on my naked backside. An unexpected frisson of desire pulses through my core at the thought. I want his cum on me.

But he's not jacking off behind me. He's ripping my leggings and panties down my legs, taking my ballet flats with them. Then he finishes taking off my bra and shirt, so I'm completely naked.

"Atlas?"

He shakes his head. Then he picks me up and lays me across the boxes with my butt right at the edge.

Grabbing me under my feet, he pushes until my knees are at my torso. "Hold them."

He is so damn sexy and his bossiness is catnip to my inner sex kitten.

I wrap my arms around each thigh, gripping with my hands to hold myself open like he wants me.

"Good," he praises in a guttural voice.

A frisson of bliss arcs straight to my core.

I am wrong. I'm not done. Pleasure tightens like a spring inside me and he hasn't done anything but put me where he wants me.

His arms wrap around my legs, his hands gripping the front of my thighs with inescapable strength. He slams his thick column of steel inside my slick channel, bottoming out on the first thrust. And his hold keeps me from sliding backward even an inch.

My nerve endings explode with sensation and my vaginal walls grip him impossibly tight.

"Such a good little pussy." He pats my mons in approval.

I am drowning in lust and an unfamiliar sense of happiness. Do I have a praise kink?

"Keep your legs where they are."

"Uh huh." It's all I can say, intelligible words beyond me.

"Good girl."

Oh, lord. Those two words in *that* tone.

One hand still keeping my body from sliding up the boxes, he reaches between us and rubs his thumb in circles over my clit as he pulls back until his swollen crown is all that is still inside me.

I mewl.

He smiles diabolically before ramming back into me, setting a punishing pace. The orgasm I deny I'm capable of is growing closer and closer.

Atlas speeds up his hips and unbelievably increases the power of his thrusts until my body shakes with every drive forward.

"Come for me," he demands, his handsome face set in a rictus of pleasure.

He's close.

I want to obey him. My body is craving the release now and my heart is set on getting another *good girl* out of him, but I can't crest this wave of pleasure.

Then he pinches my clit. I scream as I explode with the power of a nuclear blast.

He roars as his seed washes my insides with heat.

My chest heaves, my heart pounding so hard, I can feel my pulse in the tender flesh wrapped around his still hard member.

Awareness of where we are and what we are doing comes back to me slowly, but when it does, I jerk under him and start shoving at his chest. My bar manager is going to show up any minute and I do not want to be caught naked in my cool storeroom, with Atlas still inside me, when she does.

He shakes his head. "Give it some more time."

Give what? His penis? He'll be ready to go again if he stays inside me much longer. I'm not convinced he isn't ready to go now.

"We don't have time. Willow is going to be here soon."

"Who is Willow?" he asks without moving.

"She's my bar manager and more importantly, she can let herself into the building."

He grunts but doesn't move.

"I'm serious, Atlas. I don't want her finding me like this."

"She won't."

"You can't be sure."

"I will not allow you to be embarrassed." His words are a promise.

But I don't know how he'll keep it if Willow gets here before I'm dressed. Feeling compelled to trust him, I stop trying to move.

"Good girl."

Heat surges into my cheeks. I like that way too much. For several long seconds, we stay there, him deep inside me, his eyes locked on mine.

The sound of the outer door opening reaches us and I panic, but Atlas cups my face. "It will be alright. You are not doing anything wrong."

"Not sure health and safety would agree," I mutter, but my body responds to the command in his voice and settles.

Dio mio. This man.

Atlas pulls out slowly, careful of my overused lady bits. "Do not move."

He yanks his t-shirt on and tucks his still hard shaft into his jeans, but he doesn't zip them. The t-shirt won't hide the fact he's aroused, but it covers his naked flesh.

He steps out into the hallway and shouts, "Hey, Willow. I'm Atlas. Lucia wants you to start in the main area."

"You're the dude she took upstairs last night."

"And I'm the man who will be staying up there tonight too."

"I need to see my boss. You're hot and all, but how do I know you aren't a serial killer who stuffed her body in the deep freeze?"

Someone kill me now. "I'm fine," I yell, loathe to move when Atlas told me not to.

I have no idea why. I hated when Tino and his dad tried to boss me around, but this feels different. It feels right and I'm going with it.

"Do you have a deep freeze?" Atlas asks Willow, sounding weirdly interested.

"Well, no. It's a figure of speech."

A beat of silence and then, "I'm serious, Lucia, tell me something that lets me know you're okay."

"You're the one that's always telling me I need to blow off some steam." I put my hands over my face, unable to believe I said that.

No way does Willow not know what we are doing in here. But she hasn't seen me and for whatever reason, that makes it okay.

Her laughter echoes from down the hall. "Good for you!"

Atlas doesn't say anything else, but comes back into the room and closes the door behind him. I shudder to think how much extra power we used keeping it cold with the door open this long.

I didn't build a successful nightclub ignoring the little things like that.

He crosses the room to stand between my legs. "Put your feet on my chest."

Is he going to keep going? Part of me wants to. Very much. The responsible business owner knows we can't though.

He taps his chest and sex kitten wins over responsible businesswoman. I let my feet rest against his hard pecs and feel immediate relief in my strained thigh and arm muscles.

Atlas slides two fingers deep inside me. My core clenches around his hard fingers and my clitoris pulses in renewed interest. But he doesn't move them. He stands there, pressing inside me, his rugged features intent.

I can't help squirming a little. "What are you doing?"

"Making sure." He presses down on my lower belly so I can't move.

"Making sure of what?" This is getting bizarre.

"That my sperm stays inside you."

What? It's a shout inside my head, but nothing comes out of my mouth as I gape like a fish.

"No...what..." I try to get more words out, but they are locked in my tight throat.

Choosing together for me not to take the morning after pill is miles away from him actively trying to get me pregnant. Isn't it?

"What the hell are you talking about?" I am finally able to demand.

"You want my baby. I want you to have my baby."

I try to scoot back from his invading fingers. "Let me up."

"Not yet."

"We have to talk and I'm not doing it with your hand in my vagina."

"It is only two fingers. I've never been interested in fisting, but if that is something you want."

"No," I practically shout.

His dick is oversized enough. His whole hand? Not in this lifetime.

"Good. I would worry about hurting you."

How are we having this conversation? In this situation?

"Please, Atlas, you have to let me up."

He looks down at me. "I like touching you."

"I figured that out." But right now I need my brain online and it goes haywire when he's touching me. "I mean it, Atlas."

He pulls his fingers out and my body mourns the loss. *Mamma mia*. I am addicted. What am I going to do when he moves on?

A man from wealth like his doesn't have to settle. But why the heck is he *trying* to get me pregnant?

I sit up and wetness gushes from me. That's one box that is going to be unpacked, broken down and buried with the other recycling before anyone else gets a chance to see the proof of my poor decisions.

Ignoring his dictate, I clamber off the boxes in a less than graceful fashion. When my feet hit the chilly floor, a big shiver wracks my body. Standing naked in the cold storage is probably not one of my best moves.

Quickly yanking on my leggings and top, I say, "I need a shower."

And there was me thinking we could get off fast and I could go on with my preparations for tonight. I didn't factor in the lack of a condom and the mess that would make. Or how sweaty I would get either.

Sex with Atlas is messy. And overwhelming. And wonderful. But really, really messy.

Slipping my feet into my ballet flats, I grab my underwear and bra. No point in putting them on only to take them off again. Hopefully, I won't see Willow on the way to my apartment.

"Here." I shove my lingerie toward Atlas. "Make yourself useful and put these in your pocket, or something."

He takes the undergarments from me and tucks them away.

Turning back to the box, I see the wet spot testifying to what we did and cringe. I rip open the top and start putting bottles on the shelves.

"What are you doing?"

"Getting rid of the evidence." Inhaling, the scent of sex assaults me. *Caspita!* "Can you open the door, and I don't know, wave some air in here?"

The most amazing sound erupts behind me. I spin in time to see the pure amusement covering Atlas's face. His laughter is deep and masculine. Also delicious.

"You want me to get rid of the smell of our sex?"

"Yes."

He opens the door and walks out. A second later I hear the back door opening too. He comes back carrying a flattened cardboard box and using it like a fan, he waves fresh air from the hallway into the room.

Finishing with the bottles in the box my bottom was on, I break it down, flatten it and join him in his efforts.

Atlas stops, inhales deeply and nods. "Better."

I have to agree, but a trace of the scent remains. Shaking my head, I hand my flattened box to Atlas. "Will you put those in the recyclables?"

He must have figured out where we store them near the garbage dumpster to have found the one he's using.

Taking the cardboard from me, he nods. "I'll meet you upstairs."

Because he can. Because he knows my security codes.

I frown. "I need to change the codes on my doors."

"Not on my account."

Why did I know he was going to say that?

Shaking my head, I pull the door to the cool storage shut behind me. "I'll leave them for now so you can get upstairs."

"Save me some hot water," he shoots over his shoulder before jauntily walking toward the backdoor, whistling a tune I can't quite place.

And then it hits me. He's whistling "Moves Like Jagger."

CHAPTER 10

ATLAS

The shower is still running when I let myself into Lucia's apartment. The urge to join her is so damn strong, but my woman has a club to run.

After dropping my duffle in her bedroom, I clean up at the kitchen sink. Zipping up my jeans, I feel the bulge in my pocket from her panties and bra. I pull out the bra and go back into her bedroom to drop it in the clothes hamper she has there.

The panties still damp from her juices, I keep.

"Oh! Atlas. You're here." Steam follows her out of the small bathroom.

Another reason I don't join her. That room is barely big enough for me. With both of us in the shower, I doubt either of us could turn around, much less bend down. Could be fun to try though.

Lucia's hair is wrapped up in a towel and another one covers her luscious curves. I make no effort to hide my interest as she pulls lingerie from her tall dresser.

Turning, she wags her finger at me. "You stay over there, mister."

"Sure, *ílios mou*." I lean back against the wall to show her she's safe from my sexual advances.

For now.

My willpower is tested when she steps into a red silk thong and tugs it up her lush hips. When she settles her gorgeous tits into a matching bra, I growl.

Her head is down, but I see those lips of hers curve into a small smile.

"I'm being good, but if you keep teasing me, you're going to end up under me instead of in your club."

She lifts her head, her dark eyes filled with fire. "Don't even think about it."

"Seems to me you're doing your best to make sure that's all I'm thinking about."

Biting her lip, she nods. "Maybe. You deserve it though, after that incident in the cold storage."

"Incident?" I ask carefully.

"What would you call it?"

"Amazing sex."

Color surges into her cheeks and she turns away to get something out of the tiny closet. "It was more than that."

"Yeah?"

"You know it was. You *tried* to get me pregnant."

"You want a baby."

"Theoretically." She pulls another sexy red dress down her body. "Choosing not to take Plan B is very different than actively trying to get pregnant."

"Not really."

She spins to face me. "Yes, really. You can't seriously want me to have your baby."

"My mother has been on me and my brothers to give her grandchildren."

"Are you kidding me? Your mother wants to be a grandmother, so you decide to knock up a practical stranger."

I give fuck all that my mother wants to be a grandmother. Her and my dad accepted my grandfather's decision to leave me at the mercy of the bratva, telling my brothers I'd been sent away to school.

Of course, she cried and acted horrified by what had been done to me in captivity. My grandfather hadn't told either her or my dad about the videos. According to my uncle, my mom begged her father to get me back right after I was kidnapped.

He told her he would in his own time and his own way. She believed him. Trusted him. So did my dad.

Which means I will never trust either of them again.

No, my mom is not the reason. The woman I'm fucking wants a baby and she's not getting pregnant with any other man's child. "You'll be a good mother."

"How can you know that? We met last night!"

"When you know, you know." Ever since I didn't listen to that voice inside me that told me danger lurked around the corner and I got kidnapped at the age of ten, I do not ignore my instincts.

And they are telling me this woman would make an amazing mother. Not only that, but I want her to be the mother to *my* children.

It's fast. I don't care. I know what I know.

I am not letting this woman go and nothing will hold her to me with stronger glue than my baby inside her.

Convincing my family to accept her will take some doing. She's an outsider. From the look of horror on her beautiful face, convincing her is going to be even harder.

"You're serious about this," she says, her voice high with disbelief.

Keeping my cum insider her didn't clue her in? If she needs to hear me say it, I will. "Yes. I'm going to get you pregnant."

I don't tell her my plans to keep her. That might make her nervous.

"Do you always wear red to work?" Yes, it's a blatant attempt to change the subject.

There's no point in arguing about something that will not change.

"You can't say something like that and then calmly ask me about my work attire."

"Pretty sure I can."

"Atlas! Be reasonable."

"Was it reasonable not to take the morning after pill?" She has good instincts, but it's clear she's not used to following them. "You knew it was the right choice."

"I can't get pregnant."

"If that were true, I'm pretty sure you would have led with it when we talked about you not being on birth control earlier."

"Are you calling me a liar?"

"No, but you're not telling the whole story either."

"How can you know that?" She shakes her head. "Do not say it. You *do not* know me, no matter what you think."

She'll learn differently, but for now, I won't push that particular point. "Tell me why you think it will be hard for you to get pregnant."

Her face freezes in a grimace of grief, an old agony deep in her gaze. "I'm not ready to talk about that."

"Okay."

"Okay," she echoes.

"Should you take the towel out of your hair before we go back downstairs."

"We?"

"You're not spending the night around a bunch of horny, drunk men without me."

"Has anyone ever told you that you are pathologically possessive?"

"No."

Her expression is pure skepticism. "Right."

"I've never cared before if the women I was fucking wanted to fuck other men."

"Never?" she asks, her voice breathy.

"Never. My cousin asked me to introduce you because he wanted to get with you and I threw him across my brother's office."

"You told your brother and cousin about me?"

"Yes."

"And you *threw* your cousin?"

"I didn't kill him." That's restraint right there.

"Good to know."

"Don't be afraid of me. I will never hurt you."

"That's easy to say, not so easy to follow through on."

I want to know what she means by that, but Lucia refuses to talk anymore while she's getting ready. She tells me if I can't be quiet, I need to go in the other room. She needs to center herself before going down to the club.

"It's Friday night and that means all hands on deck. I'm running behind. I won't have time to come back up here and go through my usual routine to get my head in the right space to deal with a noisy, crowded club."

She doesn't like the noise and the crowds? Why the hell does she own a nightclub then?

I don't ask because I can see that she means it. Lucia needs some time to find her Zen. She's stressed and it's not all because of a busy night at the club.

My decision to get her pregnant has her discombobulated. But she's not trying to kick me out of her apartment. Hell, she's not even kicking me out of the bedroom as long as I keep my mouth zipped.

That's pretty damn telling, even if she doesn't want to see it.

Her instincts tell her she belongs to me, but her brain is fighting it.

CHAPTER II

LUCIA

Atlas helps me with my preparation and I'm grateful for two reasons. One, I'm running behind and two, his presence stops Willow from grilling me.

She doesn't even try to pretend she isn't watching us though. Every time Atlas touches me, her perfectly shaped eyebrows waggle at me and she makes a ridiculous expression of exaggerated approval.

And he touches me a lot. A hand on my shoulder. A caress over my hip as he walks by. Brushing my fingers with his when he's taking a box of inventory from me on my way to the bar. He's really got a thing about me not carting heavy boxes around.

It could be annoying, but it's not. It's sweet.

It's too much to expect Willow to keep speculation about Atlas to herself. But I don't expect my servers and bartenders to show up armed with curiosity born of knowledge.

She texted them.

My stomach knots. They all know that I took him upstairs last night. That he's still here is proof positive that my ovaries are in charge and not my brain.

The DJ arrives and my worries get tabled out of necessity. Although Chaos is a favorite with the patrons, he is not on the regular rotation. A bit of a prima donna, the DJ expects my undivided attention while he sets up. Tonight is no exception.

"Get your shit together," Atlas growls at the DJ. "Lucia has more important things to do than hold your hand."

Chaos looks Atlas up and down with a sneer. "Who are you?"

"I am Atlas Rokos. I'm in business with Constantin Petros. Change your fucking tone or this is the last gig you play on the West Coast."

Dio mio. I'm going to lose my DJ. On a Friday night.

But Chaos doesn't pick up his toys and go. He stares at Atlas like he's seeing a ghost. "*The* Constantin Petros, the nightclub owner?"

Atlas jerks his head in a nod, his jaw like granite.

Chaos puts his hands up. "Sorry, man. I didn't mean to monopolize Lucia's time. You sticking around tonight?"

"Yes." It sounds like a threat to me.

But the DJ grins. "Great! Maybe you can put a word in for me with Leon."

Who is Leon?

"Impress me and I will." His hand at the small of my back, Atlas turns me and leads me away.

"Who is Leon?" I ask out loud this time.

"He books the DJs for my family's clubs."

"Family!" Chaos exclaims behind us. "You're part of the Petros empire?"

Atlas ignores the DJ and guides me away from the sound booth.

"They must be pretty successful for Chaos to turn darn near obsequious," I say wryly.

"Successful enough." Atlas stops in a secluded corner and pulls me around so I'm facing him. "Is he always so demanding?"

"Talent usually is. One way or another." I shrug. "It's the price I pay for getting the best. Chaos brings in clubbers from all over. People will drive eight hours to be here on a night he is running the music."

The lines will be down the block tonight. I have two extra bouncers coming in.

"How did you get him to come here?"

I don't take offence at the question. My club is successful, but it's not big and I only have the one location. In the suburbs.

"One of my bartenders is his cousin." I've spent five years leveraging every person I have contact with to make Nuovi Inizi profitable.

"He'll leave for LA if Leon offers him a gig," Atlas says warningly.

"Can't be helped. Chaos refuses to sign a contract with any of the area clubs because he wants to break into either the Los Angeles or New York club scenes." Even without a good word from Atlas, Chaos is on the right trajectory to do that soon too.

Which is why I put up with his need to be the center of my attention when he plays my club.

Atlas grunts.

"Is there a reason you haven't mentioned the name of your family's clubs?" I ask.

"Zesti." He waits for my reaction.

I open my mouth. Nothing comes out. I close it. Then I try again. "Your family owns the Zesti clubs?"

There are three in Los Angeles that I know of, and he mentioned that they have clubs in San Francisco too. I'm pretty sure they have locations in San Diego as well.

Tino and his father tried to emulate their success in Detroit. They managed well enough to draw the attention of the local Irish mob and Russian bratva. My husband died trying to keep control of lucrative nightclubs that laundered money by the millions.

Cold suspicion runs up my spine. "Are you here scoping locations for another Zesti?"

Does he want to take over Nuovi Inizi?

Atlas pulls me in for a kiss. "No, Lucia. I told you, me, my brothers and my cousins moved here to build our own thing, not extend what others have already done."

I believe him, but I still say, "Promise me you're not using me to get information so you can start your own club and destroy mine in the process?"

"On my honor, I do not want to destroy your club." He presses his forehead against my own. "I promise."

Again, I believe him. Either that makes me hopelessly naïve, or a really good judge of character.

"Break it up you two." Willow looks down at her tablet. "The bachelorette party cancelled. The groom eloped with the bride's pregnant cousin. I didn't think you'd mind us refunding the reservation deposit for the tables. I wanted to check with you first though."

We usually require a minimum of twenty-four-hour notice to cancel a table reservation without charging a fee.

"We won't have any trouble filling them tonight with Chaos in the sound booth. Have Cheryl contact the waitlist before we open them up to walk-ins though."

"Will do. Barry wants to talk to you about security tonight."

I don't roll my eyes because this is typical of Barry. He has a plan, approved by me, but insists every night on going over it one last time before we open the doors.

Probably comes from being in the military.

I don't complain though. We've never had a major security incident and the minor ones get handled quickly and efficiently.

Without giving it any real thought, I take Atlas's hand and lead him toward my office where Barry will be waiting with his team.

And so it begins. Friday night at Nuovi Inizi.

I won't be able to take a full breath again until the doors shut behind the last patron.

~ ~ ~

The night is every bit as busy as I anticipated. Chaos is on fire. Probably trying to impress Atlas into putting a good word in for him with the booking agent for Zesti.

No servers call in sick. The bouncers are focused. The bartenders and barbacks sling drinks with all the flair they're supposed to.

The music is loud. We are packed to capacity.

It should annoy me having Atlas hovering like he is, but it doesn't. He knows how to stay out of the way, but he also knows how to step in and help when I need it. I've never had that.

My staff are good at their jobs, but as they say, *the buck stops here*. There are too many fires only I can put out. No doubt because of experience with his family's clubs, Atlas knows how to help me douse the flames.

I warn myself not to get used to it.

Atlas isn't a permanent fixture in my life. This thing between us is about a minute old and new relationships fail as often as new nightclubs.

~ ~ ~

But he's still there. Later that night. And the next. And the next after that. The sex is incendiary.

Even though his inexplicable desire to get me pregnant does not abate. In fact, his insistence on holding his cum inside me is a huge turn on. Not that I'll ever admit that to him.

At times I wish my body could cooperate and at others I'm grateful for whatever made me incapable of conceiving again after the miscarriage.

Because the idea of having a baby is both tantalizing and terrifying.

Especially with Atlas as the father.

Nuovi Inizi is closed Sunday and Monday, but I still have work to do.

On Sunday, Atlas leaves while I'm in my office. He says he's going home to get fresh clothes and check in with his brothers, but I fully expect a call or a text saying he won't be back today.

Not because he doesn't intend to come back, but because no matter how intense this thing between us is, Atlas can't give all his time to me.

He has a life and he's in Portland to build a business with his family.

It should annoy me having Atlas mooning like that [illegible]
[illegible] of the way, but seeing [illegible]
[illegible] I've certified that.

[illegible]
[illegible]
[illegible] knows [illegible] the fans.

[illegible] to it.

[illegible]

[illegible] later [illegible] And the next [illegible]
[illegible] legendary.

[illegible] to get his pregnant [illegible]
In fact [illegible] his cum inside me [illegible]
[illegible]

[illegible]
[illegible]
[illegible]
[illegible]

[illegible] Monday [illegible]
[illegible]
[illegible] with his [illegible]
[illegible] today.

[illegible] because I [illegible]
[illegible]

He has [illegible] to [illegible]

CHAPTER 12

ATLAS

Everyone is on the back deck when I get home. Zeus is grilling steaks and the scent of charred meat makes my mouth water.

It's not exactly barbecue weather, but it's not raining either. I don't take off my hoodie though.

"About time you showed your face." Zephyr punches me in the shoulder. "I thought you disappeared in that magic pussy."

I punch him back and he staggers. "Don't mention Lucia's pussy if you want to keep your tongue."

"It's true then, you're falling for her?" Orion hands me a bottle of my favorite beer from Santorini.

Lucia's customers aren't the only ones who like craft beer. "I'm keeping her."

"You think that's wise?" Wearing jeans and a polo, my middle brother still manages to look like a high-class lawyer.

"Don't care." This is about following my gut, and my gut says that Lucia Esposito belongs to me.

Orion's eyes narrow. "You have a job to do with her."

"And I will do it." I'll enjoy doing it. Spending time with her is no hardship.

"You think she's going to let you keep her once you start charging her club protection money?" Orion asks.

"She'll have no choice." I'm not letting her go.

Besides, Lucia will be better off under my protection in the long run. A highly intelligent woman, she will realize that once I explain things to her.

Orion takes a sip of his own beer. "Tell me about the club."

"She built it up from nothing, turning a furniture store into a bangin' nightclub. Lucia has her finger on the pulse of her clientele and the area. She keeps everything fresh."

"Fuck me," my brother breathes.

But I'm not done. "She doesn't like crowds or noise, but you'd never know it by how she is with the patrons and her staff."

"He's doing that creepy shit again." Helios glares at me.

Orion asks Zeus, "Are you seeing this?"

"I told you. He was smiling the other day and he threw Zephyr across my office when our cousin suggested getting with the woman too."

Remembering my cousin's colossally fucked up proposal, I shoulder check him and he crashes back into the table.

"What the hell? I didn't say anything," Zephyr complains.

I shrug. Zephyr is the youngest of us, and sometimes it feels like he's a lot more than two years younger than me. Maybe because he didn't make his first kill until after he was legal to drink.

"Do you smile when you are with her?" Orion asks.

I give him a look. That's a ridiculous question. Of course, I do. "What's not to smile about when I'm with the sexiest, most beautiful and intelligent woman I've ever met."

My cousins gape at each other, but Zeus and Orion are fixed on me.

"She's an outsider," Orion says the same way he'd warn me Lucia had a communicable, deadly disease.

"The fuck do I care about following the traditions of the *Ádis Adelfótita*?" Those traditions left a ten-year-old child in the hands of monsters for a year.

"It's not just about tradition. Outsiders don't understand our way of life."

"She might already be pregnant with my baby."

"*Gamo*!" That's Helios.

"Did the condom break?" Zephyr asks. "Why isn't she on birth control?"

"Remember that redhead in Athens?" Helios reminisces. "She said she couldn't use anything because she was a magnet for side effects."

"Yeah, she gave a hell of a blow job though." Zephyr shakes his head.

Zeus pulls the steaks from the grill and brings the platter over. We all troop inside and gather around the table in the breakfast nook. No one says anything about eating in the dining room.

Zeus puts the platter of steaks in the center of the table beside a cucumber salad and a basket of rolls. He's frowning, but he doesn't add to the peanut gallery.

"You didn't wear a condom," Orion guesses as he sits down.

"No."

"How do you know she's clean?" Helios asks and immediately puts his hands up. "I'm not saying anything against her."

"This lack of caution isn't like you," Orion adds, eyes the same blue as mine trying to see into my soul.

Good luck with that, brother. My soul withered nearly twenty years ago under torture and the knowledge my grandfather would rather hold on to his territory than his grandson.

"We got tested." I grab a steak with my fork and plop it on the plate in front of me before adding some cucumber salad.

I hope Gina made it. Zeus can grill, but none of us are good cooks otherwise. Not like Lucia. What that woman can whip up in her tiny kitchen is amazing.

"Your idea, or hers?" Orion asks.

I finish my bite of salad. Our housekeeper definitely made it. It has the perfect amount of feta, olives and dressing.

"What's with the twenty questions?" I ask, instead of answering my brother.

"I'm worried about you."

"Yeah, it's almost like you're human, or something," Zephyr teases.

I shrug. I don't allow emotions to be used as weapons against me, but that doesn't make me a robot. It makes me smart.

This weird lightness inside? It's okay. "I think I'm happy."

"You're volatile is what you are." Helios cuts into his own steak. "Like an elephant in musth."

"What are you? A zoologist now? The fuck are you talking about elephants?" Zephyr demands.

Helios ignores his brother. "They go into this thing when they want to impregnate a female. It's called musth and it makes them violent and unpredictable. Dangerous."

"Are you saying I'm dangerous?"

"You're the most dangerous man on the west coast, hell maybe the continent," Zeus says drily.

"That's not what Helios means." My cousin is talking about me being dangerous *to my family*.

Maybe to Lucia.

My cousin looks worried. "You're right. It's not. Your special skills as an assassin makes controlling your emotions even more important."

"I'm not going to shoot one of you." Or break their necks, or shove a stiletto through their hearts, or...okay the list could get pretty long.

I know more ways to kill than there are letters in the Greek alphabet.

"Just throw your cousin across a room." Orion's tone is hard. "Listen, brother, seeing you smile after all this time. It's pretty damn terrific, but if you lose control of your emotions after keeping them locked down so long..." He shakes his head.

"You could burn this city down and the whole state with it," Zeus says.

I frown at my oldest brother. "A few smiles and some laughter doesn't mean I'm out of control."

"You laughed?" Helios asks, dumbfounded.

My brothers and cousins all stare at me with varying degrees of disbelief.

Done with this, I surge to my feet. "You gave me a job to do, Zeus. I'm doing it."

"Sit down, Atlas." Zeus doesn't make it an order. There is almost a plea in his eyes. "Eat with us. Tell us what else you've learned."

"You want to grill the steaks? Fine. You keep trying to grill me and I'm out of here," I warn before returning to my chair.

It would be a shame to waste Gina's salad.

"I don't like the potential I see for the situation with this woman to blow up in your face and that's the last I'll say about it." Orion takes a sip of his beer. "For now."

Doesn't matter what my brothers or cousins say. I'm keeping Lucia. Hell, I'm not sure it matters what she says.

I tell them the observations I've made and the name of the distiller who sells Lucia his handcrafted ale. Too bad for Shawn, his craft distillery is in our territory. I won't mind extracting protection money from him at all.

"What did he do to piss you off?" Helios asks.

I shrug. Telling them he stands too close to Lucia might make me sound unhinged. I'm not. I'm protective. And a little possessive. Maybe a lot. Okay, yeah, definitely a lot.

I would be as happy to kill Shawn as let him live to pay us.

"There's an issue with the port," Zephyr says when I'm done giving my report.

"I thought you had it locked down," Zeus says. "We already put the offer in on the abandoned shipping yard."

"Someone else came in and made a backdoor offer. They're trying to outbid us."

"Who?"

"I don't have a name, but I saw a group of tatted up men down there today. They were with someone who never got out of the car, but they each reported to him after checking out different parts of the yard."

"What kind of tats?"

Zephyr looks at me and then back to Zeus. "I can't be positive, but they looked like bratva tats."

What the actual fuck? We spent a year investigating the Portland metro before we made our move and there was no sign of a bratva presence.

Street gangs and militia groups, but no bratva, no Irish mob and no Italian mafia. We chose our new home carefully because establishing a new territory for the *Ádis Adelfótita* isn't going to be easy.

Zeus doesn't look as shocked as the rest of us.

"You know about this?" I ask him.

"I got a tipoff that bratva activity is increasing in Portland."

"Tipoff from who?" Orion asks.

Zeus grimaces. "That anonymous guy who has been sending me texts."

We don't know who the unknown informant is. But the intel Zeus has received so far has been accurate.

"Did your CI give any details?" Helios asks.

"He's not a CI," Zeus snaps. "I'm not a fucking cop."

Unfazed, Helios says, "He's keeping his identity confidential and he's an informant, so CI."

"You're not as funny as you think you are." Zeus looks at me. "My *anonymous* informant gave me the name of a bar the bratva are hanging around. Atlas, I want you there. You have the best chance of recognizing bratva soldiers by face alone and knowing what family they are from."

I am a little obsessed with any bratva even remotely connected to Golubev. No one in my family will ever go through what I did because the bratva want something from us.

I send a message when I need to and even when I don't. Loud and clear, with dead and dismembered bodies.

"I'll do the recon, but otherwise I'll be with Lucia." I let my brother see my commitment to this family in my eyes. "If you need me, I'll be here."

Zeus nods. "I know. Zephyr, take some soldiers and set up cameras at the shipping yard. Orion, see if you can find out who made the backdoor offer. We aren't losing this port."

No piece of shit bratva are getting a foothold in our territory either.

CHAPTER 13

LUCIA

I get a text from Atlas, but it's not what I expect.

Atlas: *Want to check out a bar on the east side with me?*

Lucia: *Sure. When?*

Atlas: *Tonight. I'm on my way back to your place.*

Lucia: *I'll make dinner.*

I love cooking for Atlas. He's so appreciative, regardless of what I make, and I like keeping him to myself. I miss cooking for other people.

Letting others into my personal space is hard for me though. Maybe I'll invite Willow and Barry for dinner after I move into the new place.

I don't have to open myself up to close friendship to have work colleagues over. If you asked her, I bet Willow would say we are friends already anyway.

We're not. We can't be. She knows nothing about the real me.

My heart stutters at the thought. Because if that is true of Willow, it is equally true of Atlas. He doesn't know where I come from and that cannot change, but there's so much more I'm keeping from him.

Is it worth changing that to keep him in my life?

The weight of my secrets has never felt so heavy. Can I make myself tell him about losing the baby at least? I don't have to reveal that my dead husband was mafia.

Most regular people would never even consider that possibility anyway.

~ ~ ~

I'm finishing the last touches on my electric skillet lasagna when the door to my apartment opens.

"*Gamó.*"

A smile plays around my lips. I've figured out that means *fuck* in Greek.

Him saying it like that tells me that my current attire is having the effect I planned. I'm wearing a pair of black panties, no bra, and a frilly bib apron.

It is from a Halloween costume I wore the year before last. Sheer white organza, it is not a practical apron, but serves its purpose. Cooking naked isn't safe.

Pretending nonchalance my body is far from feeling, I sprinkle the fresh basil leaves over the top of the lasagna. Atlas starts whistling and after a couple of bars, I recognize the song. "Centerfold."

I'm already wet. Cooking naked waiting for my lover to show up will do that to me, but that whistling? It has me gushing slick onto my inner thighs. It takes everything inside me not to turn around. Swaying my bottom side to side, I put the lid back on the electric skillet and turn off the heat so the lasagna can rest.

Strong hands land on my hips sending jolts of electric energy through me, before sliding up to cup my breasts.

"I like this." Making circles with his palms, he rubs my sensitive flesh through the slippery organza.

My nipples perk under his ministrations. "I like that," I say throatily.

What this man does to me with a simple touch.

"Do you need to turn anything off?"

I shake my head. "Everything is off. The lasagna is resting. We can eat it whenever."

"Good," he growls. "Put your hands on the edge of the counter and don't move them."

Anticipation shudders through me as I obey his instructions, planting my palms flat on the countertop.

"Good girl," he rumbles in my ear, his hot breath sending sensual shivers down my neck and into my shoulders.

Kneading my breasts, he tugs at my earlobe with his teeth. I want to lean back into his hard body, but I can't with my hands where they are. I whimper.

"Problem, *ílios mou*?"

"I want to touch you too."

"More than you want to feel this?" He pinches one nipple and then the other, alternating back and forth between them repeatedly.

Something about him doing it through the stiff, but slick organza adds to the sensations and arousal arrows down my body, making my vaginal walls contract in need.

"Atlas." That is all I say, but my voice drips with need.

Making an animalistic sound, he spins me around and covers my lips with his in a bone-melting kiss.

My body softening against his immediately, I open my mouth for his questing tongue. He tastes like beer and the addictive flavor that I have only tasted on his lips. It is pure Atlas.

Skimming his hands down my body, he sends more shivers of arousal cascading along every inch of naked skin his fingers touch.

My body reacts to him so quickly and completely. One caress and I am going up in flames.

Reaching behind me, he unties the apron. Our pressed together bodies are all that is keeping it in place. I shift back a little so it can fall before pressing my now naked breasts and diamond hard nipples against his chest.

When he cups my bottom, and lifts me, my legs automatically go around his hips. He jostles me so my core presses against the erection in his jeans. Pleasure zings through me and I moan into his mouth.

Not breaking the kiss, he effortlessly carries me into the bedroom. But he stops at the bed. "You're not too sore?"

I shake my head. Am I sore? The truth is, I've been pleasantly sore since that first morning after and I love the way it feels. Every twinge in my nether regions reminds me that right now, for as long as this thing lasts, I am not alone.

I'm not only sore though. I'm also extra sensitive too. Even wearing underwear stimulates me and keeps me in a constant state of arousal.

He kisses along my jaw. "We went at it pretty hard this morning."

"I remember," I purr. "Maybe we can do that again."

My vagina pulses in agreement.

"You're so perfect for me." He lays me down on the bed and steps back to strip out of his clothes. "Don't touch your thong."

That commanding tone sends shivers of need cascading through me. I slide my hand inside the front of my panties until my middle finger dips between my wet folds.

"I said—" he starts to growl.

But I interrupt him. "To leave them on. I have. You didn't tell me not to touch myself."

Drawing the silky wetness my body has made upward, I get my clitoris wet and make light circles around the bundle of nerve endings. My hips jerk upward and I moan.

The feral sound that comes out of Atlas goes straight to my core.

He grabs my wrist and pulls my hand away from my sex and puts it in his mouth. He sucks my fingers, sliding his tongue between them.

I revel in his attention, moving my body decadently on the bed.

He releases my fingers. "You taste so good, *ílios mou*."

"Do I?"

"Taste." Bringing my hand to my mouth, he waits for me to obey.

I open my mouth and suck my own fingers in. Flavors burst over my tongue. My arousal. Him.

Tugging my fingers out of my mouth, he places my hand above my head and then slides his fingertips down my arm and over to my breast. He cups my breast and brushes his thumb over my aching nipple.

I cup my other breast with the hand not above my head, pinching my own nipple and sending sharp shards of pleasure slicing through me.

Moaning, I cant my hips upward, my core achingly empty. "Please, Atlas."

"Not yet." His jaw is taut with need, his control so close to breaking.

But he doesn't break. His erection, dark and engorged with blood, leaks pre-ejaculate and bobs in front of him like a baseball bat about to take a swing.

He tugs my hand away from my body. "Not yet," he says again. "You're not ready yet.

"I'm past ready," I argue.

Atlas smiles. And it's not one of his nice smiles. This one is all sorts of devious and it sends anticipation running along every one of my nerve pathways.

He places my hand above my head beside the other one.

Lying like this, I am vulnerable, but powerful too. I am the absolute center of his attention.

In this moment, nothing exists outside this room for either of us.

"Clasp your left wrist with your right hand."

Relishing the release of control, I do exactly as he says.

"Good girl." He says something in Greek and even though I don't understand the words, the tone makes arousal gush between my legs. "Now, close your eyes."

Letting my eyelids lower, and unable to see him now, I can only focus on what I am feeling. Both of his big hands cup my breasts, squeezing and releasing in rhythmic movements. Then he pinches my nipples and jolts of pleasure zing between them to my clit.

Gasping, I turn my head from side to side, but I don't open my eyes.

I don't want this game to end.

His hands slide away from me, and I mourn their loss, but I don't protest. I want to know what comes next.

Strong fingers grip my ankles and he pushes my legs up so my knees bend until my heels are practically touching my butt. "Spread your thighs, Lucia. Let me see my silk covered pussy."

I part my thighs and he guides my feet until I am fully open to him.

"Your panties are soaked." The air shifts and that is the only warning I get before his mouth is on me there.

He inhales my scent and groans and then he's biting against my tender flesh, but the fabric of my thong acts as a barrier, dulling the sharp sting of his teeth.

There is a snick, like a switchblade opening. Cold steel slides up my calf and a shiver of atavistic fear goes through me.

I don't move a muscle. I barely breathe as the flat of the knife glides along my skin until it presses against my center.

"Atlas," I moan.

"You are such a good girl. So damn trusting."

"Only you." I don't know why I trust him so deeply, but my certainty that he will not harm me is absolute.

"Only me," he growls. Then the knife goes under the side of my thong and cuts through the silk with barely a whisper.

How sharp is it? Sharp enough that if Atlas were to slip even a hairs breath, it would slice right through my skin to muscle.

He doesn't slip though. He drags the flat of the knife over the apex of my thighs, sending my intimate flesh quivering. And then he slices through the other side of my panties.

The silk tugs against my skin and then it is gone, my entire vulva now on display for him.

Two thick fingers press inside of me, and my vaginal walls clamp down on them, trying to suck him in deeper. When he pulls back, I whimper, but then he's thrusting forward again, pistoning in and out of my tender channel with quick, powerful thrusts.

His thumb glides over my clitoris when his fingers are embedded as deep as they can go inside me. Pleasure so deep, it is almost pain, radiates through me. I can hear myself moaning, pleading, but it is as if I am removed from it. So in tune with my pleasure receptors that I'm drunk on it, but also feeling like I'm floating beyond my body.

My eyes fly open. I need to connect to the here and now or I will be lost forever.

His eyes are waiting for mine, his gaze locking us together as intimately as his fingers inside my channel.

"Close your eyes, *ílios mou*."

I shake my head, almost frantic. "I need to see, or I'll float away."

I never knew passion like this before him, so intense it consumes me completely.

"I'll keep you here," he promises and reaches to brush his hand down over my eyes, forcing my lids to shutter.

"Atlas, I need you inside me." I want to reach for him, but I don't.

"I am inside you."

"Your sex. I need that big dick stretching me wide."

"You'll come this way first." There is no give in his voice. "You will gift me your pleasure."

The thrusts of his hand picks up pace and his thumb circles my sensitive nub with every deep penetration. Ecstasy builds inside me and I give myself over to it, once again trusting Atlas to keep me safe, even from himself.

A cataclysm of pleasure detonates inside me and I scream as my body bows upward, my muscles tensing in a pleasure pain rictus. With talented and determined fingers, Atlas drags me through the aftershocks and right into another orgasm before I've caught my breath from the first one.

Not giving me a chance to come down, he's there, between my legs, his blunt head pushing against my swollen flesh. His crown breaks through my opening and my inner walls contract.

He presses inexorably forward, forcing my oversensitive, inflamed flesh to accept the intrusion of his iron hard penis. Pleasure thrills through me as he claims my body the way I've been craving.

Every time is like the first one, and I wonder if this will be the time when I cannot accommodate his length and girth. But he bottoms out inside me, pressing against my cervix and stretching my sensitive tissues beyond what I think he can.

"You're like a damn virgin every time."

Or he's monster sized. "Had sex with many virgins?"

"None."

"Then how—"

He doesn't let me finish. "You are tighter than any other pussy I have fucked."

"Not so much with the other vajayjays you've conquered," I instruct him.

"You make me forget every single one."

I don't want to know how many there are for him to forget.

"I never wanted to keep a woman, Lucia, but I'm keeping you."

Typical arrogant man. He's not asking.

Why my inner sex kitten thrills at this, I can dissect later.

"You're going to come again," he tells me with confidence. "And you are going to soak my cock before I bathe your womb with my seed."

"You're so primitive."

"Is that a complaint?"

With my arms willingly planted above my head and my eyes voluntarily shut because that's what he wants?

"No."

"I didn't think so." He pulls back until only his head is still inside me.

I whimper at the sense of emptiness.

"Is this what you want?" He slams forward, filling me completely. "What you need?"

I can't answer because there's no air left in my lungs as he slams in and out of me with addictive force. My breasts shake and my hips jerk with every powerful thrust, each one taking me toward the precipice again.

"Please," I beg.

"What? What do you want?"

I'm so wet, that despite how tight I am around him, he slides in and out of me with ease. The sound of our intimate flesh smacking together, the squelch of my juices bathing us both is satisfying on a primal level.

"I need to see you," I gasp out. "Please."

"You can open your eyes when you come." He leans down, sliding his arms under me and gripping my shoulders to hold me in place as he rams into my body.

He surrounds me completely.

I didn't know sex could be like this. If I had, I would have been sure I would hate it. But I don't. I adore the feeling of being claimed so forcefully. I crave it.

Electric currents run along my pleasure pathways, coalescing in the center of me over and over until it explodes with sparks I can see behind my closed eyelids.

"Yes!" he shouts. "Oh, fuck. Milk my cock, take everything out of me."

Needing to see his pleasure, my eyes snap open and lock on his. Intense pleasure stares back at me and that look hits me deep in my core, lighting off another shower of sparks inside me.

His body stills, his arms locked around me like bands of steel, and he grows impossibly large inside me before a cascade of heat bathes my cervix.

If my ovaries weren't so temperamental, this would be the moment I got pregnant. The thought sends a powerful aftershock through me.

Atlas groans. "You squeeze me so tight, *ilios mou*. Even if I wanted to pull out of you, I don't think your pussy would let me."

"You know it's not exactly rational to want to get a woman you've known only a few days pregnant."

"The dark ember left of my soul knows yours."

Emotion threatens to overwhelm me. "Why only an ember?"

"It's a long story."

"And if you follow past patterns, you're not going anywhere anytime soon."

He acknowledges that truth with an inclination of his handsome head. "It's not a pretty story."

"Does it have anything to do with this?" Breaking his stricture not to move my hands, I trace the Cerberus tattoo and the Greek writing under it.

Placed over his heart, it has to be important to him.

"Yes."

"What do the words mean?" Or is that too personal? Will he refuse to answer?

"Give them nothing, but take from them everything."

"That's grim."

"I told you. Not pretty."

I wave between our bodies. "This isn't pretty either."

The way our bodies connect is too brutal for *pretty*, but it is also soul stirringly beautiful.

"If you are going to connect with my soul, I want to know why yours is only a *dark* ember." I *need* to know.

"I was kidnapped when I was ten years old."

My hands move of their own volition to curve around his neck and my legs come up around his hips as I hug him with my whole body. "I am sorry."

Wealthy families are always at risk for kidnappings. Because in the mafia, that risk is increased, especially if there's a war going on, I had training from early childhood how to react if I was taken.

It never happened to me, but I remember the nightmares after sessions for me and my brother with our instructor.

"What happened?" I ask.

"They demanded a ransom from my grandfather."

"Not your father?"

"Grandfather had what they wanted."

That's not surprising. As the patriarch of the family, his grandfather would hold the bulk of their wealth until his death.

"Your grandfather couldn't pay what they were asking?" I find that hard to believe.

His family owns Zesti, but maybe they weren't as affluent when he was a child.

"He *refused* to pay." There is a wealth of feeling in those four words. Resentment. Disillusionment. Anger.

His grandfather's refusal is still affecting Atlas today. Memory of something he said tickles the back of my mind. Family is everything to him and his brothers. Not their parents.

Clearly not their grandfather.

Atlas swallows and then speaks again, his tone low. "They kept me for a year, sending my grandfather video proof of the torture they were putting me through."

That's where the scars under the giant tattoo on his back come from. The Spartan makes sense now too. A symbol of strength and stoicism.

"A year? Were they holding you in another country?" I'm not surprised the authorities couldn't find him.

Children go missing every day and many are never heard from again.

"I got away. That's all that matters now."

"How?"

But Atlas shakes his head. "If I talk about this anymore, I'll go soft and then I won't be able to hold my cum inside you."

"I know you say you're trying to knock me up, but somehow we always end up going for Round Two when you do this."

His smile devastates my heart. "Added benefit."

My giggle gets cut off as he starts to move again. My last rational thought before pleasure takes my brain offline is that being betrayed by his family would definitely have killed part of his soul.

CHAPTER 14

ATLAS

The bar is not in the seediest part of Portland, but the businesses around it wouldn't generate as much protection money as Lucia's club all together.

"This is where you wanted to bring me?" Lucia asks as I help her out of the X7.

"My brother asked me to check it out."

"Unless you're willing to invest a lot in not only the building, but the neighborhood, anything but a pop-up club here doesn't have much of a chance."

"What about a strip club?"

Her hand tightens in mine. "You're opening a strip club?"

"We're planning a couple, yeah."

"I thought you'd do a night club."

"That's in the plan too."

"Wow, that's a lot of businesses to run. How many brothers do you have?"

"Two brothers and two cousins."

"Older or younger?"

"Does it matter for running a club? We're all well over the age to serve alcohol."

"I wasn't thinking about your suitability to run the clubs. I'm doing that thing people who date do, getting to know you."

"Are we dating?"

"You keep saying you're going to keep me, so I'm going with yes." She looks around us as we step inside the bar. "Though this is not my idea of great date night material, in case you are wondering."

It's a typical neighborhood bar. Low lighting. A little run down, but clean. A single waitress works the floor serving drinks and a bartender serves behind a bar that covers nearly the length of the back wall.

Round tables are scattered throughout the space. No booths. The hallway to the bathroom is the only brightly lit area. The bright lights send a clear message.

No dealing and no sex inside the club. In case the patrons don't get the hint from the brightly lit corridor, there is an obvious camera pointed toward the bathroom. That is unexpected.

The two tables with men speaking Russian is not, but I don't recognize any of them. I step in front of Lucia anyway, blocking her view of the bratva soldiers and their sightline to her.

I'm not supposed to engage, just check the place out and try to figure out which bratva is trying to find a foothold in the Portland metro. Having Lucia with me gives me better cover than coming alone and sticking to the shadows.

It's a solid move. So, why am I second guessing making it?

Leading her to a table as far away from the Russians as I can get, I pull out Lucia's chair for her.

She smiles her thanks, slides out of her coat and hangs it on the back of the chair before sitting down. Her back is to the Russian men, the way I want it. The location is not ideal for gathering intel, but Lucia's safety takes priority.

Even over getting the information my brother wants.

Hell. "I shouldn't have brought you here."

"It's not that bad." She smiles at the waitress approaching our table.

I don't tell her it's not about the ambiance, but her safety. I will keep Lucia from harm. Whatever it takes.

Leaving my leather jacket on because that makes accessing the knives in the hidden interior sheaths easier to get to if I need them, I sit down.

Wearing skintight jeans and a t-shirt that molds her curves and shows a slice of skin between the hem and the waistband of her pants, the waitress stops beside our table. She's easily in her late thirties, if not early forties, but she's taken pains to look younger. Mostly successful, it's the lines around her eyes that give her away.

She gives Lucia a once over, dismisses her and turns a big smile on me. "I'm Wanda Sue, but you can call me Wanda." She winks and her red tinted lips tilt in a smirk. "What can I getcha, sugar?"

"What would you like, *ílios mou*?"

Lucia looks around the bar again and then up at the server. "Do you have any craft beers?"

"This is Portland. What bar doesn't?" the waitress asks, like she thinks Lucia isn't very bright.

My sweet sunshine remains polite though. "I'll have whatever craft IPA you have on hand. With a glass."

That's my woman. All class.

The waitress nods. "And you, sugar?" she asks me.

Lucias's lips draw into a tight, flat line. Oh, she does not like this woman calling me *sugar*. Despite all the action it got earlier, my cock jerks to attention.

Jealous Lucia is our new favorite flavor.

"I'll have the same as my wife. Wait to open the bottles until you bring them to the table," I instruct her.

Lucia jerks and then she kicks my ankle under the table. "I am not your wife," she hisses at me as the waitress flounces away.

"Would you rather she kept hitting on me?" I taunt.

"A wedding ring is no deterrent for some women." She frowns. "You aren't wearing one anyway," she mutters.

"I am aware."

Lucia crosses her arms, thrusting her tits up in a temptation I have to ignore. I can't even look as long as I want to because I have to keep my peripheral vision on the Russians. And when I look at her luscious curves, it takes all of my attention.

She's wearing her signature red again. This time in a tight thin sweater with sleeves that reach an inch past her elbows. No jeans for my sun. She's got a short black skirt on that swishes around her gorgeous thighs when she walks, teasing me.

I could slide my hand up her thigh and be touching her pussy through the red lacy panties she's wearing under it. Her demibra isn't doing anything to camouflage her hard nipples either.

"You're a fucking temptation, you know that?"

"We're on a date. Isn't that what I'm supposed to be doing? Tempting you." She looks me up and down. "You're certainly tempting me."

"What are you newlyweds, or something?" Wanda Sue asks sourly as she plops two bottles of beer on the table.

Opened bottles.

"Take those away." My tone suggests she not argue.

Rolling her eyes, she says, "Jed opened them before I brought them over."

"I told you I wanted them opened at the table."

Her look asks if I'm kidding.

My glare back tells her I'm not.

One of the Russians gets up and goes down the hall toward the bathroom, only he walks right past it.

What is back there?

"I'm going to use the little girl's room while our server is getting us our *unopened* beer." Lucia stands up.

No way is she going down that hallway alone. Cameras be damned.

I stand.

"Are you going to escort me to the bathroom?" she asks with a laugh.

"Might as well drain the elephant."

"Elephant is right," she says sotto voce, but loud enough for the snarky server to hear her.

Putting my hand on the middle of her back, I walk with Lucia right past the table of bratva.

"The *pakhan's vtoroy* expects it to be handled by the time he gets back from San Francisco," one man says in Russian.

That one word confirms who they are. *Pakhan* is the head of a bratva. The fact their *pakhan's* second is in San Francisco is also a wealth of information. There are only two bratva families active in that territory.

The Golubevs in Oakland and the Semenovs, a neutral bratva that controls most of San Francisco proper. I don't recognize these soldiers as being from either bratva brotherhood.

The man closest to the wall says, "There's some company trying to buy the shipping yard. They already put their bid in."

They're talking about the abandoned shipping yard at the port on the Columbia River, and our company, Cerberus Inc. No chance they'll find us. The principals listed on the paperwork don't exist anywhere but in falsified records.

Like a lot of so-called legitimate businesses, we handle buying and selling property through a shell company based in the Cayman Islands. For us, it's not only a tax shelter, but an additional layer of security between us and the enemies that we don't want to know what businesses we own, the FEDs included.

"After tonight, we will have the leverage we need to make the broker accept our terms of sale. The port is ours," the first man replies.

That's something we need to deal with immediately. The Russians like to use threats to family as leverage. We don't, but that doesn't mean we are ignorant of who is important to the commercial real estate broker.

I shoot a text off to Zeus telling him what I heard as I follow Lucia down the hallway.

She stops at the door of the women's restroom. "I'll meet you back at the table."

I'm not leaving the hallway, but I nod anyway. No point arguing and *ílios mou* would tell me she doesn't need a babysitter. Like she tried to do repeatedly in the club on both Friday and Saturday night.

Didn't stop me from sticking close then and it won't now.

Keeping the door she went through in my line of sight, I walk casually toward the men's room and then beyond it. There are three more doors at the end of the hallway. The one on the left has a scratched and grimy plexiglass insert, allowing me to see a kitchen beyond.

A woman is loading trays of glassware for the industrial dishwasher. I suck in a shocked breath and then force my lungs to release it, shaking my head.

It's not her.

I can't see the dishwasher's face, just her profile. But it doesn't matter. The woman she reminds me of is dead, killed by bratva scum allied with the Golubevs.

My mind is playing tricks on me. I turn away and examine the other two doors, the women's bathroom never out of my peripheral vision.

Clearly leading to the outside, the center door is big and made of steel. Lifting my phone, I pretend to text and move so I lean back against the third door. Dropping one hand behind me, I try the handle and it turns. With the camera app open on my phone and set on selfie mode, I push the door open a crack.

It's another hallway. This one not lit nearly as brightly as the one I'm standing in. I catch movement on my phone screen and slide sideways so I'm leaning on the wall when the bratva soldier I saw earlier comes out of the doorway.

He jerks to a halt when he sees me. "What are you doing here?" he demands in heavily accented English.

"Checking my messages while waiting for my wife to finish in the bathroom. What's it to you?"

"Leave."

My eyes never leaving the man stupid enough to think he can order me around, I tuck my phone into my back pocket. "I'll leave when she comes out."

"Get lost." His voice is louder, like he thinks I didn't hear him the first time.

"Fuck off."

"Hurry up, Boris." The man who said they were going to get leverage on the broker tonight is standing at the other end of the hallway.

He looks at me, but what should be a cursory glance takes everything in. I know because I'm doing the same thing. Boris is only a couple of inches shorter than my six and a half feet. He's twice as broad though and should be a lumbering ox of a man.

But he holds himself with a readiness that I recognize. He won't go down easily. His compatriot is coming closer, the movement overtly casual but he's a predator.

Like recognizes like.

These bratva soldiers have an edge the Golubevs I've been hunting since my teens don't.

I flick my wrist with a minute movement and my stiletto slides into my palm.

"I told this asshole to get lost, but he says he's waiting for his woman to come out of the toilets."

Boris's friend narrows his eyes at me while I pretend not to understand what they are saying.

Lucia steps out of the bathroom as the bratva soldier comes abreast of the door.

She gasps and stops short. "Oh."

"Hey, sweetheart." I move quickly to get between Lucia and the dangerous man standing too damn close.

Her smile belies the worry I can see in her eyes. "Ready to get that beer?"

No fool, she can sense the tension in the hallway, but she's acting like she doesn't.

"Are you the asshole that told Wanda Sue you would not drink the beer she opened?" This man's accent is even thicker than his pal's.

"What's it to you? She your girlfriend, or something?" More likely his interest is in the bar's nightly take.

This place is either paying protection to the Russians or owned by them. They're too at home here for it not to be under their control one way or the other.

"You order beer. She serve you beer. You pay."

"Fine." If Lucia wasn't standing two inches behind me, I would argue. "Let's go, sweetheart." Shifting sideways, so both men stay in my line of sight, I take Lucia by the arm.

She's stiff and glares at the Russian man. My feisty Italian lover does not like my easy capitulation. As a club owner who makes sure her staff offers stellar customer service, she takes it personally when others do not.

Anger is coming off her in palpable waves. If I don't get her out of here, she's going to start something I'll have to finish.

Not that I mind killing these two, but Lucia doesn't need to see me do it. She doesn't know I'm Greek mafia yet and she will *never* see Dímios in action.

My phone vibrates with a text, but I ignore it. The situation is too volatile to let my focus splinter even a single shard.

The two Russians follow us until we're out of the hallway and then they veer toward two more bratva standing near the tables they'd been sitting at before. They talk together in tones too low for me to catch.

Not that I'm lingering by their tables. I'm hurrying Lucia toward ours. When we reach it, I don't pull her chair out, but grab her coat and help her into it.

Then with my left hand on her arm, I pull out my wallet with my right and extract a twenty to toss on the table.

She glares at me. "Oh, hell, no. You are not leaving that bad excuse for a server a ten-dollar tip." Pulling her arm from my grasp, she digs through her purse.

Holding up two fives and two ones, she says, "This covers it."

It's not an extravagant tip, but it's still twenty percent.

She grabs the twenty and hands it back to me.

"Keep it," I tell her, refusing to take the money. "You're not paying for the beer we didn't drink."

"Don't be a chauvinist."

"I brought you to the bar. I pay."

"So, if I invite you someplace, I get to pay?" she asks suspiciously.

I shrug. It's not something that has ever come up for me before. I don't date and the few times I have had drinks or dinner with a woman before fucking her, she never balked at me paying.

"Why do I get the feeling that shrug means *no*?"

"Because you're intuitive like that."

"Don't try to charm me into keeping your money. It's not going to work."

I smile. She's the only woman, hell the only person, who has ever accused me of being charming.

"And keep those bedroom eyes to yourself. I'm angry."

"That is a challenge I am willing to take on." Once I have her out of this bar and away from the bratva soldiers.

She rolls her eyes at me, but pink tinges her cheeks and her breathing speeds up. Guiding her toward the door, I keep a watch on the men who are still talking.

Some of them are looking this way. Two guesses who they're talking about right now and the first one doesn't count.

CHAPTER 15

ATLAS

As soon as we get outside, I rush Lucia toward my X7. It automatically unlocks when my RKE is within a few feet so I can yank her door open as soon as we reach the truck. I grab her by the waist and lift her into her seat, then slam the door and jog around the SUV to the driver's side.

Pressing the button to start the car, I bark. "Seatbelt, *ílios mou*."

"I told you that's not on right now," she huffs, mistaking my urgency for a desire to get back to her apartment for sex.

Not that she's wrong. I always want sex with her. Right now, I want to get her away from men, who would kill her without a second thought, more.

"Now." I start backing out of the parking spot as the men come outside.

Boris is watching my truck like he's memorizing the plates. He probably is. It won't do him any good.

We don't register our vehicles under our own names. No one in our business with a healthy sense of self-preservation does.

Lucia does up her seatbelt. "*Caspita*. You could have waited until I was buckled."

Keeping an eye on my rearview mirror for a tail, I voice activate a call to my brother.

It connects and before he can speak, I say in Greek, "You are on speaker and Lucia is in the car with me."

At the sound of her name, she gives me a questioning glance.

Traffic isn't heavy, but there are a few cars on the road with me. Unless they pulled out of the bar parking lot with their lights off, the Russians aren't one of them.

They don't know who I am and have no reason to follow us. However, they recognize I am a dangerous man and if they are as well trained as I believe they are, they'll pay attention to that.

Neither of the soldiers liked that I was hanging around in the hallway by the bathrooms, which tells me that the rooms behind the other door are worth looking into.

"What is going on?" Zeus asks me in Greek. "Did you overhear anything else useful? Do you know who they are going after tonight?"

"No. My guess is either the broker's wife or mistress." The information Zephyr compiled did not list any children and the man's parents are living their retirement dreams out in Arizona.

"Helios took his team to the broker's home. Zephyr and his team are on the way to the mistress's apartment. "

"He thinks the mistress is the target?" If he didn't, my youngest cousin would have insisted his team be the one to go to the broker's house.

The port deal is his baby.

Lucia's arms cross and she looks out her window. Away from me.

"Stay with Lucia. We'll handle the bratva bastards."

I wasn't planning on leaving my woman, but don't bother telling Zeus that. No reason to get my *anax* pissed at me if I don't have to.

"Be careful," he warns me. "We don't know how many soldiers they have in the city."

We have five teams of 3 to 5 men. We're working on recruitment, but if the bratva have a large contingent of soldiers, we'll be stretched thin.

My brother hangs up and I tell my phone to send a group text to my team.

Atlas: *Get a hotel room near Nuovi Inizi. Bring your kits. 3 days.*

I am telling them to bring their weapons and at least three days' worth of clothes.

Theo: *Something going down boss?*

A year younger than me, Theo is third generation Greek mafia, but his father left the Drakos outfit in Chicago to join the *Ádis Adelfótita* when he married the daughter of the *anax* in Sacramento.

In the wrong place, at the wrong time, Theo had been taken by the white supremacist under my kill order. He and his mouth-breathing cronies were beating the hell out of Theo for looking too much like his biracial mother.

His Cerberus tattoo is on his neck, so I knew right away he was a member of the *Ádis Adelfótita*.

After killing my target and his shithead friends who thought they could lay hands on one of my brothers, I took Theo to a mafia doctor. It took him six weeks to recover from the beating.

He asked to join my team while he was still in the hospital.

Atlas: *Just left a bar infested with bratva.*

Bobby: *What family?*

Bobby is a straight up product of the American foster care system. I recruited him to the *Ádis Adelfótita* when he was sixteen. That was eight years ago, and he's been loyal to me ever since.

Atlas: *Don't know.*

And I hate not knowing. When I get back to the club, I'll instruct my team to cover Nuovi Inizi in shifts while rotating in groups of two to stake out the bar Lucia and I left. We need intel.

Yesterday.

Michael: *This got anything to do with why Zephyr and Helios's team took off loaded for bear?*

Michael's mother is Greek mafia. His father is a professor at USC. After six years in the Army, Michael decided he'd rather beat up and kill people for the mafia than the government. According to him, we're more honest about our motivations.

I don't follow politics, so I wouldn't know, but he's been an asset to my team for the last two years.

Atlas: *Yes.*

Bobby is the only one who had to learn to speak Greek and now he's fluent. We do all of our texting in Greek as a matter of course.

With every text my phone reads out to me over my car's speakers, Lucia grows more visibly irritated. Her whole body is turned away from me by this point and her posture is rigid.

She huffs out a sigh after the last text. "If you miss having someone to talk to in Greek so much, maybe you should go home and hang out with your family in person."

"I'm not going anywhere but back to the club with you."

"Maybe I want some time to myself."

No chance in hell.

Seeing an empty parking lot for an industrial building, I yank the steering wheel to the right and pull the SUV into it.

"What are you doing?" Lucia demands.

Not bothering to answer, I pull my truck around to the back, so it's not visible from the road. Once I maneuver it so I'm facing the way we came, I put it in park, but leave the engine running.

"What are we doing here? Why did we stop?" Lucia is looking at me finally, her dark eyes snapping with annoyance.

"You are angry."

"You think?" she snarks back.

I don't take the bait. "Yes. What I want to know is: why?"

"Oh, I don't know. You take me to a dive bar where the service sucked and you paid for beer we didn't drink. If it was busy, I could understand the server forgetting and opening our bottles, but the only people there were those two tables of thugs."

Thugs is right. Lucia has good instincts, even if she's too innocent to know what they are telling her.

"You're mad because I paid for the beer?" If I had known it was going to cause me grief with my woman, I would have taken the bratva bastards out back and eliminated them. "It was ten bucks. Twelve with tip."

"You gave me twenty, so essentially that's what you paid because we both know you'll get sneaky about not taking the extra eight dollars back once we get to the club and I can break the twenty."

She knows me pretty damn well for such a short time being together.

"What is this really about?"

"You talked to your family in Greek to exclude me."

And then I see it behind the ire. Hurt.

"I wasn't trying to exclude you." Just maintain her innocence about the reality of my business.

Yes, I'm keeping her, but even I realize it is too early to start inducting her into the mafia life. Some wives never know about the *Ádis Adelfótita* and their husband's true vocations. I don't fool myself that Lucia can be kept in the dark indefinitely.

She's too smart.

"That's not what it felt like." She sighs. "I learned to speak Italian before English. My mother preferred it, but she taught me and my brother not to speak it in front of our friends and exclude them."

"You have a brother?"

"Not anymore."

Shit. He's dead. "I'm sorry."

"Me too."

"Were you close?"

"When we were kids." She wraps her arms around herself. "But not for a long time."

"You still miss him."

Moisture pools in her beautiful brown eyes. "Yes."

Shit. Fuck. Damn. "Don't cry."

She blinks furiously and turns her head away. "I'm not."

That is worse. Dealing with her tears has me tied in knots, but having her turn away so I won't see them? That is fucking excruciating. Any other woman and I'd be glad for it, but not Lucia.

I cup her cheek and turn her face back toward me, brushing at the wetness trickling from the corner of her eye with my thumb. "Cry if you want, but don't turn away from me."

"Why not?" She sounds genuinely confused.

"I don't like it."

"Most men would be relieved."

"I am not them."

Lucia gives me an assessing look. "When I turned my face to hide my emotions, did that make you feel excluded?"

A pit yawns before me. I'm not a fool. I know the parallel she's drawing for me.

"I will try not to speak in Greek around you."

"It's not speaking in Greek that bothers me, it's you having whole discussions that exclude me."

"My family and I are used to talking about business in Greek, *ílios mou*."

"I like when you call me your sun. Sweetheart is more generic. Why did you start using it at the bar?"

She noticed? Of course, she did. Lucia is as observant as I am.

"It seemed appropriate." For reasons of expediency and hiding my identity as a Greek man from the bratva.

I am not ready for them to know who I am. They will soon enough. They'll be aware exactly who they set themselves against. Right before Dímios wipes them out.

"Well, I like *ílios mou* better." She pronounces *my sun* with a perfect accent.

I smile. "I will remember that, *eromenis mou*."

"What does that mean?" she asks breathily. "Only you said it with that tone you usually use when we're making love."

"It means *my lover*."

Her eyes soften and small puff of air gusts out between her lips. "Oh. I like that too."

"Sometimes I will talk business in Greek. It is not meant to hurt you."

She sighs and turns to kiss the palm of my hand.

My muscles clench from that small act of affection, my cock swelling to aching readiness in seconds.

"I miss my family more than I realized. Having you talk in Greek to yours brought home that I don't have that anymore. I am alone."

"No. You are with me now." She will never be alone again.

Tilting her head up, her parted mouth invites my kiss. I give it to her, plundering her sweet heat with my tongue. She grabs at my shoulders and tries to press forward but the seatbelt stops her.

She scrabbles at the release and breaks the kiss with a curse when she can't get it to disengage.

Breathing heavily, I put my hand over hers. "Stop. I'll get us home and you can ravish my body then."

"Ravish? Who says that?"

That would be me. "I read a lot."

"Romance novels? Because I'm pretty sure they're the only ones that are going to mention ravishing."

I shrug. Some of them are seriously hot and when I'm in the mood to get myself off instead of searching for pussy, they work better than porn. All that emotion that I don't let myself feel is a huge turn on.

"Really? You read romance?"

"Sometimes."

"That is unexpected."

"The erotic kind," I explain.

"That makes more sense."

"What do you read?"

"I used to read romance, all kinds. For the past five years the only reading I've done is invoices and tax statements though."

That is going to change. The woman needs time to relax and I'm going to make sure she gets it.

"Who is your favorite author?"

She names an author I've read before, and I like that we have similar taste.

"Do you read thrillers. *Did* you?" I correct myself.

"Yes."

I name an author this time and she smiles. "I love his books."

As I put the X7 into gear, I say, "He's one of my favorites too."

For the rest of the drive, we list favorite authors and books. There are only a few we don't have in common.

"I need to download a couple of those." Reading is a good way to decompress when I'm off the job.

She pulls out her phone. "What's your email address?"

I tell her.

She goes silent, tapping away at her screen. I hear a notification from my phone.

"I sent you some books."

"You bought me books?" I ask. Has anyone ever bought me a book?

"By those two authors I was telling you about."

One thriller and one spicy romance. "With you around I don't need the romance."

"Maybe it will give you ideas."

Fuck me. She wants to play. "Do you think I need them?"

"No, but I wouldn't want you to run out of inspiration."

"You are the only inspiration I need." I grab her hand and put it over my hard cock.

She squeezes. "Good to know."

I whistle "Don't Worry, Be Happy" and Lucia gives me what would be a heart melting smile.

If I still had a heart.

CHAPTER 16

ATLAS

Lucia is passed out from pleasure and exhaustion beside me when the text comes in from my brother.

Zeus: *Bears neutralized. Need you at the warehouse.*

We bought the rundown warehouse before we even started looking for a place to live. Priorities.

And having a place to interrogate and intimidate is high on the list for men like us.

Atlas: *One hour.*

I send a text to Theo, who is on guard duty for the club tonight.

Atlas: *Inside. Guard the door to upstairs.*

Theo: *You going to the warehouse?*

One of the other soldiers must have let him know about the successful operation. Theo hadn't been happy to learn that he and the rest of my team were on guard and recon duty when shit was going down.

He'll get over it. They do what I need them to do.

Atlas: *Yes.*

Theo: *I'll watch over your woman.*

I don't bother to reply. Theo will be waiting for me outside the backdoor when I get downstairs.

After a military shower, I dress in a black t-shirt and jeans, strap on my weapons and pull on my leather jacket over the holstered gun and the knives strapped to my forearms. There's another knife in the sheath in my right combat boot and a gun strapped to my ankle.

The inside of my leather jacket is lined with throwing knives on both sides.

From now and until the bratva threat is neutralized, we will all be heavily armed wherever we go.

My body is a deadly weapon. Up close and personal, I can take out an enemy quietly and effectively without hardware. A shot to the head is more efficient in distance situations though. My throwing knives are best for incapacitation, or slowing down my prey.

Every tool has its purpose.

Lucia is still sleeping when I finish dressing and come out of the bathroom. The light is off before I open the door, so I don't wake her. It works, but I risk rousing her anyway when I lean down and kiss her lips softly.

Her mouth molds to mine, even in her sleep. When I pull it away, those pretty lips go lax again and I smile.

This woman.

There is no way I am ever letting her go.

~ ~ ~

When I reach the warehouse, there is no sign of anyone else. As it should be. I drive around the back and open the bay door with my remote. It looks rusted into place and decrepit. But it is made of reinforced steel and swings up on silent hinges.

I pull my X7 in next to Zephyr's bright yellow Lambo. My truck is more useful for transporting bodies, something important in my line of work. It's also a hell of a lot less of an attention seeker.

From the other vehicles parked in the warehouse, it looks like Zeus and Helios are here as well.

I go down to the basement, the top selling feature for this property. It is not on the blueprints filed with the planning office and the access is now hidden behind a bank of broken down filing cabinets that look like they haven't moved in the past two decades.

Following the sound of murmuring voices, I find my brother and both of my cousins in the interrogation room. Two men are stripped naked and hanging by their wrists from a chain in the ceiling.

Satisfaction unfurls in my gut when I see that one of them is that fucker that got me in trouble with Lucia for insisting I pay for the beer. Lucia's safety and my family's interests made the timing bad for taking him down earlier, but now?

I'm going to have some fun.

"I don't think I'm ever going to get used to seeing you smile," Zephyr grouses as I walk closer. "Although this one looks damn evil."

"I'm looking forward to *talking* with the prisoners."

"Oh, shit, what did they do to you?" Helios asks.

I shrug.

"You! I knew you were trouble," the Russian on the right says malevolently.

"Good instincts," I acknowledge. Then look him up and down and shake my head. "Bad choices."

The man on the left spits toward me. "When my bratva is done with you, you'll all wish you'd shot yourselves in the head."

"Strong words for a man about to cry for his mommy," I say with disinterest.

My toolchest is designed for garage tools, but the things I keep inside the grey metal drawers are a lot more interesting. Or their use is.

"Hell," Zeus says. "You're pissed."

I shrug. "Do I look angry?"

"No, you look like an emotionless psychopath, but we both know that's not you."

I'm feeling emotion right now. Most of it, rage. These fuckers came into our city and they want to disrupt our plans. Plans my brothers and cousins and me have spent years developing.

"What are you doing in Portland?" I ask them.

"Fuck you." The man on the left spits at me again. His saliva falls short and splats on the cement, but the disrespect is there regardless.

"I would teach you some manners, but there's no point when you're never leaving here alive."

"If you're going to kill us anyway, why should we tell you anything?" the man on the right asks.

A more intelligent response, if shortsighted.

"Because there's a world of pain in difference between a clean death and a dirty one. I can keep you alive for days and you *will* talk." I have only run across one man who didn't respond to any of my interrogation methods.

Serbian, he was a tough mofo that earned my respect if not my mercy.

These two? They're professional, but they aren't immune to pain. I'll prove that to them soon enough.

I open the top drawer on my tool chest and pull out the blackjack that belonged to my grandfather. My dad's father, not the asshole who left me with the Golubevs for a fucking year.

Pappous gave it to me when I turned thirteen and spent the next two years training me how to use it with lethal efficiency.

"First lesson. Don't spit at the *palach*." When I mention the title the Russians have given me, the bratva scum both jerk in their chains. "So, you know who I am."

"*Palach* is a bogeyman. There is no assassin acting as executioner to the bratva."

"Tell that to the dozens of your brothers I sent to hell when you meet up with them later." I smack the man who spit at me with my blackjack at the right angle to knock two of his teeth out.

He grunts but doesn't cry out. Anticipation sends my blood rushing through my veins. I like a good challenge.

Two hours later, my muscles burn from a good workout, and I have a sheen of sweat on my arms and chest. Bloody and missing some teeth and fingernails, both men are covered in red blotches that will bruise if they live long enough.

My methods of interrogation ultimately cause them to shout their throats hoarse, but the information they reveal is minimal. Not useless though.

Knowing they are from Russia and do not plan to stay in Portland tells me they are acting as temporary muscle to help take over territory for a US based bratva. They stubbornly refuse to tell me which one, but I already have a good idea. And there is a long road of pain driven revelations between here and death for them.

Helios is doing a deep dive based on their vehicle registration. It's not a rental and it isn't owned by a shell company. Not good planning.

The man who owns it lists an apartment address in SE Portland as his home. Zephyr is hitting it now with his team.

I will be surprised if they find anything but an empty unit, used solely for the purpose of filing paperwork. But I recognize the name on the registration. The man is dead. I killed him two years ago.

Using his credentials is a forward-thinking security move. Too bad I know his bratva and all their connections as well as I do. The dead man was a shot caller for the Golubev Bratva.

Sure, it could be someone else with the same name, but I don't believe in coincidences.

So, the Golubevs, not the Semenovs. The *Ádis Adelfótita* will be able to maintain our truce with the Semenovs.

Maybe I should have expected this. The Golubevs are moving their territory north, where they believe they won't have syndicate competition. Portland would be a good location to rebuild their decimated ranks, especially with help from their bratva brethren from the homeland.

If we did not live here.

But what they do not realize is that they are trying to relocate to territory now claimed by their enemies, the *Ádis Adelfótita*. Worse for them, their *palach* now calls Portland home.

Coincidence? No.

It is Nemesis at work. They would have been safer staying in California. Because I am Dímios, the instrument of Nemesis.

Knowing they are from R[illegible] and [illegible] tells [illegible] temporary [illegible] to help [illegible] a US-based [illegible]. [illegible] not only [illegible] tell me what [illegible] and that is a [illegible] dead [illegible].

[illegible] doing a [illegible] based [illegible] and [illegible] by a shell company [illegible] planning.

[illegible] with [illegible].

I will be surprised if [illegible] for the purpose of [illegible] paperwork. But [illegible] two years ago.

[illegible] The dead [illegible] was shot [illegible].

Still, [illegible] with [illegible] name, but I don't [illegible].

[illegible] not [illegible]. The [illegible] the [illegible] news.

[illegible] I should have [illegible]. The [illegible] work [illegible] the [illegible] in the [illegible].

[illegible] here.

But what [illegible] [illegible] now [illegible] and home.

[illegible].

[illegible] would have [illegible] California [illegible] of [illegible].

CHAPTER 17

LUCIA

After a night of intense lovemaking, we sleep in. Or I do. Atlas isn't there when I wake up, but there's a text on my phone.

Atlas: *I'll be back to take you to lunch at 1:30.*

The door to my office opens at precisely 1:30. Atlas stands in the opening, his gaze locked on me. "Ready?"

"Let me just finish this beer order."

"You need more of Shawn's ale?" Atlas asks, his tone sneering when he says my supplier's name.

"No. This is my monthly order for the national brands. My clientele likes craftsman ale, but the margin on it isn't as good as what's mass-produced."

"I notice your liquor is higher end than I expect in a nightclub."

"We don't serve rotgut and because of that we are busy on nights the local bars are practically empty."

"But aren't you losing margin on the other nights? And you're closed on the quietest nights already."

She shrugs. "I'm not serving top shelf, but what is the point of offering my customers swill, I wouldn't serve a guest on a bad day?"

"You see your customers as guests?"

She closes her laptop and stands up. "Yes. My staff are trained to see them that way too. We're more than a dance club to spend a couple of hours getting wasted with your friends. Nuovi Inizi is an experience."

His expression is blank, but I see the minor tells around his eyes and the edges of his lips. He thinks I'm wrong, but he keeps his mouth shut.

"Thank you for not trying to educate the little woman." Tino and his father would never have held back.

They assumed they knew better.

"Your success speaks for itself. I wouldn't presume to question the method that got you here."

"But you don't agree with it."

"We don't see the club business the same way, but there's more than one way to build a business. If your goal was to have multiple locations, your methods would have to reflect that."

"One club is plenty for me to handle." It pays for Lenny's care and provides me a decent livelihood.

That is enough.

"Even with only one club, I think you need a general manager to take some of the load off of you."

"That's in the long-term plan." But can't happen right now. Not if I want to buy my house.

Having a home that isn't an efficiency above my nightclub is more important to me than having more time in my day to revel in my aloneness.

Though I'm not alone right now.

I grab my purse. "You ready to go?"

"Not yet." He pulls me into a kiss.

My brain is fuzzy from pleasure when he pulls his head back. "I like this look on you."

"What look is that?" I tease in a sultry tone that only came into my repertoire after meeting him.

"The just kissed and thinking about fucking look."

"Accurate."

Growling, he lays another lip-lock on me that sets fire to my core.

This time I'm swaying on my feet when our mouths break apart. "Maybe we should go upstairs and see if you can't keep me looking like this for the rest of today."

I'm caught up on paperwork. There are always things I could be doing, like updating our social media accounts and looking into new suppliers. But I deserve time off too.

Atlas looks tempted but shakes his head. "You need to eat."

"I had breakfast." My stomach chooses that moment to snarl loudly.

I guess my body doesn't count a single croissant eaten a few hours before as adequate sustenance.

He takes my hand and tugs me out of my office. "And now you're going to have lunch."

Once we're in his SUV, he asks me where I want to eat. "You know the area better than I do."

"There's a family-owned Italian restaurant a few minutes away. Let me call and see if they have a table." Listening to him talk and text in Greek with his family last night triggered a hunger for the familiar.

He thinks my brother is dead, but Rocco survived the war with the Irish and the bratva. When I'm overwhelmed, or sometimes really tired, I consider calling him. I let myself imagine that his love for his sister will be bigger than his loyalty to the don.

But that's a pipe dream.

If I want to keep Lenny safe and happy where he is, if I want to avoid another mafia marriage, Rocco and my parents have to continue to believe that I'm dead.

Does that hurt? Yes.

But the alternative would hurt even more. Or that's what I tell myself. Honestly, if Lenny's welfare wasn't part of the equation, there are times I would pack it in and return to Detroit. To my family.

The lunch rush is pretty much over, and the small Italian restaurant has an open table. I give them my name and ask them to hold it for us.

Over lunch, Atlas asks my opinion of the different businesses in the area. And he listens with rapt attention when I give it.

For a woman raised to accept the very traditional role of first mafia daughter and then wife, his interest in my thoughts and opinions is heady stuff.

"Are you and your brothers really considering opening a strip club near that bar we went to last night?" I ask Atlas, making no effort to hide my disapproval of the idea.

He gets a strange look in his eyes I can't quite decipher. "It might be a strategic move."

"I'm not so sure about that." Those thugs last night sounded Russian.

Which in and of itself is not concerning. There are over 40,000 Russian, Ukranian and other immigrants from the Baltic states in the Portland Metro. Many came to Portland to escape religious and other types of persecution.

I considered starting Nuovi Inizi in the Dobro Pozhalovat, a predominately Baltic neighborhood in East Portland, before ultimately deciding on my current location in Portland's west suburbs.

Before making the decision, I did my research on Portland's large Baltic community. There was no bratva presence when I did it.

What is concerning is that the men from last night had familiar tattoos. Ones like those the bratva that killed my husband and father-in-law wear proudly.

"There are places in and around the city that would be more profitable." Not to mention safer. "Besides, if you're working all the way over there, when will I see you?"

He keeps saying this thing between us isn't temporary. Well, if it's not, then him working across the city and with more than a couple of suburbs between us isn't going to be conducive to seeing each other.

"Running the club won't be my job."

"I thought you were doing this with your brothers."

"And cousins," he corrects while topping off my wine glass. "We each have our roles to play. Mine isn't management."

"What do you do?"

"Facilitate."

I'm not sure what that means, but no doubt he and his family have a system.

"You've been spending so much time with me, I'm not sure how you are facilitating anything."

"I worked this morning."

"That's where you went? Were you looking at properties?" Hopefully not near that seedy bar.

If those are bratva soldiers, no one working, or living in the vicinity of that bar, is safe. Especially not the Baltic immigrants building a life for themselves here.

Like all organized crime, the bratva prey on their own first, exploiting and drawing from the population for new recruits.

Worse is the potential for human trafficking. The bratva in Detroit traffic humans for both the sex and employment slave trade.

The very thought of it nauseates me.

Not all bratva generate income from human trafficking, but chances are any bratva looking to establish territory in Portland does. It's a matter of the path of least resistance. The city ranks in the top twenty for human trafficking in the US.

"What's wrong?" Atlas leans forward, his hand outstretched. He lays it against my forehead. "No fever, but you look sick."

"I'm fine." Just nauseated at the idea of my city being infiltrated by a syndicate willing to buy and sell human beings.

A sparkle comes into his glacial blue eyes, warming them. "We'll stop at the pharmacy on the way to my house."

His meaning sinks in and everything inside me seizes. With longing that won't be fulfilled.

It makes me grumpy. "Forget it. Even if I were pregnant and we both know I'm not, no way would I be morning sick yet."

The nausea didn't kick in until I was six weeks along, which my mom thought was early. It didn't go away when I hit the three-month mark either. I was miserable right up until the sixth month. I only had one month to enjoy being pregnant. I'd be nauseated every day of my pregnancy not to have lost my baby at seven months.

"We *don't* both know you aren't pregnant."

"Well, I do."

"You're not on birth control."

"I told you I probably can't get pregnant." And when he accepts that, will he dump me?

Chance of rain 90%.

"Probably is not *can't*."

Leaving his ridiculously optimistic viewpoint aside for the moment, my brain screeches as the rest of what he said penetrates. "What do you mean *your* house? We're going back to my place."

"Zeus wants to meet you."

"You want me to meet your family? Already?" Wow.

"Yes."

"I'm not sure I'm ready for that."

"What's there to be ready for? I'm not asking to fuck you in the ass. I'm taking you to meet my brother."

That he considers backdoor sex a sign of deeper intimacy than meeting his family is something for me to unpack later. Also, that he considers it a natural progression of our sexual relationship.

CHAPTER 18

ATLAS

The look on Lucia's face says the last thing she wants is to meet my brother. Should I mention it won't only be Zeus?

Helios and Zephyr are dealing with the fallout from last night, but Orion should be at the mansion.

Deflection seems like a good strategy right now. "You ready to explain that *probably* to me yet?"

She's silent so long, I think she's going to refuse, but then she huffs out a long breath of air. "I was married."

Dark fury that another man called her wife rises up in me. I don't care if it is reasonable. Lucia is mine.

The only thing keeping me sane in that single word, *was*.

My jaw so tight, my back teeth are grinding, I ask, "Where is he?"

"That is not the question I expected you to ask."

Too bad. I repeat it. It is the question I want answered.

"In the cemetery."

The man is dead. Good. Lucia's soul is not dark like mine. She would not like it if I had to kill the man she married.

I pull the SUV onto the freeway. "Did you try to get pregnant with him?"

The idea is doing nothing to abate the rage inside me.

"I got pregnant the first year we were married, but I..." She pauses, her voice thready. "I tumbled down the stairs and lost the baby."

"I am sorry." Not words I usually say, but in this case, they are the only ones that matter.

How the hell did her husband fail to protect her from something like that happening? Or did he cause it?

My grip on the steering wheel is so tight, I'm surprised it doesn't crack under the pressure. "Did he push you?"

"No." Something in her voice tells me that's not the whole answer.

"Did the fall do damage to your reproductive system?"

"I don't know. Maybe. After I healed from the miscarriage, we didn't use birth control, but I never got pregnant again, not in two years."

"How often did you have sex?"

"I don't think that's any of your business."

"Tell me."

"Hardly ever," she huffs, crossing her arms under those generous breasts.

I reach over and run my hand along the tops. "Why?"

"He got busy with...with work and I..." Her voice peters out like she ran out of battery.

"You what?" Am I being intrusive? Hell, yes.

She'll get used to it. I'm not going anywhere. And I want to know everything about her.

"It was hard for me. Having sex with him. I think he suspected it. Losing the baby so late in my pregnancy was hard on both of us."

"But he's the reason you lost it." It's a shot in the dark, but I'm a damn good night sniper and I expect it to hit my target.

Her gasp and the way her body goes stiff tells me it does. "I never said that."

"He didn't push you down the stairs." She said that. "Were you running from him when you fell?"

Maybe I can find a necromancer to bring the bastard back from the dead and kill him all over again. This time with my own special nuance.

"I didn't fall."

Gamó. "Tell me."

"Lenny is my brother-in-law. I can't believe I'm telling you this. He was in an accident when he was a child and suffered a traumatic brain injury. I was supposed to watch him when my husband and father-in-law were out of the house."

Traumatic brain injury can mean a lot of things. "What was the impact of the injury on Lenny?"

"He lacks impulse control. He'll get fixated on an idea and lash out at anyone who prevents him from following through."

She doesn't have to spell it out. With her being her brother-in-law's primary caregiver, that person would have been Lucia, more often than not.

"He's an adult now?" I ask.

"Yes."

"And when you lost the baby?"

"Yes."

"A large man?" Even an average size man would be bigger than Lucia, but a large one would be damn near impossible for her to control physically.

"Yes." Her voice is soft, laden with old grief.

"Your bastard of a husband expected you to care for and protect his brother who was an adult sized male?"

"Yes."

"What happened?"

"Lenny wanted something I wouldn't give him. We fought. I tried to get away. He shoved me. The stairs were too close, and I went flying. When I woke up, my baby was gone."

And those bastards probably blamed Lucia for not being able to handle Lenny. She said her husband is dead. Is her father-in-law?

"How did your husband die?"

"A workplace incident. Something went wrong at the club and both he and his father died."

I am not a good man. I hope those bastards suffered before death. "That's why you came to Portland. You left your old life behind."

"Yes."

I can't stand the pain that single word holds, and I pull off at the next exit. We're close to the mansion, but I'm not ready to take her there. I discovered a park with a sunken rose garden when I was doing recon for the area. Finding a parking spot on the street near it, I pull in, maneuvering the X7 to fit between two cars.

I turn it off and get out. Lucia is still sitting in her seat with her seatbelt fastened when I come around the passenger side of the truck and open her door.

I reach over her and press the button to release it, and then carefully pull the belt away from her as it retracts. "Come on."

She looks past me. "Where are we?"

"Someplace I can hold you while you talk."

"A park?" she asks, like that's the strangest place I could have brought her.

I wrap my arm around her waist and pull her close. "Yes, a park."

The roses have bloomed and died already, their bushes in hibernation for the winter, but it is still a peaceful place. A few walkers and joggers power along the path that runs the perimeter of the park, but only a couple of people are in the sunken garden itself.

Exactly what I wanted.

"I didn't know this was here. I've visited the Rose Garden in Washington Park, but no one ever mentions this place. I bet it's beautiful in full bloom."

"We'll come back in July and you can see."

"That's nine months away. You keep talking like we have a future."

"Because we do."

"Isn't it too early to be sure about that?"

"How long did you know your husband before you knew?"

She makes a strange sound before she shakes her head. "We knew each other our whole lives. Our parents were matchmaking before I learned how to walk."

"Is that why you married him?" Had she loved the man who put her and their baby in such a dangerous situation?

"Family expectation was a big part of it, but I fell in love with Tino. He was handsome and sophisticated."

"He was older than you?"

"Only a couple of years, but he had way more life experience than I did at twenty."

"Were you happy?" Can she be happy with me?

She'll have to learn to be.

"For a while."

"Until the baby?"

"Things were hard before that. We argued over getting Lenny professional help. Tino and his dad were adamantly against it."

"Why?" Was it money? But somehow Lucia had ended up with enough money to start a nightclub.

"They were old fashioned Italians. Everything was supposed to be taken care of by the family."

Sounds like the mafia. Only family takes a backseat to the wellbeing of the syndicate. Not for my uncle though. For him, family comes first.

What happened to me shaped all of us, Constantin, Zeus, Orion, and even Zephyr and Helios. They weren't part of the rescue, but they learned how little our grandfather valued us and how easily he controlled our parents.

"You deserved better."

"So did Lenny. He was devastated by the loss of the baby. It set him back for a long time." She sounds sad.

"You have a lot of empathy, don't you?"

"Not so much anymore, but back then, I cared too much about the people in my life."

She's saying she cared about that piece of shit she was married to. "Are you saying you don't care now?"

"I don't have people in my life now."

Bullshit. "You have me."

And when she is pregnant with my kid, I'll be her shadow. A man who knows so many ways to kill also knows how to keep someone safe.

She takes care of her employees too, not just her club. They care about her. Does she not see that?

Lucia's laughter is hollow, but there's a thread of amusement there. "Do you make these pronouncements expecting everyone to fall in with your plans, or is it just me?"

Zeus is *anax*, but my crew looks to me first for orders. As it should be. When I tell them what to do, of course, I expect them to obey. When I told them we were moving to Portland, I assumed they would make the move without resistance.

Theo told me I should have asked them. I told him to fuck off and get his place packed up.

Lucia's face is tilted up toward me. "That look on your face. It's definitely more than me."

"Only the people closest to me." I don't care enough to tell other people how it's going to be. Not even my parents.

"How did we get so close so fast?" she asks, not like she's denying it, but finds the closeness hard to believe. "It's only been a matter of days."

I shrug and start us down the wide cement steps leading into the sunken garden. "Sex."

She smacks me in the stomach with the back of her hand and then yelps. "That hurt."

"I'm sorry?" She hit me. Not the other way around. That will *never* fucking happen.

"You should be, having such a hard stomach."

"You like my muscles." She spends enough time touching them.

"You got me there."

We walk in silence until we reach the fountain in the center of the rose garden. Lucia stops and watches the water shoot into the air until the pattern starts repeating. Then she sighs and pulls my other arm around her, holding both of my forearms.

It's not a good position to protect her from, but it's not an impossible one either. She seems to want to be surrounded by me. So, I give that to her. Maybe she's cold. Her coat more fashionable than warm.

I stay alert to our surroundings. My instincts tell me we are alone and not being watched.

"I want to be a mom. I don't know if my body will let me."

"You have to have sex to get pregnant."

"We had sex, but not very often."

"Repeated occurrences increase the chances for most things."

"But..." She stops talking and grips my forearms harder. "You really think I can?"

"I think if you are worried, we go back to the private clinic and have them run some tests."

"I'm not sure I want to know. If something inside me was damaged, it will bring it all back."

"And if nothing is wrong with you except an inept dead husband."

"Tino wasn't inept."

"So, the way you respond to pleasure with surprise so often has nothing to do with his ineptitude. Right."

"It's been five years."

"Which might explain your sexual hunger, not how shocked you are by the things I do to make your body sing."

She turns in my arms and looks up at me, doing her best to frown. "You are so darn arrogant."

"Confidence is not arrogance when it is justified." I have absolute confidence in my ability to kill and make this woman come until she passes out.

Both of which I have proven over and over.

"I'm nervous about meeting your brother."

"Brothers," I admit.

"Both of them will be there? I thought Orion was a lawyer. It's Monday. Isn't he at his office?"

"He'll be there for dinner."

"Oh. So, now I'm nervous about meeting both of them. Do you all live together?"

"Yes. My cousins live there too." She doesn't need to know about our men who live on the grounds too.

They won't be at the house. Theo, Michael and Bobby want to meet her, but their recon job at the bar is the reason I have Lucia with me.

I need all three to infiltrate the bar. Unlike some of the specialists that came up under my grandfather, me and my brothers never send our guys in without enough backup. Neither do my cousins.

Which is why we've never lost a soldier from our teams. Doesn't mean we won't. Death is a part of this life. I should know, I'm usually the one dealing it out.

But it will not be because of us.

"That's a lot of men in one house. Do any of your brothers or cousins have significant others?"

"It's a big house. And no, they're all single."

CHAPTER 19

LUCIA

He says *they're all single* like he's not. With anyone else, I would worry he'd slipped and was revealing a committed relationship to me.

But that's not it.

Atlas considers us a couple. I'm his and he's mine.

It's surreal. So, why does it feel so right?

I'm still asking myself that question after we finish our walk in the rose garden and he drives us to his home.

He uses his phone to open the gate, but there are guards on either side. And I can see others patrolling the grounds.

How rich are these men?

Wealthy enough to worry about their security. Then what is Atlas doing running around without a protection detail? I ask him.

He laughs. "I don't need anyone else to protect me."

"You can say that after what happened to you as a kid?"

"Anyone coming after me is signing their own death warrant."

"I guess you took a lot of self-defense courses after you got back home."

"Something like that."

"It worries me that you see yourself as invincible. You aren't. No one is."

"If you say so."

"I mean it, Atlas. It's obvious you and your family are worried about security. You shouldn't be going to clubs alone, much less picking up strange women."

"You are not a strange woman."

"It's not so nice from the other side is it?"

"What?" he asks with barely restrained patience.

Yep. Not so nice when he's the one getting chastised for not being cautious. "Being told you aren't careful enough about your own personal security."

"Lucia, it is my job to protect you, not the other way around."

I laugh. I can't help it. "This isn't the stone age and you aren't a caveman, no matter how much you might act like one in the bedroom. Watching out for each other goes both ways."

With an arrested expression, he puts the SUV into park and turns it off in front of the ginormous mansion he apparently lives in.

"How do you stand being in my tiny apartment when you have all this?" The house is easily twice the size of the home I left in Detroit and that place was ten thousand square feet of opulence.

"You're there."

"There you go, saying the perfect thing again."

"Come on, I'll show you around."

"That sounds good." At least it will get me out of meeting his family immediately.

Or that's what I think until we walk into the marble tiled foyer. Another man with the same dark hair and blue eyes as Atlas is standing there and his expression isn't friendly.

He's sizing me up.

I slide my hand into Atlas's bigger one. He squeezes and whistles "Don't Worry, Be Happy" under his breath.

It makes me smile and I'm able to greet his brother. "Hello, you must be either Zeus, or Orion," I extend my hand.

"That's Zeus," Atlas says, shifting his body between me and his brother, forcing me to abort my attempt at shaking hands. "He's the oldest."

"I remember."

"Were you whistling?" Zeus asks Atlas.

Atlas shrugs.

I roll my eyes. "He likes to whistle, as I'm sure you know." And he uses the songs as messages.

Or is that just with me? Maybe he doesn't pick his music to communicate with his brothers. Maybe he just whistles tunelessly around them? The thought makes me go warm and squishy inside.

This man is so dangerous to my heart.

"My brother hasn't whistled since he was ten years old," Zeus says accusingly.

But what is he accusing me of? Bringing out the musical side to Atlas?

I stand up straighter and give Zeus my best mafia princess look. "You wouldn't know that by me."

The older man's eyes widen fractionally. Is he not used to women standing up to him? Then we are in for a long and probably unpleasant evening. Because I am no pushover.

Not anymore. Not that I ever was one, but I let Tino and Antonio Sr. convince me to take on responsibilities I did not want. Not only that, but I strove to do them well so I wouldn't disappoint the two men.

I worried more about what Agustino Sr. thought of me than my own father.

Now, my father believes I'm dead and I refuse to twist myself into a pretzel to impress any other man. Even Atlas's older brother.

His tune changes from "Don't Worry, Be Happy" to...is that "We are the Champions"?

"Knock it off," I admonish Atlas. "I'm not fighting with your brother."

"If you were, my money would be on you."

"What the hell, Atlas?" His brother sounds annoyed. And a little disbelieving.

Removing his hand from mine, Atlas slides it up, under my hair, to clasp my nape. "Lucia is a strong woman," he says, like he's explaining. "And she has the advantage of having me on her side."

There's a warning in his tone that I can't miss. Which means, neither can his brother.

"Are you threatening the *anax*?" someone asks from my right.

I turn my head and yet another ridiculously gorgeous man with black hair and blue eyes is walking toward us.

"Did your parents use PGT before doing IVF, or something?" The level of masculine beauty in this foyer is absurd.

"What is PGT?" Zeus asks with narrowed eyes.

"Preimplantation Genetic Testing," the other brother says before I get a chance to answer. "Why would you ask that? A lot of siblings look alike."

Is he seriously trying to pretend he doesn't realize how good looking he and his brothers are? I mean, sure Atlas takes the hotness up to nuclear levels, but no way are his brothers having any trouble getting dates.

"You are Orion, the lawyer if I'm remembering right." I don't bother to offer my hand to shake this time. Zeus wasn't particularly keen, I could tell and then there's the Mr. Possessive-Pants with his hand on my neck

Orion jerks his head in assent and glares at Atlas. "What else have you told her?"

"The only thing that matters."

Oh, crap, he's going to say it in front of his brothers.

"What's that?" Zeus asks this time.

"That she's mine."

He said it. Heat flashes up my neck and into my face. Neither brother seems any happier about Atlas's claim than I am. Though their reaction leans toward anger, not embarrassment.

"Are you sure you're not triplets? I mean, you've all got that swoony black hair and blue eyes thing going on. Chiseled jaws and handsome features that could have been carved by Michalangelo himself. Don't even get me started on all that height and muscles." I fan myself and not only because I'm hot with mortification from Atlas's words. "You even scowl the same."

Zeus and Orion turn those matching frowns on me.

Atlas pulls me around to face him and yep, he's got the hot Greek daddy glare going on too. "You do not think my brothers are swoony."

"You're the swooniest." I pat his chest and then let my hand rest against his heart under his leather jacket, because, well...I want to.

"Is that even a word?" Orion snarks.

I ignore him, staring up into my boyfriend's eyes and trying not to drown in the intensity I find there. "I don't think your brothers are happy you are dating. Do we have to stay for dinner?"

I thought mafia men gave off dangerous, primal vibes. *Caspita!* The men in the life I knew back in Detroit had nothing on these uber wealthy Greek brothers.

Zeus grunts. "We are not unhappy Atlas is dating."

"Shocked more like." That's Orion. No surprise the lawyer is the snarky one.

I don't answer, but look up at Atlas appealingly.

"You will not find my brothers attractive."

"You're still stuck on that?" I don't roll my eyes, but it's close. "You're acting like a caveman again, just in case you wondered."

"I am the only man you will find sexually desirable."

"I didn't say I found them sexually desirable," I practically shout. I can't believe he said that. "You're the only one that makes my panties wet."

Did I say that? Out loud? In front of his brothers? Oh, well.

In for a penny, in for a pound. "I said they are good looking. Which they are. Until Orion opens his mouth and then the appeal wanes quickly. The jury is still out on Zeus."

A crack of laughter sounds behind me.

"Hey!" Orion says, sounding offended. "Women like my mouth fine."

"Well, of course they say that when you pay them enough," I say without turning around.

Atlas bursts into laughter, which is what I was going for. He was looking way too unhappy about the similarity in looks between him and his brothers. I can't help they are hot, but I don't want to bang them.

I tug his head down so I can whisper in his ear. "Five years, Atlas. *Five years*. I wouldn't have broken up with B.O.B. for your brothers."

"Remember that," he says in that growly voice that soaks my panties.

Porca miseria. I have no hope of getting through this evening with a modicum of dignity intact.

"Whose Bob? Do we have to get rid of someone?" Orion asks.

I jump and shove myself away from Atlas. Orion moved closer while I wasn't looking and I practically run into him.

"What are you, part bat?" I demand. "And also, have you heard of the concept of personal space? As in, you are standing in my bubble."

Orion takes an unexpected step back. I didn't expect him to listen to me and react so easily. He doesn't give off cooperative vibes.

It's not far enough for Atlas. He tugs me another two feet away from his brother, taking the opportunity to divest me of my coat and slide off his own jacket. He opens a hidden door in the wall and hangs them both up in a freaking walk in coat closet.

"Who is Bob?" Zeus asks when his brother comes out of the closet and shuts the door, leaving the wall looking as seamless as before.

An earthquake opening up a fissure in the floor I could sink into would be welcome right now. You could fry an egg on my cheeks at this point.

"I assume she named her vibrator," Atlas says when I remain silent.

"That did not earn you any good boyfriend points," I mutter.

"B.O.B.?" Orion asks, like he's amused. "I get it now. Battery operated boyfriend."

"You would have earned a gold star for your ability to state the obvious, but the need to spell it out is your fault because you were listening to a private conversation. So, no gold star for you."

"You're standing in a foyer with two other people. That's hardly private."

"Have you heard of the concept of whispering? Clearly my words were not meant for your bat ears."

"Your woman is mouthy," Zeus says.

"Not usually. Apparently, you all bring it out in me." I haven't been this willing to pop off with what's in my head since me and my brother were kids. When we were still close.

Training to become a mafia princess included learning to stifle any and all sarcasm. It wasn't considered ladylike. I'm kind of glad it's back.

Too bad my brother isn't here to use it on, but Atlas's brothers will do as stand ins.

Sudden emotion wells up inside me at the thought.

I turn to look up at Atlas and poke him in the chest. "You'd better mean it, when you say you're keeping me," I say fiercely.

He can't offer me a family and take it away. I won't survive that.

"My brother never says anything he doesn't mean." Zeus doesn't add that's what has him worried, but it's in his tone.

I'm worried about this thing between Atlas and me too. It's fast and incredibly intense. There's the whole what-happens-when-I-don't-get-pregnant thing too.

If he dumps me, I will hunt him down and shoot him in the knee. Too bad for him, my father taught me to shoot when I was ten, right alongside my brother, who was only eight at the time.

I take Atlas's hand and tug. "You said you'd show me around this place."

"It will have to wait," Zeus says. "Gina made dinner and it's ready now."

"Who is Gina?" I ask Atlas as he starts walking down a hallway off the left of the foyer.

"Our housekeeper."

"She has to clean this place *and* cook for you all? When does she sleep?" I ask, "I'm pretty sure there are labor laws against hours like those."

Atlas smiles and shakes his head. "She has two people working for her."

I look down the long hallways with several doors off of it. "Not sure that's enough. Especially if they're picking up after you all and not just doing the deep cleaning."

"You're inordinately interested in our domestic staff arrangements," Orion says. "Did you do work as a maid?"

"I was married. Same difference." I had a service that came in weekly to do the deep cleaning, but I did all the cooking for the Revello family. "It was a traditional household."

"Where is your ex-husband?" Zeus asks, his tone dark.

"That's the first question Atlas asked too."

"And your answer was?"

"In a cemetery."

Zeus nods, like that's good.

I roll my eyes this time. "You do know that the customary response to learning someone is a widow is to say you are sorry for her loss, not look like you're pleased by the death of another human being."

"Was it a loss?" Orion asks way too perceptively.

"I loved my husband." It's the truth, if not all of it.

"Do you love Atlas?"

CHAPTER 20

LUCIA

I ignore Orion's question as we walk into the dining room.

Not merely because it is ridiculously intrusive, but also because I don't know the answer. I mean, I think I *do* know the answer, but my brain rebels against me feeling something so deep for Atlas after a matter of days. It's not possible. Love builds over time.

At least that's how it was between me and Tino. We always knew we were going to get married, and I knew him as well as I knew my own family. It was natural to love him. Tino was a charismatic, smooth guy.

Atlas is not smooth. The more time we spend together, the more I realize he is more caveman than charisma. I guess I like cavemen, because I'm falling into the deep end of my emotions.

The sound of chairs scraping across the dark hardwood floor brings my attention back to where I am. The dining room is huge, with a table that would easily seat twenty.

"Planning to do a lot of entertaining?" I would have thought they would be too busy starting their clubs.

I know from experience that doesn't leave a lot of time for anything else, much less dinner parties for twenty guests.

"Why do you ask?" Atlas pulls my chair out and waits for me to sit down before practically lifting it up with me on it to scoot me closer to the table.

This little show starts a slow burn of desire in my core.

"The size of your table."

Atlas looks at the long table that wouldn't look out of place in a palace. "Sometimes, we meet with our men in here."

They must have a pretty friendly relationship with their security team if they have their meetings in the family dining room.

Yanking the chair to my right several inches closer, Atlas sits down and puts his arm over my shoulders.

Orion shakes his head. "Are you going to piss a circle around her next?"

"Nice," I snark.

Orion narrows his eyes at me. "Do you have brothers?"

"I did. One. Rocco was two years younger." And right this minute, I miss him like a lost limb.

"I am sorry for your loss." Orion's voice rings with sincerity, his expression serious.

"He was lucky to have you for the time he did," Zeus says.

And my eyes tear up. What is it with these Rokos men? Assholes one minute and then worming their way into my heart with the right words the next.

I turn my head away, hiding my emotions from them, and stand up. "Excuse me. Where is the restroom?"

Atlas isn't having any of it. He grabs me and pulls me onto his lap. "You're not going to the bathroom to cry alone."

I don't ask how he knew what I planned. This man notices everything about me.

"Men aren't comfortable around a woman in tears." I learned that lesson quickly after the loss of my baby.

Neither Tino, nor his father wanted to see me cry. My own father and brother weren't any better.

Atlas puts his fisted hand under my chin and tilts my head back so I can't hide my emotion from him. "We talked about this."

"Your brothers don't need a crying woman ruining their dinner."

"Who told you that?" he asks, his voice hard.

"Whoever it was is an asshole." That's Zeus.

Atlas grabs the cloth napkin from his place setting and gently dabs at the moisture on my cheeks. "Let me guess, your first husband."

"He was my only husband," I say with some asperity.

I don't have a string of dead husbands in my past. I'm no black widow.

"Until now."

"Don't say things like that."

"Why not? If they are true?"

I shake my head and squirm, trying to get up. Hardness that is not his muscular thigh presses against my hip and I stop moving fast. How long has he been this way? Do his brothers know?

"Losing a sibling is devastating. If you need to cry, cry," Orion says.

And he knows, doesn't he? He lost Atlas for a whole year when they were children.

"We're not weak men. We can handle a woman's tears." Zeus's tone brooks no argument.

Was Tino weak? I would have staunchly denied it five years ago, but looking back, I know he wasn't the husband I needed. Meeting Atlas has forced me to look at the past through different eyes.

There's no ignoring the stark difference between the two men.

"I am not Tino," Atlas says, reading my mind.

"No, you aren't. In so many ways," I whisper under my breath.

"He sure as hell isn't," Orion says, like he's judging my dead husband and not favorably.

Zeus grunts in agreement. It must be his go to sound. Another thing he has in common with Atlas. I wonder if Orion does it too.

"The more I learn about Tino, the more satisfying I find it that you don't think I'm like him, but I want to know exactly what you mean by that," Atlas says.

Bat ears is another common genetic trait, it seems.

I sigh. "I'm not spending dinner talking about my dead husband. He is in the past. I am also not eating sitting on your lap."

"Why not?" His arm settles over my lap like a steel band.

The silent message is clear. I'm not going anywhere.

"It's not polite, Atlas."

"I don't care."

"Maybe your brothers do."

"It's weird, I'll give you that," Orion says.

I frown at Atlas. "I told you."

"It's not that you're sitting on his lap," Orion clarifies. "It's that my baby brother wants a woman in his personal space at all."

Is Orion trying to imply that Atlas, Mr. Handsy himself, has an issue with people in his personal space? Because I don't believe it. He's always invading mine.

Not that I mind.

Somehow, I find myself sharing a plate of food with Atlas. But I draw the line when he tries to feed me.

"I have my own fork," I say with asperity, grabbing said fork. "I'll stab you with it if you try to feed me like a child in front of your brothers."

"Does that mean you don't mind him doing it when we aren't around?" Orion again.

I give him the stink eye. "None of your business."

There are so many lies of omission in my life that I will not lie about anything else. And the image of sitting in Atlas's lap with a blindfold over my eyes, and my hands tied together, while he feeds me has my ovaries sending messages to all my other lady bits.

I'm so wet, it's a miracle I don't slide right off Atlas's thighs.

"You will tell me whatever is putting that look on your face later."

I shove a bite of delicious chicken cooked with artichokes and tomatoes into my mouth and chew with gusto. Not answering him. N. O. T.

Under the cover of the table, Atlas shifts his arm. His hand settles on my knee, but it doesn't stay there. He starts sliding those thick fingers up the inside of my leg.

I squeak.

"Did you meep?" Orion asks.

"Will it offend you if I deck your brother?" I ask Atlas.

"No. I'll hold his arms for you."

"Not necessary." I level an ire filled glance on Orion. "I've taken down bigger men than him."

All three men growl. In unison. Excuse me while I expire from arousal. "You know, I'm not attracted to your brothers, but that growl in stereo? Seriously hot."

"You should never have been put in a situation you had to take a man of any size down." Atlas makes the pronouncement more appropriate for a different era, but his brothers nod in agreement.

All three men look ready to take on my past.

My inner feminist takes a nap and I revel in all this testosterone directed toward my protection.

Atlas doesn't even grumble about my comment regarding the hotness of his brothers. He's too busy looking furious about my past. He knows about Lenny and he hates I was put in the position I was.

I hate it too, especially on the anniversary of my baby's death. But I despise it as much for Lenny. He deserves to be happy and his life in Detroit was a lot of things. Dangerous. Chaotic. Uncertain. Happy was not among them.

"Newsflash, it is the twenty-first century, gentlemen. A woman can take care of herself," I am compelled to say. Even if knowing I don't have to is sweet like honey to my soul.

"Not my woman."

"Your caveman is showing again."

"You mean it ever goes into hiding?" Orion snarks.

Zeus shakes his head, like his brothers are too annoying for words. My father used to do that when Rocco and I were acting up and feeding off each other.

These men are all adults, but the dynamic is so precious, it hurts.

I don't get time to dwell on that heart pain though, not with Atlas's hand moving inexorably higher on my thigh. Another inch and he's going to feel my soaked panties.

I'm regretting my decision to wear the short sweater dress with thigh-highs and no tights. I'm way too accessible to that wandering hand.

"Why a nightclub?" Zeus asks.

Ah, we've reached that part of the evening. The grill-the-new-girlfriend over dinner phase.

"It is what I knew."

"You worked in a nightclub before coming to Portland?" Zeus probes.

I'm adept at avoiding answering questions I don't want to, but there's not harm in answering this one.

"I did the books for the nightclubs my husband and his father ran." Both the ledgers the government saw and the real ones. "I couldn't help learning a lot about the business side of things in the process. When I left, I knew my best chance at making the life I wanted would be running a nightclub."

It wasn't what I wanted, but it was what I knew. The only thing I knew that could make the kind of income I needed to take care of both me and Lenny. Unless I wanted to start my own criminal enterprise and without the support of a syndicate, that option was way too risky.

"Considering how many fail in the first year, you must be good at it." Zeus doesn't sound like he's giving me a compliment. "Do you have silent backers?"

"Not that it's any of your business, but no, I don't. Nuovi Inizi is 100% my responsibility." After paying ahead five years for Lenny's care, I invested the rest of the money I drained from Tino's accounts in the Cayman Islands in Nuovi Inizi.

"And fully your triumph." It's not Atlas who says this, surprisingly, but Orion.

Maybe we'll get through the evening without me doing him bodily harm.

"It is. Lucia is a damn fine businesswoman." Atlas's fingertip brushes over the gusset of my panties and ecstasy fizzes over my labia and up into my core.

It is all I can do not to squirm.

I grab Atlas's wrist. Too little. Too late. Why didn't I stop him before he reached fingertip to vulva contact?

"You must have done your research before opening the club where you did."

I nod, not about to open my mouth when embarrassing noises might come out instead of words.

"Atlas said you have some recommendations for us in regard to buying our own clubs," Zeus says leadingly.

Shoving another bite of food into my mouth, I nod again.

Atlas's finger slides under the fabric between my legs to touch my naked lips. *Dio mio*. I am not going to make it through this dinner.

"What are they?" Zeus asks.

He wants me to answer him? Now? I accidentally, on purpose stab Atlas in the hand with my fork while ostensibly going for another bite. He grunts.

He grunts!

Is it murder when it is provoked? Asking for a friend.

"You okay there, Atlas?" Orion asks, his voice laced with laughter.

Oh, he knows something is going on.

Torture just got added to the table along with the murder possibility. I may have left behind the mafia, but I haven't forgotten everything I learned.

"I think I need to sit in my own chair," I say from between gritted teeth.

Atlas's hand slides back down my leg and he lifts his fingers right up to his mouth. I watch in mortified fascination as he sucks my juices off of them.

O-M-G. My mouth parts and I gasp as desire rips through me with the power of a tsunami.

Kissing my forehead, Atlas says, "Answer my brother, Lucia."

I look toward Zeus, cringing inwardly at the judgement I'm going to see in his face. What kind of woman lets her boyfriend touch her like that at the dining table? Not one raised to be a perfect mafia princess, that's for sure.

Zeus isn't looking at me with disgust though, he's looking at his brother with concern.

What is that about?

"Answer me first why you and Orion seem so worried about Atlas dating." I wait in silence for one of them to answer me.

"When Atlas was ten..." Zeus looks to my boyfriend, like he's asking permission to continue.

Atlas shrugs. "I told her already."

"You told her?" Orion asks, sounding dumbfounded.

I get that it's early to be talking about such heavy stuff, but we both laid our past bare for the other. Well, my past is almost bare. I haven't mentioned the whole mafia connection. How do you tell someone your family is part of a century old criminal syndicate?

"Yes." Atlas takes a bite and chews unconcernedly.

My whole body is still buzzing with the electric current caused by his shenanigans.

Zeus gives his brother a strange look before saying, "When Atlas came home, he was different."

"Inevitable after spending a year going through what he did." I shift my hips, trying to alleviate the ache between my legs without being obvious about it.

"For fuck's sake, let the woman sit in her own chair, brother," Orion says with exasperation.

Atlas's arm contracts around me like he's stopping me from leaping form his lap. "I like her where she's at."

"This." Zeus waves between me and Atlas. "This is what I'm worried about."

"I told you your brothers would be uncomfortable with me sitting in your lap for dinner." Let's not mention the inappropriate touching that I very much want to go back to.

In private.

"They'll survive." Atlas has zero concern about the awkwardness of the situation.

"You're really stubborn."

Atlas shrugs.

"Before he met you, Atlas hadn't smiled in years," Zeus says.

Orion nods in agreement. "I hadn't heard him laugh since before the kidnapping."

"He's happy." And being with me makes him that way.

Warmth unfurls inside me and I want to hug Atlas so hard. When have I ever been the source of someone's happiness?

Never.

"I didn't know he *could* be happy." Zeus doesn't sound all that joyful about it himself. "What happens when you two break up?"

Hearing the question from someone else's lips throws my own worries into perspective. It doesn't matter how long Atlas and I have known each other. He's the puzzle piece that has been missing from my life, and I'm the one that completes the picture in his.

"We're not going to break up."

"Glad you finally realize that." Atlas rewards me with a bite of crisp asparagus from our plate.

I take it off the tines of his fork and savor the perfectly prepared vegetable. So much for feeding myself.

"Well, at least you are living in the delusion together," Zeus says acerbically.

"There are things you don't know," Orion says, clearly not content to let things lie.

Zeus lays down his own fork and pushes his plate away. "That's for a later time." His tone is one of command, not suggestion.

I don't mind. Atlas will tell me what he needs to in his own time. How can I expect anything else when I'm hiding so much about the woman I used to be from him?

CHAPTER 21

ATLAS

After dinner, which my brothers managed to make ridiculously awkward by implying I'm emotionally stunted to Lucia, I give her the tour of the house I promised.

She loves the media room and sighs over the indoor pool, but when we get upstairs, she says, "I want to see your room now."

Grabbing her hand, I drag her down the corridor to my suite and press my palm to the reader beside the door before swinging it open.

We've both been on a razor's edge of desire since dinner. It's time to take care of it.

"You have biometric security on your bedroom?" she asks with disbelief.

"It's more like an apartment within the house."

Her perfectly shaped brows draw together in a frown. "You don't trust your brothers?"

"They're two of only a handful of people I do trust. The lock is there for everyone else."

"Like your housekeeper?"

"And everyone else who comes inside the mansion."

"I guess after what happened to you that level of paranoia makes sense, but it must be exhausting."

"Security is second nature to me now."

"Were you like this before you were taken?"

"I don't remember." I was a kid. I came home a made man at the age of eleven, no longer a child, but not an adult either.

"Your brothers are really worried about you. I'm assuming you don't date a lot."

"I don't date ever."

"That's hard to believe considering how quickly you went from one-night-stand to committed couple who don't see other people."

"I knew you were mine the first time our eyes met."

"I want to scoff at that, but it felt like that for me too." She sounds worried about that.

And she doesn't even know the half of why she should be. The fact that we got together so quickly is nothing compared to the identity of the man she's dating.

Dímios. The executioner.

It is inevitable that she will eventually find out about my connection to the Greek mafia, but she never needs to know how many men I have killed. Or how much more blood I will spill in the future.

She looks around my space and her eyes widen as she takes everything in. "You weren't kidding when you said apartment. This living room is three times as big as mine. You even have a freaking kitchen."

"More like a snack area." There's a stove that I never use, a small fridge and a wall of cabinets and drawers.

"It's bigger than my kitchen and I bet you never cook for yourself."

"That's a bet you would win." I'm not interested in talking about how my meals are prepared right now. "Tell me what put that look on your face at dinner."

"What look? There were so many ranging from embarrassment to confusion, not to mention trying my hardest to hide how turned on I was by what you were doing."

"It was definitely a turned on look. And it was before I started touching you under the table."

"Oh." Lucia looks away. "That."

Definitely that if this is the effect remembering what caused it is having on her. "What were you thinking?"

"You were trying to feed me."

"I did feed you." She kept forgetting to eat because my damn brothers were talking to her, so I had to feed her a few times to remind her about the food on our plate.

She swallows. "Yes. You did."

"So?"

"So, I liked it," she says in a small voice.

"So did I."

She ducks her head, her dark hair falling like a curtain over her cheeks so I can't see her face at all. I don't like it.

Pulling her around to face me, I lift her chin so her eyes have to meet mine. Their chocolate depths are swirling with emotion. And desire.

Fuck me.

"It turned you on when I fed you?" I'm surprised. She'd made a big deal about wanting to eat with her own fork.

"Yes, but thinking about you doing it...a different way, turned me on even more."

"What way?"

"I had this picture in my head."

I pull her close with one arm while cupping her nape with the other, keeping her face tilted up. "What did that picture look like?"

"I was sitting on your lap."

"Were you dressed?"

She shakes her head.

My cock, which is in a perpetual state of readiness around her, goes painfully hard. "What were you wearing?"

"My panties and bra."

"The ones you have on now?" Sheer crimson stretchy fabric, the bra barely contains her generous tits. Her matching thong reveals her shaved pussy lips and showcases her ass.

"Yes."

"And?" I don't ask what I'm wearing because it doesn't matter. My clothes aren't going to stay on for much longer.

"And I'm wearing a blindfold."

My knees about buckle. "What else?" I ask hoarsely.

"Handcuffs, or a tie, or something, but my hands are bound behind my back."

"*Gamó*."

"What do you think?" Fear and lust fight for supremacy on her beautiful face.

"What are you afraid of?"

"You thinking I'm a freak."

"I think we didn't eat dessert."

She frowns, opens her mouth and then snaps it shut again. Swallows. And then, "Oh."

It takes me only a few seconds to tear off my clothes and Lucia watches me the whole time with blown pupils.

"Take off everything except your bra and panties."

She grabs the hem of her tight dark red sweater dress and tugs it up slowly, revealing her body inch by inch. Her thong is so wet it sticks between her pussy lips. My mouth waters to taste her, but that's not what is happening right now.

Stopping as the hem of her dress reaches the underside of her breasts, Lucia lets out a small puff of air.

"Finish it," I say in a guttural tone usually reserved for interrogations.

She shivers like she can feel the barely leashed violence behind it. Not that I will do her harm, but I am going to fuck her so hard, she'll need to sit on a pillow tomorrow.

She tugs the soft red knit up a sliver at a time until her pebbled nipples poke at me through the sheer fabric of her bra. Stopping when her body is revealed but her face is hidden by the dress, she puts herself on display, making herself vulnerable to me.

My plan to have her undress herself going up in the fiery inferno of my need for her, I step forward. We pull her dress the rest of the way off together.

I toss it away from us before cupping her generous mounds. "Your tits are beautiful."

"I'm glad you think so."

"You never told me why the red." Not sure why my brain offers that as a distraction. "Is it because you're so passionate, *eromenis mou*?"

I need to get a handle on the lust surging through me, or I'm going to rip off her soaked panties and destroy the matching bra. Finding out why she always wears red is as good of a brain interrupt as anything else. Or should that be little-brain interrupt?

She shakes her head. "The shade of red that represents passion is brighter. Besides, I didn't even know this kind of desire lived inside me before we met."

My little brain likes hearing that. Too much. "So what does that dark red mean?"

"A lot of things, but the one that matters to me is courage. Making the choices I did that led me here took a lot of it. Wearing something crimson every day is my way of reminding myself I have the courage I need to get through whatever comes."

Gamó. "When I think you can't get any more perfect, you do." And as distractions from my lust go, this discussion is a total bust. "Take off your boots."

"Aren't you going to help me?" she teases.

"I'm busy." I could play with her rack for hours. I pinch both nipples at the same time. "Be my good girl and do what I say."

She shudders.

She loves being called a good girl. It fucking fascinates me. She is my good girl though, even when she's being bad.

"I need to bend down to get my boots."

Nodding, I release her tits and step back. "Turn around, I want to watch your ass."

Blushing, she turns. That blush makes me want to throw her over the couch and drill her without mercy, but we've got plans.

She squats to take off her boots, popping her ass cheeks out and putting the crotch of her panties stained dark from her arousal on display.

"Never wear tights again," I order.

She shakes her ass a little. "Like my thigh highs, do you?"

"Yes." The way they stop midway up her juicy curved thighs and frame her ass and pussy gets me every damn time.

She tugs off first one boot and then the other, before straightening her legs. She does not lift her torso, effectively leaving her bent over and touching her feet.

She stays that way until I am breathing heavily from the view of her ass. "You're a fucking tease, Lucia."

Standing, she turns and sweeps her long hair back over her shoulders so every inch of her luscious tits is on display for me. "I'm not teasing, I'm tempting."

"Stay there."

"You're so growly."

Jogging down the hall to my bedroom, I don't answer. I grab two of my silk neckties that will not survive the night. There are a box of zip ties in my equipment room I use for jobs, but I am not binding her tender wrists with a zip tie.

There's a sex toy store near her club. I'll have to drop by and get some leather cuffs, maybe some other bondage equipment. Being restrained for me excites *ílios mou* and that means I need bindings that won't hurt her.

When I get back in my suite's living room, Lucia is standing exactly where I left her. Her eyes are hazy with desire, her nipples diamond hard peaks and the perfume of her arousal permeates the space.

Staying there because I told her to is turning my woman on.

I approach her in silence, my eyes eating up her delicious body. I don't ask if she's ready. I can tell that she is. Stopping behind her so my aching cock presses against her back, I cup both of her naked shoulders. I'm holding a tie in each hand and the ends dangle, brushing along her silky skin.

She moans. I slide my hands, still holding the ties, down her arms, leaving gooseflesh in my wake. She moves restlessly when the ends brush against her legs.

So beautiful. So fucking responsive.

Trailing my hands up her torso, I cup her tits again and play with her nipples until she's leaning against me for support. She's making those little sex noises that act like tinder to the fire inside me. I want to bend her over and shove my cock deep inside her tight, wet pussy.

My dick is drooling, leaving a streak of precum on her back. Rocking forward, my boner slips against her slickened skin. If I don't stop, I'm going to come all over her back and that is not the plan.

I force myself to step back.

She sways and I catch her hip with one hand. "Can you stand?"

"I don't know."

"Try."

She shivers.

Gamó.

I let her go, but give it a beat to see if she's steady. She doesn't sink to the floor.

"Good girl." I squeeze her ass.

"Atlas," she says in a breathy, barely there voice.

Wrapping one of my ties around her head twice, I blindfold her, and tie the ends together behind her head.

"It's dark."

"Good." It should be. I'm an expert at blindfolding targets.

Next, I create a double loop with my other tie, before pulling one of her hands back and sliding it in the right loop. She offers the other one before I can grab it.

Smiling at her eagerness, I slide the loop over her hand and secure the tie so that it will not tighten if she yanks against it but will not loosen either.

"Stay there."

"What are you going to do?"

"Get our dessert."

She swallows and nods.

I know exactly what I want to feed her. My brothers prefer *kaimaki*, traditional Greek ice cream with swirls of cherry preserves and infused with rose water. It's too sweet for me. I like lime sorbet and Gina makes sure I always have a pint in my freezer.

No surprise, the pint of gourmet sorbet is there, when I open the freezer. I grab it and a spoon and put them both on the coffee table. Then I return to my sweetly patient lover.

Too sweet for a man with a dark soul like mine, but I am not letting her go. I sweep her up into my arms.

Gasping, Lucia contorts her body, trying to hold on, but her hands are secured behind her back.

Holding her tightly against my chest, I say, "Relax. I will not drop you."

She instantly stops squirming and rests against me. "I know."

I sit down and settle her on my lap facing me, maneuvering her thighs on either side of mine. The scent of her pussy juices are even stronger with her legs spread.

My cock bobs and my mouth waters. My favorite sorbet isn't what I want for dessert. "You make me so fucking hard."

CHAPTER 22

LUCIA

Blindfolded, with my hands tied behind my back, I should feel vulnerable. Maybe even scared.

I'm not. Not even a little. I feel empowered.

I'm so excited, my heart is going to beat out of my chest. The strength in the hard thighs under mine only makes me feel safe.

"You are so beautiful like this." Atlas's voice is even deeper than usual.

My inner muscles involuntarily contract and pleasure pulses in my core. Shifting side to side, I try to get some relief.

Atlas grips my hips, stopping the movement. "Ready for your dessert?"

Dessert? All I want is him. "Dessert later."

"No chance." His laughter is a little diabolical. "You want this *eromenis mou* and I will give it to you."

"Why does that sound like a threat?" I ask, panting.

His big hand presses against my bottom and he jerks me forward until the soaked gusset of my panties is flush with the base of his sex. Vibrating with sensation, my clit rubs against his iron hard tool.

"Not a threat. A promise." He kisses me, licking my lips before pulling his head away.

I extend my neck, trying to chase that sexy mouth.

He wraps my hair around his fist and uses it as a handle to pull my head back. "Open your mouth."

My lips part of their own volition.

A cold spoon touches my bottom lip. "Taste."

Shivers of arousal cascade through me as I obey. Flavor explodes across my tongue. Lime. Sweet. It's sorbet. The frozen treat melts almost immediately in the heat of my mouth.

The next thing to touch my lips is not a spoon, but the blunt tip of Atlas's finger. Covered in the sorbet.

I suck the dessert off his appendage without having to be told and somehow the saltiness of his skin mixes perfectly with the sorbet to create my new favorite flavor. He feeds me bite after bite with me taking longer and longer to suck his finger clean.

Desperate to touch him, I yank against the tie around my wrists. It doesn't give.

I let his finger go with a pop and ask, "Aren't you going to eat any?"

"Yes."

"Do you want me to feed you?" Please untie me.

"Yes," he says gutturally.

He reaches behind me and does what I'm craving, removing the tie binding my hands. But I have no chance to enjoy my new freedom before I find myself on my back on the couch.

Atlas shoves my thighs wide apart and arranges my hands in the crooks of my bent knees. "Hold them."

"I want to touch you." I'm not whining.

I'm stating, in a sort of pleading tone. Is pleading better than whining? Does it matter when I feel this good?

"You want me to control your body," he says, his tone deep and commanding.

Dio mio. He is right.

Unable to see him because I am still blindfolded, I clasp my legs tightly and pull my thighs even further apart for him.

He hums his approval and then my panties yank tight against my hips before the fabric gives way completely to the strength in Atlas's grip.

Pulling the ruined underwear upward, he tows the thin strip of fabric that sat between my butt cheeks up between my nether lips. It drags against my clitoris before he rips the torn panties completely off my body.

Wetness gushes from my core. Not being able to see makes everything I experience so much bigger. We are definitely doing this again.

"I'm going to leave a wet spot on your couch," I pant.

"Good. Every time I see the stain, I will think of you like this," he growls.

Nothing he could say could turn me on as much as knowing he thinks about me when we aren't together. It is not out of sight, out of mind, like it had been in my marriage.

Freezing cold against my clit shocks a scream out of me. My legs automatically try to snap together to protect my tender bundle of nerves. Atlas's head and shoulders are there though. His hot mouth covers my clitoris and he sucks, nipping gently. Then, swirling his tongue around my clit, he warms my chilled flesh.

He pulls back. "Pussy and lime sorbet. My new favorite flavor."

I laugh.

"What?"

"That's what I thought when I sucked it off your finger."

He grunts.

Oh, caveman. Why are you so damn sexy?

Another dollop of frozen confection lands against my clitoris and I cry out. He doesn't put his mouth on me right away this time but holds my thighs open while the chill permeates my sensitized bud.

I squirm as the sorbet slowly melts against my heated flesh, sending a message to my nerve endings that I cannot decide is pleasure or pain.

"Please, Atlas."

"What do you want, *eromenis mou*? Do you want me to finish my dessert?"

"Yes," I practically yell.

"Soon." He runs his finger through my slick folds. "So pretty."

"Atlas," I wail.

There is no warning before he shifts and his mouth is back on me. He licks all over my vulva, before gently sucking one of my labia into his mouth. Holding it carefully between his teeth, he runs his tongue along the plump and sensitive flesh.

Porca miseria! I am not going to survive this.

I realize I said the words aloud when he stops eating me and lifts his head.

"Yes." His voice so fierce it sends a shudder through me. "You will survive and thrive."

His visceral reaction beats against me, but I do not know what he wants from me. I want his mouth back on my intimate flesh. I thrust my hips upward in silent supplication.

"Say it," he demands.

My brain addled by unfulfilled pleasure, I can only cant my hips again, seeking more of his mouth.

"Say you will not die. I will not let you."

His sheer arrogance gets through my arousal fogged brain. "Pretty sure that's not your decision. You are not God."

"I am your lover," he says, like that's something more powerful. "I will never let you go."

If anyone can hold onto me by sheer will alone, it is this man.

"Don't let me go." It's a plea for so much more than sex, but I do my best not to acknowledge that. Even to myself.

"Say it."

"Not dying right now. I need." Him. His mouth. A climax.

The original Atlas held the weight of the world on his shoulders. This Atlas could give the ancient son of Titan a run for his money in stubbornness though.

He proves it by taking me to the edge over and over again, no matter how much I beg for and demand my release. Only when my body is covered in a sheen of sweat and tears of frustration leak from my eyes does he finally allow me to come.

Two big fingers drill into my intimate tunnel while he suckles my clit with the strength of a vacuum. My orgasm blasts through me like a case of C-4 going off. I scream so loud and so long, my throat hurts.

Feeling light-headed, I sink, boneless, into the couch. My body is so replete, even the aftershocks of my seismic climax can't make my muscles tense again.

Fingers work behind my head and then the tie is being removed. Light assaults my eyes and I wince, closing them.

"Look at me," Atlas orders. "I want your eyes on me."

It takes a few seconds for my eyes to adjust to the light and then I'm able to focus on him. His handsome face is set in rigid lines, his gaze feral. I release one of my legs so I can wrap my fingers around his turgid erection.

Rearing up, he puts his hand over mine and jacks himself off with our combined grip. Our eyes are locked the whole time, his showing an intensity of feeling that cannot be mere lust.

"Yes, like that," he says, as if I have anything to do with the strength of our grip, or the speed of our hands moving over the hard column of flesh.

Then his face sets in a rictus of pleasure and he shouts my name, ejaculating all over my vulva. Globs of his warm semen hit my sensitive flesh and send residual waves of pleasure through my core. He keeps my hand wrapped tightly around his sex as he prolongs his own pleasure.

"Keep your hand there," he demands as he removes his own to rub his essence into my nether lips, scooping some on his fingers, pushing it inside me.

Tingles of pleasure, that can't quite turn into arousal in my exhausted body, follow his fingers' path.

I am connected to him on an intimate level I never experienced in my three-year long marriage.

Why this man? How is the bond between us so strong already?

~ ~ ~

I wake up surrounded by familiar heat in an unfamiliar bed. The mattress is harder than mine and bigger.

Atlas's bed is huge, like the man it belongs to. The man whose arm holds me so tightly, my body is flush with his. The need to pee forces me to try to squirm out from under the heavy appendage.

His hold tightens and pulls me back into his heat.

I groan. "Atlas, I have to pee," I hiss.

Mumbling, he nuzzles my hair, keeping me close in his sleep.

It should feel claustrophobic. I used to hate when Tino smothered my body with his in sleep. But I like this. Too much. Atlas's hold makes me feel safe. Warm. Secure.

My bladder isn't going to let me revel in the pleasant feelings though. If I don't get out of bed soon, it won't be my arousal or Atlas's cum leaving a wet spot soaking through the sheet to the mattress.

I pinch his forearm. Hard. "Atlas." My voice is loud in the dark and silent room. "Let me up."

"No."

"I have to pee."

Grunting, he sits up, pulling me with him and proceeds to guide me out of bed and to the bathroom without turning on any lights.

Plopping down on the toilet just in time, pee gushes out, splashing into the water below my butt.

"Sounds like Multnomah Falls down there," Atlas says in a sleepy grumble.

"You could have let me come to the bathroom alone."

"I like being with you."

"In the bathroom?" I roll my eyes in the dark. "How pleasant for you."

"All the time I spend with you is pleasure." He yawns. Loudly.

I can't believe how good his words make me feel, but I snark, "Obsessed much?"

The subtle shifting of his body and the air around us lets me know he's shrugging.

"Seriously, Atlas, your brothers are going to get sick of you being with me so much."

"They'll get over it." His tone implies he doesn't care if they don't.

I'm sure that's not true though. He, Zeus and Orion are really close. That was made abundantly clear to me from the moment I met the oldest brother and all through dinner.

It's only a guess, because they weren't there, but I suspect they are as close with their cousins. After all, the five men moved up from California together for a joint business venture.

"You're lucky." My voice reveals my grief at the estrangement from mine, and I wince.

For five years, I have done my best not to think about my family, but being around Atlas with his brothers makes my heart ache missing my own.

His big hand lands unerringly against my neck and curves around it possessively. "Why are you sad?"

I wipe and stand, lowering the lid before flushing. "You and your brothers remind me of what I lost."

"Now you have two brothers to annoy you, not one." He reaches out and suddenly a dim light above the sink goes on. "And two cousins who will be up in your business, whether you want them to, or not."

"Don't say things like that," I say sharply as I wash my hands with jerky movements. "They're not my family."

"They will be. Once we marry."

"We're not engaged." No matter how right things feel with Atlas, I'm not jumping blindly into the deep end of this thing between us.

That's a good way to drown.

CHAPTER 23

ATLAS

Lucia is quiet when we wake up. I fuck the thoughtful right out of her in the shower, but she's back to staring off into space by the time she gets dressed in her clothes from the night before.

Knowing she's going commando is doing nothing for my ability to control the urge to touch her.

I'm cupping her ample ass when we reach the kitchen, where my family is eating breakfast. Seeing everyone there, Lucia squeaks. She jumps away from me, smacking my hand away from her ass.

Worse, she insists on sitting in her own chair. When I go to grab her and put her in my lap, she threatens to turn me into a eunuch with her fork. My cousins and brothers find this hilarious, laughing like hyenas.

Zephyr shakes his head. "Woah, you'd better watch out for this one, Atlas. She's a firecracker."

"Talking about me like I'm not here is a good way to learn how big I can explode like one," Lucia says sweetly to my cousin.

Laughter erupts from the peanut gallery while Lucia pretends to ignore my annoyance. Zeus, being Zeus, formally introduces her to our housekeeper, Gina, and my two knucklehead cousins.

"Too bad Atlas saw you first," Zephyr says, because he clearly wants an early grave. "If you ever decide to upgrade models, keep in mind that I'm younger and have more stamina."

The asshole won't have any stamina when he is dead, will he?

"Yeah, not buying that, even if you gave me the nickel to do it." Lucia smiles at Gina and takes a laden plate of breakfast from her. "Thank you."

"Getting a peek at my *stamina* is worth more than a nickel," Zephyr claims then shouts as his chair tilts backward from my foot lifting it under the table.

He crashes to the floor.

"What happened? Are you alright?" Lucia asks while Gina rushes over to help Zephyr up.

Grinning like a fool, he winks at *ílios mou*. "I'm fine. The chair had a mind of its own there for a second."

"More like a nudge from Atlas." Gina glares at me.

I shrug.

"Did you knock his chair over?" Lucia's brows are drawn together in confusion, like she's trying to figure out how I did it.

Long legs and strength can accomplish a lot.

I grab a fresh roll from the basket on the table. "He had it coming."

"Atlas!" Lucia looks at me with shock while the hyenas around the table laugh again.

I roll my eyes at her. "He's fine."

"That was uncalled for." Lucia glares at me.

Irresistibly drawn to those pursed lips, I kiss her until she forgets she's mad and kisses me back.

"Save it for the bedroom," Orion snarks.

Lucia goes stiff and yanks her head away from mine. She forgot where we are. I like that so much, I decide I won't kill my cousin today.

"I can't believe you knocked your cousin's chair over. What are you, twelve?"

"He offered to show you his cock. He's lucky he didn't end up with a knife in his junk."

"You can't say stuff like that, even as a joke," Lucia admonishes me, standing up like she's going to check on Zephyr's nonexistent injuries herself.

I give my cousin a look to let him know how much I do mean my words and he waves her off. "I'm fine. It's nothing."

Smart man.

Tugging Lucia back into her seat, I ask, "What time do you have to be at the club today?"

She looks up at me, worry darkening her gaze. "Have you considered therapy? I think you might have anger management issues."

Orion turns his laugh into a cough, but Helios nearly falls off his own chair in hilarity.

Ignoring them, I take Lucia's hand in mine. "Been there. Done that. My mother made me go after my rescue."

The psychologist was connected to the life and even she couldn't know it all. I read once that for therapy to work, you have to be honest. Since there was more that I couldn't tell her than I could, the sessions were doomed to fail.

"This is as good as it gets."

I don't know what Lucia sees in my face, but hers goes all gooey and she caresses my cheek. "It's pretty darn wonderful from where I'm sitting."

"You'd better keep her, Atlas. She's the only woman with rose colored glasses tinted enough to see you as boyfriend material through them," Orion offers his two-cents.

Lucia turns a censorious glare on my brother. "I have twenty-twenty vision and you should be more affirming of your brother."

While she and Orion trade barbs, Zephyr joining in to back them both up, Zeus gives me a disapproving glare which I ignore.

My cousin knows better than to say shit about Lucia seeing his stamina. He had his warning in Zeus's office last week.

"What time do you need to get to the club?" I ask Lucia again, when I'm on my second cup of coffee.

She sighs. "I should be there already. I'll need to leave right after breakfast. I can get a rideshare though, if you have things to do."

"I will drive you." Like hell is she getting into a car with a stranger. "You work too much."

"Whereas you are not working enough," Zeus says.

When Lucia bites her lip and starts looking guilty, my hand itches to toss a throwing knife at him. I would hit him in the fleshy part of his arm. He is my *anax* and brother, after all.

"I'm doing everything I'm supposed to," I remind him.

He tips his coffee cup to swallow the last sip and then sets the empty mug down. "Are you though?"

Enough of this shit. I stand up. "Let's go, *ílios mou*."

"It sounds like Zeus needs you. Let me get a cab back. It's not a big deal."

The look I give my brother should set his head on fire.

He doesn't see it because he's frowning at Lucia. "You aren't taking a damn cab back to your club."

Finally, he says something that makes sense.

"Don't worry about Zeus," Orion says to Lucia. "If he's not busting somebody's balls, he's not happy."

"For that, you can drive Lucia home. I need to meet with Atlas."

I'm about to tell him to shove his meeting right up his ass when I notice the expression on Lucia's beautiful face. She looks stressed. I don't like it.

"You okay, *ílios mou*?" I ask her.

"I don't want to cause trouble between you and your brothers."

"You're not causing any trouble," Zeus and I say at the same time.

Lucia smiles. "Have you thought about taking that act on the road?"

"I'm happy to drive you home," Orion says. "I want to see Nuovi Inizi. Atlas has talked it up and I want to see if it lives up to the hype of a man whose dick is addicted to the owner."

"It does," I say.

Lucia gives my brother a look. "Do you talk to your mother with that mouth?"

"As infrequently as possible."

Aw, hell, now Lucia is giving my brother her compassionate look.

"If you touch her, I will cut off your fingers," I warn him in Greek.

"I'm not about to touch your girlfriend," he answers me in English.

Lucia beams at him. "Thank you for speaking in English."

"Keep making her smile at you like that and we'll need a new lawyer because you'll be six feet under." I stick to Greek.

Lucia doesn't need to hear my threats. Only Orion does. He knows they're more like promises.

~ ~ ~

"She's got you tied up in knots," my brother says.

"Stop trying to be an agony aunt and tell me why I had to let Orion drive Lucia to the club."

"I want to check in with you."

"Not this shit again. I am fine. Yes, I want to keep her. No, that doesn't change who I am or what I do for the *Ádis Adelfótita*."

"Maybe it should."

"What the hell do you mean?"

"Do you think Lucia will be able to accept you as Dímios?"

"She never has to know about my job as executioner. She'll know I'm an enforcer soon enough."

"Not as soon as we planned. I want to take care of the bratva problem before we start collecting protection money. Securing the shipping yard has to be our top priority right now."

A flood of relief I don't understand washes over me. It shouldn't matter *when* Lucia finds out I'm an enforcer for the Greek mafia. She's going to accept it because there is no other choice.

But I'm still glad I have more time to get her as addicted to my cock as I am her pussy.

Or get her pregnant.

[illegible] "Thank you for speaking to him."

"[illegible] will [illegible] won [illegible] that and we'll need a new [illegible] you [illegible] Creek."

[illegible] no hearing [illegible] knows [illegible]

"[illegible] knows [illegible]"

"Stop trying [illegible] and tell [illegible]

[illegible] to the [illegible]

[illegible] with [illegible]

[illegible] I want to keep [illegible] who I [illegible]

[illegible] should [illegible]

"What [illegible] you mean?"

"Do you think [illegible] will be able to accept [illegible]?"

[illegible] know [illegible]

[illegible] I want to [illegible]

[illegible]

[illegible]

[illegible]

"But [illegible] I have more [illegible]

[illegible]

[illegible]

CHAPTER 24

ATLAS

It's early on a Wednesday night. The club isn't packed yet, which is why they stand out like nudists at a convent.

Three of the bratva soldiers we saw at the bar the other night are looking over Nuovi Inizi with greedy eyes.

What are they doing here?

When their gazes land on Lucia in her signature red wrap dress that shows off every banging curve and two inches of mouth-watering cleavage, that greed gets tinged with lust.

A crimson wash of anger darkens my vision until all I can see are their bloody, lifeless bodies in my mind's eye. Moving so that I am between Lucia and them, I text Bobby, my guy watching from the outside tonight.

Atlas: *How the hell did three bratva get past you?*

Bobby: *Didn't get past me, boss. Just texted you to tell you they are on the way in. Do you want backup?*

Alone, I wouldn't need backup against three men. No matter how well trained. But Lucia is here. So is her favorite bartender. Hell, she'll be upset if *any* of her employees get hurt. Only way to guarantee that doesn't happen is to lure the assholes outside.

Atlas: *Call in Theo and Michael and meet me by the back door.*

The bratva bastards make it easy, coming toward me on their way to Lucia. I bump into one, lifting his gun on contact. The clueless bastard doesn't even realize it, but he does shove me and start yelling at me in Russian.

"Watch out, bitch."

I smile at him, a Dímios smile and he frowns. One of his friends backs up a step. The other looks at me warily.

"Your brothers cried like the little bitches they were when I killed them," I say in Russian.

Fury turns all three men's faces even uglier than they already are. The one I bumped jumps toward me, but I spin away, grab his arm, whip him around and shove his own gun into his side. His body now acts as a shield between me and his buddies.

"What's going on?" Lucia asks from behind me.

An unfamiliar feeling makes my heart pound.

Fear. This woman has a nose for trouble, or a magnet drawing it to her. She attracted me, didn't she?

Turning slightly so I can see her, I keep my body between her and the bratva soldiers and tighten my hold on the man acting as my shield. "Nothing for you to worry about, *ílios mou."*

Her eyes narrow. "He was yelling at you. In Russian."

She heard that? She doesn't understand Russian, or she would have asked questions at the bar that night. Lucia is too curious and intelligent to have done anything else.

"No big deal. I was surprised to see them in the club and bumped into Ivan here." I've got no clue what the man's real name is, but Ivan will do.

Other than the name, I'm careful to tell Lucia the truth. Something inside me roars like a beast at the idea of lying to her. There's a hell of a lot I'm not telling her, but that isn't the same as telling her something that is not true.

That feels like a betrayal and I won't do it.

"Right?" I dig the gun harder into the Russian's side.

"*Da*."

"English, asshole," I bark.

"Yes."

"Friends of yours?" Lucia asks, her dark eyes glowing with curiosity.

"They want a word. I'm taking them outside," I answer ignoring the actual question. "Right?"

"*Da*. Yes," my hostage corrects himself when I squeeze my fingers together on his shoulder, pinching the nerve there. "We talk outside."

His voice is hoarse with pain, but he also doesn't sound terrified. His two compatriots get self-satisfied looks on their faces when they hear we are going outside.

Which tells me three things. One, they all speak English. Two, they think they can take me. And three, the Golubev Bratva's kill order on me is about as effective as a paring knife against a machine gun.

Not a single bratva soldier I've run into has recognized my face. If these three recognized me, they would not be so eager to go outside with me.

Maybe I killed the soldiers who were tasked with researching me. Chances are good, considering how many I have taken out.

Regardless of the reason, the bratva know nothing about who their *palach* is and the bounty they have on my head is worthless. Not one of them knows what their bogeyman looks like and that has already cost three of them their lives.

Tonight, it will cost three more.

After I find out what the hell they think they are doing in Lucia's club.

"You can use my office if you want," Lucia offers.

My innocent, too-generous-for-her-own-safety sun.

"Thank you, *ílios mou*." I don't care if these men know her importance to me. They won't live to utilize the information. "We'll be fine outside."

"If you're sure."

I nod. "I might be gone a while. We have a lot to catch up on."

"Take your time." The guilt is there in her voice. Again.

It pisses me off, but I can't deal with it right now.

My woman needs to get over this idea that spending time with her is a hardship. Not only am I doing my job for my mafia, but even if I wasn't, watching over her would be my priority.

Especially with the infestation of bratva in the area.

I guide the men outside. My grip on their friend making me the Pied Piper for the other two.

As soon as we step out the door, I shove my hostage to the side and follow, keeping a firm hold on him. When his friends come out the door Bobby and Theo grab them, pressing guns to the back of their skulls to keep them docile.

We force them away from the back entrance to the club. When we are on the other side of the dumpster, I signal to my men to stop. No one using the back parking lot will see us here and garbage isn't taken out until after closing.

The employees that smoke are the only potential problem and I don't plan to be here long enough for it to become an issue.

I don't have to tell Michael what to do with our captives. This isn't our first rodeo and my team works together like a well-oiled killing machine. He slaps duct tape over their mouths and then zip-ties their hands behind their backs and their feet together at their ankles.

"I want you inside the club, keeping an eye on Lucia," I tell Michael in Greek when he is done.

He nods and disappears through the door we came out of with his usual silence.

I toss my keys to Theo. "Get the SUV."

The three trussed up men are now watching me with wariness. Is it the Greek? Or how quickly we incapacitated them?

"You thought you were the baddest motherfuckers in the area, didn't you? But now you know you're three little bitches about to spill the secrets of your brethren."

The one I called Ivan glares daggers at me, but one of his friends looks worried. He'll be the one to break, but not until after I prove with his friends how far I'm willing to go to get information. He's the kind who is impacted as much, or more, by seeing torture happen than being hurt himself.

We toss the three on top of each other in the back of the SUV and secure the specialty cargo net over them before shutting the tailgate. They aren't going anywhere.

Theo drives while Bobby keeps his eye on the prisoners. I call Zeus.

"What's up, little brother?"

"I'm on my way to the warehouse with three bratva soldiers."

"The fuck? Where?" He means where did I come across them?

"At the club."

"I'll be there in twenty. Don't start without me."

There's a lot we can do without *getting started*, so I don't argue with my *anax's* order.

When Zeus arrives, we have the three men hanging by their zip tied wrists from the rafters. Their feet are bare, making access to toenails and the fragile bones in their feet easy. Right now, their toes can touch the floor enough to take pressure off their shoulder joints. One turn of the winch and they lose even that level of comfort.

I'm ready to turn it.

I despise the Golubev Bratva and their allies. For what they did to me as a kid, but also because they make most of their money from human trafficking.

"Hey, brother. We've already done introductions. They know my name but aren't ready to return the favor." Though I have not told them I am the bratva killer their brethren in California refer to as *palach*. "I'm calling them Larry, Curly and Mo."

"You and your old movie references. Do they even know who the Three Stooges are?"

"Does it matter?" Sure, the psychological advantage of them knowing I am insulting them every time I use the names would be welcome.

But there's a psychological benefit to me calling them by names other than their own in and of itself. It implies they aren't real people to me. That they don't matter.

Zeus shakes his head at me. He approaches the dangling men.

"You are hellishly unlucky, aren't you?" he asks in Russian. "To walk into the club where your *palach* is hanging out with his girlfriend."

"He is not our executioner," the one I dubbed Mo says with misplaced bravado, completely missing my brother's inference to their *palach*.

"You are allies to the Golubev Brava." I throw my knife up high, letting it flip three times before catching it again. "I am death to you."

"What do you have against our Golubev brothers? They have no enemies in this state." This is Curly and he accompanies his words with a globule of spit landing on the floor a few inches from my boot.

Pig.

"Wrong." I punch him in the nuts with my knuckle duster while stabbing into the flesh of his thigh with my knife. "They are trying to establish territory in the same city as their greatest enemies."

Curly screams and jerks in his bonds, his toes losing their hold on the floor. He screams again when the weight of his body pulls against his strained shoulder joints.

Huh. Might have pulled one or both out of their sockets with that move.

"I was going to let you watch me play with your friends." I wipe the blood off my knife on his shirt. "But then you had to spit."

Curly moans.

"What no warmup?" Zeus asks.

"I have places to be." Almost as lethal as I am, I trust Michael to watch over Lucia.

That doesn't soothe the itch to get back to the club, so I can protect her myself.

Mo and Larry look at Zeus and me with dawning understanding. "You are Hades Brotherhood," Larry says.

He's been silent until now. He didn't react when we hoisted him up. No empty threats like his fellow soldiers when we ripped the duct tape from their mouths. No curses or insults.

"Curly's not the boss of your crew," I say. "It's you."

The man stares back at me with dead eyes. Eyes that before I met Lucia would be a mirror of my own. I don't know what Larry sees there now. His death? Yes. But a dead soul? Not so much.

She's fanned the dark ember of my soul into a flame. Though I'm pretty sure the fire is from hell, and it only burns for her.

"You are *palach*." He eyes me up and down. "You have killed many of our Golubev brethren."

"They started the war." And I will finish it.

"When they kidnapped a child from the Hades Brotherhood."

"You know your history."

He inclines his head, showing no discomfort in his situation, but his shoulders have to be burning. With normal interrogation techniques, he might crack in a week, or two. If we can keep him alive long enough to torture him effectively. My eyes scan the other two men.

Mo is the one I'm betting on, but does he have the information we need?

"The Godfather of the Night did not care enough to ransom the child back. How is the offense worth making mortal enemies of the bratva?" Larry asks.

My grandfather didn't value my life, but my uncle did and still does.

Content to let me do my thing, he ignores the San Francisco Golubev *pakhan's* demands to turn over the executioner. He also ignores the *pakhan's* offers of money and territory in exchange for a promise of safety for his men from the *palach*.

Never going to happen and Constantin will never ask for it.

"The only mortality being faced in this war is by the Golubev scum." There are no innocents among the Golubev Bratva soldiers and their allies.

Every one of them stinks with the shit clinging to them from the skin trade. They kidnap, torture, buy and sell human beings. Adults and children alike.

Larry's eyes narrow fractionally at my words, reflecting raging fury before it disappears and his gaze is once again soulless.

Interesting. The reaction was there, even if it is gone now. For a man like him to react implies a more personal connection than allies.

I do not lose my cool when allies of the *Ádis Adelfótita* are threatened. But for my brothers? And now, Lucia? I will burn down cities.

CHAPTER 25

LUCIA

When Atlas doesn't come back inside after thirty minutes, I go outside to look for him. There's no one there. Not the men he said he wanted to talk to.

Not Atlas.

His swanky SUV is gone from the parking lot too.

I text him.

Lucia: *Where are you?*

Biting my bottom lip, I wait for him to answer. Five minutes later, I go back inside. Where is he? There's no reason to be worried. Atlas is a grown man and can take care of himself.

But what if those men are bratva? I should have told him my suspicions so he would be more cautious.

Only how do I explain my ability to spot Russian criminals without revealing my own past, or making up some ridiculous story that would feel like acid on my tongue to tell?

I do one of my usual walks around the club to take the temperature of the room. It's more crowded than it was earlier, and people are having fun.

The dancefloor is more than half full. Two men have stripped off their t-shirts to dance with their oiled pecs on display. Atlas will be mad when he sees them and if he follows the pattern he's set, he'll demand they put their shirts back on, or leave.

But he's not here to go caveman on my customers.

My phone buzzes in the hidden pocket of my dress. I pull it out.

Atlas: *Had to do some work for my brother. I may not be back tonight.*

Disappointment fills me, but my text reply is all happy, happy.

Lucia: *Okay. Talk soon. [smiley face emoji, kiss emoji]*

Atlas: *I will be there tomorrow morning, if not before. Be good.*

I take a picture of the shirtless men dancing and send it.

Lucia: *Maybe I'll do a little dancing myself. [dancing woman emoji, devil emoji]*

Atlas: *[dancing man emoji, knife emoji, knife emoji, knife emoji]*

Laughter bubbles up in me.

Lucia: *You should have said goodbye.*

I'm the one that told him he shouldn't neglect his work to spend time with me. I can hardly complain about him listening to me. But it was rude to leave without even texting me that he was going.

What kind of work is he doing this late at night though? Maybe Zeus wants Atlas to check out a club he's thinking of buying.

I wish Atlas had asked me to go with him. I would have left Willow in charge and gone.

ATLAS

Fuck.

I should have texted her I was leaving. Now, she's dancing with shirtless men. I send a quick text to Michael.

Atlas: *Keep the naked men away from Lucia.*

Michael: *She's talking to patrons at the reserved tables. Nowhere near the dancefloor.*

The little tease. But nothing says she'll stay away from the dancers. I need to hurry this damn interrogation along.

Feeling stabby after my text conversation with Lucia, I turn to my brother and say in Greek, "I don't think these bratva are *allies* of the Golubevs. They're family."

"How big is the Golubev Bratva in Russia?" Zeus asks, knowing I've done my homework.

"Big enough to be a problem." This is about more than relocating their rapidly dwindling California counterparts. It has to be. "They want something here."

My brother nods. "We know they want the port, what we need to know is why."

There's a lot we need to know, and I'd bet my bank account in the Caymans that Mo has all the answers. Getting him to talk is the tricky part.

Pulling open the second drawer down on my tool chest, I examine the vials lined in neat rows before grabbing the one in the center. It is a cocktail I helped our chemist perfect before we left California.

It decreases inhibitions while increasing a sense of fear and visualization. Twenty minutes after I administer a strong enough dose, the blood dripping from a single cut will be warped by Larry's mind into a gushing river.

Knowing how to use it, requires knowing how it works, so I administered it to myself and had my brothers put me through various scenarios.

The drug magnifies everything. Pleasure and pain. Fear and euphoria.

I give a starter dose to Mo and Curly, but twice as much to Larry. He'll be hallucinating within thirty minutes on the outside and won't be of any use answering questions until he starts coming down. It's then, he'll be at his most vulnerable.

"You think we haven't trained for this?" he asks when I stick the needle in the vein running down the inside of his elbow.

I don't bother to answer. Him believing I'm using something like sodium pentobarbital will only make the real reaction to the drug harder for him to handle.

Extracting information is 10% torture and 90% mind fucking.

Larry starts screaming warnings about monsters and the devil to his bratva brothers thirty minutes later as I slice another shallow line down Curly's chest.

Curly barely reacts to my cut, but his face drains of color as he watches his leader lose his mind.

"Don't worry. I didn't give you as much as I did him. Tell me what I want to know and I won't."

Curly spits at me. Again. I dodge. It's a defiant act by a desperate man. And gross.

Blood doesn't bother me, but spit? Is so fucking unhygienic.

Giving Curly time to let his panic grow, enhanced by the drug in his system, I focus on Mo.

"Ten bucks says Mo pisses himself," I say to my brother.

Mo shakes his head and moans. "No. Leave me alone."

Zeus shakes his head. "Not taking that bet."

"I'll bet dinner with Lucia you can't make it happen in under five minutes." Orion saunters into the warehouse.

I signal to Theo and Bobby. "Get back to the club and watch over *ílios mou*."

Now that my brothers are both here, my team can focus on what I prize most. Keeping my woman safe.

"You have got it bad, brother," Zeus says.

"She could be pregnant with my baby," I remind them. "Not taking any chances."

"But are you taking my bet?" Orion pushes. "Or has fucking one so often made you a pussy?"

"I want your car if I win." Lucia needs a car.

Sure, I could buy her one, but taking my brother's is more fun. Besides, it can take up to a year to get the make and model of his Mercedes E Class fitted with armored body and bulletproof glass.

My woman needs her own wheels *now*.

Orion's eyes narrow. "You think eating dinner with Lucia is worth my car?"

"Yes."

"Fuck. You're on." He taps his phone. "Timer is running."

It only takes a minute and a half. I cut Mo's clothes from his body and then make two shallow slices near his testicles. When I offer to castrate him and save the world from his progeny, Mo pisses down his leg.

"Shit. I thought he was going to hold out longer than that," Orion complains. "He seemed calmer than the other two."

"While showing me the whites of his eyes. You can taste his fear in the air."

Orion sniffs and grimaces. "The only thing I smell is his piss."

"There's a reason you're the lawyer and I'm the head enforcer." I pull out the scraping tool and pliers I use to remove fingernails.

"I thought it was because you're so good at killing people."

"That too." Not that Orion is a slouch in that arena.

He doesn't have as many kills as me, but he's no choir boy.

Mo is crying when I place the tip of my blade under his chin. "What were you doing in Nuovi Inizi?"

"We wanted to meet the owner. Heard it was a woman."

That was more than I heard before that first night. "Where did you get your intel?"

"Shut the fuck up," Curly yells.

"You shut up. It's not your balls he's threatening, is it? I'm not telling them anything important anyway. He knows the bitch owns the club already."

All information is important, but more important is the fact that once someone starts giving answers, it gets harder to stop when faced with escalating pain.

"Do not call my woman a bitch." I punch him in the jaw, satisfied when blood and teeth spray out of his mouth.

"Don't break his jaw so he can't talk." Zeus frowns at me.

Curly does some very creative cursing in Russian.

He's realized they aren't getting out of here, but Mo keeps looking toward the door as if he's expecting to be rescued. Not going to happen. Even if they've got trackers embedded in them somewhere, we've got the signal jammers on.

Zeus's guy has a program running that has their phones pinging off cell towers all over the city while he downloads their data too.

"Why did you want to talk to Lucia?" I ask with a friendly punch to the kidneys.

Mo groans. "Protection money. Clubs are good targets."

I am aware.

"The club is nowhere near your bar."

Curly jolts, like he's surprised we know about the bar. Which goes to show how unobservant he is. Because I saw him at the bar. He sure as hell doesn't remember seeing me.

What did they think happened to the men that went after the real estate broker's mistress? They went on a journey to find themselves?

So, I ask.

"We thought it was a street gang. We've had a few run ins with them."

They're trespassing on gang territories? Or businesses? Or both?

I learn it's both. After some not so gentle persuasion.

"The gangs aren't running protection rackets," Mo offers when Curly clams up.

He doesn't want his ball sac peeled off. I explain how it works in detail that makes him heave and then start vomiting words.

"You can't protect businesses all over the city." Not unless they have a damn army over from Russia.

"They pay to stay safe from us." Mo looks at me like I'm not very bright.

But that's not how the *Ádis Adelfótita* operate. When we charge a business tithe for protection, we protect them. And not just from the disasters that might befall them if they refuse. Which is why I've been doing so much research on the businesses we are taking on.

Geographical location is important, but so are the threats they face. We're not stepping into gang neighborhoods until we've got the numbers to take what we want and protect it when we do.

CHAPTER 26

ATLAS

"We need to make recruitment a priority," I say to my brothers.

Orion narrows his eyes. "Agreed. We should offer a bonus for bringing in foot soldiers."

"Already on it," Zeus says. "Constantin is sending us a contingent of soldiers. Some may choose to stay in Portland, but as long as they are here, it is our responsibility to bankroll them."

Good. It's one thing to fly under the radar while we establish our control in a city with no syndicate presence. It's another to be ready to go war.

"Our brothers will hunt you down like pigs in the street," Curly spits.

I know their real names now, but I'm sticking with Larry, Curly and Mo.

"Like you hunted us down after we dispatched the team you sent to that woman's condo?" Orion asks with derision.

"They were soldiers."

"You implying you're something more?" I ask, sounding bored.

Better to get the information I want.

"Not us," Mo says.

"Shut up," Curly shouts.

"You said it first." Mo looks over at Larry. "They'll send an army from Russia to avenge him."

That's worth knowing.

"Who is he?"

"The *pakhan's* son."

Not the *pakhan* in California. New to his position after losing his father, because of me, *his* son is only a child. Curly is talking about the Golubev *pakhan* in Russia.

What is his son doing here in Oregon? Proving himself? But by doing what exactly?

"What is he here to do?" I ask Mo.

He doesn't answer. I turn the crank on the winch, lifting them until the three men dangle above the floor. Finally breaking for real, Curly screams and begs me to lower him back down. "My shoulders, my shoulders," he whimpers.

"Answer my question."

"The *pakhan* wants the port to bring our cargo in."

"What cargo?"

Neither Curly nor Mo are willing to tell me. Not even after I crank the winch twice more and threaten Mo's testicles again. It takes a surprising amount of bloody and painful persuasion to get the answer.

When it comes, it's not a surprise, but rage boils through my blood at the confirmation of what I suspect.

They're moving people. The *pakhan's* son is here to establish one end of a new east-west pipeline for human trafficking. Worse, they have plans to use Nuovi Inizi as a source of inventory. Lucia's DJ program brings patrons from the surrounding counties and even states.

"Better to take women from out of town than locals," Curly wheezes.

I grab my weighted baton, bring it up over my shoulder and swing down against his tibia. The bone cracks and he howls. I didn't think he had that much vocal juice left in him. One broken end of the bone makes a lump under the skin on his calf.

What these men would have done to my beautiful lover when she refused to let them use her club as part of their flesh trade, has me swinging my baton again. Curly's scream this time sounds like it's coming from the bowels of hell. Where I plan to send him.

"What is your problem?" Larry demands with more lucidity than he should be capable of.

His pupils are still blown. That last scream must have given him a shot of adrenalin.

"No fucking syndicate is moving into our territory to buy and sell humans." Zeus throws a one-two punch to Larry's kidneys.

The *pakhan's* son screams unintelligible things about fire, proving he's still well under the influence of my drug cocktail. A well aimed kidney punch can feel like you're being skewered with a hot fireplace poker, I guess.

Leaving him to writhe in his agony, Zeus takes a turn at questioning the other two.

Curly is barely conscious, but reveals that the current contingent of bratva soldiers isn't as large as we thought. Only a handful of Golubevs from California are here. I've decimated their numbers so much they can't afford to send more than that to Oregon until they make the move out of California entirely.

According to Curly, that move is supposed to happen once the shipping yard is secured. Which is never going to happen. There are only two dozen soldiers here from Russia. I like my odds.

As expected, Larry gives up more intel as he comes down from the drug cocktail I injected him with. He knows the names of all the major players, what they are supposed to be doing and where they live.

Helpful.

It would be more helpful if his location directions referred to neighborhoods in Portland, not St. Petersburg. There are drawbacks to using the drug.

He also knows who the contacts for the rest of the pipeline are and those he gives to me in a more coherent revelation.

"You've got to help him. He's dying." Mo tries to shout, but his voice is more of a whisper at this point.

I look dispassionately at Curly. He's pale and barely breathing. I must have damaged a large vein, or an artery when I broke the bone. His lower legs are purple and swollen. Internal bleeding.

"You're both dead. You just haven't stopped breathing yet."

"But we told you what you wanted to know." Mo cries, snot and tears mix with the blood on his face.

If he wants mercy, he'll have to ask for it in the afterlife, because he's not getting it here. "What were you going to do with Lucia?"

"Who is that?" Mo tries to wipe his face against his dislocated shoulder and only ends up spreading his blood and snot around.

"The club owner."

"Oh, her." His eyes go shifty.

I make a shallow cut under his right testicle and wait for him to stop screeching before saying, "Yes, her. What are the plans for her?"

"Ivan wants her."

"Who is Ivan?" No surprise one of the bratva pigs is really named Ivan.

I picked that name to give to Lucia earlier for Mo because it's so common.

"The *pakhan's vtoroy.*"

Larry didn't mention Ivan, which shows how well he trained to withstand interrogation. Knowing that makes me suspicious of the rest of the intel we got from him. We will have to verify it. Discreetly.

"What does Ivan want with Lucia?"

"He likes curvy women with dark hair."

They've been watching Lucia? I would have noticed. "How does he know what she looks like?"

"The recon team we sent in three months ago. They took pictures of the club and its owner."

Before we set our sights on Nuovi Inizi. Timing. Sometimes it is off like a bitch. If we'd moved earlier, I would have known about the bratva presence before they got more entrenched in the city.

"Ivan usually likes them younger, but she's a beauty though. Thought about trying her out myself." Mo's admission earns him another punch to his balls.

He moans, but is in too much pain to react like he did the first time.

"What does he do with these beautiful curvy brunettes?" Every word out of my mouth is a bullet that makes Curly flinch.

"He fucks them."

Ivan is now at the top of my kill list.

"If he really likes them," Curly mumbles. "They last longer."

"And if he doesn't?"

"He kills them while he's fucking them. His movies make the *pakhan* a lot of money, but it's the *vtoroy's* viciousness that got him so high in the ranks." Mo is rambling now, his words barely intelligible and all in Russian.

But I have *very* good hearing and I catch it all. "Where is Ivan?" I ask in a deadly tone.

"California."

So, he's still in San Francisco. "When will he be back in Portland?"

"Don't know." Mo drools blood and spit out of the side of his mangled mouth.

I ask again with more persuasion, but get nothing. Mo is not high enough in the food chain for that kind of information.

We ask Larry about Ivan's return. He tries to hold back the information, but now that I know he hasn't been as forthcoming as I thought, I change my interrogation tactics. Eventually, he tells us Ivan is supposed to return to Portland in two days, via private jet arriving at one of the smaller airports west of the city.

Not only will his men not secure the shipping yard like he wants, but when he gets back, a good number of them will be dead. I can accomplish a lot in two days.

Not that it will matter to him. He is going to die. The only question is how much information he will part with before he does.

When I am done questioning Larry, I clean up my tools and then myself.

"We should take a page out the Golubev playbook and find out if the *pakhan* values his son more than Grandfather valued me." I clean the blood from my hands and forearms with the essential oils wipes I keep in my toolbox.

The smell of blood doesn't bother me, but most people prefer the scent of mint and tea tree oils. I'm sure Lucia will.

"You want us to keep him a hostage until they cede Portland to us?" Zeus asks.

"Oregon, but yeah, that's the idea. We can see how the *pakhan* reacts to getting videos of his son being tortured."

"It's not a bad idea," Orion muses. "The containment cells are operational."

Every part of the warehouse is ready for business. The interrogation rooms, containment cells and the incinerator in the basement that burns at 1600°. Hot enough to cremate human remains in under two hours.

We also have three levels of climate-controlled storage in subterranean rooms accessible via tunnels from the basement.

The only thing we need now, are more soldiers.

"We kill and incinerate Mo and Curly."

"Curly is already dead," Orion says.

I look over and see my brother is right. "Saves me a bullet. Larry goes in a cell."

"His name is Dimitri."

"I give a fuck." I throw away the wipes in a paper trash bag that will be tossed in the incinerator along with Mo and Curly's bodies.

Zeus grabs one of the wipes and rubs it on my face. "For now, we let the *pakhan* wonder where his son is and who has him. It sounds like they've already made enemies with more than one street gang. The bratva will start their searching there."

I knock his hand away. "I haven't been a kid in a long time."

"Didn't think you'd want to go back to Lucia with blood spatter on your face."

He's right, but I'm not about to say thank you.

"So far, none of the bratva even know we are here," Orion says. "We should capitalize on that."

"Yes," Zeus agrees.

I do what I'm best at. I kill bratva soldiers.

"We need them neutralized," Zeus says to me, thinking the same thing. "It's time for you to go hunting."

"I'll start tonight." At the bar.

"Take your team," Zeus orders.

"I need men watching Lucia and the club."

"They aren't going to send another team there before they even realize this one is missing. And once they do, they'll be busy looking for their *pakhan's* son."

"That search could lead them right back to the club." It's what I would do. Trace the last known steps of one of my missing men.

"I'll drop in on the club tonight," Orion says. "But I'll post a man in and outside the building."

"Text your men," Zeus orders me.

I frown. "They aren't leaving until Orion shows up."

"Then I'd better get going." My brother takes off.

"My guys will handle this." Zeus waves his hand toward Larry, Curly and Mo. "Start with the soldiers. Bring in the shot callers in a couple of days so we can interrogate them for updated information."

"That was my plan." But I shoot Mo in the head before I leave.

I promised him death and I always keep my promises.

CHAPTER 27

LUCIA

I spy a familiar dark head near the entrance and my heart skips a beat. He's back. I skirt the dancefloor and the quickest path to intercept him.

When I get close enough to see his face, disappointment mixes with surprise inside me. It's not Atlas, but his brother, Orion.

His lips tilt in a mocking smile. "Don't look so happy to see me."

"Are you here to check out the competition?" I ask, when what I really want to know is where his brother is.

"Competition?" He lifts a single dark brow in question.

I roll my eyes. "Nuovi Inizi may be a stand alone club and not part of the Zesti empire, but we do alright."

"More than alright by the look of it." His blue gaze so like his brother's takes in the now crowded club and the busy waitstaff serving drinks. "You should charge a higher cover to get in. This place is worth it."

"Thank you. The cover goes up by 25% on Friday and Saturday night and I charge for table reservations besides the minimum drink order required."

He nods, clearly approving. "So, not just beautiful, but smart too. Atlas is a lucky man."

"Come on, I'll get you a drink." I turn to lead him back toward the bar, ignoring his blatant flattery.

Willow is working the bar and turns to us after handing a customer their drink.

She eyes Orion up and down. "There are two of them? Why didn't you say so, boss?"

Her implication she finds Atlas hot irritates me. "Flirt on your own time," I tell her.

Willow's eyes widen and she puts her hands up. "Didn't mean to step on any toes."

Crap. That's not the impression I want to give. "No toes to step on. I'm dating Atlas, not Orion."

"Maybe you should give me a try, make sure you're getting the best brother?" he teases.

Unless my instincts about them are way off base, and they never are, Orion would sooner walk in front of a car than try to poach his brother's girlfriend.

That doesn't mean the annoying man won't flirt to get a rise out of Atlas.

"Put a sock in it, Romeo," I tell Orion. "Atlas isn't here to get a rise out of."

And by the way, where exactly is he? Not asking. Not. I am not that needy, clingy girlfriend.

"I'll have my usual," I tell Willow. "What can I get you?" I ask Orion.

"Do you have plomari?" He asks about a traditional and high rated brand of ouzo.

"Drinking ouzo is a little cliché of you isn't it?"

"I am Greek." He shrugs. "Why should I settle for anything less?"

"We have Metaxa. Will that do?" We carry Ouzo 12 too, but I suspect he wants the less common brand.

His eyes light up with surprised approval. "Very nicely."

I signal to Willow to pour him a shot.

"Ice, or no ice?" she asks him.

"No ice."

"A purist, huh?" She pours a finger of the clear liquid that smells faintly of black licorice into a rock glass.

"No one has ever accused me of being pure," he purrs.

Willow hands him his drink. "I bet."

Ignoring their banter, I take a sip of my cranberry juice and soda water. The fizzy bright tang slides over my tastebuds.

"Where's your table?" Orion asks me.

It's my turn to shrug. "I don't sit down long enough to keep one free for me."

"No VIP area?" He swivels his head from side to side, like he'll find one if he looks hard enough.

There's a space upstairs, but buying my house takes precedence. "Not yet."

The renovations needed to make it something more than a few extra tables with a view of the dance floor will take a significant monetary outlay. Not to mention the additional staff necessary. The VIP area is something that will have to wait for the next phase of my business plan.

"I was hoping to get to know you better," Orion says. "But this shouting every word isn't working for me."

"Come on." I lead him to my office, unlocking the door when we reach it.

Orion follows me inside and puts his drink down on my desk before throwing his arm over my shoulder. "Smile."

"Watch it. You're going to make me spill my drink."

He snaps a selfie before I realize what he's doing and then steps away quickly, a devious expression on his face.

"What was that for?" I demand. As if I don't know.

"Letting Atlas know what he's missing."

"He's doing his thing for your brother," I chastise as I lean back against my desk. "Do you think it's fair to tease him?"

Orion shrugs and grabs his drink. "Where would the fun be if I couldn't give my baby brother a hard time?"

He saunters over to the chair near my desk that Atlas likes to use and sits down.

Looking down at his phone while his fingers are busily sliding across and tapping on the screen, he says, "It's a lot quieter in here, but I still think you need a VIP area."

"We don't all have a ridiculously rich family backing us with a gazillion dollars for a startup business. Expansion upstairs, including the VIP area will come when I have enough saved up to do it without taking out a loan."

Extra debt means that if something unforeseen happens, Lenny's place in his facility is in jeopardy.

I'll never let that happen.

And I have my employees to consider now too. Expanding too quickly puts everyone's livelihoods at risk.

"Atlas would lend you the money. I doubt he'd even charge you interest." There's something in Orion's tone.

I shake my head. "No chance. I don't need my rich boyfriend offering me money and I would appreciate you not suggesting it to him."

"Why not?"

"I've built this place on my own. I'm proud of that." Owning a nightclub isn't my dream, but it is what I need to do to keep me and Lenny safe and Nuovi Inizi is a success. "I'm not giving anyone else a stake in my club."

"Taking a loan isn't handing over the reins to your business."

"I don't want to owe anyone, least of all my boyfriend."

Orion's phone buzzes and he looks at the screen, his eyes flaring before he schools his expression.

"Was that Atlas?"

Orion nods, giving me a long look. "He's a little intense where you're concerned."

"You think?"

"And what about you?"

"What about me?" I ask with my brows raised and arms crossed.

"You never answered my question."

"Which one would that be?"

"Do you love my brother?"

I knew this would come up again. Nothing about any of the Rokos men makes me believe they give up easily. "Not something I am going to discuss with you."

"Just tell me you're serious about him."

"Is this you asking me what my intentions are?"

"Yes."

"I don't know what is happening between me and Atlas," I say honestly.

A thunderstorm of negative emotion blows over Orion's features.

"I mean at first, I thought it was a one-night stand. But it wasn't. I'm not sure what it is, but Atlas isn't the only one feeling things intensely."

ATLAS

If my brother doesn't watch himself, I won't only be killing bratva soldiers tonight.

That fucking picture, with his arm around Lucia. I texted him a warning. Keep his hands to himself or I will break every bone in them. Unlike Orion, I don't have a sense of humor. He knows I mean it.

His response was a picture of my sun leaning on her desk. The angle of the shot indicates he's at least four feet away from her.

His hands might survive the night.

Not like the bratva I'm here to kill.

Itching to get back to Nuovi Inizi and Lucia, I pull into a parking lot of a closed paint store across the street from the bar. I park my X7 in the shadows and put a single earbud in before turning on the app on my phone for monitoring the bugs my guys planted.

The devices have been acting up since the guys placed them. Like there's interference. The Russians could have jammers in the bar, but then the feed would only produce static. Not this interrupted shit. Maybe they've got equipment close by that causes interference.

Doesn't matter. I'm able to tell there are four guys at one of the tables talking. A deep, impatient voice demands the others tell him where Larry, Curly and Mo are. None of the others know.

The surly man, who is probably one of the shot callers, thinks they had a run in with a street gang. He expects them to prevail. Unfortunately for him, two of his men are already dead and in our incinerator.

Larry-slash-Dimitri is cooling his heels in one of our basement cells.

Orion was right about them believing the gangs are responsible for their brethren's disappearance. My brother is a smart guy. Hopefully smart enough not to take any more selfies with my lover.

Knowing he is there watching over her, even if he's being an ass, helps. But this fucking anxiety. This need to be with her and watch over her. It's like nothing I've ever experienced.

It's a damn good thing we're putting her club under our protection. How hard is it going to be to convince her I'm moving in?

Knowing my sun, she won't make it easy for me.

She'll let me do anything to her body, but she holds onto her independence fiercely. Better to stay the nights and start leaving my clothes there. No conversation that will make her think she has to assert her autonomy necessary.

There are only a few cars in the bar's parking lot. I run the plates on all of them while I am waiting for Theo, Bobby and Michael. Two of the vehicles are registered under the identity the bratva are using as a front.

Grabbing what I need from the kit in the back of my SUV, I look around to make sure no one is watching. My truck is hidden from the street by one side of the building. I lope across the nearly empty four lane street, stopping when I'm on the side of one of the bratva vehicles away from the bar.

I listen for anyone coming outside who might see me. There is nothing. No door opening. No crunch of shoes on asphalt.

In my earpiece, I can hear the bratva inside the bar still debating about going to look for Larry, Curly and Mo.

My vote is yes. It will make it easier to covertly eliminate them.

With another look around to make sure I'm not being observed, I place trackers and remote devices that will blow the tires on both vehicles.

Then I go back to my SUV and wait.

Theo's truck pulls in next to mine before the bratva come to an agreement on what to do. We all get out to confab quietly.

"I've got trackers on the two vehicles I could identify. When they leave, Theo, you and Bobby follow the silver sedan. It's tracker VD048 on the app. Michael, you're with me."

Fifteen minutes later, the four men exit the bar. Three got into the blue pickup truck I'd put a tracker on. An older man they referred to as boss, got into the silver sedan.

If we are lucky tonight, Theo and Bobby will track the shot caller back to their real domicile.

I am going hunting and plan to have three more bodies for the incinerator before dawn.

CHAPTER 28

LUCIA

Atlas climbs into my bed in the early hours of the morning, his body warm and hair damp from a recent shower. His arms go around me, pulling me close to him. Under the clean scent of the shower gel he prefers is a faint whiff of mint and...is that tea tree?

Weird, but I'm too tired to worry about making sense of it.

A few minutes later, I'm too turned on. Atlas touches me everywhere, his big fingers gentle but insistent between my legs.

When he slides into me from behind, I moan. Setting a leisurely pace, he acts like he has all the time in the world. He doesn't pull back very far, using short, deep and slow thrusts to keep me on the cusp of orgasm, but never quite taking me over.

My body is on fire and I undulate against him. It's not enough though.

I reach between my legs and press my middle finger against my clit. Ecstasy shoots outward from the bundle of nerves, making my womb contract. Shivers of pleasure travel up and down my thighs.

His hand grabs mine, pulling it away and I cry out in protest.

"You want something?" he asks, his voice husky in my ear.

"I want to come."

He wraps our fingers together. "Do I ever leave you hanging?"

"Now. I want to come now."

"You're not ready."

I'm so ready, I'm vibrating with it. But instead of arguing, I touch myself with my other hand. It's more awkward because that arm is under me, but I'm able to reach my pleasure button and I push it.

Circling the bundle of nerves and then scissoring my fingers around it, my orgasm builds.

"Uh...uh...uh..." Atlas tuts, grabbing that hand too.

He guides it up to his neck, shifting my body as he needs so he can. He pulls my other hand up. "Clasp them behind my neck," he growls in that bossy voice that sends arousal arcing along every nerve ending.

All the while, he keeps up that maddeningly slow rhythm with his hips. His thrusts take him deep inside my body, his oversized sex stretching me perfectly, on the pleasure side of pain.

I interlock my fingers behind his neck.

"Good, *eromenis mou*. So good for me. So good to me." His hand travels up and down my body.

Squeezing my breast, pinching my nipples, caressing my neck, trailing his fingers down my inner thigh, he touches me everywhere but where I need him most.

"Touch me!" I plead.

"I am touching you."

"There, I need you to touch me *there*."

"Here?" His fingertip barely skims over my clitoris.

"Yes," I moan.

He does it over and over again and I'm sure it's not enough. I plead and shift against him, but I don't move my hands. He doesn't change the slight pressure of his touch.

I am mindless with pleasure when my climax hits me out of nowhere. Screaming, my body arches and somehow he moves his hand enough to keep the same light touch. There is no respite from the pleasure, it builds to a second crescendo almost immediately and I scream until I am hoarse as shudder after shudder of ecstasy works through my body.

Then he shoves forward, buried so deep in my body his scrotum presses into my bottom. His hand clamps down on my tender flesh and pleasure wars with pain as my overstimulated clit reacts to the firmly possessive touch.

He comes shouting my name and holding my body so tight, it feels like he'll never let me go.

Like so many times before, he refuses to pull out after, his still hard erection holding his essence inside of me.

Exhausted from my prolonged pleasure, I fall asleep with him still inside me.

~ ~ ~

He's still wrapped around me when I wake up late the next morning. We shower together, have breakfast and he accompanies me to my office. I settle down to work, but he gets a phone call and takes it out in the hallway. He comes back later, to take me for a late lunch at a local restaurant.

That sets the blissfully happy pattern of the next few days. We spend the day mostly together. During breakfast and lunch, Atlas works on getting to know me. He is keenly interested in my opinion on the local economy, my plans for my club and anything else I want to talk about.

He never acts bored with me and although he's a little more taciturn, I love listening to him talk.

Especially about his brothers and cousins. I swear he acts like he's not telling funny stories, but their dynamic cracks me up. He's gone in the evenings and late into the night working with his brothers, but Atlas always wakes me up to make love in the early hours of the morning.

ATLAS

Ivan does not come back to Portland when expected. He flies to Moscow instead. It's not a surprise, considering how many of his soldiers I kill before he is supposed to arrive.

Apparently, he doesn't think Portland is safe for him. He's right. But him running back to Russia won't stop me hunting him down and killing him.

He is a threat to Lucia, so he cannot live.

At first, the bratva soldiers remain, beating the bushes to find their boss, Larry. Dimitri if you want to be accurate. Their search makes my hunting easier because we haven't found their base yet.

They don't return to the bar either, but they are out on the streets at night, roughing up gang members and making more enemies. I am the predator, keeping to the shadows, tracking them, and killing them one-by-one.

When the gangs start hunting them too, things get more fun for me. I have to find the soldiers first.

"Do not start killing gang members," Zeus says, glaring at me, like he knows I'm going to argue. "We're still deciding which gangs we want to negotiate alliances with and you're not going to make that decision unilaterally with your gun."

"Or your knife," Orion drawls.

I roll my eyes. "It's like you two don't trust me, or something. When have I ever been caught doing my job?"

And the only way I have to kill a gang member is if I get caught.

Before the *pakhan* can send major reinforcements, it is time for implementing the Hostage Plan.

A week after my interrogation of Larry, Curly and Mo, we send a video to the *pakhan* in Russia. It shows him the *enthusiastic* hospitality of *Ádis Adelfótita* toward his human-selling piece-of-garbage son.

Three days and three more videos later, the *pakhan* agrees to parlay with Zeus. It takes another recorded session between Larry, me and my tools, but ultimately, the *pakhan* proves to care more about his son's wellbeing than my grandfather cared about mine.

The *pakhan* over all the Golubev bratva agrees to our terms. Leave Oregon and stay the hell away from *Ádis Adelfótita* territory here. Constantin has given Zeus permission to negotiate the withdrawal of the American Golubev bratva from California.

That discussion is more heated, but finally, the *pakhan* agrees that his bratva will cease all organized criminal activity in California. They have six months to sell their legitimate businesses and get out of the state.

He agrees to put a leash on the *palach*, me. I will not kill any more Golubevs during the transition as long as they keep to the terms.

"One breach of this agreement and the entirety of it becomes null and void," Zeus says.

The *pakhan* nods. "Yes, yes. Just release my son."

"He will accompany your men when they leave," Zeus says.

"At least get Dimitri medical treatment."

"We have a doctor on standby to treat him."

Relief washes over the *pakhan's* features, something Zeus would never allow to show. He doesn't let his enemies see his emotions. The *pakhan* shouldn't either. If Zeus was without honor, he would have the leverage now to demand more concessions.

"There is one final detail," the *pakhan* says.

Zeus doesn't show his anger at the Russian man trying to renegotiate the terms of the deal. If he is angry. The *pakhan* opening up negotiations again, leaves Zeus free to ask for more too.

"As a token of good faith, turn the *palach* over to us. He has murdered many bratva from our family. Making an example of him will ensure the commitment of my people to our agreement."

"As a *token of good faith*, I will not send the executioner to Russia to kill your men off one-by-one. It is your job as their *pakhan* to make sure your men abide by the terms of the agreement, not mine."

"Do not threaten us," the *pakhan* snarls in Russian.

"It is not a threat. It is an outcome you can avoid. Whether you will, or not, remains to be seen."

"Your *palach* is a danger to my bratva. He cannot be allowed to live."

"Your men have nothing to fear from their executioner if they abide by the terms of our agreement and stay out of our territory in the future. If they don't, it won't be the *palach* that they have to worry about."

That is true for everyone but Ivan. But when I go to kill that bastard, I won't leave anything for them to trace the hit back to the United States, much less our mafia.

"If you expect us to act as allies, you must make this concession."

"At no time have I implied an ally relationship. We don't do business with human traffickers. This agreement is for a truce and it only extends so long as all of the conditions are met."

"You do not have the position of strength you think you do. I could send over an army and destroy your Hades Brotherhood in a single day."

"You could try, but the only syndicate that will be destroyed is your bratva."

Someone says something to the *pakhan* but the words are too low to understand.

The man slams his fist down on his desk. "A truce. For the return of my son."

Zeus nods, in complete control of his emotions. "Since you have reopened concessions, you have two weeks instead of a month to vacate Oregon and three months for your American brethren to get out of California."

That cuts both departure times in half.

Zeus cuts the connection while the *pakhan* is still sputtering.

"You don't trust him to keep his word, do you?" I ask before my brother can say anything.

"No, but this buys us time to build our numbers, so when they come for us, we're ready to destroy them."

I nod.

"You heard me give my word."

"That I won't kill any more of their men as long as they get the hell out of our territory and stop doing any business in it? Yes."

"They may not be men of their word, but we are. You don't kill another bratva in Oregon or California unless they break the truce."

"I won't be the one that breaks terms." But neither of us is convinced the Golubev Bratva is as determined to keep their word as we are.

Men who make human beings a commodity have no honor and cannot be trusted.

~ ~ ~

Over the next two weeks, I take my turn watching the bratva still in Portland while they put their properties up for sale and vacate the apartments they rent. Cars are sold or returned to leasing agencies and business is cancelled.

The listening devices we planted in the bar were found a few days after we took Dimitri, but that doesn't stop us watching them. We always have someone inside the bar they congregate in.

The *pakhan* is probably scrambling to figure out another port to use for the human smuggling operation. Too bad for him his partners won't be available to do business. Zeus agreed to let the bratva live, but not their partners responsible for establishing the other segments of the new route.

CHAPTER 29

ATLAS

Carrying the two items I bought today while taking my turn watching Dimitri's second in command.

The man seems to be obeying the terms of the agreement, but I take nothing for granted. When he goes into a sex toy shop, I follow.

He informs the owner that she will have to work with suppliers from another state to get what she wants to order from them. The bratva are smuggling sex toys from China so they aren't subject to tariffs or commodity restrictions.

It's a lucrative market. We should be in it too and I text as much to my brother before purchasing a pair of pink satin lined leather cuffs and matching sleep mask, clearly intended to be used as a blindfold.

Lucia is in her office when I get to the club. It's Sunday and she doesn't work tonight. The perfect time to play with our new equipment.

Her beautiful gaze lights up when she sees me standing in the open door of her office. "Atlas." The way she says my name sends blood surging to my cock. "You're back."

I hold up the handcuffs and sleep mask, dangling from my forefinger. "Time for a break."

Her eyes dilate and her lips part as she starts to breathe shallowly, but she doesn't get up.

"Come, *eromenis mou*. You have been working all day." It's not a shot in the dark.

"I need to finish this..."

Shaking my head from side to side, I stalk toward her. "You can finish tomorrow. You didn't even take a break for lunch."

The tracker I put on her phone shows she has not left her office since I drove away this morning.

"How do you know that? Did Willow rat me out?"

"Willow didn't have to. I know you, Lucia." I don't mention the tracker. It only confirmed what I already suspected.

And she doesn't need to know about all the measures I take to keep her safe.

Her smile is blinding. "Yes, you do."

I put my hand out toward her

Getting up from her chair, she takes it. Her eyes are focused on the leather pieces in my other hand though. "Are those new?"

"Yes." I am surprised she feels the need to ask. "I will never use something on you that has touched another woman."

A small puff of air escapes her mouth as she shivers. "Good."

"Is anyone else here?" Bobby says there isn't, but I want confirmation from Lucia.

She shakes her head, her silky dark hair swaying over her shoulders. "Willow left an hour ago."

"Any deliveries scheduled?"

"We have two cases of spirits that should arrive in a couple of hours," she says.

"I will take care of it."

"There's no need. I know you think I can't lift a case of liquor, but I promise I can. I'll accept the order."

"You'll be tied up." I watch for when the meaning of my words penetrates.

She gulps and darts a look down at the handcuffs. "Tied up...by those?"

"Yes."

"In two hours?"

Longer than that if I have my way, but I simply nod.

"Okay."

Predatory satisfaction settles deep inside me. "Take off your clothes."

She doesn't ask any questions, or demur with a false sense of modesty. Not my beautiful, adventurous lover.

Lucia unbuttons the front of her jumpsuit and then slides down a hidden zipper before pushing it off her shoulders and down her body to pool around her feet. She's wearing a black lace bra and panties under the crimson red jumpsuit.

Reaching out, I unclip the front closure of the bra with a flick of my wrist. The stretchy lace separates and her gorgeous tits spill out in all their glory. Looking like perfect little raspberries, her nipples are already hard and flushed with blood.

"You are beautiful, *eromenis mou*." My mouth waters to taste her sweet raspberry peaks.

She slides the boy short panties that leave half of her ass bare down her thighs and then steps out of them and the jumpsuit. She's so graceful, she manages to keep her sexy black heels on and stands before me naked except for them.

She knows seeing her in only her heels turns me on. Not that I need anything more than her presence, but the way they make her legs look a mile long makes my cock surge painfully against the zipper of my jeans.

"Lift your arms and put your hands out." My voice is low and guttural.

Her small, elegant hands rise putting her wrists exactly where I want them. I run my fingertips down her arms and she shudders.

"So damn responsive."

"To you."

I like the implication she wasn't like this for the man she married. Shoving thoughts that make me murderous away, I buckle a cuff on one of her wrists and then do the other.

The lightweight chain between them is about six inches long, preventing immediate strain on her shoulders from the cuffs.

Lifting the sleep mask, I ask, "Are you ready?"

"Yes." Her voice is barely above a whisper, but it does not waver.

I put the blindfold on her, running my fingers through the silky strands of her hair after tightening the sleep mask so it will not slide off.

Wrapping the long tresses around my fist, I gently tug Lucia toward me. "We're going upstairs."

"Okay."

Bending down, I grab her clothes and hand them to her. "Hold these."

She curls her bound hands upward, tucking the clothing between her forearms and her torso.

I adjust the position of her arms so her breasts are completely unfettered and then guide my sun out of her office by my hold on her hair.

LUCIA

The darkness behind the blindfold is not absolute, but it doesn't have to be. I can't see anything. No shapes. No obstacles in our path. Not where we are going. Not the expression on Atlas's face.

I'm so wet, my thighs are slippery. Just from having my wrists restrained and the blindfold put on me. Atlas's hold on my hair only adds to my arousal.

The hand not guiding me cups my breast, tweaking my nipple and I gasp.

"Is your pussy wet for me?" he asks, his mouth near my ear.

Moaning, I nod.

"Use your words, *eromenis mou*."

My lover. I am that. His. In every way. Yes, it's fast, but it's right too. I have never felt this way. Not with Tino. Never.

I trust Atlas implicitly and I have no fear as he guides me through the club and up the stairs.

"Yes, my pussy is wet." I never use that word, but saying it sends a jolt of pleasure straight to my core.

Is it the naughtiness of it? Or simply that I'm telling Atlas about how turned on he makes me?

He growls and slides that errant hand down between my legs, his long fingers slipping between my slick folds easily.

We keep walking, even though his fingers delve into my hungry cooch. *Dio mio.*

The things this man does to me.

He plays with me as we cross the club and stops only to put the code in to unlock the door. Then his fingers are back, rubbing over my swollen clit as we mount the stairs. The shift in our bodies as we go up each stair jostles his fingers, giving and then taking away the friction I'm craving.

His big bulge rubs up against my bare bottom every couple of steps too and I can't help pushing back into him. Wanting more, knowing I can't have it.

Yet.

He opens the door to my apartment, guides me inside and then both of his hands fall away from me.

"No," I protest.

"Be a good girl and stay there."

Porca miseria! Can he say anything in that voice that won't turn me on?

I hear him moving around the kitchen and then his steps take him to the bedroom. I remain where I am, my body vibrating with need as images of what is to come play through my head.

The cuffs on my wrists tug and I realize Atlas is back, right in front of me and he's pulling on the chain between the cuffs.

"Everything is ready. Come with me."

Everything? What is everything?

"*Che cosa?*" I ask in Italian.

Before I can get my befuddled brain to translate to English, Atlas stops and his lips press almost reverently against mine before the kiss turns carnal and I find my leg up around his hip as I seek the stimulation I need against his denim clad leg.

He breaks the kiss and gently shifts my leg so my foot is once again on the floor.

"No," I moan.

His hand cups my nape. "Trust me."

He waits and I realize he wants my agreement.

"I do," I tell him. With my body and my heart.

He gets us over to the bed and pulls me into his lap, so I am straddling him. A sweet, fresh scent makes my mouth water as something cold presses against my lips.

"Open." He's being bossy again.

And it's making my core go molten. If I were a nuclear reactor, I would be in danger of exploding from the heat.

My lips part without a thought from my brain and a cold morsel settles on my tongue. A grape. I chew and swallow before he kisses me again. But as soon as it gets interesting, he pulls his mouth away and puts another piece of fruit against my lips.

It's a chunk of pineapple this time. He keeps kissing and feeding me until I'm humping mindlessly against his jean covered erection. I eat each bite without thought waiting for the kiss that follows.

Until he doesn't stop kissing me and his hands play with every erogenous zone.

I tear my lips from his. "*Per favore*, Atlas. *Ho bisogno di te*."

"What part of me do you need, *brava regazza*?" he asks, calling me good girl in Italian.

So, I answer him in kind, telling him I need his cock. "*Ho bisogno del tuo cazzo*."

"Not yet. I'm still hungry." He flips me on my back on the bed and yanks the chain between my cuffs upward.

I hear a small click and try to pull my hands down, but I can't. He's attached the cuffs to the bed somehow. A thrill zings through me and I tug harder, my heartbeat speeding up when there is no give.

So turned on I cannot form words, I moan and twist my head side to side, unable to see what Atlas is doing because of the blindfold. Every nerve ending tingles with anticipation for his next touch.

Strong, warm hands push my legs apart and guide my knees upward. "Hold yourself open for me."

Fluid gushes from my core as I do what he says.

And then he feasts. On me. Two thick fingers press inside me while he licks up my labia. He draws them out and shoves back in as he swirls his tongue around my clitoris. He eats me out like he's starving.

Something not as hard as his finger presses into my opening. It's strange but he pulls it out before I can figure out what it is. He shifts between my legs and then he traces my lips. The scent of my own arousal mixed with the sweeter scent of pineapple calls to something primal inside me as he wets my lips with my juices.

The he presses the pineapple piece into my mouth. "Taste yourself. You're sweeter than the pineapple."

He moves again and his mouth is back at my core, his teeth tugging gently on my swollen nether lips. He presses something inside me again, but follows it with his tongue and then he eats the piece of fruit saturated with my arousal.

He nuzzles my monz, inhaling deeply. "Your honey is delicious."

Nothing but garbled sounds make it past my lips.

"I know, *pethi mou*." He sucks and licks and nibbles on my most tender flesh until I am writhing and straining against my restraints.

I need more, but I will only get what he gives me. And that revs my engine, making my body purr like a million dollar sportscar.

His mouth pulls away from me, but he has three fingers inside me slowly pistoning in and out of my tight, wet channel.

"Do you know what *pethi mou* means?"

I shake my head side to side gasping as he keeps me on the precipice of coming with his fingers. If he would just touch my clitoris. A single caress with his thumb is all it would take.

"It means my death. You are the death of me being alone. Your light fills my darkness, *ilios mou*."

"You...are...not...dark..." I gasp out.

His laughter is drowned out by my scream as his thumb finally finds my clitoris and I climax. He forces me into another climax almost immediately, never letting up with his hand.

And then he's on top of me, shoving his hard shaft into me, stretching the tender walls of my vagina in a delicious pleasure tinged with stinging pain. It morphs into unfathomable bliss as he thrusts deeper than he should be able to go.

His balls slap against my bottom and I mewl. It's too much, but he won't let up.

"You can take it. Give me one more climax, *eromenis mou*. I know you can." He pounds into me, grinding his pelvis against my over sensitized clit.

Ecstasy washes over me, wringing a hoarse cry from my already strained throat, my entire body convulsing.

"That's right, *brava regazza.* Milk my cock, draw my seed into your body. Take it all." His filthy words of praise fall on me like warm rain.

My inner muscles grip his hardon as his hot seed shoots inside me.

Sometime later, he undoes the cuffs, rubbing my shoulders and arms before taking off the sleep mask. He shadows my face with his body so the light does not hurt my eyes as I blink, trying to adjust.

"You are so perfect for me, Lucia." My name on his mouth sounds like the sweetest endearment ever.

I wrap my arms around his neck and inhale his earthy post-coital scent. "I could never have done all that with Tino."

It's probably against all sorts of dating rules to bring up the dead husband while naked with the current lover, but I need Atlas to know that what we have is special. Profound.

"Why?" He slides to the side of me, his gaze searching my face for something.

I'm not sure what he wants to see, but I give him the truth. "I didn't trust him like I trust you."

Even before we lost the baby.

My gaze skims down his body and a laugh is startled out of me. His jeans are shoved down around his hips, his still partially engorged penis laying against his hairy thigh.

"What?"

"You never got your clothes off."

"I was busy." He strips now, but climbs back onto the bed with me.

Neither of us makes a move to shower.

"You are mine, *ílios mou*. I will never let you go."

His fervency should make me nervous, but it doesn't. It tells me that this thing between us is mutual. We're both all in.

CHAPTER 30

ATLAS

"Our offer has been accepted on the shipping yard." Zeus looks at me like he's trying to see something in my face.

I take a draw from my beer. "That's good."

Zeus called an in-person meeting with me and Orion. I don't like leaving Lucia, but we've got eyes on the remaining bratva in Portland and Theo is watching over her from outside the bar.

I need to introduce her to my crew soon. They will be part of her life, like they are part of mine. Besides my brothers, they are the only men I trust Lucia's safety to.

"It's a step toward getting us back on track," Zeus says.

Finally. The bratva issue took a lot of time and resources we weren't planning for.

"You want me to finish setting up our protection racket." It is as important for potential money laundering outlets as the income it will provide.

"Constantin wants us to build numbers and make a move to establish our physical territory." Zeus's expression is even more constipated than usual. "That means getting the protection racket up and running."

"Okay, I've got it locked down. I know exactly which businesses to start with and how wide to go with our territory." My discussions with Lucia have paid off. My beautiful lover is a font of information.

"If Lucia balks, we get her to sell the club to us. Constantin agrees."

A pit yawns inside me. None of us trusts the Golubev *pakhan*. The recent conflict with his bratva makes establishing our territory now imperative.

But Zeus is talking about *forcing* Lucia into cooperating with the *Ádis Adelfótita* laundering money through her club, or selling Nuovi Inizi to us.

That is not going to happen. "We are not taking her club from her."

"Then get her to cooperate."

"I'm not threatening Lucia." I stand up and lean over my brother's desk to let him see my rage close up and feel how much I mean my words.

"Fuck her into compliance, for all I care, but we need Nuovi Inizi working with us," Zeus says harshly.

"Piss off!" I slam my knuckles down onto his desk. "I am not touching *ílios mou* for any other reason than that I want her bangin' body."

Not to threaten her and sure as shit not to fuck her into submission. No matter how fun that might be in fantasy scenario.

Instead of lurching to his feet and taking a swing at me like I half expect, Zeus rubs his eyes the weight of his position in the lines of fatigue on his face. "Then use fucking logic and *convince* her. We can't get our own clubs up and running soon enough for what we need."

We have twenty soldiers coming up from California to fill our ranks. Even after we recruit the numbers we need, some may decide to stay. All members of the Hades Brotherhood need jobs to do and a source of income. Nuovi Inizi is pivotal to all of it.

Because I made it that way.

But how is Lucia going to react to having her club become such an integral part of the Greek mafia? We're beyond setting her up to pay a protection tithe now. Too many of our plans hinge on access to the club. Access to her and her knowledge of the city.

"We have to expand our numbers now for all our safety. Including hers," Orion adds when I scowl in silence at my oldest brother.

Zephyr and Helios haven't said a word during the discussion, but both are looking at me like they're wondering if they can trust me. Like my loyalty is in question.

Fuck that. Fuck them. And fuck this situation.

Maybe I have been hoping we could figure a way around charging Lucia a protection tithe, much less using Nuovi Inizi in any other way. So, the fuck, what?

Lucia's club is about to become our contact spot like that seedy bar on the other side of Portland has been for the bratva. A move like that makes Nuovi Inizi ours even if her name stays on the deed to the building.

Gamó.

"Your girlfriend is a savvy businesswoman," Orion reminds me. "She'll understand what has to happen once you tell her what the bratva planned to do with her club."

Like hell I'm going to tell her that. Unless I have no other choice. She doesn't need to worry about something that never happened and I will not allow to happen in the future.

"No one is going to hurt her," I warn my brothers.

"Of course not," Orion says but the look on Zeus's face puts our middle brother's assurance into question.

Orion ignores Zeus's glower and appeals to me. "Her business must be brought under *Ádis Adelfótita* oversight for Nuovi Inizi to have all of our protection."

"If she refuses to pay a protection tithe and does not want to sell, we will buy in as partners," Zeus offers his version of a compromise with cold finality.

My *anax* is only willing to go so far to appease my woman. The *Ádis Adelfótita* comes first.

What I don't say is that Lucia will be forced into cooperation, taking a partner she doesn't want or selling the business she worked so hard to build over my dead body and maybe theirs.

LUCIA

I'm so happy, I'm fizzing with it. It's the final walkthrough of the house before closing.

"You need to sign off on the repairs the seller made and then the final paperwork will be drawn up by the bank," Elaine says. "The inspector has already approved them."

He is leaving as I arrive and tells me that everything looked good. But as the homeowner, I'm expected to give my authorization as well. I like that, so I don't mind taking time from my day to essentially rubber stamp what the inspector said.

I only wish that Atlas could be here with me. It's an important milestone for me, and I want to share it with him. He's way more important to me than he should be after only a matter of weeks, but there's no help for it.

The heart wants what the heart wants. And the dreams I thought dead are coming to life again inside mine. But he's working with his brothers today and I could hardly ask him to tell them no when he spends so much time with me already.

Walking into the master bedroom where one of the windows had to be repaired, my gaze automatically goes to where we made love on the floor.

There's a tell-tale spot on the carpet. Elaine doesn't notice it. I doubt the inspector did either. It's very faint, but I know where to look. Atlas's fluids mixed with mine, right under where the bed will sit.

Does it make me sick that I want to leave it there? Something private and secret just for me. A memory no one can take away.

Reveling in joy stronger and deeper than any I have felt before, I have to stifle the happy laughter the sight of our cum stain on the carpet elicits in me. Me and Atlas together.

A sign of things to come, of a future not filled with the loneliness of the last five years.

Lenny has a home he loves and feels safe in, and now I will have mine.

"You look really happy, Lucia. Clients like you are the reason I am in real estate."

"Honestly?" I ask with a smile. "I'm bubbling over with it like a bottle of champagne somebody shook before popping the cork."

I wasn't sure this could ever happen for me. No matter how much I want this, Lenny's care and safety must come first. He doesn't have anyone else to look out for him.

But I am finally able to buy a house that's mine. It's a place where I can be myself. Not the mafia princess I once was. Not the nightclub owner I don't really want to be. But simply the woman I am deep down inside in my own space.

"Everything came together like you needed it to," Elaine says.

It's such a typical realtor saying, but she means it. She's not only here for the commission. Especially on such a small property.

"When I started Nuovi Inizi I was pretty sure I could make a go of it, but not certain I could bring in enough to pay for my brother-in-law's care."

Elaine knows about the facility because my contract to pay for Lenny's care came up when the underwriters started digging into my finances to determine if they would approve a mortgage for me.

"So many new businesses fail," Elaine says with her usual enthusiasm. "But you have the club making enough profit to cover his care and the mortgage for this place. You should be really proud of yourself."

I grin. "I am."

I might wish I could do something else, something quieter, but I've made Nuovi Inizi work for me and I'm proud of that. Maybe even more proud than I would be if it was my dream. I did the hard thing and succeeded.

As another successful businesswoman, Elaine's approval feels good. When I explain everything about Lenny to Atlas, he'll respond in the same way.

We walk back through the dining-slash-living area bathed in light from the autumn sunshine coming in through the large picture window.

It feels like a bright, happy omen.

My house. My home. A place for me.

I sign the papers for it tomorrow, and I can't wait.

~ ~ ~

Wearing my favorite red wrap dress, I'm still buzzing with excitement hours later.

The club is hopping and soon we will be at capacity. My staff are all where they are supposed to be. The DJ is here and spinning tunes.

Atlas said he will be here before close tonight. I can't wait to tell him about signing the papers and taking possession of my new home tomorrow.

He lives in a mansion. Is it a pipe dream to think he'll want to share my little house with me?

He spends every night in my even smaller apartment, I remind myself. The house will be an improvement.

Am I really going to ask him to move in so soon? I should wait. I should wait, but if he does what he is doing now, he'll be my de facto roommate without me ever asking. I want it to be my choice.

I need him to know that I want him there.

My gaze flicks to the entrance for the millionth time tonight, but this time I am rewarded with the sight of Atlas. There are three men with him. I recognize two of them. They've been in Nuovi Inizi before, when Atlas wasn't here.

I'm pretty sure I've met all of his family in Portland. Only, the way they all walk close together, it's clear they don't mind being in each other's personal space. Which means they know each other pretty well, even if they aren't family.

It's strange they never introduced themselves to me when they were here before. Had Atlas not told them about me?

They break through the crush of bodies and I notice how they are dressed. Unlike his usual attire of tight-fitting dress shirt and slacks or dark jeans, Atlas is wearing a charcoal grey, tailored suit. Open at the neck and with no tie, his black button up shirt reveals the strong column of his neck.

My brows furrow as my eyes take in how his companions are dressed the same way. Their suits are a rung down on the designer ladder, but nowhere near off the rack.

I go cold inside, a fist squeezing my heart so tight if it was a piece of coal, it would become a diamond.

Atlas looks like Tino used to when my husband went out to work. The suit is probably Hugo Boss and not Armani like Tino's, but that attitude Atlas wears it with is all too familiar. Confidence oozes off him in overwhelming waves.

The look he gives to the people stepping out of his way is both expectant and arrogant. He's used to intimidating others. How am I only just now noticing that?

Because my ovaries have been overriding my common sense since the first moment our eyes met.

That emotionless expression on Atlas's face is eerily familiar too. Every made man I knew back in Detroit had perfected that cold and detached air.

Suddenly everything clicks into place in my brain.

Atlas coming to Portland with his brothers and cousins. They're here to build a business all right, but they aren't simple nightclub owners like me.

They're mafia. Freaking *Greek* mafia and they are claiming territory in the city I have made my home.

Why didn't I know? When Tino and his father talked about Zesti, they never mentioned the clubs are owned by a syndicate. I should have realized though. My husband and father-in-law would never have admired a completely legitimate business the way they did Zesti. Much less want to emulate them.

Atlas's blue eyes warm slightly when they catch mine, but he doesn't smile. Why should he? He's not here for me. He's working.

Nausea rises in the back of my throat, and I force myself to swallow. The only way I get through this encounter is if I can pretend to be as disconnected from my emotions as Atlas.

If I have a single doubt about what Atlas is, the three large men flanking him pound the final nail into the coffin of any hope he's a regular guy. I've known men like them before. I grew up around them. They are like the men my father has working for him, some of whom I even called uncle.

The way these men's watchful gazes take in my club's patrons, the tense set of their shoulders, like they are ready to spring into action...it all spells one thing.

They are the muscle. Not that Atlas needs any, but like my dad used to say, it's all about perception.

Atlas stops in front of me, and I want so badly for him to say something, *anything* that tells me my instincts are wrong. To do something to show me everything hasn't changed. But he doesn't go to kiss me like he usually does.

"Lucia." He reaches for me. Finally.

But I jerk back so his fingers do not connect with my skin.

Surprised, he stares at me in silence and the longer it drags on, the more certain I am of why he's here tonight. It's not to see me.

Inside, my brain is screaming, *this cannot be happening*, but I smooth my face into a blank mask and turn to head toward my office. This discussion isn't taking place in front of my employees and patrons.

Not for Atlas's sake, but for mine.

The prickles on the back of my neck let me know that he is following me. I'm careful to maintain enough distance that he cannot touch me though.

Not that he would want to. His need to play besotted boyfriend is over.

CHAPTER 31

LUCIA

When we reach my office, I hurry to unlock it before Atlas catches up. However, his hand lands against the small of my back, burning me through my dress.

Getting the door open, I leap forward, away from him and rush to get behind my desk, though I don't sit in my chair.

One of his men follow him into my office. The other two remain outside in the hall.

"Shut the door." I'm impressed with how even my voice is when every word coming out of my mouth feels like glass shards shredding my vocal cords.

Giving me a look like he's trying to figure something out, Atlas waves toward his man. A moment later, the door shuts with a soft bang. I don't see it. My eyes are fixed on Atlas, and I watch him like he's a cobra and I'm a mongoose.

I am not helpless, but neither am I foolish enough to dismiss the danger my deceitful *ex*-lover represents.

Not anymore. I should have listened to my instincts about the danger I sensed lurking around him. How did I trust him enough to tie me up and blindfold me?

We didn't just do it once either. Atlas showed up one night with a pair of leather cuffs and I let him use them on me. More than once. I have to swallow back bile again at the memories.

He's mafia. A criminal.

He probably has more blood on his hands than Tino ever did. Because Atlas doesn't run nightclubs. Unless I'm badly mistaken...again...he runs the protection racket. Like my dad.

These men are his collections team. They're here to set up *protection* for my club, for a price. Like my dad and his men did to so many businesses in Detroit, probably still do.

"Are you okay, *ílios mou*?"

"Don't call me that." My fingernails dig painfully into my palms with my hands fisted at my sides to stop them shaking. "I am not your sun."

Though I sure illuminated plenty for him. I see everything so clearly now and the need to vomit increases.

He's been using me to get information on the area, the businesses, and my club. And all the time I took his interest as proof of his affection and respect, when in fact, it is the opposite.

"Introduce me to your friend," I say.

With a frown Atlas, steps toward me, like he's going to come around the desk.

Panic screeches through me and I lift one hand in a stopping gesture. "Don't come near me."

Atlas has the effrontery to look wounded. If I had a knife right now, I'd really wound him. I'd cut out his black heart and let it die right next to mine.

The other man rubs his hand over his closely cropped black hair, a gold pinkie ring glinting under the light. "Maybe I should go out in the hall with Bobby and Michael."

But I shake my head vehemently. "No. You stay."

The man looks toward Atlas who gives a miniscule jerk of his head. Watching me like I'm a dangerous animal set to attack, the man takes a seat in the chair furthest from my desk.

"Introduce me." I jerk my head toward the other man in case Atlas is in any doubt who I'm referring to.

"This is Theo, Lucia, a fr—"

"I know what he is," I interrupt. "I just didn't know *who* he is."

The fizzy bubbles of happiness have all popped, leaving my insides hollow and my heart aching.

He does not smile, and I wonder if any of his smiles were ever real. His gaze is unemotional, and I know the warmth I thought I saw there was fake.

There's no point in dragging this out. "How much?" I ask.

His glacial blue eyes flare with surprise, like he's shocked I realize why he's here. He doesn't have to give me the spiel. I've heard it all before from the other side.

"What's the name of your outfit?" I ask, pain and fury a dangerous cocktail inside of me.

I want to hit him.

But you don't strike out at made men unless you're prepared for them to strike back, twice as hard.

When he looks at me with confusion, I say, "Syndicate. Mafia. Whatever the fuck you want to call it. I've never heard of the Rokos Mafia."

I would have remembered if I had, and it would have saved me a lot of pain. And even more disappointment. If only he had told me what he wanted from the start. Why did he have to use me like he did?

My body aches like I have the flu.

"You said fuck."

So? "You say it all the time."

"You don't." His eyes narrow.

"How does that matter?" I demand. "Just tell me what outfit you are with."

I hate being in the dark about anything now that I know what a big secret he has been keeping.

"We are part of the *Ádis Adelfótita*." Atlas still looks like he can't believe I know what he is.

I look at him blankly.

"The Hades Brotherhood."

"A Greek syndicate?" It sure sounds Greek. He and his family are Greek.

"You're not the..." I trail off. "Does the Greek mafia have dons? Or godfathers?"

"My uncle is the Godfather of the Night. He rules the entire West Coast territory."

"Even territory you haven't claimed yet. There were no syndicates here when I moved to Portland."

"How do you know?" That is from his cohort, Theo.

I ignore the question. "Your uncle told you to set up protection territory here?"

"No. Zeus is my *anax*."

So, like a don, while the Godfather of the Night is like the Godfather in the Cosa Nostra. However, the Italian Godfather is the head of the entire Cosa Nostra in the United States and his uncle's territory is the West Coast.

Does it go up into Canada?

My brain is focusing on the minutia so I don't have to deal with the hurricane of pain from Atlas's betrayal.

"How much?" I ask.

"How much what?" he asks back.

His tone is neutral, but the words taunt me. He knows exactly what I'm talking about.

"Don't. Just don't." I inhale as deeply as I can, letting the air out of my lungs slowly in an attempt to keep my roiling emotions under control. "You know I'm talking about protection money. You've got two soldiers standing outside my office to make sure I don't leave before agreeing to your terms."

"Bobby and Michael are out there to make sure we aren't interrupted."

Is that supposed to imply a difference? If it is, I don't see it.

"How do you know why I'm here?" he asks and then glares. "Did the bratva approach you while I was gone?"

Theo makes a scoffing noise. "Nobody got past us, boss."

I refuse to answer. I will *not* explain how I know what is going on. Atlas deserves no explanations from me.

When neither Atlas nor I break the silence between us, Theo says, "10% of net profits."

Theo must be Atlas's second. He wouldn't speak for his boss otherwise. He's got the made man stoic mask down pat, his brown features showing not a single emotion.

The protection tithe could be worse. It could be 10% of my gross takings. Regardless, the money they want is too much for me. Not that they'll see it that way, or care if they do.

"We'll be checking your books to make sure you aren't shorting us. You don't want to steal from us." Theo's voice is laced with threat.

Atlas turns a glare on him before looking back at me. Something roils in the blue depths of his eyes, but he says nothing to deny the other man's words.

Something inside me shatters. My ability to trust. My hope for the future. My soul. I don't let it show though. I am stronger than that.

I am stronger than either of these men will ever know.

"When is the money due?" My tone is cool and my voice doesn't break. I'm proud of that.

Theo sighs dramatically when Atlas remains silent. "One of us will come by every Sunday to collect."

I nod my understanding. It's Wednesday. That means my first official payment is in four days. I'll have to make sure I have enough cash on hand to cover it.

"We'll take our first payment now," Theo says and I wonder why Atlas came at all if his soldier is doing all the talking. For intimidation factor? "Whatever cash is in your till."

I want to refuse, but I can't. I want to say I'll have to pay again in four days, can't they wait? But they don't care if it is fair, or even reasonable. Only that I pay what they consider I owe them for doing business in the territory they now claim.

I know this game. My dad tried to keep work away from his family, but I was a curious child. I overheard plenty when no one realized I was around.

This is how it works. If I were a restaurant, they would be asking less because profit margins are lower. If I owned a casino, it would be more.

They don't care that I was going to buy a house. They don't care that I have to pay for Lenny's care. Nothing matters but me paying them what they require for their protection now that they have moved into the city.

If the payment meant closing the club, they'd adjust it, or force me to take them on as partners and change the way I do business to bring the profit margins up.

Sure, they'll keep the other gangs and syndicates at bay, as long as they're the strongest. Not that anyone else was demanding money or making problems for me.

"Were those Russian guys the other night bratva?" Is Atlas moving in on Nuovi Inizi before they get a chance to?

Atlas knew them. Said the one guy's name was Ivan. He took them outside and I haven't seen the three men back in my club since.

Theo gives Atlas another long-suffering look and then answers my question. "Yes."

"Were they here to claim my club for their syndicate?" I direct my question to Atlas and dare him with my eyes to let Theo answer for him again.

"Yes," Atlas says with a frown.

He doesn't want to talk about this. Too bad. It's my life going into the crapper because organized crime finally decided Portland has potential.

"You'll be better off under our protection, believe me," Theo says, his dark brown gaze earnest.

"You think? Considering the fact that you are here demanding payment for that protection, you'll understand me not taking your word for it."

"They would have taken more than money from you," Atlas says through gritted teeth.

"So, you say."

"It is the truth."

I let him see how much I believe his so-called truth. "Why should I believe you about anything?"

"I have no reason to lie to you." Atlas's handsome lying face demands I believe him.

Not going to happen. "Your credibility is suspect."

"You need our protection," Atlas grounds out. "Larry, Curly and Mo coming here shows how much."

The bratva soldiers are named after the Three Stooges? No way. It must be some kind of code Atlas uses. "You told me that one guy's name was Ivan."

Something terrifying flashes in Atlas's gaze when I say the name Ivan.

"They won't be a problem for you anymore," he promises. "Neither will Ivan."

I guess I'm supposed to take his word for that too. So not happening.

"You lied to me and used me for my own good? Is that it?" I ask, sarcasm dripping from every word. "Newsflash, it's never for my own good."

The surprise on his face is almost amusing. Only nothing is funny right now. My lover is my extortionist. Nothing funny about that.

"Okay, lets go rob my till." I wave toward the door.

I'm not moving until they do. I don't want to be within two feet of either Atlas, or his man, Theo.

"We aren't robbing you," Atlas says forcefully.

"To-may-to, to-mah-to." He can call it protection money, but he's stealing from me. And we both know it. "Let's get this over with."

CHAPTER 32

LUCIA

Atlas and I stare at each other, both waiting for the other to move. Too bad for him, I'm stubborn as hell. I'll wait here until the club closes if I have to, but I'm not walking past him.

"Come on, boss. Let's get the money and go. It sounds like Miz Esposito has things to do."

Like scream into my pillow until my throat's raw.

Atlas puts his hand out to me and a laugh that has zero humor in it barks out of my throat. I shake my head and lift the hand he wants to hold with my middle finger extended.

Theo makes a sound between choking and laughing.

I stare daggers at him. "I'm glad someone finds this situation amusing."

His face slides into a stoic mask and he turns to open the door.

Atlas doesn't move. "Why are you acting like this? You'll get more out of this relationship than you'll lose by it."

"Says you."

"I did my calculations."

"Based on?" I know what he had to have done.

Get on my computer and look over my books. Will he admit it?

"Your password for your computer is the name of the club." He sounds put out by that.

Like he supposedly was when he realized I used the same number combination on the lock downstairs as my apartment? That's going to change tonight. Both of them.

I will set two *different* unlock codes he has no way of guessing.

"Are you trying to imply it's my fault you betrayed my trust and got onto my computer and looked at the club's ledgers?" I'm glad there's nothing about Lenny's care home on the computer.

Would it change anything if Atlas knew about Lenny? I shake my head. It wouldn't. So, I'm glad I never told him all my secrets. I gave enough of myself to this man.

"I didn't say that."

"You implied it."

"Your protection tithe won't take too much out of Nuovi Inizi," he says, clearly unwilling to argue. "We'll launder money through the club and within a year, you'll make it back in the fees we pay you. With our contacts, you'll save money on stock too. If you make a few changes, your profit margin will increase too."

"You've got it all worked out, don't you?" I mock angrily.

He calmly nods. "Yes."

"Only you didn't take into account that I don't want to launder money for criminals, much less use your contacts to get a better price on alcohol."

"Boss, we've got two more stops to make tonight," one of the men from the hall says.

Frustration bleeds through Atlas's blank mask. "We'll talk later."

Later never.

Finally, he leaves my office and I follow, locking the door behind me. I skirt around the wall of men in my hallway and head to the bar. Walking to the end, I signal to Willow to release the lock on the access.

Betrayal eats at my gut like acid. I go behind the bar and straight to the till. Feeling so brittle, one wrong word or touch will shatter me into tiny glass fragments of my former self, I avoid the bartenders and barbacks.

If there wasn't Lenny to look after, I could tell them all to go to hell. Especially Atlas. The lying, conniving snake.

But it's not just me. If I want to keep Lenny where he is, I can't afford what Atlas and his crew will do to bring me in line. A fire in the bathroom. Armed burglary. Things that will not destroy the club but will cost me enough and cause enough fear to make me amenable.

For my own sake, they could burn my club to the ground. I wouldn't pay a single cent to a man who used his body and my weakness for it to manipulate me into giving him access to my knowledge and my business.

Because it isn't just for my sake, I open the till and pull out most of the large bills. Leaving a few along with the smaller ones so my bartenders can continue to make change, I shut the drawer. I stack the money together and exit from behind the bar.

Ignoring his lackeys, I walk over to stand directly in front of Atlas, getting closer than I have since he walked into my club.

Glaring up at him, I offer the stack of money. I make no effort to hide what is happening. If the Hades Brotherhood wanted to keep this little extortion agreement a secret, Atlas and his crew should have waited to approach me until the club was closed.

For a breathless second, he makes no move to take the money. A curl of hope unfurls inside me. Maybe he's going to say this was all a mistake. He'll tell Theo and the others my club is off limits.

Atlas's hand comes up and those ridiculous pipe dreams turn to ash.

"You told me there was a dark ember left of your soul, but there is no smoldering fire there, just darkness," I hiss.

He flinches, but the hurt I see in his expression must a trick of the club lights. A heart as dark as his can't feel pain.

I smack the cash onto his palm and immediately yank my hand away. Or try to.

His fingers curl around mine too fast for me to pull back and his other hand comes down over the top of mine. "It's going to be okay, *ílios mou*. You'll see. I will protect you."

I flinch when he calls me his sun. Of course, he didn't listen to me when I told him not to. I can't stand having my hand trapped between his. Because even knowing what I know, the electric connection between us is not gone.

My fury only seems to heighten it.

"Those words might mean something if you weren't stealing my money to pay for that protection." I jerk at my hand.

He lets me go.

I look at Theo. "Nuovi Inizi is closed on Sunday. Come by at three and knock on the back door if you want your payment."

Theo looks at Atlas, but his boss is looking at me and I am *not* looking at him.

"I'll be here at three," Theo says finally and Atlas doesn't correct him.

The last tendril of hope dead inside me, I turn and walk away from them without another word.

But I don't get more than two steps before a hand lands on my shoulder. I know who it is. I jerk away from his touch and spin to face him, letting him see my fury, but not my pain.

His blue gaze traps mine. "This is business. The money..." He shakes his head. "It's not personal."

Is that supposed to make it better somehow? "Don't worry, I am under no delusion that we have anything personal between us. I'll have the money for your men on Sunday."

If Atlas comes instead, I'm not sure I'll be able to refrain from stabbing him in the eye.

His mouth works like he wants to say something but there is nothing he can say that I want to hear.

"Your guy said you have other businesses to shake down tonight." It's a not-so-thinly veiled hint for him to leave.

"Theo can take lead on the last two stops."

Oh, heck, no. Atlas is not sticking around here. "Then I guess you had better head home to check in with Zeus."

What did he call him? The *anax*? Men in his position are usually older. Men my dad's age, or older. Like almost always. There *is* a thirty-five-year-old don for one of the Five Families in New York, but that's unusual.

Zeus is around that same age, but I'm not asking Atlas how old his brother is.

I'm never asking him anything personal again.

"Are we done here?" I ask, finished with subtle hints.

He hands the money over to Theo, who tucks it away inside his jacket.

"Our business is done." He reaches for me.

I jump back, nearly tripping in my need to get away from him, to stop him from touching me. "No."

"I am not your enemy."

Is he really that clueless? "You are the very definition of my enemy."

"No, I am not. I will always protect you. Your club will thrive. I promise."

"You mean like you protected me tonight?"

His mouth snaps shut, something like guilt flashing in his gaze. It's too late for guilt. He already gutted me. Remorse won't change how he used me. How he played me.

This situation is bringing back memories I buried five years ago.

Tino's face superimposes over Atlas's and I see my husband the first time he wanted to have sex after I lost our baby. Tino's touch made my skin crawl and I nearly vomited. He'd slept in the guest room that night and for a month after.

Eventually, we'd reconnected. I'm not sure I ever forgave him.

I may never forgive Atlas for using me the way he did. If only I reacted to his touch like I had Tino's at first. Instead, even now, my body yearns to lean toward Atlas, to put my hand back in his.

Not happening. My ovaries are done calling the shots.

"I suppose it's too much to hope that you'll never come back, but if you do, it won't be for me. Because I never want you to talk to me again, much less touch me." Without drawing him a map to the exit, I can't be any clearer.

His jaw like granite, Atlas glowers. "We are not over."

We so are, but I'm done arguing.

"Leave." I will not plead with this man. I will not let him see me cry, but the tears are burning the back of my eyes and making my throat tight. "Now."

He clenches his jaw and nods. "I'll be back later."

No words left, not even *no*, I shake my head.

Finally, he turns to leave.

My shoulders drop from around my ears as I take the first full breath since I realized what he was doing here. I will him not to turn around again and for once, I get my wish. Atlas and his crew make their way across the club, other patrons unconsciously stepping aside to clear a path for the predators among them.

How had I not seen the hunter lurking in Atlas's eyes? I cringe at my own willful ignorance, because it was willful. Atlas is apex predator through and through. I made myself see something else when I looked at him. Something human and trustworthy when he's neither.

"You alright, Lucia?" Willow is standing right next to me.

How long has she been there?

"I saw you give your boyfriend the money from the till. Not trying to tell you how to live your life, but lending money to him like that could come back to bite you in the ass."

I spin to face my bar manager, unable to believe she thinks I would do something so foolish.

Opening my mouth to tell her just why I gave Atlas the money, I snap it shut again. Atlas and his mafia aren't the only ones who would be in trouble if the cops get involved. And I don't know if I can trust Willow not to call them.

She doesn't understand that if they're collecting protection tithes, the Hades Brotherhood have local law enforcement and probably at least one prosecutor and judge in their pockets. The only one that will be damaged in the long term is me.

I've been very careful to keep my name and image out of databases. Everyone back in Detroit thinks I'm dead and I'm going to keep it that way.

Doing my best not to let my inner devastation show, I shrug at Willow. "Sometimes, you just have to do what you have to do."

"Love makes fools of us all." Willow squeezes my shoulder in commiseration.

Love, or our ovaries.

CHAPTER 33

ATLAS

I throw Theo up against the side of the SUV. "Why the fuck did you tell her we'd be checking her books?"

"It's what we always say. So, they don't try to cheat us." Theo cocks his head, like he's trying to figure me out.

I'm not the one doing stupid shit.

"Yeah, boss. You always say it's better to threaten them before they get greedy than to have to punish them after," Bobby adds. "Better for business relations."

"Lucia isn't just a business owner. She's my woman." And they know it.

Michael looks at me levelly. "I'm pretty sure she doesn't see it that way."

"If she's yours, why are we shaking down her club?" Theo challenges me.

I shove him away. "Because our *anax* ordered it. I shouldn't have to explain that to you."

This whole damn night is a shitshow of epic proportions. I wanted to do Nuovi Inizi last, take my time explaining the protection tithe and how it will benefit Lucia and her nightclub in the long run.

I knew she'd be upset to learn how much I've been hiding from her. I planned to explain all of it. Well, almost all.

She doesn't need to know about Dimios.

She didn't give me the chance to explain anything. Somehow, she knew why we were there before I said a word.

How? Has she paid protection money before? To one of the gangs? She never said anything about it.

Like you never said anything about being part of a syndicate?

I ignore the voice in my brain to scowl at my crew.

"She's pissed, but she knows she's mine." I dare any of them to argue.

None of them do.

"Let's get the last two businesses set up." Neither owner had been around when we showed up earlier.

We're hitting both at closing.

"Theo, you and Bobby take the Vietnamese restaurant. Michael, You're with me."

Staying at the club would have meant waiting until tomorrow to hit the second location. We never go in alone.

Lucia needs time to cool off.

And I need time to figure out what to say to make her understand. Nothing I have said so far did the trick. She doesn't want to do business with criminals.

Gamó.

I'll change her mind. Once I figure out how.

I'd ask my brothers for advice, but Zeus is the one who insisted I collect the fucking protection tithe to begin with and Orion is better at poking the bear than soothing it.

I don't even consider asking my cousins. Both are man whores like Zeus used to be before he turned into The Monk. And the way they looked at me in my brother's office, neither understands how important Lucia is to me.

I'll figure it out. Lucia is mine and she's staying that way even if I have to cuff her to my bed.

My cock twitches at the image in my head. She would look beautiful spread eagle on my bed, her hands and ankles tied down.

LUCIA

Refusing to give in to the emotional pain that wants to take me to my knees, I force myself to work the floor like I do every night. I talk to patrons, check in with the DJ, help my bartenders keep the inventory stocked behind the bar and answer questions Willow can't.

All-in-all a typical Wednesday night. Only tonight, when it's time to clear the club, I am militant about getting everyone out. I instruct the DJ to make the announcement and then switch to soft jazz. We turn the lights up and I tell the staff and bouncers to hurry people on their way.

I want time to lick my wounds in solitude, if not peace. There is no peace trying to wrap my head around Atlas's betrayal.

Whether they can sense the mood under my calm exterior, or they're ready to go home themselves, everyone does their closing tasks quickly and without the usual joking around. When they are all gone, I lock the door, arm the alarm and then think better of it.

I turn it back off and reset the code to one Atlas doesn't know. I use the date of Tino's death. Another day when my world exploded around me.

Once the alarm is set, I head upstairs. On the way, I change the code on the door to the stairs to the date I married Tino. A reminder of the past and how naïve it is to trust a man with my heart. When I reach my apartment, I reset the unlock code to Lenny's birthday. This time it's a reminder of what is at stake and what my priorities have to be.

Walking inside the small space, I immediately regret coming upstairs. I should have slept in my office, even if I had to do it on the floor. Atlas's leather jacket is lying over the arm of the small sofa. His duffel is against the wall. The scent of his cologne lingers in the air but it's the memories that hurt the most.

The two hand-cast ceramic mugs he bought from the Farmer's Market because I like them sit on the counter waiting for our morning coffee. The table where we share breakfast and other things. My disloyal brain throws up an image of me riding him while he sits on one of the chairs at that small table.

It plays like a high-definition video in my head and it's not a fantasy, but a memory.

Another memory assaults me. Us making lo—having sex against the wall. Over the back of the couch. Him eating me out on that same couch.

I try to shake the memories loose, but the images won't stop and my heart shreds in my chest knowing I will never experience that level of sexual pleasure again. Worse, I will never know that kind of emotional intimacy.

It was fake for him, but it wasn't for me.

It wasn't for me.

My legs fold under me. There's no one here to see me give into weakness. I let myself fall to my knees, the tears I've been holding back for the last three hours coursing down my cheek.

I worked my butt off so I could buy that little house, that tiny part of the world that was just for me. But giving the Hades Brotherhood 10% of my net profit doesn't leave enough money to cover Lenny's care and the mortgage on the house. Not without strapping me so tight there will be no money left for emergencies.

And there are always emergencies.

For five years, I have worked long hours with no days off in order to get to a place where not only can the club profits support Lenny's care going forward, but I can take on a home mortgage and live a life away from the club.

Where I can take a day off here and there. But the only way the club stays solvent is to reinvest, to expand, to follow the plan. That plan only works with enough money.

I can't do that. It's not fair to the people who work for me not to be prepared for the unexpected. They're all relying on me to keep Nuovi Inizi going.

There is no point in putting it off. My realtor won't be in her office this late and I'm hoping she won't answer her work phone either. I want to leave a message. Maybe it will hurt less to say what needs saying that way.

I call and relief flows through me when the call goes to voicemail.

"I am sorry, Elaine." So, so sorry. As much for myself as the work she's wasted on this listing. "I have to cancel the purchase on the house. I know that means I give up my earnest money, but I have no choice."

I will lose thousands between the earnest money and everything I have paid for the appraisal, inspections and repairs for the underwriters to approve the loan.

It does not matter.

Nothing matters now.

ATLAS

It takes me longer to get back to Nuovi Inizi than it should. Zeus calls and wants a report on tonight's activities. In person.

There's no putting it off until tomorrow. My brother is in a piss poor mood and pulls the *anax* card. Our meeting takes twice as long as it should because Zeus refuses to take anything at face value.

By the time I'm back in my X7 and headed toward Lucia's place, my mood is as black as my brother's.

After the second attempt to turn off the building alarm, I realize Lucia changed it on me. *Gamó.*

Bringing up the disarming app on my phone, I get it started in time. I hope. When the beeping stops and the little light on the panel turns green, I let out my breath.

After the fiasco with the alarm, I am not surprised to find out she changed the unlock code on the door to the stairway. There's no app for this. It requires my analog skills at lock-picking. Same with the door to her apartment.

I would be happy my woman finally listened to me about changing the codes on her doors, except she did it to keep me out. Opening the door, a strange sound reaches me.

Like there's a wounded animal in Lucia's apartment.

The wounded animal is her. *Ilios mou.*

Halfway between the door and her bedroom, Lucia kneels on the floor, curled into herself. Her shoulders shake with her sobs.

What do I do? I am the executioner. Comfort is not in my skillset. But I cannot leave her like this.

First, I have to get her off the floor.

Squatting, I get one arm under her legs and wrap the other around her back. Lucia goes rigid before I can stand and throws herself away from me, landing on her side on the floor.

The skirt of her wrap dress rides up, showing every inch of her gorgeous legs. But the horror in her beautiful brown eyes throws a bucket of ice water on my libido.

"What are you doing here?" she demands, her voice hoarse.

How long has she been crying?

"I came to see you."

"I changed the locks." She scoots back and uses the wall behind her to help her stand, but she keeps her wary gaze on me.

What does she think I'm going to do?

"Criminal." I point to myself. "Remember?"

Her eyes darken with accusation. "How could I forget? You need to leave."

"We need to talk."

"There's nothing left to say. You used sex to get access to me and my club. You used me." Her voice breaks on the last word and more tears track down her face. She swipes at her cheeks angrily. "Just go."

"I'm not leaving you like this." Does she think I'm a monster? Sure I don't want the answer to that question, I don't ask it.

"Why not? You got what you wanted."

"I want you."

"Stop," she shouts hoarsely. "Just stop. No more lies."

"I never lied to you." I left a lot of shit out, but I never flat out lied to her.

"Like hell you didn't."

That voice of hers is killing me. I go into her kitchen, fill the electric kettle and turn it on.

"What are you doing?"

"Making you tea with honey and lemon." It's what my mother gave us when our throats were sore when me and my brothers were kids.

She yanks on my arm, trying to pull me from her kitchen. "I don't need tea. I need you to leave. Now."

I'm a big guy and even though she's furious, she's not shifting my body unless I let her. And I am not leaving her like this. I'm not leaving her at all.

"You are mine to take care of," I explain.

"I am not yours. Not one bit of me." She throws my arm from her and goes to the door. Opening it, she glares at me. "Get out."

"No." I turn back and open the cupboard she keeps her tea in.

I don't want to give her caffeine this late at night, so I grab the ginger tea. After I put a teabag in the mug she keeps out for her morning coffee, I turn back to face her.

Her eyes are puffy and red from crying, but her glare is sharper than my favorite knife.

Shrugging out of my suit jacket, I watch her eyes narrow. I hang it on the back of the chair I sit in when we eat together at her little bistro table. My shoes go next.

"What are you doing? Stop undressing. You aren't staying."

"We already had this discussion," I remind her.

"You refusing to leave is not a discussion."

"You insisting I leave when you are upset isn't one either."

She barks out a laugh. "Are you trying to convince me that you care you hurt me? You knew!"

"I knew what?"

"That you were using me. You knew you planned to steal from me. You knew it would hurt me."

"The protection tithe isn't stealing. We aren't the bratva. There are benefits to being under the protection of the *Ádis Adelfótita*."

"Like being poorer?" she snarks.

I hold onto my temper. She's not herself and she doesn't understand, but she will.

"Like being protected from the bratva."

"What difference does it make if it's you extorting money from my club, or them?"

"They didn't just want money." I hate having to tell her this. It will upset her, but she has to see the truth. She needs me.

"Oh, really? What else did they want? A better place to hang out than that dive bar with the terrible service?"

"They wanted to use your club as a hunting ground for women." I spell it out for her. "They wanted to give you to Ivan to use and abuse before he killed you making a snuff film."

"Ivan, the man in the club that night?"

"No. That man's name is actually Dimitri and his is the son of the *pakhan*. Ivan is his father's second in command. The *vtoroy* has a type and you're it."

Remembering what Mo and Curly said, fury boils through me. Lucia is my woman. I will protect her, and I will kill anyone who is a danger to her. Including Ivan.

"I'm supposed to take your word for that?"

"Why would I lie?"

"Oh, I don't know...because it's what you're good at."

"Damn it, Lucia, I didn't lie to you."

"You said you and your brothers were in Portland to start a business."

"We are."

"You're here to claim territory for the Hades Brotherhood."

"That too."

"You told me you're a facilitator for your family."

"I am." And an assassin. Sometimes the killing is part of the facilitating.

"You told me you weren't using me to get information," she says like she won the argument.

She didn't. "I promised you I was not trying to use your knowledge to compete with or destroy your club. I didn't."

"I guess our definition of destruction isn't the same."

The kettle boils and clicks off. I pour the water in her mug and let it steep while I find the honey and a lemon. "Destruction is destruction, Lucia. Yes, the tithe will lower your profit margin at first, but we'll get you making more money than you ever were before."

"Don't talk like we're a team. We aren't."

Pain pierces my chest. I've been having these aches all night. I need to up my cardio, or something.

I slice a wedge out of the lemon and put the remainder in the little lemon keeper she has in her fruit drawer. Lucia has weird but cool shit in her kitchen. Probably because she likes to cook. She's going to love having a full kitchen again when she moves into the house she's buying.

I need to find out when she takes ownership so I can get an alarm system installed and other security measures implemented on the property. I've already looked into the houses on either side. Neither are for sale, but I don't anticipate a problem convincing the owners to change that.

If I'm going to be living there, I want my men living in the other properties.

[illegible] of the [illegible] little lemon [illegible] she has [illegible] fruit [illegible] kitchen. Probably because she likes to cook. She's going to love having a full kitchen again when she moves into the house she's buying.

[illegible] relationship has changed [illegible] on the [illegible]

[illegible] Neither [illegible]

[illegible]

I'm going to be away [illegible]

CHAPTER 34

LUCIA

My hand gripping the edge of the door so hard, it hurts, I watch Atlas make me tea.

Once he has the honey and lemon juice stirred in, he adds a single piece of ice to cool it down enough for me to drink without burning the roof of my mouth.

Too bad he isn't as worried about causing me emotional pain as physical.

What is wrong with him? He's acting like we're still together when we both know he was using me and my weakness for him to get information for his damn Hades Brotherhood.

Atlas lifts the mug. "Do you want to drink this in here, or in the bedroom?"

I want him to leave, but that doesn't look like it's happening until I drink the damn tea.

Leaving the door open, I approach the table. "In here."

I'm not inviting him into my bedroom. My body is still reacting to his like he's safety, affection, sex and everything good in between, but my mind? My mind knows the truth.

Atlas is my enemy, not my boyfriend. No matter what my ovaries try to tell me. Those little buggers are in a timeout for leading me into this situation in the first place.

He puts the mug down on the table and then takes a step back, like he knows I won't sit down until he does.

He's right.

As I shuffle over to the dinette chair, I'm in a nightmare, every move at the treacle slowness of a dream. Only, unlike in my dreams, I feel every ache in my body and heart.

Atlas watches me, his gaze never once wavering as I sit down.

Taking a sip of the tea, I realize how thirsty I am. All that crying. It's not like me. I didn't lose it like that even after I learned of Tino's death. How can I be more devastated by Atlas's betrayal than the death of my husband?

The tea helps the soreness in my throat with the side benefit of settling my stomach that has been roiling since Atlas and his crew showed up in the club earlier. No way am I going to admit that to my ex-lover though.

Atlas leans against the counter, his arms crossed over his chest, and watches me drink.

I pretend not to notice.

"When do you take possession of the house?" His deep baritone shatters the silence.

Glaring at him, I consider which is better: not to answer at all, or to tell him it's none of his business.

I go with, "None of your business."

There won't be any signing of the papers.

"I know you are angry right now."

"Do you? How astute of you."

He frowns. "We can work this out."

Yeah, not happening. "There is nothing to work out."

"I am not giving up on us."

"There is no us!" The shout strains my already abused vocal cords. "There is no us," I repeat in a near whisper before gulping down hot tea.

It soothes my throat and I concentrate on that sensation, not the ache in my heart.

"There is an us. You are mine. I am yours."

"No." I shake my head.

There is so much more I want to say, but not enough to croak it out through a strained throat. He and the Hades Brotherhood cost me my home.

Laundering money for the Greek mafia is a losing proposition for me. The risks outweigh the rewards big time. If the authorities come knocking, it won't be Atlas and his brothers that end up under indictment. It will be me, their associate with no actual affiliation to their syndicate.

I know how these things work and I am expendable to them. To Atlas. Especially to Atlas. How can I be anything else when he was willing to use me like he did?

Regardless of how I feel about it, the Hades Brotherhood isn't going to let me refuse to launder their money through Nuovi Inizi. That's not how it works. They targeted my club and I'm still in their crosshairs.

Looking around my small studio apartment, at the life I thought I was changing, an idea begins to form. A solution to my dilemma that has the side benefit of being something that will infuriate Atlas.

I'm pretty sure his brothers aren't going to be any happier. That only makes my plan more attractive to me.

I am a woman with agency and tomorrow they will all learn how powerful that agency is. Under the layers of pain and betrayal, an ember of joyful vindication burns deep in my chest.

Finishing my tea, I stand and leave the mug on the table. "I'm going to bed. Let yourself out like you let yourself in."

Not waiting for Atlas to answer, I head to my bedroom and shut the door once I am inside. There is no lock, but I'm too tired to care.

I want to sleep, but I force myself to take a shower. I need to wash the work and stress sweat off my body. Not wanting to go to bed with wet hair, I pile my long tresses into a messy bun on top of my head before I step into the shower.

After drying off, for the first time in weeks, I pull on my comfy pajama pants and a sleep tank top.

Climbing into my bed, I'm so tired, I ache with it. But my mind still spins with everything that happened today and what it means for my life.

The sound of movement filters in from the outer room and I realize Atlas hasn't left. It's then I notice that the pillow he usually sleeps with is missing from the bed and so is the throw that I keep at the end of it.

The stubborn, arrogant man plans to spend the night. On the couch. That is at least a foot too short for him.

A grim smile tilts my lips.

Neither of us is going to get much sleep tonight.

~ ~ ~

I wake feeling safe, warm and surprisingly rested. The source of the heat against my back does not register at first, but then the weight circling my waist does.

Swearing, I throw myself out of the bed.

Atlas came into my room last night. After tossing and turning between stress dreams, I didn't even wake up. My body has not gotten the memo that he cannot be trusted.

He sits up instantly, looking around for a threat. "What?"

"What are you doing in my bed?"

"Your sofa is too short." He finger combs his tousled hair away from his face.

"For you."

"I was the one trying to sleep on it." He looks and sounds disgruntled. "I finally came in here a couple of hours ago."

It's the first time I've seen him wake up grumpy like this. Poor baby really didn't sleep well on the too short sofa. Sucks to be him.

"You have a bed the right size for you at your house. You should have gone there, not come into my bedroom uninvited."

"I didn't touch you."

"You sound proud of that fact."

"I am."

I roll my eyes. "Your arm was over my waist when I woke up and your hard dick was pressing against my back."

He doesn't look even a little bit sorry, just disappointed he wasn't awake to experience our unintentional cuddling. Unintentional on my part anyway. The jury is still out on his intentions.

Yawning, he stretches his arms above his head. The covers slide down his muscled body and I swallow the moisture that pools in my mouth from the desire to taste his salty skin. Wetness pools somewhere else too, but we aren't talking about that.

Tilting his head first to one side, and then the other, he rolls his shoulders. "If you really want me to pay penance, make me sleep on that damn sofa a few more nights."

The idea is intriguing. I cannot lie. But I'm not giving him a chance to make up for his betrayal. If things go the way I want today, I won't care if he sleeps on my sofa a hundred nights. I won't be here to see it.

I rub between my heavy breasts, trying to assuage the instant pain that thought causes in my chest.

It's a good plan, damn it.

"I'm going to take a shower. Want to join me?" Atlas climbs out of the bed completely nude.

I spin away, but not before I get a full monty view of his morning erection. A condition I have happily taken full advantage of in the past weeks.

Not today. *Not ever again*, I remind myself.

Self harrumphs, not in the least impressed.

Pulling open the drawer with my leggings, I pull a pair of fleece lined black ones out. "I showered last night."

"Don't make breakfast. We'll go out," he says as he disappears into the bathroom.

Can he really be that oblivious, or is he pretending everything is fine because he's hoping eventually it will be? And why does he care? He got what he wanted.

Or at least he thinks he did.

The Greek mafia is about to find out that messing with a Cosa Nostra princess is dangerous.

Dressing quickly, I quietly sneak out of my bedroom when the shower goes on. The keys to Atlas's SUV are in the dish he's taken to using for them. Predictability can be a good thing.

I grab the keys, careful not to clink them together in my hand and head downstairs.

In my office, I take the sheaf of papers sitting in the printer tray and tuck them into my tote style purse. I created the sales contract on my phone last night during one of my restless bouts and then sent it to the printer.

Before Atlas joined me and I slept like a baby. Not something I want to analyze right now.

Opening the safe, certainty settles over me as I spy the manila envelope with legal documents I had drawn up, signed, witnessed and notarized as soon as I took possession of Nuovi Inizi's building. I stuff the large envelope in my purse too.

I grab one last item from the safe. My gun and the belt holster that will be hidden by my oversized sweater. After checking and loading it, I put the belt on and slide the twenty-two into the holster.

Thirty seconds later, I'm climbing into the driver's seat of Atlas's luxury SUV.

CHAPTER 35

LUCIA

When I arrive at the Rokos mansion, I roll down the window to talk to the guard. I recognize him as one of the men that was here guarding the gate when I came with Atlas the first time.

I dismissed all that mafia security as typical for billionaires, which it probably is. But I willfully blinded myself to the other similarities between the Greek mafia and the Cosa Nostra because I didn't *want* to see syndicate when I looked at the Rokos lifestyle.

It wasn't just willful ignorance though. It has been decades since the Russo mafia moved into new territory. The idea that a mafia family would expand like Atlas and his brothers are doing for the Hades Brotherhood never occurred to me.

"I'm here to see Zeus," I tell the guard.

His eyes widen fractionally and then almost comically when he realizes whose vehicle I'm driving. He's surprised I'm here with Atlas's SUV and no Atlas. But the days of that fake relationship are over.

"Does Zeus know you are coming?"

"No. Why don't you tell him I'm here?"

The guard talks into the comm unit on his shoulder, listens to the response and then the gate opens. Driving through, I hear the gate close behind me and apprehension slithers down my spine.

I am not trapped. I am here of my own volition. This is the plan.

Parking in the same spot Atlas used, I turn off the SUV and hop out of the truck. Gina opens the door before I have a chance to ring the bell.

She smiles like she doesn't work for a bunch of extortionists. "Good morning, Ms. Esposito. Atlas isn't here, but if he said he would meet you, I'm sure he'll arrive shortly."

"I'm here to see Zeus." I don't return her smile and my tone isn't friendly.

I can't help feeling like Gina is part of the conspiracy to keep me in the dark until Atlas extracted all the useful information from me that he could.

And didn't I make it easy?

"Zeus is in his office," Gina says, her smile slipping in the face of my lack of friendliness.

"Would you mind showing me where that is? It wasn't part of the tour Atlas gave me."

"Of course, but let's hang up your coat before we go."

I shake my head. "I'd rather keep it with me."

When I'm ready to leave, I don't want to have to wait for my coat to be fetched before I can do so.

Gina cocks her head. "If you're sure?"

"I am."

Without any further questions, the housekeeper turns and leads me down a hall to the right of the foyer. Zeus's office is at the end.

Gina knocks lightly on the door.

"Come in," Zeus calls from inside the room.

Opening the door, Gina steps back so I can get past her into the room. "Ms. Esposito is here to see you."

"Thank you, Gina."

The other woman leaves without another word.

I don't look at Zeus right away, but give myself a moment to gather my thoughts while I take in the room. It's more traditional than I expected considering how modern the décor is in Atlas's suite.

Large windows look out into the well-manicured backyard. The wall behind me is lined with heavy wood bookcases filled with books, and the large executive desk Zeus is sitting behind looks like a well-preserved piece of the past. Two leather wingback chairs face the desk and there are two more chair pairings against the walls on either side of the desk.

Plenty of space for him to have meetings with his brothers and cousins.

Nothing about the office screams crime boss of a syndicate, but the weight of the atmosphere makes it easy to believe Zeus does both legitimate and back alley business here.

"Atlas isn't here." Zeus lets the words drop between us like a challenge.

I raise my brows in response as I pull off my coat. "I am aware. I left him showering in my apartment."

"He will be worried when he realizes you aren't there."

"You want me to believe you haven't texted him already?" I tsk and shake my head. "All evidence to the contrary, I'm not that gullible."

"Atlas didn't—"

"Stop, right there," I interrupt, my hand up. "I am not here to talk about Atlas."

Zeus's eyes narrow. "Then why are you here?"

"I have a business proposition for you."

If he is surprised, he does not show it.

He waves to one of the wingback chairs facing him, inviting me to take a seat.

I do so, crossing one legging clad leg over the other, placing my coat over my lap. Sliding my hand under the hem of my red tunic style sweater, I unlatch the holster and draw the gun out under the guise of adjusting the coat.

Unwilling to allow him to see my grief or even a glimmer of my nervousness, I refuse to fidget. My hold on the twenty-two secure but loose, I force my breathing to remain steady.

Taking out my phone, I show him that I'm turning it off. "I'm going to assume you have a jammer going so nothing we say here can be listened to or recorded regardless."

He inclines his head but does not answer.

"Good, I'm not interested in wading through euphemisms."

His lips tilt the tiniest bit at the corners, like he finds that amusing.

Then he's back to the serious, stoic eldest brother, crime boss persona. "If you are here to try to talk me out of the protection money—"

"That's not why I'm here."

"Whatever your reason for being here, this conversation should include Atlas."

"Why? He's not my boss. Is he yours?" I taunt.

Zeus frowns, but he doesn't take the bait. "He is your boyfriend and that makes private conversations between us problematic."

"One, he is most emphatically *not* my boyfriend." I tick off on my finger. "Two, I'm here to offer you a business proposition, not the other kind."

Heartbreaking sex with one brother in the Rokos family is my limit.

"Glad to hear it."

Lifting my purse, I pull out the sheaf of papers I grabbed from the printer in my office before I left the club.

I lay them on his desk. "I'm here to offer you a very good deal to buy my club."

Glacial blue eyes flare with surprise that is gone quickly. I have shocked him. Good. Last night I got a shock too. We will both survive.

"Here are the terms." I push the sales contract toward him.

I am not a lawyer, but with my experience doing the paperwork for the mafia clubs as well as a template I bought off the internet for the sale of a viable business, I am confident I have my bases covered.

It offers him the club and the building it is in at a steep discount from fair market value, with one stipulation. He agrees to take over payment for Lenny's care.

Zeus reads through the document, taking his time. When he is finished, he looks up at me and there is a question in his eyes. "Who is Lenny Smith?"

He says the name Smith in a way that makes me know he is aware it's an alias. I don't care. There's nothing linking Lenny Smith to Leonardo Revello.

"Someone I am responsible for. Once I sell the club, I will not be able to continue to pay for his care long term."

"Why should I take on this burden?"

"Think of it as protection money." I make no effort to hide the irony in my tone.

"Explain," he says, no amusement in his voice.

Oh, it's not so fun having the shoe on the other foot, is it, Mr. *Anax*?

"First, if Atlas told me the truth, then the Hades Brotherhood plans to start at least two nightclubs in the Portland Metro. Nuovi Inizi is already established and owning it gives your organization a material foothold in the territory you are claiming."

"That may be true, but I don't need to take on this unending debt, to get it."

"Yes, you do." I let the implication of my words settle between us. This is a nonnegotiable clause to the purchase agreement.

"You called it *protection*?"

I'm not ready to go there yet. "I am aware that clubs are perfect for money laundering, and Atlas has implied that is part of your plans for Nuovi Inizi. However, as long as I own the club, it won't be."

His brows draw together in an expression so like his brother's it hurts to see it. "Why not? Your cut would more than cover the expense of Lenny Smith's care."

He's not wrong there. Although I don't know what mafia business they have already established, I do know how organized crime works. If they don't already need it, the Hades Brotherhood will soon require a place to clean millions of dollars in dirty money each year.

"At first, maybe. But eventually I end up dead or in prison as a fall guy for your syndicate. And then who looks out for Lenny's interests?"

"That's a dark prediction for the future."

"But not an unrealistic one."

"You think Atlas would allow you to be made a fall guy?"

"I have absolutely no doubt." After last night, there is no place for trust between me and Atlas Rokos, or his brothers.

They were all part of the conspiracy to use my knowledge and set me up to pay protection.

Zeus doesn't like my answer. Tough. Sometimes the truth hurts.

"If I turn down this offer?" he asks.

"Then you can negotiate with the new owner for both protection money and the money laundering scheme." Although it's unlikely the Brotherhood would willingly let me sell the club to someone else.

Zeus's expression changes subtly and an atmosphere of menace fills the room. "You seem to be under the misapprehension that you can sell the club without our approval."

I was expecting this, but that doesn't stop the frisson of fear that goes down my spine. The Rokos men can be intimidating when they want to be. But I was raised around scary men and trained from childhood to hide my fear.

"I know there are things you can do to stop me selling, to cut me out entirely," I acknowledge.

"Then why are you here?" The *wasting my time* goes unsaid, but I hear it anyway.

I don't let his anger faze me. "Because, unlike the owners of the other businesses around me, I have a failsafe."

The sense of menace goes up a notch.

I'm not worried. Zeus is the *anax*. Like a don, he will not make any rash decisions. He will hear me out, if only to make sure he has all the information he needs before he deals with me. And my backup plan *is* full proof. Once he hears it, he isn't going to kill me.

The tense silence stretches between us.

"What kind of failsafe?" he finally asks.

I start with an explanation. "In another lifetime, I was a Cosa Nostra princess. I had a don."

A husband. And a family. I had people and many of those people are still alive.

Once Lenny is protected and his future is secure, can I go back to my family? Do I want to?

"That explains how you knew what was going on last night without having it explained to you." Zeus measures me with his gaze. "Does Atlas know?"

"Do I really need to answer that? If he knew, so would you."

An odd expression goes over his face, like maybe he's not sure of that.

Wishful thinking. I won't indulge in it. Atlas lied to me. He used me, I remind myself.

He's 100% on his brother's side in all this.

"What is your supposed failsafe?" Zeus asks again.

There's no *supposed* about it. If his mafia was better established in their territory, they might risk it, but not when they're getting up and running.

"In the event of my death or disappearance, the original of these documents will be delivered to the don." I put the manila envelope onto his desk.

The originals are with a firm of lawyers with whom I have weekly check in protocols. If I don't contact them via our agreed upon method, they send those documents to Don De Luca in New York, a man powerful enough to guarantee Lenny's safety.

"What are these documents?" There is no mistaking the anger in his tone now.

"You can read them for yourself." I indicate the envelope he will have to reach across his giant desk to get.

I won't be moving it closer to him. I'm not in an accommodating mood.

"You tell me."

I roll my eyes at his domineering order, but in the interest of expediency, I comply. "First, there is a letter explaining Lenny's whereabouts and copies of his diagnosis and treatment plan from an eminent neurologist."

Zeus makes a continue motion with his hand.

"Second, there is a witnessed and notarized will that leaves the club and any of my assets in a trust for Lenny, administered by the don."

His eyes narrow at this, but Zeus doesn't say anything.

"Last, there is an enduring power of attorney for all business matters related to the club and Lenny. Whether I disappear or die, the don will have legal claim to Nuovi Inizi."

"You believe we would disappear you?" Zeus asks, clearly offended.

Too bad. So sad. Send your brother in to seduce a woman into spilling information and making herself vulnerable to racketeering, and that woman doesn't trust your intentions toward her. *Shocking*.

Zeus shakes his head when I don't bother to answer what should be a rhetorical question. "My brother may want to chain you to his bed, but he won't do it."

Memories of the times Atlas handcuffed me to my own bed assail me. He made good use of the handcuffs he bought after he tied my hands to feed me up in his suite.

It takes all my mafia princess training to stifle my reaction to the x-rated movies playing in my head.

"If the don receives these documents, it will give him and the Cosa Nostra a foothold in your territory. Something your Hades Brotherhood cannot want right now."

Zeus doesn't look worried. Even a little.

I narrow my eyes and study him. No, not even a tiny tell to show my failsafe concerns him. Why?

"You want me to believe you put all of this in place since last night?" he asks derisively answering my *why*.

"You think I'm bluffing." I nod toward the envelope. "Look inside. You'll see I'm not."

"I don't need to. You're a smart woman. I'm sure you did your best to make the documents appear legally binding, but there was no time between last night and this morning to get them witnessed and notarized, much less set up to be delivered to a Cosa Nostra don."

My hand tightens on the gun and I have to force myself to relax my hold. No matter how pleasurable I might find shooting Zeus, I'm not going to.

Unless I have no other choice. "You're making a dangerous assumption, especially if you believe I'm as smart as you say."

"What's that?"

"That I wouldn't have set this up already."

He shakes his head. "It's a good bluff, but I don't believe you. This little drama isn't necessary regardless."

Little drama, my ass.

Shooting him is becoming more *necessary* by the second. Not for my safety, but to assuage my anger.

How angry would Atlas be if I shot his brother? I don't have to kill Zeus. Maybe maim him a little. And why the hell do I care what Atlas will think?

Zeus stands up and comes around the desk. He leans against it right in front of me. "Your club is in my territory and you will do what I say. If that means laundering money, you will do it. If that means running whores out of your back room, you will do that too."

The kid gloves are off and instead of being afraid, a sense of power courses through me. It's the familiarity of it all. He has no idea who he is dealing with. I might have been a naïve fool with his brother, but I'm no pushover. I was raised in the mafia, not the suburbs.

"No. I won't." I stand up and glare at him, moving until I'm out of striking range before revealing the gun in my hand.

CHAPTER 36

LUCIA

"What the fuck, Lucia? Put that away." Atlas's voice comes from the door.

I swiftly move back so I can cover both brothers. "I won't ask how you got here so fast. I don't care. Go stand by your brother."

"You're not going to shoot me." Instead of doing as I said, Atlas stands *between* me and Zeus.

Taking a two-handed grip to steady the gun, I aim at his torso. "I won't shoot to kill, but I will incapacitate you." I drop the aim a few inches. "Or maybe I will castrate you, stop you from seducing other women into being your dupe."

"I think she means it brother," Zeus says. "Right now, she's less likely to shoot me."

I nod. "Your *anax* is right, but that doesn't mean I won't shoot him. Now move further away from me, Atlas. If you rush me, I will pull the trigger and I won't be aiming to wound."

"You are hot with a gun in your hand, *eromenis mou*."

"I am not your lover. Not anymore."

"We'll have to agree to disagree." He sounds so darn complacent. I'm tempted to shoot him just because.

Atlas must see something in my face because he moves closer to Zeus. He still keeps his body between me and his brother though.

Protecting the boss. It's what a good soldier does.

"Do not make the mistake of thinking that because I fell for your brother's lies, that I am weak," I say to Zeus, ignoring Atlas acting like a wall between us. "I put the failsafe in place the week after I opened the club so that Lenny would always be taken care of."

"What do you think, brother? Is she bluffing?" Zeus asks Atlas.

I expect Atlas to ask what about, but he doesn't. He looks at me, trying to read my sincerity. My honesty about this is not something I need to hide. I let him see my sincerity as well as my hurt anger at his betrayal.

Atlas winces. "It seems like she's telling the truth, but she could be lying. She hid her affiliation with the Cosa Nostra from me."

My brows furrow. "How..."

Atlas points to an earbud in his left ear. "Zeus had me listening to the conversation from the time you came into his office."

"You told me you had a jammer," I accuse Zeus.

It never occurred to me he wouldn't use it. His business is the one that cannot come under scrutiny, not mine.

"I do have one. It isn't turned on." Zeus returns to his chair. "Please lower your gun, Lucia. You do not need it."

"I'm supposed to believe you?"

"Atlas would kill me if I so much as threatened you, much less touched you."

I make a production of showing my patent disbelief at that statement.

Atlas growls. "Damn it, Lucia, you know you're safe with me."

That's the trouble. I *do* feel safe with him. I have since the first moment. But that safety is an illusion.

"Sit down over there." I indicate one of the chairs across the office from me. "Then I will lower my gun."

Atlas doesn't hesitate to do what I say. He sits back and even puts his right ankle up on his left knee, the picture of relaxation. His stance is a stark contrast to his brother's looming presence only minutes ago.

The reason I felt the need to draw my gun in the first place.

"We have a lot to talk about." Atlas looks at me as if he expects me to agree.

I roll my eyes. Heart-to-hearts with the conniving jerk are so not happening.

"You're part of a mafia family?" Atlas asks, his tone casual.

Oh, so, not a heart-to-heart, but more intel gathering. There's no point in trying to hide what I've already admitted to.

I lower the gun to my side, but I don't put it back in its holster. "I was."

"Why didn't you tell me?"

"Are you being real right now?" Are we even on the same planet? "Why would I have?"

"We are lovers. Lovers tell each other stuff like that."

"You mean like you told me that you're part of a Greek mafia and came to my club to scope it out for your protection racket?" I scoff.

"That was different."

"Yes, it was," I breathe, furious all over again. "Me not telling you about my ties to the Cosa Nostra had no malice behind it. My past cannot hurt you, but you can't say the same about your present. Can you?"

"I didn't mean to hurt you."

Undeserving of an answer, I ignore that supremely ridiculous statement.

Shifting my gaze to Zeus, I say, "If you kill me or even kidnap me, that document packet will be delivered to the don."

"You set up a check-in protocol?" Zeus's tone sounds admiring.

I don't answer the question. The less they know about that, the less able they are to dismantle my precautions.

"Like your syndicate, the Cosa Nostra is always hungry for new territory and the don won't hesitate to claim it." It's a bald-faced lie.

The Cosa Nostra hasn't had a major expansion of territory for over a decade, and it has been even longer in Detroit.

"If you wanted the mafia taking care of Lenny Smith, you wouldn't be working so hard to do it yourself," Zeus says, clearly thinking he's got a point.

But I'm not letting him believe that. "The don might not keep him in his facility because of the entrenched belief that *it stays in the family*, whether that's good for family or not. But Lenny won't be homeless, and they won't hurt him on purpose."

That doesn't mean my brother-in-law won't be hurt, or that he might not hurt someone else if he is put back into a family household. Yes, that makes me feel guilty, but not enough to stay here and run Nuovi Inizi for the Hades Brotherhood. Whether they buy it, or not, my club won't be mine anymore.

I am emphatically not running sex workers out of my club. Atlas tried to tell me he saved Nuovi Inizi from being taken over by the bratva and used as a hunting ground for women. As if.

"Who is your don?" Zeus asks me.

"Does it matter? Do you want any of the Cosa Nostra to have a foothold in your territory?"

"Why give up a club you've worked so hard to build? You would make so much more money stay—"

"As a glorified manager? No, thanks," I interrupt him to say. "I'm not running your money laundering or a brothel out of the unused space upstairs. Like I said, I have no intention of ending up dead or in prison."

"No one is going to kill you," Atlas barks out, sitting up, all pretense of insouciance gone. "And you will never be a fall guy for the Hades Brotherhood. As my wife, you will be protected."

"Did we get married and I don't know about it?" I ask with sarcasm. "Only, I think I would remember."

"We aren't married yet."

"Or ever," I tell him flatly and turn back to his brother. "Do we have a deal?"

"Would you stay and run the club if you have my word you would be protected, married to Atlas, or not?" Zeus asks.

I don't know why he would offer that, or if I could trust him if he did. But it does not matter because it's not going to happen.

I am done.

"You can either agree to buy the club. Now." I'm not giving him time to come up with a plan to counteract my failsafe. "Or not. If the only way out is for me to give it to the don, then that's what I'll do."

The mafia will take care of Lenny. I did my best to protect my brother-in-law, but I can't do that from behind the bars of a prison cell. One way, or another, Lenny's safety will end up reliant on someone else.

Better I control who that someone is and what they do for him, than leave it to chance. Lenny deserves better. I deserve better.

"I'm not afraid of Russo," Zeus says mildly, like he's letting me down gently and letting me know he's aware I'm from Detroit. "He couldn't hold onto his territory; he's not taking mine."

Zeus knows I learned about running a nightclub from my husband and that my husband is dead. If he knows about the clubs in Detroit being taken over by the Irish and the Russians, he can easily work out that my husband is one of the men that died trying to protect them.

Which means he also knows who my husband was and probably who Lenny is too.

"Who said anything about Don Russo? Five years ago my husband and his father were murdered during the mob-bratva takeover," I say like I'm telling him something new. "Russo couldn't protect my husband. Why would I trust him to protect my brother-in-law?"

"You named a different don as his guardian and owner of the club," Atlas says, drawing my attention back to him.

Though, if I'm honest with myself, and I try to be, he's been the center of my focus since arriving. No matter who I'm looking at.

"Only the most powerful don in the Five Families. Everyone knows that when Don Caruso dies, Severu De Luca will be named Godfather of the Cosa Nostra."

Finally, Zeus looks like he's listening and not just humoring my *little drama*.

"If I buy the club, I want three months for you to train the new manager," Zeus says in a complete about face.

"No. I'm not staying."

"You want me to keep Leonardo Revello in that fancy facility? You will train your replacement." There's no give in Zeus's tone.

Worse is the look of utter implacability in his eyes.

Nausea roils in my stomach and I have to breathe shallowly so I don't throw up. Stress. It's a thing.

But the last thing I want is to stay in Portland where Atlas is. I shake my head.

"You are a very intelligent woman, Lucia Cattaneo."

Making a sound like a wolf facing its enemy, Atlas surges to his feet and takes a step toward me when Zeus uses my married name. "Do not call her that. She is not a Revello."

"Calm down, Atlas. The man is dead."

But Atlas doesn't look calm. He's one misspoken word from tearing Zeus's office apart.

What is wrong with him? He knows I am a widow. And I am not *his*, no matter what he says.

"As I was saying, Lucia, with a brain like yours, you know that negotiation requires compromise. I'm not taking over your club without you offering a smooth transition."

"You talk like you have room to negotiate in this."

"Do not make the mistake of believing I don't."

His words send unpleasant shivers along my nerve endings. I listen to my instincts telling me to take the win, even if it comes with a transition period. I'll just have to avoid Atlas.

Like I did last night. Right. That's going to work *really well*.

"Thirty days," I counter.

Zeus's eyes narrow. "Two months."

"Thirty days," I reiterate firmly.

"What happens if I don't pay for your brother-in-law's care? The facility isn't going to hire a lawyer and sue me for it," he points out.

So arrogant, like his brother. But he's right.

"So much for your word," I say sarcastically.

Probably not smart to taunt the criminal boss, but I'm so done with this conversation, and I have run out of fucks to give.

"You can't hold Lenny's care over my head. The facility knows to contact the don if his fees aren't paid." They'll contact me first, but Zeus doesn't need to know that. If I can't pay the fee, then they will contact Don De Luca.

"So?" Zeus asks, clearly unperturbed by the possible outcome.

I shake my head. "Funny. Despite how he used me, I would have said that Atlas had a sense of honor and you by association."

Zeus doesn't look so uncaring now. He's scowling at me. So is Atlas.

I ignore the wounded pride of both men. "If the facility has to contact the don, you will be in default on the terms of our contract. Don De Luca will have legal recourse to take the club from you."

Whether he exercises that recourse is anyone's guess, but one thing I know for sure. Severu De Luca puts *la famiglia* first and he won't allow Lenny to end up on the street.

"You're determined to make sure this guy is taken care of." Zeus's gaze fills with speculation.

Atlas is vibrating with emotion, though I'm not sure if it is anger, or something else. "Why is he so important to you?"

"He's my family."

"But he cost you your baby."

I wince, wishing I hadn't told Atlas about what happened. The dirty betrayer doesn't deserve my confidences, but I didn't know that at the time.

"It wasn't Lenny's fault."

My heart came to terms with his role in my baby's death a long time ago too. I tried to forgive Tino and Agustino Sr. too. But I couldn't forget the price my baby and I paid for my husband and father-in-law's choices.

"It sure as hell wasn't yours."

"Of course not." Though a small part of me has always shouldered some of the blame.

Watching over Leo, as he was known at the time, was my job. I was supposed to anticipate his needs and protect him from himself. I failed and failed my baby too.

Atlas moves like he's going to touch me and I jerk away. The gun knocks against my thigh and I almost drop it. I tighten my grip now slick with sweat. If I'm not careful I'm going to shoot someone accidentally.

The Rokos brothers might deserve it, but I could shoot my own foot if my grip slips again. Sighing, I unchamber the round and put the gun back in its holster.

"I made a promise to Tino, and I care about my brother-in-law," I say, my emotions even more raw than they were earlier. "I've done my best to take care of Lenny, but I'm not giving up my own freedom for his."

If that makes me a bad person, so be it.

Nausea rises again and I force myself to hide it. Okay, I'm not as insouciant about this as I want to appear.

I need to be out of this office. Away from Atlas and anyone named Rokos.

CHAPTER 37

ATLAS

Lucia pales, sweat beading on her upper lip.

I want to kill the demons putting that look on her face, but they are me and my brother.

"Thirty days," I say. She's not going anywhere, and a month is plenty of time to convince her of that fact. "And we will adhere to the terms of the contract."

Zeus looks at me and I let him see that I'm willing to go to war over this. He jerks his head in agreement. "Thirty days and we will pay for Lenny's care."

Lucia lets out a soft breath, but then she glares at my brother. "You won't be using Nuovi Inizi for any money laundering until I'm gone."

He opens his mouth to say something. Probably to argue. He is my *anax* and my brother, but Zeus is a few seconds away from my fist in his face.

Showing more courage when confronted by my brother than most made men, *ílios mou* puts up her hand and shakes her head. "No. I am not giving you the leverage to force me to stay and manage the club for the Hades Brotherhood."

She has a very Machiavellian mind. I like it, but I don't like her lack of trust. Even if I earned it.

"We aren't trying to trap you into staying to manage the nightclub." I don't care if she manages the club, unless that's what she wants and then I'll make sure she gets Nuovi Inizi back.

It's not her business that will work as leverage to keep her here. Though her move to force my brother to buy Nuovi Inizi and take on the financial responsibility for Leonardo's care is hella unexpected.

Lucia will stay because my plan to hold onto her has a lot more heft than my brother's. If I'm right, her pale face and obvious nausea have more to do with pregnancy than the stress of confronting my brother.

Ilios mou is not afraid of anyone.

"I told you," I remind her. "I will protect you."

"Like last night?" she scoffs.

"Yes. Getting Nuovi Inizi under the protection of *Ádis Adelfótita* is necessary to keep you and your employees safe." I'll protect her with my life, but that's not enough.

She doesn't want Nuovi Inizi used in human trafficking, even if she doesn't own it anymore. She cares too much about her employees and even the patrons. I can't protect the club and her alone.

I need my brotherhood behind me.

"Right." Her voice drips sarcasm. "Until they get arrested during a raid by the vice squad."

I remember what Zeus said to her about running sex workers out of the club. He was pissed, but he still shouldn't have said it.

"We'll use the strip clubs to run the a la carte sex trade," I inform Lucia with a glare for my brother. "We only use our nightclubs for the escorts to meet their client dates, for *their* safety. Transactions are never done on site."

"That's not what Zeus said."

"He was angry and pushing your buttons." My brother doesn't like his authority questioned.

He barely tolerates it from me and Orion.

If I know my brother, Zeus is angry that Lucia rejected me last night too. Even if he told me it served me right for letting my softer emotions rule me.

I told him to fuck off. There's nothing soft about what I feel for Lucia. It's hard, raw and primal.

Zeus does not need to protect me from Lucia or myself. Because I am not letting her go. She is *ílios mou* and I am not going back to the darkness.

"This time he threatened me. What happens the next time your *anax* gets angry? Maybe he drops me in it. I'm not going to let that happen." She sounds tired.

She was restless last night until I joined her on the bed. She thinks I came in there for my own sake, because of the short sofa, but I heard every toss and turn of her body.

Worried she would not get enough rest, I laid down beside her and took her into my arms. She settled immediately after that. No matter what she thinks she knows about me, her body trusts mine.

Her mind needs to get on board though. Or things are going to get awkward with the whole pregnant with my baby thing.

"That will never happen," I tell her. "You need to trust me to take care of you."

She stares at me with rampant disbelief. "You cannot be serious. I *do not* trust you and that isn't going to change now. Because now I know what you are and if there's one thing I've learned about made men, it's that I can't trust you to put my safety first."

"Who taught you that?" Zeus asks, mining for information.

That's my *anax*. Always looking for an angle to use. What he hasn't figured out yet is that I'm not going to let him use any angles against my woman.

"Besides your brother?" Lucia asks drily.

"Yes, besides Atlas."

I'm glad my brother doesn't try to argue that Lucia can trust me. She's stubborn and him getting in her face about it will only solidify her position.

She shrugs, her hand pressing against her stomach. "Who didn't?"

The nausea is getting worse. I need to look up remedies. Or take her to the doctor today. Yes, that's a better idea. They'll make time for her at the clinic.

The head of the clinic started his practice in L.A. with a loan from *Ádis Adelfótita*. He knows the importance of not crossing my family.

"That's not an answer," my brother pushes.

I stand up. "Leave it." I cross the room to Lucia. I can't watch her struggle with discomfort from a distance.

"I don't owe you an answer," she says to Zeus, pretending not to notice my approach.

That's better than her running away.

"Tell me anyway."

"That's something else you Rokos men have in common. You're all pushy." She looks at me now, censure glinting in her brown gaze.

"Then you know you might as well answer my question."

Lucia sighs. "My father, my brother, my husband, my father-in-law, and the list goes on. Every single mafia man who had a chance to put me first didn't." Her eyes catch mine and don't let go. "Including you."

She's wrong. Like last night, she's dismissing the truth of how precarious Nuovi Inizi's position is with at least two syndicates vying for territory.

The Russians are gone. For now. We can't trust the *pakhan* not to try again with bigger numbers though.

"Do we have a deal?" Lucia asks Zeus, her voice strained.

"Yes." My brother reads through the papers in front of him and then sends a text. "I will pay for Leonardo Revello's care in the facility, but his don deserves to know where he is."

"What?" Lucia jumps up and shoves past me to glower down at my brother across his desk. "You can't tell him. Even if Don Russo is willing to leave my brother-in-law where he is, Lenny's grandfather won't be. Agustino Sr. was a stickler for keeping it in the family, but his father is militant about it. He's totally old school."

"Lenny has a living grandfather and you've had sole responsibility for his care since his father's death?" I put my hand on the small of Lucia's back.

For a single breath, she leans back into me. But then she pulls away and shrugs. "I told you, his grandfather is old school. I wouldn't put it past him to kill Lenny to protect the Cosa Nostra."

"His own grandson?" Zeus asks.

"Considering your grandfather's protection of the Hades Brotherhood is the reason your brother's back is riddled with scars, I'm surprised you have to ask that question." Lucia casts a concerned glance at me.

Like she's worried I'll be hurt by her bringing up the scars. I'm not surprised she figured out the real circumstances behind my captivity, now that she knows the truth of my background.

I didn't lie to her about it. I left some stuff out. Like she did. My mafia princess.

She'll be the perfect wife for me.

After a perfunctory knock, Orion and Zephyr come into the office. Helios is right behind them.

"Let me look at the contract." Orion puts his hand out. "If everything is in order, Atlas and Zephyr will sign as witnesses and I will notarize it."

Zeus jerks his head in the affirmative.

"I need some air." Lucia spins around and pushes my cousins out of her way to get to the door.

I follow.

When we get in the hall, she looks to the right and to the left, her face creased with worry. "Which way?"

The bathroom. She's turned around and doesn't remember where it is.

I grab her hand and lead her to the guest bathroom closest to Zeus's office.

Lucia barely makes it to the toilet before throwing up bile. There is no food in her stomach because she skipped breakfast. I assumed she would have grabbed something before sneaking out of the apartment.

"You can't miss meals right now," I tell her.

She rinses her mouth with water from the sink. "Breakfast was not a priority for me this morning."

"No, stealing my SUV and meeting with my brother was."

"I *borrowed* it."

"Without my consent." She needs her own car though.

And as soon as I'm not sure she'll use it to run, I'll have Orion sign the title to his G-Wagon over to her.

"Do you see a chop shop anywhere around here? I didn't steal it, but I can drop it in one of the gang neighborhoods for you if you want."

My gut clenches. "You aren't going anywhere like that alone."

"You're not the boss of me." Wilted and leaning against the sink now, her words lack oomph.

"You keep thinking that."

"I know that. Even if I was still your girlfriend, you wouldn't be my boss."

"You're not my girlfriend," I agree.

She winces, hurt flashing in her dark eyes, but she ducks her head, hiding her reaction.

"You are *ílios mou*. You bring light into the darkness of my soul. You are the flame that burns there." I sound fucking poetic.

Her head snaps up, her eyes wide and disbelieving in her pale face. Then she shakes her head. "We are not talking about this right now."

Fine by me. No matter what Zeus thinks, I am not suddenly wrapped up in soft emotions. Acknowledging them once is enough.

"You didn't tell me you are mafia," she accuses.

I shrug. "Neither did you."

"I'm not mafia. Not anymore."

"You used the threat of Cosa Nostra involvement to get what you wanted from my brother. You're still mafia."

"You have an answer for everything." She doesn't sound impressed by that. "But what is your answer to my broken heart? That it shouldn't be broken."

I snap my mouth closed on my instinctual response, because that is exactly what I think. Her heart shouldn't be broken. If she trusted me, it wouldn't be, but according to her, it is.

That damn pain twinges in my chest again.

"I want to go home." She looks at me like she's waiting for something.

For me to move? That's not happening. She's fragile. She needs my support. "Don't you think we should go to the doctor first?"

"I don't need a doctor for stress nausea," she dismisses.

"Are you sure that's all it is? You've been tired the last few days and getting up later." I looked up symptoms of early pregnancy so I could watch for them.

She rolls her eyes. "I own a nightclub. Running it can be exhausting."

"Are your breasts tender? I noticed your areolas are darker. Your reaction last night and today could indicate hormonal based emotions."

She looks at me with confusion and then dawning understanding.

"You think I'm pregnant? And that's why I'm so angry with you?" Her voice rises steadily until she's almost shouting. "I'm angry with you because you betrayed me, not because I'm hormonal."

"Okay, but you have other symptoms of pregnancy. You haven't had a period since we met." That was eight weeks ago.

It only took a few seconds to realize I wanted her and one night to know I am never letting her go. And if I'm right, less than two months to get her pregnant.

The primal part of me is very satisfied by that fact.

"I...you...you got me pregnant on purpose!" She's definitely shouting now.

"Yes." I have made no attempt to hide my desire to do so.

"But I thought..." She shakes her head then the confusion disappears completely as her temper ignites. "You knew. You knew everything I didn't know and you got me pregnant anyway. You bastard!"

Every curvy inch of her vibrates with outrage.

Pain explodes in my cheek and my head snaps back. I don't expect the punch, or the shove that comes after so she can scoot around me to get out of the bathroom.

My feisty woman has a helluva right hook. I'll wear her bruise tomorrow.

I follow her down the hall whistling.

CHAPTER 38

LUCIA

The infuriating man is whistling again. I know this song. "Love is a Battlefield." Aargh!

I spin around and point at him. "Knock that off."

His brows raised, his handsome face the picture of innocence, or as innocent as a made man can look, he stops whistling. Shaking my head, I turn back around and stomp toward the front door.

The whistling starts again. It takes me until I reach the door to recognize it. "My Girl" by the Temptations.

Are you kidding me?

Refusing to give him the satisfaction of a reaction, I storm outside, only to stop at the SUV when I realize my purse and coat are still in Zeus's office. Along with the contract. That I still have to sign.

Porca miseria.

I don't know how long I stand there staring at the truck, telling myself I need to suck it up and go back inside to get my stuff.

Then the sound of whistling reaches me. He's still on "My Girl" like a smart speaker set on repeat.

"Why didn't you get in the truck? It's too cold to be standing around outside without your coat." Atlas sounds so dang reasonable.

Not at all angry I punched him in the face.

My hand still hurts. I shake it and wince. I'm not so lucky.

He notices. Of course, he does.

"You need to ice that. Here, put on your coat and then get into the truck. I'll be back with an icepack." He hands me my coat.

Avoiding looking at him, I take it and slide into the sleeves, grateful for the near instant warmth. It's a bright autumn day, but the air is chilly enough to cause gooseflesh to erupt on my arms.

I put my hand out for my purse. "My bag."

"Here." He holds it out toward me, dangling it from his big hand by the straps.

I reach for it, but he doesn't let go.

My gaze snaps to his face. There is a red mark on his cheek that will bruise, but no swelling that I can see.

His blue eyes are waiting to snag mine with that invisible tractor beam I swear he has. "There you are."

I roll my eyes. "Here I am. Now, will you let me have my purse?"

He releases it and because I'm tugging on it, I stumble back a step.

Reaching out, he grabs my arm. "Steady."

"Don't touch me." I jerk away.

His big body swells with affront, but he lets me go. "Orion said you can sign the contract tomorrow."

Of course, Atlas asked when he grabbed my coat and purse. He thinks of everything, except telling me who he really is before I find out on the other side of a demand for protection money.

"I'd rather get it over with." Though the idea of returning to Zeus's office makes my stomach roll again.

Atlas shakes his head. "He'll bring the contract by the club tomorrow. We have somewhere else to be."

What is he talking about? Then it hits me. The doctor. He wants to take me in for a pregnancy test. "I can just pee on a stick."

He hums, but I can't tell if he's agreeing or humoring me. "I'll get that icepack."

"Get one for your face too." I don't tell him it's not necessary. My hand is throbbing.

Besides, there's a chance I can get out of here the same way I arrived. Alone and driving his truck.

He heads back into the house without responding, probably thinking he's too tough to ice his cheek.

Men!

Disappointment makes my tender stomach clench, but there's no surprise as I dig through my bag only to determine that his keys are missing.

I could call a rideshare, but Atlas will be back by the time it gets here and will just follow me. If he doesn't scare the poor driver off all together.

He's intimidating on his best days. The Greek mafia enforcer pretty much only smiles around me. It took me a while to realize that, but the more I see him interacting with others, the more obvious it is.

Today is not one of his calmest. The driver might not recognize the leashed violence in Atlas's strong body, but her atavistic instincts will.

Why are so many rideshare drivers women? It feels like it wouldn't be the safest job to have.

And why is my mind taking me on a tangent?

Because I don't want to think about what Atlas pointed out in the guest bathroom.

I might be pregnant.

Even thinking the words fills me with stress, making the nausea rise again. Swallowing back the urge to retch, I force my mind away from an image of my stomach swollen with child.

Like I was before. Only this time, giving birth.

Dio mio. I have to stop thinking about this.

In desperation, I move toward the SUV. Feeling more than a little contrary, I consider climbing into the driver's seat. But I am also feeling lightheaded after my bout with nausea in the bathroom. Another symptom of pregnancy?

Don't go there. But my brain refuses to go anywhere else.

My hands come up of their own volition to press against my breasts. Tiny jolts of pain twinge through my generous mounds. Sighing, I pull my hands away.

They *are* tender and my bras are fitting more snugly lately.

What if I am pregnant?

Everything has changed since my epiphany that I still want to be a mother. I no longer own Nuovi Inizi, or won't once I sign the papers tomorrow, but neither am I responsible for the cost of Lenny's care.

With the sale of the club, I'll have enough to start over somewhere else. If I live frugally, I can even stay at home with the baby until he, or she, starts school. I will have to get a job at some point though.

None of this takes into account that I *didn't* visit a sperm bank to get pregnant. If I am pregnant, I have no doubt about who the baby's father is.

Atlas.

Moving away and starting over again would mean taking the baby away from him. Can I do that in good conscience?

No matter how angry I am at him, there is no world in which I allow my baby to pay for my mistakes.

What kind of father would he be? Protective. That's for sure. Bossy. That's a given. Will he expect our child to become part of the Hades Brotherhood, or marry to be advantageous to it?

One thing is certain. I may no longer be part of the Cosa Nostra, but I was raised in it. And I'm not afraid to raise my child adjacent to Atlas's life as part of the Hades Brotherhood.

I am terrified of what that means for me though. Will Atlas insist on marriage, if only for name's sake? He's Greek mafia. In the Cosa Nostra, certain old fashioned ideas are still rife.

If my father knew about my pregnancy, he would give Atlas two choices. Death, or marriage.

A shiver skates up my spine at the thought of my father and Atlas meeting. How would that even work? Do I call my parents and say, "Ta da, I'm alive?"

Questions whirl through my brain, one after the other until I start feeling sick again.

"Why aren't you inside the SUV?" Atlas demands.

I look at him. "What if I'm pregnant?"

"Then we will be parents."

"You make it sound so easy." For him, it probably is. "You don't have to carry new life inside your body." And worry if that life will survive to be born.

"I will worry about both you and the baby until you give birth safely. But I will protect you both with my life."

That's like a pathological thing with him. He sees protection money as an investment, not merely a payment for doing business in a syndicate's territory. My dad has the same attitude.

Papà says the mafia provides a service for what they charge their *clients*. Does Atlas see Nuovi Inizi as a client, or a cash cow?

It doesn't matter now, I remind myself. Because as of tomorrow, I will no longer own it. And in thirty days my obligation to the club and its employees will be finished.

Grief should be weighing me down, a sense of loss. I worked hard to build Nuovi Inizi into what it is, pouring my time and energy into it to the extent I have no life outside of the club. Not before Atlas anyway.

But I never wanted to own a nightclub. If I could have made enough money to support both Lenny and me with an office job and no crowds, I would have.

Opening Nuovi Inizi was the only legitimate way I knew to make enough money to pay for Lenny's care. Now, Zeus is responsible for the financial part of it.

Unexpected relief washes over me.

I'm not alone taking care of Lenny anymore, even if my partners in it are unwilling.

I will continue to personally oversee my brother-in-law's wellbeing. He's my family even if he doesn't want to see me. For whatever reason, being around me riles Lenny up. The doctors think it is wrapped up in the loss of my baby.

At first, that hurt. I gave up the life I knew and the rest of my family to protect Lenny. To keep my promise to my dead husband, if in a way he would not have expected or necessarily condoned.

But starting Nuovi Inizi took all my time and energy and being discouraged from visiting Lenny took away the guilt of not being able to.

I get weekly emails with pictures and a daily diary of his care and commentary about his mood, health and interactions. I make unscheduled visits to the facility every few months to check on my brother-in-law in person. Though he does not see me.

"Zeus won't tell Don Russo about Lenny, will he?" I ask Atlas as he opens the passenger door for me.

"No."

"You're sure?" My hand hurts and I don't want to use it. So, I sit back and allow Atlas to buckle my seatbelt like he usually does, doing my best not to breathe in his masculine scent. "He sounded like he might."

"He won't."

"Why are you so certain?" I expect Atlas to say because he knows his brother, or something.

What he actually says is, "I told Zeus I would kill him if he upset you by doing that."

The serious and determined note in Atlas's voice tells me he's not joking.

"You threatened to kill your brother?" My voice rings with disbelief I cannot hide.

"Yes." Atlas settles a cloth wrapped icepack on the back of my hand. "Hold this in place."

I do as he instructs because it's what is best for my hand, not because he tells me to. "But you wouldn't, and he has to know that."

As their *anax*, Zeus is the one person none of the Hades Brotherhood would consider killing. Especially his own flesh and blood.

"I would and *he* knows me well enough not to doubt that like you do."

"But the mafia comes first."

"No." He closes my door before I can respond to that ridiculous denial.

Once we are off the property, Atlas asks, "Why are you so determined to keep Leonardo in that facility? You implied him staying there keeps him free, but isn't it the opposite? Are you enacting your revenge against him for hurting you?"

"What?" I gasp. "No! I can't believe you think that of me."

"It's what I would do."

"Well, I'm not you."

"No. You aren't. You're filled with kindness and grace. I deal in cruelty and death."

"Is that how you *facilitate* for your family?" I ask with bite.

"Explain about Leonardo," he says without answering, but his silence is answer enough.

If he's in charge of racketeering for the Greek mafia in Portland, then he hurts people. Even kills them when necessary.

"He goes by Lenny."

Atlas shrugs, like Lenny's preference for what people call him doesn't matter. And I suppose it doesn't under the circumstances. Atlas will never meet my brother-in-law.

"When Tino and Agustino Sr. died, I became responsible for Lenny's wellbeing, not just his care. I had promised Tino to keep Lenny safe as if he were my own brother."

Atlas makes a sound of displeasure. He really doesn't like me mentioning my dead husband.

Possessive much?

Ignoring the little flare in my belly that thought gives me, I continue my story. "After Tino and his dad were killed and our house was blown up, Lenny and I were presumed dead. Incinerated in the blast."

"That explains how you got away from the Cosa Nostra, but not why you wanted to leave."

I'd already told him all the reasons, but not in connection to the action, so I spell it out for him. "First, the only way I could get Lenny the specialized medical help he deserved was to take him away. Second, I knew if I stayed in the Cosa Nostra, eventually, I would be expected to marry again. To make more Cosa Nostra babies."

"The Detroit Cosa Nostra are backward," Atlas says with judgment.

"The Detroit mafia, my family and the Revellos especially, have very traditional views of the roles for men and women. I was allowed to work, but only to get me over my grief after losing my baby." Tino would have expected me to quit my job as bookkeeper if I had gotten pregnant again.

"So, you ran?"

"Yes. Tino left me money in offshore accounts no one else knew about. It was his failsafe for me."

Atlas growls again.

"I was married once. He left me money to start a new life." Even if that was not how Tino expected me to use the money. "Get over it."

"What about Leonardo? How did he end up at the facility if you weren't trying to get rid of him?"

"Don't judge. Living with family isn't always best for someone with challenges like Lenny's. Living with me only agitated him. Hoping to figure out why, I took Lenny to a renowned clinic that specialized in traumatic brain injury."

"What did they say?"

"Lenny's diagnosis wasn't great, but it wasn't awful either. The damage to his brain meant that he would never mature emotionally past his current state, and he would always be prone to outbursts."

"That sounds all not great."

I like that he doesn't say bad because Lenny's condition isn't *bad*. It *is* challenging though.

"Untreated, his outbursts would grow worse and more frequent." I go silent, remembering how I felt when the doctor told me that. My fear for Lenny, my renewed grief for the loss of my baby, the result of one of those outbursts.

"I knew I wouldn't be able to keep Lenny safe, or the people around him on my own."

"You should never have been put in the position of needing to."

"That's easy for you to say, with your brothers and cousins to back you up." Even if I agree in principle, I don't tell Atlas that. "Regardless, there *was* treatment available. Inpatient treatment. The doctors were adamant. There could be no question that Lenny needed supervised living both for his safety and to ensure he got the most out of treatment."

"Did it work?"

"If you mean by work, did his moods and behavior stabilize? Yes. Lenny loves living there. He thrives under the supervised conditions. Lenny gets to spend more time doing things away from the facility than he was ever allowed to leave while living in the Revello home." In Detroit, he was a virtual prisoner.

In his current situation, he goes to the movies with friends. He shops at the game store and goes out to buy his own clothes.

"My brother-in-law is allowed every bit of autonomy he can manage without compromising management of his condition."

"Don't call him that."

"He's my family. I'm not going to pretend otherwise."

"Then call him brother."

"You're offended by me calling him my in-law?"

"It doesn't offend me. It fills me with rage."

The violence of his feelings should scare me. It doesn't. I know to my very core that Atlas will never physically harm me. Break my heart? He's already done that. So, yeah.

But break my person? Never. "Why does it make you angry?"

"It reminds me that you belonged to another man."

"Your caveman is showing again. I belong to myself."

"Yes," he agrees easily, surprising me. "But you are also mine."

And that last claim doesn't surprise me at all. Though it does exasperate me. "I told you, I'm not your girlfriend anymore. If I ever was. Not after last night."

"And I told you: you're something more important."

"Your sun. Your light." I sigh, frustrated with myself more than him because the claim touches me when it shouldn't.

Not after the way he used me.

"Yes." His tone leaves no room for argument.

But I'm good at wedging in places I shouldn't. "Can you use your light like a naïve fool?"

"I did use you to gain information and insight into the area," he admits without a tinge of remorse.

Glaring at him, I say, "I know."

"Stop frowning at me. I don't like it."

"Should have thought of that before you made me your dupe."

"You aren't my dupe or a fool," he says with all the exasperation I felt moments ago. "You are intelligent and knowledgeable enough to be a resource and an asset."

"Maybe you should be a spin doctor instead of a facilitator." He sure makes my gullibility sound like something better. "But believe it, or not, no woman aspires to be an information asset to the man she has allowed into her body."

"I didn't have sex with you for information."

"Yeah, right," I sneer.

"We made love because neither of us can keep our hands off the other. Your pussy is made for my cock. Your womb meant to carry my babies. My strength exists to protect and cherish you."

These damn maybe-pregnancy hormones. I swipe at my cheeks, but fresh tears wet them again. His use of the term *made love* robs me of my ability to think, much less retort coherently.

And the rest? The rest shatters something inside me, something I refuse to examine.

CHAPTER 39

ATLAS

"This is the wrong exit." They are Lucia's first words in ten minutes.

"No, it isn't."

She sighs. "It is unless you want to add twenty minutes of slow traffic on surface streets before we get to my club."

"Our club now," I remind her, pushing for a reaction.

I don't get one. "Whatever, you know what I mean. There's a pharmacy right off the exit nearest the club if you're wanting to stop and get a pregnancy test."

"Do you want to keep Nuovi Inizi?"

"That's no longer an option, and don't change the subject. Why did you take this exit?"

I am not trying to change the subject, but I want to know how she feels about selling her nightclub to us. "What if it was an option?"

"To keep the club?" she asks derisively. "We've been over this. I'm not laundering money for your mafia. I'm not running sex workers out of my club, even if it's their job of choice. I am not, under any circumstances, setting myself up to take the legal fall for you and your brothers."

"I will never let that happen."

"Two days ago, I might have believed you. Now, where are we going?"

Willing to leave the discussion for now, but not forever, I say, "I had Zeus call and make an appointment with an OB at the clinic we had our tests done."

"You told your brother you think I'm pregnant?" she practically shrieks.

"Fuck, Lucia. I could have lost control of the car with you shouting like that."

She snorts. "Not likely. I can't believe you told Zeus I might be pregnant."

"If you are, it won't stay a secret for long." Eventually, she'll start showing.

I wonder when. I didn't look that up. I have more research to do on pregnancy. A lot more if I want to keep her safe like I promised. That includes keeping her and our baby healthy.

I have a lot of questions for the doctor.

"It's not a secret," she huffs. "It's just *my* business."

"Our business." Lucia will not cut me out of our child's life, or her own.

Though I don't expect it to be easy to convince her of that. She took learning I am the head enforcer for our mafia badly. She never needs to know about my job as top assassin for the *Ádis Adelfótita*.

"Fine. *Our* business. But *not* your jerk of a brother's."

Her easy acceptance that I have an interest in her pregnancy loosens something in my chest that has been tight since the night before. "I thought you liked my brother."

"I did. He's a grump, but I liked Zeus." Sadness permeates her tone. "Before. Now, I know he never saw me as anything but a source of income and information. Like you."

I promised myself I would be patient with her, but this shit has got to stop. "I never said that."

"You didn't have to. Your actions said it for you. So did theirs. Zeus showed his true colors today."

"My brother is a short-tempered asshole on his best days." He used to be the charming one. Before the bratva killed his fiancée. "Today was not one of them. You blackmailed him into taking over the cost of Leonardo's care and it pissed him off. How did you expect him to act?"

Me promising to kill him if he told Don Russo about Leonardo's whereabouts, and by default Lucia's, only turned a bad mood into a vile one. But Zeus grudgingly admitted his threat was empty. He has no plans to tell the don.

"Oh, poor Zeus, having to do something he didn't want to. I wouldn't begin to know how that feels." She crosses her arms and stares out the window away from me.

"We all do things we don't want to, *ílios mou*."

"I'm not your sun."

"You bring warmth and light into my world even when you're mad at me."

"Stop saying stuff like that."

"No."

We drive in silence for a few minutes before she sighs. "I thought your brothers liked me too; it hurts to know it was all an act. Orion reminded me of Rocco and for a little bit I didn't feel so alone."

"My brothers do like you."

"You all put on a good show, I'll give you that."

Is her stubborn insistence on attributing the darkest motives possible to our actions from pregnancy hormones, or is it Lucia? My woman does have a temper and there's no signs of it cooling since last night.

Only time is going show her how wrong she is. "You said Rocco is dead."

Did she lie to me?

We know about the Revellos because they owned clubs that got taken over by the bratva. Information is power and we keep tabs on key players. That Tino Revello's wife and brother died in an explosion after his clubs got taken is also in our files. Who his wife was is not.

Now, I know it is Lucia. But I don't know what family in the Detroit Cosa Nostra she comes from. She's too smart to have gone back to her maiden name. That would make her too easy to track down.

"I didn't lie, but no, Rocco isn't dead. I said my brother is lost to me, like my parents. Which they are. I couldn't keep in contact with them and get Lenny away from the backward thinking mafia. My father would have insisted on Grandfather Revello making the decisions for Lenny's care."

"It's the way families like ours work. And you gave yours up to make sure Leonardo gets the treatment you think he needs. Why?" The promise she made to a dead man doesn't cut it.

"The day I lost the baby was as traumatic for Lenny as it was for me. He wanted me to have that baby so bad. Even more than Tino. He talked to my stomach all of the time. It destroyed him when his actions led to me losing the baby."

"How did he know they did?"

"He has the mind of a twelve-year-old, not a two-year-old. He lacks maturity and impulse control, but he can put two and two together. If he hadn't, his father made sure he knew. Agustino Sr. thought it would help Lenny control his rages to know what they cost the family. All it did was ensure that Lenny was as hurt by the outcome of that day as I was."

"Asshole."

"I didn't grieve his death like I did Tino's, that's for sure. And Agustino's father is even worse."

I don't need to hear how she grieved her asshole husband's death. He was as responsible for her pain and loss as her father-in-law.

"What will happen to you if your don finds out you've been hiding and keeping Leonardo hidden?"

"If you weren't lying, then he isn't going to find out."

Taking a second to control the anger her words elicit, I pull into the clinic parking lot.

"I was not lying," I bite out. "My brothers risked their lives as fucking children to rescue me when I was kidnapped, and I am prepared to kill Zeus if he rats you out to Don Russo."

Or at least make my brother wish he were dead. Not that Zeus will do that, threat, or no threat. But I had to have his vow and I used the threat of death to get it. Because it is important to Lucia.

"You wouldn't kill your brother." Her derisive tone scrapes my last nerve.

Getting out of the car, I don't bother to answer. She's determined to piss me off with her lack of trust. Showing some measure of self-preservation, Lucia waits for me to come around to open her door. My anger ratchets back a notch.

When she refuses to take my hand to get out of the SUV, it climbs right back up again. I grab her around the waist and lift her out of the truck.

She gasps. "That wasn't necessary."

"I disagree."

"You can be so infuriating."

"I do not have a corner on that market."

"Are you saying I annoy you?" She tries to avoid my hand.

But I catch hers and hold onto it. "Your determination to mistrust everything I say and do is pissing me off, yes."

"Poor you."

LUCIA

I realize the second the words leave my mouth that I've pushed Atlas a step too far.

His big body swells with the fury he's clearly been doing his best to bank and he yanks me around to face him. As angry as he is, he is still careful with me.

"No, Lucia, I am not poor, because I have no intention of going without."

I don't know how he gets that interpretation of poor, but we are so not going there. "If you thin—"

His mouth cuts off my words. The kiss is brutal, but my traitorous libido responds. I kiss him back, giving angry passion for angry passion until someone behind us clears their throats.

"Uh, if I could get inside." It's a woman's voice.

I try to jump back from Atlas, but he holds onto me, shifting us both out of the way of the heavily pregnant woman. One arm around my waist to stop me from moving, Atlas opens the door for her with his other hand.

She smiles her thanks and then winks at me. "Lucky you."

I don't feel lucky right now. My heart is one slice away from bleeding out. Knowing I am in love with a man who is only using me is devastating my usually resilient spirit. If I'm pregnant, Atlas is going to pretend to want me. I just know it.

"You don't have to pretend," I tell him. "I'm not going to try to keep you out of the baby's life if I'm pregnant."

"What exactly am I supposed to be pretending, *agape mou*?" he asks, his voice dangerously soft.

What does *agape mou* mean? Normally, I would ask, but not right now. Because I'm not sure I want to know.

"To want me," I answer his question.

He jerks my hand to the front of his jeans and presses it against the massive bulge there. "That is not a pretense."

"Atlas!" We're right in front of the clinic. "Anyone could see."

"Let them."

I try to jerk my hand away, but only succeed in sliding it down his erection. Heat burns in my cheeks. "Let go."

"No. Admit it."

"Admit what?" But I know.

"This is not fake. I am hard for *you,* and I don't care who knows it."

"Fine, you're hard for me. After the last two months, I'm convinced you can get hard in a stiff wind."

"Only if that wind carries your scent."

"You have to stop saying stuff like that."

"No, I don't."

"You're so stubborn."

"And you aren't?"

I shake my head. "Come on. Let's find out if our lives are permanently entwined."

"They're already that, *agape mou*. Believe it."

Taking a page out of his book, I don't bother to answer that provocative statement.

Thirty minutes later, I sit in stunned silence as the doctor tells us that I *am* pregnant.

"I didn't think I could get pregnant," I tell him.

"Why is that?"

When I explain, the doctor frowns. "We'll do an ultrasound and run some extra tests to see if there is anything to worry about. I would also like to see your medical files from your first pregnancy."

I curl my fingers into my palms in stress. The mafia doesn't recognize HIPPA guidelines and my previous obstetrician is a Cosa Nostra doctor. The private hospital where I lost the baby has ties to the mafia as well.

"You will need to sign a release, but we should be able to get them immediately," the doctor blithely continues, unaware of my growing agitation. "Unless your previous obstetrician does not have digitized files."

Atlas, who has been grinning at me since getting the news, goes rigid and shifts his now glacial gaze to the doctor. "You think her reproductive system could be compromised?"

"Honestly? From what Ms. Esposito has described, no. However, it is always better to err on the side of caution."

I agree. Of course, I do. I don't want to risk this baby's health in any way, but I don't want to reveal my whereabouts to the Detroit Cosa Nostra either. Much less the fact that I am alive.

But can I withhold my baby from my parents and brother? It's one thing to let them go on thinking I'm dead, but another entirely not to tell them about a grandchild.

My mother wanted to be a grandmother so badly the first time around. From social media, I know that my brother has not married yet and there are no grandchildren for my parents to dote on.

The weight of everything presses down on me.

"Do you have the equipment?" Atlas stands up, looming over the doctor's desk. "Or do I need to take her to the hospital?"

The silver-haired man makes an obvious effort not to lean away from Atlas. "We have the best ultrasound machines available here in the clinic, but your wife—"

"We aren't married," I rush to correct.

"Your...um...partner, needs to hydrate. If you could drink four cups of water over the next hour, Ms. Esposito, the ultrasound images will be clearer."

I remember how that full bladder feels with the ultrasound wand pressing down on my stomach and grimace.

Atlas frowns at me and demands, "Is that necessary?"

"If we want the best diagnostic results, yes."

"It's fine, Atlas. I've done this before."

"Water with no bubbles is preferred, but you probably remember that from your last pregnancy. You'll want to avoid carbonated beverages going forward to decrease the chance of painful heartburn."

"Where do you want to spend the next hour?" Atlas asks me. "Here or at a restaurant?"

"Here is fine."

"Get her some water," Atlas demands. "I have some questions for you while we wait."

The doctor stiffens at being ordered around, but he texts someone on his phone and a couple of minutes later, a woman comes in with a sixteen-ounce glass water bottle. It has the logo for the clinic on it and a pretty lavender lid.

Atlas has already started asking his questions.

Flipping the lid back, I drink from the water bottle, happy to discover the liquid is chilled, if not ice cold. Room temperature water is supposed to be better for hydration, but I don't like it.

Atlas is still asking questions when I indicate the empty water bottle to the doctor. He nods and puts his hand up to pause his discussion with Atlas.

Sending another text, he gives Atlas a bemused look. "You weren't joking when you said you had some questions."

"Why would I joke about something like that?" Atlas asks, his voice flat.

He really doesn't show much animation with other people. Unless you count intimidation.

"I don't remember ever answering as many detailed concerns with another spouse...uh, partner," the doctor hastily corrects at my glare.

The nurse comes in and takes my water bottle away.

"Do *you* have any concerns?" the doctor asks me.

I blink at him, still processing everything Atlas has asked and the doctor has answered. "I don't think so."

"Are you sure?" Atlas turns to me, his gaze probing. "Just because you have been through this before doesn't mean you won't have questions."

"Did you read that in a book?" I ask wryly as the nurse returns with my second sixteen ounces of water.

I take the bottle from her and immediately start sipping.

"It's in one of the brochures I read while we were waiting for the results." If Atlas is embarrassed to admit he read the brochures, it doesn't show.

Tino wouldn't have read them on a dare. And if he had read them, he never would have admitted it. Not macho enough.

Apparently, Atlas has no such issues.

"You have enough questions for both of us," I tease and then suck in my lips.

I don't want to be teasing him. Finding out I am pregnant does not undo his betrayal. What it does do is raise the question: why did Atlas want to get me pregnant in the first place?

And that is not a query I am going to make in front of the doctor.

CHAPTER 40

LUCIA

After I finish my water, we are led to a room housing a high-tech ultrasound machine. It has two screens and enough buttons and dials to double as a plane cockpit.

Atlas refuses to leave the room when the nurse instructs me to change into an exam gown.

"You're being unreasonable," I assure him.

He leans against the wall, a silent testament that he is not budging from the room. "I will turn away if you want, but I'm not going anywhere."

"What do you think is going to happen to me here?"

He raises his brow at me.

"Fine. Stay, but avert your gaze."

"Why? I have seen every inch of your body and tasted it too."

Not about to touch that statement with a ten-foot pole, I remind him, "You said you would."

His gaze burns into me for long seconds but then he turns his head. I quickly strip out of my clothes and put on the exam gown. It is open in the front but has enough fabric to wrap over itself and protect my modesty.

Which seems really important right now.

Ten minutes later, I realize that my modesty has nothing on Atlas's on my behalf.

"Transvaginal as in vagina?" he asks the doctor in clipped tones.

"Yes. And transabdominal refers to the ultrasound we will do via Ms. Esposita's abdomen."

"The fuck you are touching her vagina." Atlas moves his body between me and the doctor. "Get a female doctor in here."

"Mr. Rokos, vaginal exams will be a regular part of your wife's...uh..." He gives me an apologetic look. "Uh...partner's prenatal care. Nevertheless, the ultrasound will be performed by an ultrasound technician."

The doctor speaks patiently, like he expects Atlas to calm down once he is shown reason.

I have no such expectation. Now that I know Atlas is a mafia made man, so many of his idiosyncrasies make sense. The one thing the doctor should not expect is a rational response from my caveman when it comes to another man seeing, much less touching my most intimate flesh.

My caveman? No, *not* mine. But still very much a caveman.

"If you would be more comfortable stepping out of the room," the doctor has the lack of foresight to suggest.

Atlas grabs him by the shoulder and shoves toward the door. "The only man leaving this room is you. Get a woman doctor in here. Now. And if she can't perform the ultrasound either, you'd better get a woman technician too."

"While I appreciate your concerns..." The doctor is still talking when Atlas pushes him out of the room and closes the door behind them.

I can't hear what is being said through the door, but Atlas comes back into the room a few minutes later. "Their top female OB-GYN will be in shortly. She will be performing the ultrasounds and taking over your care."

"I never doubted it for a minute."

"If he touched your pussy I would have to kill him."

I roll my eyes. "Of course you would. How did I not realize you are a made man?"

"Knowing that you were raised in the mafia, it *is* strange that you didn't suspect anything."

His words flay my conscience and I sigh. There is nothing like willful ignorance. "I didn't put the pieces together, that's for sure. I didn't want to."

He cocks his head, like he's wondering about that but he asks, "Are you happy about the baby?"

"Yes."

"Even though I am the father?"

That is a question I'm not ready to answer. Atlas being my baby's father means I cannot walk away from him completely. That should not cause a flutter of relief in my heart.

Avoiding that emotional quagmire, I say, "You aren't the only one who decided not to use birth control."

"That's not an answer."

"Yes, it is. I am an adult and I take responsibility for my choices."

"And you chose to get pregnant with me."

"Yes." I trusted him too easily, but that is on me. "What I don't understand is why you chose to get me pregnant."

The door opens, interrupting whatever answer Atlas would have given. Part of me is thankful. I'm not sure I want to know if I'm a convenient womb to carry the next generation for the Rokos mafia.

A tall woman with long blond hair and wearing glasses comes into the room. "Hello, I am Dr. Lida MacGowen."

"MacGowen is an Irish name," I say suspiciously. Don't tell me that the Irish mob is moving in on Portland too.

"Yes, it is. And Esposito is of Spanish origin."

"Italian," I correct, still looking at her with suspicion.

Atlas cups my neck. "Relax, *ílios mou*, she's not part of an Irish syndicate," he tells me in perfect Italian.

"That day when I told you to get out of my house, you understood me fine," I accuse.

That triggers another memory. Him calling me good girl in Italian. I was so lost to passion, it didn't register then, but now I realize he's understood every word I've spoken in Italian since we met.

"Why didn't you tell me you speak Italian?"

"Calling you *brava regazza* didn't clue you in?"

"I was too far gone at the time to register it," I admit. But I remember now and I also remember how good it made me feel.

Why this man? Why does he have the key to my every lock?

"That is good to know," he replies in English, reminding me it is rude to carry on a conversation the doctor cannot understand.

"I apologize," I say to her.

"It's fine. It must be nice to be able to share a private conversation in front of others. But I didn't realize Rokos is an Italian name too?"

"It's not," I say.

"It's Greek," Atlas adds, pride infusing his tone.

"But you speak Italian?" she asks as she sets up the equipment.

"Yes." Atlas makes no attempt to explain.

The doctor doesn't seem offended. "We are going to start with the trans-vaginal ultrasound. It will give us a more detailed picture of certain parts of your reproductive system. It also offers the most likely chance of seeing Baby at this stage."

While it's small, the wand up my vagina is every bit as uncomfortable as I expect it to be. However, the 3-D image that comes up on the monitor is fascinating.

The doctor explains everything we can see, including a bunch of medical terminology that basically says I'm healthy and so are my reproductive organs. A whoosh-whoosh repeats in a rapid pattern.

The doctor smiles. "That's the baby's heartbeat."

Tears wash into my eyes as I grin up at Atlas. "Our baby."

I'm such a sap, but he looks utterly flabbergasted. "That is our baby?" he asks, like he didn't believe it the first time, or the second time, it was said.

"Yes." The doctor moves the wand inside me, clicks a couple of things on the space age instrument panel. "According to the measurements you are eight weeks along, Ms. Esposito."

"Eight weeks?" I ask faintly. That means I got pregnant the first time we had sex without a condom.

Like it was meant to be.

"I told you," Atlas says to me.

"You've told me a lot," I remind him.

"Your body was made to carry my baby. You got pregnant on the first try."

"We weren't trying that first time."

He shrugs.

"Your partner has a bit of the Neanderthal in him, doesn't he?" Dr. MacGowen asks.

"You have no idea."

~ ~ ~

Atlas calls his brothers to tell them about the baby as soon as we are back in his SUV.

"So, my brother knocked you up, huh?" Orion asks, humor lacing his tone over the vehicle's speaker system. "I guess you were doing more than playing Parcheesi on all those sleepovers."

"No, we played Monopoly."

"Pretty sure that's not how you got yourself a Greek bun in the oven."

"Half Italian," I reply with a snap.

"Don't Worry, Be Happy" is a low-level background noise as Orion and I trade barbs.

"Is my brother whistling?" Orion asks, his tone astonished.

I roll my eyes. "Yes."

"You sound happy brother," Zeus speaks for the first time.

"Can you doubt it?"

"Does this mean Lucia isn't planning to leave Portland after she trains a manager for Nuovi Inizi?"

"I will not withhold the baby from Atlas." My temper burns bright, but I'm not vindictive. "I am not that woman."

"That's good to know."

"Uncle Orion has a certain ring to it."

"Like a doorbell," I snark back.

"When are you going to introduce Lucia to your crew?" Zeus asks.

"They're waiting for us at the club."

That's news to me and butterflies start step-dancing in combat boots in my tummy. "I met three of them last night."

It's not a memory I want to hold onto.

"That was different."

"How many men are on your crew?" I ask.

"Three full-fledged members of *Ádis Adelfótita* and we are testing four more for potential initiation. They won't be at the club."

"You're recruiting for your crew? Why? Is the bratva fighting over territory?"

"Not now," Atlas replies.

Which is not reassuring because it implies they could be in the future.

"We have a truce with the *pakhan* in Russia. He has ordered his men out of Portland."

"Back to Russia? Or somewhere else nearby?" I ask.

"Good question," Orion says with grudging approval.

"Two of the men flew to Seattle, but the *pakhan* thinks we believe they all went back to Russia, or California." Atlas maneuvers around a slow car in the center lane on the freeway.

"California?"

"The Golubev Bratva have just over two months to sell or close their business and other assets before leaving the state," Orion adds. "They agreed to stay out of *Ádis Adelfótita* territory."

"And the Hades Brotherhood doesn't claim Washington as part of their territory."

"No, but British Columbia and Oregon are. There's only so much the bratva can do hemmed in from the north and south." Zeus's words imply the problem is taken care of, but his pensive tone indicates something else.

"We won't let them get to you," Atlas promises.

"Should I be worried?"

"No."

But I remember what Atlas said about the bratva coming to my club to shake me down. A frisson of fear makes the hairs on the back of my neck stand up.

As angry as I am at him and his brothers for doing the same thing, I don't fear them.

The bratva is something else all together. They showed no conscience, much less pity, when taking over Cosa Nostra territory in Detroit. They blew up my house, believing I was in it.

It was a different bratva family, but if the Golubevs approach bratva business the same way, I really do owe Atlas my gratitude for keeping them out of Nuovi Inizi.

I have no plans to tell him that though.

CHAPTER 41

LUCIA

"I'm surprised you took the time to assess my club too," I tell his crew when Atlas formally introduces me to them, letting them know I remember seeing them in the club before last night. "Atlas had access to everything."

Including the profit and loss ledgers for the Nuovi Inizi. What could his men add to his already minutia level knowledge?

Bobby puts his hand on the back of his neck and looks over to Atlas, who is giving his stoic face. "Uh, yeah. We weren't here for that."

Did they come to check out the woman their boss is...*was* banging?

"Why were you here then?" I dare them to tell me but they all stand there like silent robots.

Deadly robots if the aura they give off is to be believed. And I'm done ignoring my instincts.

I turn to Atlas. "Why were they here? Did they want to know what the woman you duped looked like?"

Atlas's jaw ticks and I am ridiculously pleased with myself for getting to him so easily.

"No, ma'am." Michael's hair is cut short, a high and tight like a Marine's and he talks like one too.

Ma'am. For crying out loud.

"Then why?" I demand.

"We were here to protect you when the boss was out hunting those bratva bastards," Bobby blurts out.

He's the youngest and most impulsive of their little group.

I shoot a glance toward Atlas, but he's letting his men speak for themselves. He's made it clear that as long as they don't get too close, he wants me to get to know them.

"We weren't the only ones watching over you," Theo adds when I don't respond to Bobby's revelation.

Why is he telling me this? Atlas's crew should be more circumspect, shouldn't they? They're doing their version of talking their boss up.

A tendril of warmth unfurls inside me. His crew wouldn't want to talk him up if they didn't think he wanted me. Which means they never thought he was banging me for information.

Putting that away to take out and examine later, I turn to Atlas. "Hunting?"

He shrugs.

"Atlas is the Golubev Bratva's *palach*." Bobby's youth shows in his enthusiastic hero worship of his boss. "No one has ki—"

"The guys will be with you when I am not," Atlas says, cutting Bobby off.

Theo smacks Bobby on the back of the head and the younger man turns on him instantly, his entire demeanor changing. Gone is the affable young man proud of his boss's accomplishments, whatever they are, and in his place is a stone cold killer.

"The fuck?" Bobby demands.

Theo barks something at Bobby in Greek and the other man's eyes widen. He looks from me to Atlas and then back at me again.

He asks Atlas something in Greek.

Michael simply stands in stoic silence during this interaction, his attitude one of watchful readiness. I'm not sure what he's watching for in a closed nightclub, but his behavior is familiar.

Maybe if the Detroit Cosa Nostra had men like that on their payroll, that final night in Detroit would have gone differently. But Augustino Sr.'s men were like his son. Fourth or fifth generation mafia with an attitude of entitlement and certainty no one would be brazen enough to storm their kingdom.

They'd been wrong and unprepared for warfare when it came to them. Atlas will never be caught unaware like that. The fact he went hunting for the bratva, rather than waiting for them to try to attack him and his brothers shows how different he is from the Revello men and my former don.

Atlas shakes his head. "English from now on, when Lucia is around."

"Unless we need to keep things private," Theo says.

It's not a question, but Atlas nods.

Maybe it's time I learn Greek. I give Atlas a sugary sweet smile that makes him flinch.

"It's a good thing we aren't a thing," I say conversationally. "I don't want to be part of a world again where I don't have a voice because I have ovaries."

Even if those ovaries go gaga over Atlas. His eyes narrow, tension emanating from his big body.

"That's our cue to leave. It was good to meet you under less stressful circumstances, Lucia. When you can't get ahold of Atlas, call one of us. We'll be watching out for you." Despite the evidence of last night, Theo is clearly the charmer of this crew.

"I don't have your numbers."

"I put them in your phone," Atlas says without the slightest qualm.

Putting my hand out, I say, "Give me your phone."

He doesn't hesitate, opening it before he hands it to me.

Shock at his easy capitulation surging through me, I grab the phone and open his contacts. It only takes a minute to add Willow, Barry and my head server to them.

"What are you doing?" Bobby asks when Atlas doesn't.

"Putting the staff manager, bar manager and head of security for Nuovi Inizi in Atlas's contacts." I smack Atlas's phone back into his hand. "Tit-for-tat."

"Are you going to go through my computer too?" he asks, understanding immediately what I mean.

"Yes. When I'm done, I will have invaded your life as thoroughly as you have invaded mine." It's not an empty threat and I hope he knows it.

"Good."

He doesn't mean that. He can't. But the challenging expression in his blue eyes defies me not to believe him.

"I am not going to shut up and have babies," I warn him. "And I'm not going to marry you because I'm pregnant."

One marriage for duty's sake is enough in any lifetime. I might have loved Tino by the time we married, but I realized after losing the baby that he never loved me.

He married me to continue the Revello line. Out of both duty and necessity. Agustino Sr.'s uncle had lost his position as capo because he and his wife hadn't been able to have children.

That's how Agustino became a capo and took over running the clubs. Tino made it clear he wasn't going to let that happen to him.

If I get married again, it will be because the man I'm marrying loves me.

We aren't in the Cosa Nostra and I'm not a good little mafia princess anymore. Even if the father of my baby is the nephew of the freaking Godfather of the Night for the Greek mafia on the west coast.

"Good to meet you, Lucia." Bobby is backing up fast, Theo and Michael moving right along with him. "See you later, boss."

They leave via the hallway to the backdoor.

Atlas's focus is 100% on me though. "Make no mistake, *eromenis mou*, you will marry me. If I have to kidnap you, fly you to Vegas, roofie you and get married with the fucking video package as proof of the deed. You're my woman and the child inside you is my child."

That absolutely should not turn me on and make my heart pitter-pat. Should not. So, why does it?

"Not if it means going back to being a mafia princess who is seen and not heard," I snap right back.

"The Cosa Nostra in Detroit might be stupid enough not to value your smarts. But I appreciate your brain as much as I incessantly crave your body."

"Your mafia might be Greek, but you can't tell me they're so different from the Italians, not with your crew slipping into Greek to protect the *little woman* from knowing too much."

"Protection is right. The less you know, the less of a target you are."

"That's not why you cut Bobby off when he was talking. What kind of hunting do you do? What does *palach* mean?"

"You don't want to know."

"Oh, but I do," I assure him.

"Leave it alone, Lucia."

"Not going to happen. You've been picking my brain for weeks. Now it's my turn."

"I never pushed you to tell me something you didn't want to."

"Are you saying you never will because I don't believe you. Either this thing goes both ways or it doesn't go at all." Darn it. I didn't mean to imply there is a *thing* between us, but I'm not taking the words back either.

"Dimios." He heads toward the door to the upstairs.

"What is dimios?"

"Who I am."

Dimios is a name? "Why do you have so many names?" Dimios. Palach. They have to mean something. That's how it works in the mafia.

Without answering me, he stops at the door and waits for me to key in the code to unlock it. Atlas, or is it Dimios? Whichever, he makes no effort to hide that he's watching the movements of my finger over the keypad with keen interest.

Since he can pick the lock as easily as use the code, I don't bother trying hide which buttons I press.

Standing in my apartment, for the first time, the space feels too small with him in it. He won't be here long, I soothe myself. But we do have things to discuss. Like the baby and what having a child together will look like for us.

"Sit down. Do you want tea?"

Slipping out of my coat, I lay it over the back of the sofa. "I would rather have coffee."

"Caffeine isn't good for the baby."

I sigh. "I know. Herbal tea is fine."

I don't know why I'm letting him act like a host in my apartment, but I'm suddenly tired. The last two days catch up to me and I flop down onto the sofa.

He fills the electric kettle with water. "Dimios means executioner in Greek."

Ah, so not a name so much as a title? "What does *palach* mean?"

"I dispense justice."

By dispense justice does he mean punish, or kill? Dimios-slash-executioner implies the latter. But what does *palach* mean exactly?

A cold chill works its way down my spine. "That sounds like you're more than an enforcer."

He shrugs.

"Are you? More than an enforcer?" I press.

He's silent so long, I don't think he's going to answer, but then he says, "Yes."

"What more?"

"I am the executioner."

"For who? Enemies of the Hades Brotherhood?" I guess.

"Sometimes. The Golubev Bratva is the syndicate that kidnapped me when I was ten."

Air whooshes out of me as I process this. He's saying that he dispenses justice on his own behalf too, killing his enemies. The tattoo on his back makes so much sense now. A Greek Spartan warrior conquering the symbol of Russia, a bear.

Wait. Another truth hits me. "The same bratva that you just made a truce with?"

"Yes. They wanted to make turning over the *palach* part of the terms."

"*Palach* is Russian for executioner, isn't it?" A picture is starting to form and despite his betrayal, my heart hurts for the little boy he was and the killer he became.

"I started when my uncle and brothers came to save me. I made my first kills that night."

"You were only eleven!"

"Yes."

"When did you start executing them again?"

"I never stopped. I hunted the Golubev Bratva soldiers who participated in my torture over that year first. I learned my skills on the backs of their corpses."

Atlas began slaying his enemies at the age of eleven and never stopped.

"Are there any left?"

"Of the men who kidnapped and hurt me? No. Golubevs? Obviously, yes. I only killed bratva connected to my capture, or ones who tried to do business in our territory."

"Killed. That's what Michael was going to say."

"Yes. No one has killed more bratva than me."

I shiver. "Who named you Dimios?"

"Constantin."

"Your uncle."

"Yes. For the first few years, only he and my brothers knew what I was doing. Later, when Constantin took over as *Nonós tis Nýchtas*, he made me an official assassin for *Ádis Adelfótita*."

Legitimizing what his nephew was doing anyway. "He was protecting you."

"Yes."

"If your grandfather knew you were doing unsanctioned killings, you would have been punished."

"I would be dead."

A man who left his ten-year-old grandson in the hands of monsters for a year would not have hesitated to kill that same grandson for disobedience. For some in the mafia disobedience equals betrayal.

"I don't want to live in the mafia world again." That brutal world where a child is sacrificed for power and the broken man he becomes could be killed by his own people for seeking the vengeance due him.

"I am sorry."

Because he knows I have no choice. I can remain "dead" to my family in Detroit, but because the baby inside me is Atlas's, I will always be connected to his Greek mafia.

"Why did you *want* to get me pregnant?" I don't get it. The consequences are lifelong for both of us. "You were fucking me for information. Why connect our lives inexorably like this? What was the point?"

"The point was keeping you. Pregnancy is an unbreakable bond between us."

I shake my head in useless denial. This man sees only one way forward. To take what he wants and keep it by whatever means necessary. He's utterly ruthless.

He wanted me locked down. So, he went for the jugular in terms of cementing our relationship.

Knocking me up. "You said you were sorry."

He nods, clearly unwilling to repeat the words.

"If you were really sorry, you would have given me a choice. You would have told me about what you are before getting me pregnant."

"You got pregnant before either of us made a conscious decision. I am not sorry I got you pregnant. I am sorry you don't want to live in my world."

"But I can't leave it."

He hands me the mug of tea. "No."

"What if I ran? I disappeared from one crime family. I can do it again." Especially without having to worry about Lenny's long term care.

"If you run, I will follow."

"To drag me back." I curl my legs up under me. "I don't know how many men you have killed, but you've done a great job of assassinating my future."

"I won't drag you back."

I don't believe him. "What then?"

"My role as Dimios is not locked into a geographical location."

Is he saying what it sounds like? "You're saying you would chase me, to what...visit your child?"

"I am keeping you."

It's not the first time he's said it, but maybe it is the first time what he means is truly sinking in. "But what about your brothers?"

"I wouldn't be able to continue as their head enforcer."

"You would leave your family for me?" I shake my head decisively. Not possible. "I don't believe you."

"We'll work on that."

CHAPTER 42

LUCIA

Orion brings the contract for me to sign the next day as well as his cousin Helios to begin training as my replacement. The club isn't open on Monday, so I start Helios on learning inventory and suppliers.

Atlas isn't happy when I sign the papers, but I ignore his brooding presence.

Over the next week, teaching Helios the ropes of running Nuovi Inizi goes surprisingly smoothly. He picks things up quickly and gets along with the staff. By the end of the week, I'm convinced it won't take a full month to train him.

Atlas is always here and when he's not, one of his crew is. He doesn't bring up marriage again though.

Which does not disappoint me.

I'm not great at lying to myself and can't help wincing at that whopper. No matter how angry I am at him, how used I feel, the thought of building a life without him, or having him only on the periphery is way too depressing.

"Doesn't Atlas trust you?" I ask his cousin.

Helios shrugs. "Sure, but he knows my focus isn't your safety."

So, Atlas makes sure someone is always here that sees my safety as a priority. Because of the baby?

What else am I supposed to think?

Other than his threat to kidnap and marry me, we haven't discussed what being coparents will look like. As determined as he is to invade every aspect of my life, when I start asking questions about the future, there is always someone, or something else, that needs his attention.

Every night I go to bed alone, but every morning I wake up wrapped in his arms.

The first morning, I cut up rough about it, but Atlas pointed out that like the night before, I didn't fall into a deep sleep until he joined me. I still don't invite him to sleep with me. I don't even invite him to stay on my sofa, but Atlas does what he wants.

He doesn't initiate sex. Neither do I. No matter how out of control my ovaries are from my pregnancy hormones. I know why I don't, but I don't know what is holding him back.

He's already proven that I'm easily seduced by him. I might think he doesn't want me anymore, but when I wake up in his arms it is always with his raging hard erection pressing into my back too.

"Shit, cousin, you need to get laid," Helios says after Atlas bites his head off about asking me to order the craft beer for the weekend.

Atlas glares at me.

"What did I do?" I demand.

It's not my fault that Shawn is interested in me. I don't do anything to encourage him. Not that he is as pushy lately. In fact, if I am there when he makes a delivery, he keeps a wary eye on Atlas and respectful distance from me.

"I think it's what you won't do," Helios says. "Have you cut my cousin off since we took over your club?"

"One, my sex life or lack thereof, is none of your business. Two, you didn't take over my club. I sold it to Zeus."

The look Helios gives me says he doesn't see the difference. But there is one. I took my fate into my own hands and forced Zeus to buy the club with the stipulation that Lenny would always be taken care of.

I am not powerless.

"You ready for lunch?" Atlas asks me, his tone clipped.

"Wow, how can I turn down such a charming offer?" I roll my eyes. "Yes, I'm ready."

The best way to control my nausea after waking is to snack throughout the day. If I don't each lunch soon, I'll need a granola bar, or something if I want to maintain my new normal.

"Let's go upstairs." Atlas lifts a to-go bag from my favorite Italian restaurant up.

"When did you get that?" I follow him up to my apartment.

"I had Bobby pick it up."

"Thank you."

He grunts.

I shake my head, having to stifle a weird urge to smile. He's kind of cute cranky. Knowing he's in a bad mood because of me is just a bonus.

Again, not powerless.

We plate the food together and Atlas puts it on the table while I get us both a drink. "Cranberry-cherry juice okay?"

He shudders. "Water is fine."

I hide my smirk. He doesn't like any form of cranberry juice, but it's my favorite drink.

After placing both beverages on the table, I sit down.

"When are you moving into your house?" he asks.

The impulse to smirk, much less smile, leaves like a puff. "I'm not."

"What do you mean you aren't? Did something go wrong with one of the repairs?"

Looking away from him, I swallow back emotion at the loss of my dream. "I canceled the purchase."

"Why?" he growls.

"Why the heck do you think?" Now I meet his eyes, my own filled with the temper coursing through me. "I couldn't afford it once you decided to take a cut of Nuovi Inizi's profits."

"But you sold the club to us. You have enough to buy the house outright now."

"I had already texted my realtor to cancel the sale when I realized the only true option was to sell the club to your brother."

"It wasn't your only option."

I give him a look that says, *right*. "My only safe option."

"I will never let you be the fall guy for our business," he practically shouts. "That was never the plan. You can run Nuovi Inizi and I will always keep you safe."

Jumping up from the table, he starts pacing in the tiny confines of my kitchen.

"That's not the only reason."

He stops and glowers at me. "What else?"

"I didn't think I was pregnant and had no intention of staying in Portland after I trained Helios."

"Where were you going to go?"

"Does it matter? Away from here."

"Because of me."

No reason to sugarcoat it. "Yes."

"And now?"

"Now what?" I don't know what he's asking.

"Are you going to run?"

"What would be the point? You already said you'd come after me." And no way am I escaping the Hades Brotherhood's assassin.

He's a hunter. His men said as much.

I have no intention of becoming prey.

"You hate me."

Do I? "A week ago I would have agreed," I admit.

"But now?"

"Now, I've spent the last week only sleeping well when you sneak into my bed. You take care of me and it's not all about what's best for the baby. You rub my feet and tell your cousin to figure stuff out himself when it is my job to teach him."

"But none of that changes that I used you to get information."

"No." I sigh. "None of that changes why we met."

"Does *why* we met matter so much?"

That's the million dollar question I've been asking myself. "You hurt me."

"I didn't mean to."

"Maybe not, but I don't think it would have mattered to you if you realized what the outcome would be."

"The hell it wouldn't have. If I knew asking for a protection tithe would cost me you, I never would have done it. I would have protected you and your club no matter what. You have to know that."

Part of me does, but part of me is still struggling with it. "I want to believe you because it hurts thinking it was all about using me."

"It wasn't." He drops on his knees in front of me. "Damn it, Lucia, the second I saw you, I knew you were mine. Maybe that's where I messed up. I thought you had to feel something that strong too."

"I did," I admit, my voice hoarse with emotion.

"Then why the hell do you doubt me when I say I will leave my brothers to be with you? That I will protect you with my life? I will never let you be hurt."

"Because no one has ever put me first like that. They're your family."

"*Agape mou*, you are my sun." He grabs both sides of my face and presses our foreheads together. "You are my future."

I want to believe him so badly, it scares me.

~ ~ ~

Two days later, Atlas takes me out to the parking lot. "I have something for you."

When we get outside, there is a metallic silver Mercedes parked near the back door. A soft chirp sounds and the quiet snick of door locks disengaging follows.

Atlas holds a black key fob with the silver Mercedes logo in the center out to me. "It's yours."

"You bought me a car?" Shock and excitement course through me. The luxury sedan is beautiful.

"I won it from Orion in a bet, but I had it detailed so his cologne won't assault you every time you drive."

He talks like his brother wears some cheap aerosol spray crap. When in fact, like everything else in Orion's life, his cologne is expensive and classy. However, Atlas knows my nausea can be triggered by smells.

So far, that doesn't include sophisticated men's colognes, but he's not taking any chances.

"What kind of bet gets you a car?" Unable to help myself, I open the driver's side door and peek inside.

The custom grey leather interior is pristine. I inhale. Atlas is right. I don't smell his brother's cologne. Or anything. Nothing to trigger the pregnancy nausea.

Nice.

"It was about how efficiently I can do my job."

Considering what Atlas's job is, I don't ask for more details. "Were you going to give him your BMW if he won?"

"No. He wanted dinner with you."

"Atlas!" I glare over my shoulder at him. "You cannot bet my time."

"You like to cook."

"That's not the point."

"I knew I would win, so it wasn't really a bet," Atlas dismisses.

"I'm surprised your caveman nature didn't balk at promising your brother dinner alone with me, even if you were confident you'd win."

"I never said it would be alone."

That sounds more like the Atlas I know.

"Whatever." I slide into the driver's seat and adjust it to fit my frame. "No more bets about anything to do with me."

He shrugs. Which is not a promise. "It got you an armored car nine months before a new one could be delivered."

His tone says it all worked out so what is my problem?

"Is Orion driving a regular car?" I ask, worried. "Is that safe?"

He's the family lawyer, which makes him a target on two fronts.

"Don't worry about my brother," Atlas grumps, his possessive nature reasserting itself. "He's fine. He can drive one of the security vehicles until his new car arrives."

CHAPTER 43

LUCIA

A few days later, I am working in my office on payroll.

It's not something I need to teach Helios. He'll be using a bookkeeper going forward. So far, they haven't recruited anyone local with the skill set. For now, the payroll and monthly bookkeeping will be done by someone in California.

The Hades Brotherhood can't hire a regular accountant any more than the Cosa Nostra can. With the mafia, there are always two sets of books. Those for the tax man, and those for the syndicate with record of all money laundered through the club and where it came from.

I haven't suggested myself for the job because I'm still wary. Bookkeeping is a lot safer than running one of their front businesses, but there is still risk. Lessened significantly if the Rokos brothers protect me, like Atlas promises.

I want to trust him, but I'm scared that if I do, he'll hurt me again.

Both our secrets are out in the open, but I wait for the other shoe to drop. Are there still things I don't know about him? Will Atlas start treating me like Tino now that I'm pregnant?

Chance of rain, less than 20%.

My ruthless enforcer still asks my opinion about things, even though the Hades Brotherhood have made their move to secure territory and taken over my club to do it.

So does Zeus. Which is weird. He can be a jerk when challenged, but apparently one that respects my intelligence. He even told me he would never threaten to run sex workers out of Nuovi Inizi again and that he shouldn't have done it the first time.

It's not an apology, but it's an admission of wrongdoing by a man with the same authority and power as a don.

Orion is the same snarky man with the typical god complex of an influential lawyer. He doesn't tell me he's sorry. He tells me to stop dicking his brother around and to get over myself.

The attitude is so much like Rocco that I start to cry. Orion gives me an awkward hug to comfort me and tells me not to be such a crybaby. It's like these Rokos men are intent on proving that I'm part of their family, whether I like it, or not.

"Hey, boss, you look pensive." Willow stands in the doorway of my office, or rather Helios's office.

"Come in sit for a minute." Other than announcing the change in ownership to the employees, I haven't talked to Willow about what's happening.

She relaxes in the chair closest to my desk, no stress or anger evident in her posture. "I guess you weren't loaning your boyfriend money that night, huh?"

I shake my head. "Not exactly, no."

"At first, I worried you were being coerced into selling. You worked so damn hard to make this place a success." Willow eyes me thoughtfully. "But every day that Helios takes on a little more responsibility, you get more relaxed."

"I do?" It surprises me she can tell. I put a lot of effort into hiding my real emotions behind an even-tempered façade.

"Not sure anyone else has noticed, but I've worked for you since you opened this place."

I nod, encouraging her to go on.

"In the beginning, I saw how hard it was for you to deal with the crowds and the noise. You tried to hide it, but it was there in a tightness around your eyes. The way you never wanted to socialize outside of work because you needed time to regroup away from people."

That isn't the only reason I hold myself distant from Willow and the others, but it is part of it.

"You don't think I'm being forced to sell?" I ask, to make sure.

Atlas and his brothers don't need that kind of gossip spreading about them.

"Nah. The more I think about it, the more this move makes sense for you. Besides, that overgrown boyfriend of yours is way too protective to let anybody push you into doing anything you don't want to."

"I'm not exactly a shrinking violet," I argue. "I can stand up for myself."

"Absolutely. Still, it doesn't hurt to have someone like him gaga over you."

"How is everyone doing with the transition?" I ask.

Willow shrugs. "Helios is a cool guy. A little scary sometimes, but I feel like that's a common family gene."

I can't help laughing. "Agreed."

"As long as you're happy, Lucia, we're all doing great. Helios said they want to open more Nuovi Inizis around Portland. They'll be looking for management and I'm keen."

The Hades Brotherhood are going to open other clubs under the Nuovi Inizi name? Not Zesti? I remember Atlas said they wanted to make their own way, but building on what I started is still a very cool thing for them to do.

Warmth expands inside my chest.

Why didn't Atlas tell me? Not that we talk about a whole lot lately. He's busy training new mafia guys. There are a lot more members of the Hades Brotherhood hanging around the club than I even realized were living in Portland.

"I'm glad you're happy about the transition. It's the right thing for me," I tell Willow. "But I didn't want to leave you all in the lurch."

"You so haven't. Helios made it clear that no employee you hired gets fired unless they screw up. Even though they've got their own people, they're finding places for all of us here, or in the new clubs."

"That's good to know." And something I wish Atlas had told me.

He's drawn back into the shell I didn't even know he had until our fight. He's so careful with me, but there's a barrier between us and I'm not sure how to take it down. I've only realized in the last couple of days that I want to.

Very much.

After my chat with Willow, Atlas finds me and tells me it's time for lunch. Today, he has grilled chicken salad and breadsticks ready for me when we get upstairs.

After we finish eating, he herds me toward the bedroom like he has every day for the past two weeks. Atlas expects me to nap, which is ridiculous. I'm not a child, but somehow, I always fall asleep and wake up feeling better. I don't get as tired at night while the club is open either.

I have a feeling that as soon as Helios is fully trained on closing, Atlas will suggest I go to bed earlier. By suggest I mean, carry me up the stairs if I don't go of my own volition.

Like the caveman he is.

I walk into the bedroom and stop short, my breath seizing in my chest.

Crimson leather cuffs sit in the center of my bed with a sleep mask in the same color beside them. My heartbeat stutters.

There is a message here, not just in the presence of the cuffs and blindfold, but in the color of them. Atlas had to have bought them special and he knows what crimson symbolizes to me. Courage.

Atlas is asking me to be brave. To take a risk. On him. On us. He stands so close behind me that I can feel the heat of his body. My thighs clench. My nipples ache. My lips part for kisses that haven't been offered, or welcome, in two long weeks.

Big hands cup my shoulders, their warmth seeping into me. "It is time for you to remember that you trust me, *agape mou*."

"What does that mean? *Agape mou*?" I ask him, finally ready to know.

"My love." He pulls me back against him and wraps his arms around my front. "Some people use it like darling, but I have never called another woman *agape mou*."

Does that mean he loves me?

"You want to have sex."

He thrust his hips forward a little so his hard erection presses into my back. "What gave me away?"

Wrapping my arms with his, I sigh softly. "I'm afraid."

"Of the handcuffs?" he asks, his tone heavy with emotion.

"Of being hurt again."

"I cannot promise not to hurt you, *ílios mou*. My soul died a long time ago. You resurrected it, but that doesn't make me perfect. Or even a different man."

Something in his voice tells me he wishes that were not the case. But I don't want a different man. I want the heart of the one holding me right now.

"I bet you called my OB and confirmed which sex positions are okay for me right now."

"I did, but then I called another doctor too."

"Why?"

"Doctor MacGowen isn't a fan of anal."

My whole body flushes. "You want to..." I let my voice trail off, unable to give voice to the tantalizing picture in my head.

It's not something I ever wanted with Tino, but my panties are soaked from thinking about Atlas touching me in that forbidden place.

"Take your ass? Yes. I want to own every part of your body, Lucia."

"And the other OB said it is okay?"

"I talked to six of them and all of them said yes as long as we go slow, use lots of lube and stretch you so there is no chance of tearing. Like I wouldn't do that anyway. What kind of monster hurts his woman when he's claiming her body?"

Uh...the kind that she asks to? I don't know, but I do know some women love pain with pleasure and others hate it and I'm somewhere in between. Though I doubt I would ever be okay doing anal without lube.

And right now? Pregnant?

I'm totally on the side of caution and care. "Okay."

CHAPTER 44

ATLAS

"Okay."

Lucia's voice hits me in the solar plexus with the power of a punch. She is saying yes.

"To the blindfold?" I need to confirm.

"Yes."

"To the handcuffs?"

Her body shudders. "Yes."

"To me claiming your ass?" Every muscle in my body goes taut waiting for her answer.

"*Yes.*"

I don't wait for her to change her mind. Pulling her top up and over her head, I start undressing her.

Her hands come behind her to pull at my belt, her fingers brushing over my rigid cock.

I groan. That feels good.

The clasp on her bra releases with a flick of my fingers and I peel the sheer, stretchy fabric away from her generous curves. "You know how much this bra turns me on."

"Mmm hmm." She's still trying to get my belt unbuckled.

I'm enjoying the feel of her hands sliding over my engorged penis too much to help her.

"Are you wearing the matching panties?" I ask with a puff of warm breath in her ear as I cup her tits, brushing my thumbs over her swollen nipples.

She moans out an affirmative.

Picturing the sheer thong revealing the bare lips of her pussy is enough to make my cock start drooling. Good thing I have clean boxers to change into later.

I pick her up and put her on the bed, so I can take her boots and socks off. Running my fingers down the center of her arches I revel in how she gives a whole body shiver at the stimulation.

"I want your tits in my mouth."

"Then hurry up and get us naked," she demands.

A predatory smile curves my lips. "There will be no rushing this."

"It's been two weeks, Atlas!"

"I am aware." If I didn't rub one off every morning in the shower, I would explode from sexual frustration.

It's a near thing regardless.

Yanking my clothes off, I watch her squirm on the bed, her fingertips sliding over the handcuffs and then away again. She wants to be bound. She loves it, but it makes her shy sometimes.

Lucia is it for me, whatever iteration she gives me of herself. The sexually confident siren or the demure angel. Both are her. And both are mine.

Once I am naked, my cock sticking out like a flag pole from my body, I tug Lucia's leggings down her legs one slow inch at a time.

"Come on, Atlas. I know the other has to take time, but not getting undressed."

For all her complaining, she doesn't take matters into her own hands. She trusts me to take care of her, even if she isn't saying so out loud.

Or maybe she is. She did say *yes*.

I leave her panties on so I can look my fill at how they cling to her puffy pussy lips because of how wet she is. "You are so beautiful, *eremenos mou*."

"So are you." Licking her lips, she stares at me with eyes glazed with lust.

This woman.

Kneeling on the bed, I grab the handcuffs. "Give me your wrists."

She offers them without a murmur, the scent of her arousal permeating the air around us.

I buckle one around her wrist and then the other, before attaching them with an eight inch leather cord. Positioning her in the center of the bed, I put a pillow under her head.

The crimson chain I attached to the headboard earlier this morning rattles when I pull it out from where I have it tucked behind the pillows.

Lucia's head jerks up at the sound and her eyes widen when she sees the chain. "You really want me to be brave."

"Maybe I need the reminder to show courage in our relationship." I've been giving her space, but that wasn't working.

I realized I wasn't initiating sex because I was afraid of Lucia's rejection. Fuck that. I don't give into fear. That's not the man I am.

So, I bought the handcuffs from a specialty shop that only sells by appointment. The leathersmith was willing to dye the natural cuffs crimson to match the silk blindfold I brought him. I painted the chain myself.

"What are you afraid of?" she asks, cutting straight to the heart of it.

"Your rejection."

"But I'm so easy for you."

"The past two weeks haven't felt easy," I let her know.

"No, they haven't." She smiles softly. "This is what we both want."

Pulling her cuffed hands above her head and attaching them to the chain, I say, "You know what this means."

"Deeper intimacy than meeting your brothers."

She remembers.

"Yes."

"I've never had anything in my butt. Not even a finger," she informs me.

I almost come right there. "You're a virgin."

"In that way, yes."

Fuck me.

She laughs. "I think it's going to be the other way around."

I said that out loud. I'm losing it. "Let me get the blindfold on you."

"Okay."

Her sweet acquiescence goes straight to my cock and I have to kiss her. She lets me sweep her mouth with my tongue, relearning the taste I've been missing for too long.

When I break the kiss, we're both panting and she's writhing on the bed, her legs splayed wide in invitation. My beautiful lover is so needy right now. Just the way I want her.

I trace her lips with my fingertip after I get the blindfold on her. "Can you see anything?"

"Muted light."

It's not a blackout blindfold, so that's to be expected. "Good."

I cup her breasts again, squeezing gently. "You're all mine to play with."

She arches up toward my hands. And I pinch her nipples in reward. I use everything I have learned about her body to bring her to the brink of orgasm before I rip her panties off, shove her thighs wide and feast on the pussy denied me for fourteen days.

Her scream of release is music to my ears, but I don't stop. Only this time, I cover my finger in lube and circle her asshole over and over. She undulates, clearly enjoying the stimulation of the nerve rich tissue. Some women don't like this.

I knew *eromenus mou* would. And she does. I suckle her clit as I press a fingertip inside her. She moans, canting her hips between my mouth and hand. Not trying to get away from either, but get more of both.

I finger fuck her with one digit until her passage is completely relaxed around my finger. Then I add another, pushing her closer to her second orgasm with my mouth. But she likes having her ass played with and it's not me compensating with the pleasure to her pussy to make up for discomfort in her ass.

She's enjoying both, her ass muscles milking my fingers like her pussy does when she comes. She's so tight. I scissor my thick digits, stretching her for what comes later. We have a ways to go before she'll be able to take my cock.

It takes another climax and a third finger before she's ready for me.

But it's only when she pleads, "Please, Atlas, I want you inside me. There. I need you," that I move up her body and kiss her again.

Forcing my tongue into her mouth so she can taste her own honey, I gorge on her sweetness. She moans and kisses me back, sucking on my tongue. Her earthy delight in our combined flavors turns my crank until I'm revving in the red zone.

I've got to take this slow, no matter how aroused she is, or how turned on I am.

Turning her over, I position a firm pillow under her hips. My mouth waters at the sight of her full, round ass on display, the lube glistening at her crack. I pull her ass cheeks apart and groan at the sight of her pretty stretched hole.

After slathering more lube on the steel monster between my legs, I press my weeping head against her sweet little pucker.

She goes still under me, but doesn't ask me to stop.

So, I don't. "Press out, *brava regazza*. It will make it easier for me to go in."

I'm so hard, there isn't going to be any trouble with me penetrating her backdoor, but I don't want to hurt her. She's going to feel nothing but pleasure giving this virgin hole to me.

She does what I say and my head pops inside. Her muscles clamp around me in a near painful grip. I press forward about a half an inch.

She groans.

"Too much?"

"Not enough. Give it to me, Atlas," she pants. "Make me yours."

"You're already mine," I growl, but surge forward because I can't not.

She gasps as I enter heaven. Are those angels singing? No, it's my woman's sweet little moans.

I pull back and she cries out.

Stilling, I force my raging body to wait until she's ready.

But she slams her ass toward me. "Do that again. It feels so good."

I get halfway inside her before I pull back this time.

A decadent moan of pleasure snakes out of her as I withdraw until only my head is inside her.

We do this over and over until I'm finally seated fully inside her tight virgin channel. No one else has ever felt her velvety heat around them like this and no one else ever will.

The thought unleashes the last of my restraint and I fuck *ílios mou* until she burns me as hot as the sun I call her. Reaching around to play with her clit, I rub circles and brush my finger side to side.

Her ass muscles grasp at my cock, revealing how much she enjoys this.

"Harder, Atlas, more!"

I give it to her, sliding in and out of her lubed tunnel, fucking her with all the power of my bigger body until she screams out her climax. Her ass milks me and drives me right over the edge until I'm coming deep inside her bowels, claiming her in the most primal way possible.

I wait for my breathing to regulate before pulling out slowly, relieved to see nothing but lubricant on my cock. No blood. I did not tear her. With the way she shouted for more, I didn't think it was likely I was hurting her, but I'm still satisfied to see the confirmation.

After I remove the blindfold and handcuffs, I pull her body into mine, surrounding her with my heat. Her hair is sticking to her forehead and temples with sweat, her breathing coming in shallow pants.

I rub her back in soothing circles until she nuzzles into me and says, "I need a shower."

"We both do." We shower together in her tiny stall.

We're going to have to move into the mansion until our house is built because we need a bathtub. Right now my sweet girl needs to soak and she can't.

Doing the next best thing, I bathe her with soapy hands. No wash cloth or loofah to abrade her delicate skin.

When I go to wash her backdoor, she balks. "What are you doing?"

"Washing you. What does it feel like?"

"Uh, that, but I can wash myself."

"You are mine to care for, *ílios mou*."

She relaxes her tightly clamped thighs. "Okay."

"That's becoming my new favorite word," I tease her.

Smiling, she washes what she can reach of my body with soapy hands. We cherish each other in the shower until the water cools.

I pull her out and gently dry her body before rubbing a towel vigorously over my own.

She wraps her arms around me and lays her forehead against my chest. "Thank you."

This woman. "The pleasure is mine."

"It was both our pleasure, but it was more than that."

"Yes, it was." And I'm glad she acknowledges that.

[illegible] nothing, she wanted more. She can reach orgasm [illegible] with [illegible] fingers.
We cleaned each other in the shower until the water [illegible].
I pulled her out and gently dry her body [illegible] and [illegible] on [illegible]
[illegible]
[illegible] in my arms [illegible] and [illegible] her [illegible] my [illegible]
[illegible]
[illegible] The pleasure is mine."
It was the first pleasure, but it was not the last.
[illegible] I'm glad she acknowledge [illegible]

CHAPTER 45

LUCIA

Atlas's phone rings in the bedroom and he ignores it as our souls connect in the silence between us, the steamy bathroom our refuge from the world.

The ringing stops, only to start all over again a few seconds later. Then my phone starts up.

I lift my head. "We should probably answer. I don't think they're going to stop calling otherwise."

His jaw taut, like he wants to say something, he nods and steps away.

I follow him into the bedroom. Atlas grabs his phone. "What?" he barks.

He listens, his body going rigid, an emotionless mask dropping on his face as he carries on a conversation in rapid fire Greek.

He hangs up and starts yanking on clothes. "Get dressed, we have to go."

Urgency laces his voice and I don't hesitate to tug on fresh underwear and then my legging. I don't bother with a bra but grab a t-shirt to pull over my bare breasts. Even with the sense of urgency surrounding us, my sensitized buds zing with pleasure at contact with the soft cotton.

I yank one of Atlas's hoodies on and zip it up halfway. It smells like him and helps the tension in my body ease. While I put on my socks and boots, Atlas slides his arm through his shoulder holster and adjusts the gun.

After grabbing a brush and a scrunchie, I swipe my phone from the table and grab my purse. "Ready."

"Is your pistol still in there?" Atlas takes my hand and pulls me after him.

"Yes."

"Good." Tugging me into the kitchen area, he grabs a gun and extra ammunition from the top of one of my cupboards.

When had he put that there? I don't ask.

Now is not the time to discuss his tendency to make himself at home in my apartment. The fact that he feels the need to grab the extra gun when he's already wearing one in a shoulder holster, says whatever is happening is serious.

He slips the extra ammo into his pocket and holds the gun up and ready. "Hold onto the back of my shirt. I need to know you're there."

With no thought to argue, I slide my hand under his jacket and grab his shirt.

He jogs out of the apartment and down the stairs. I stay with him the whole way. Helios, Theo, Bobby and Michael are all downstairs in the club when we get there.

"I'll get her to the mansion." Helios reaches out like he's going to take my arm. "You need to go hunting."

"I'll hunt down the walking dead men *after* I get her safe," Atlas snarls. "You, Bobby and Michael stay on our six. Theo, you're driving my SUV."

He hustles me outside and into the SUV's middle seat while the other men get into another SUV parked behind the club.

Atlas gets in beside me. "If I say down, you bend over and keep your head below the line of the window. If I say floor, you unbuckle and get on the floor, curled into as tight of a ball as you can."

"Okay." Childhood training comes back and I sit slanted sideways so my head is not a target.

"*Brava regazza*."

It's a totally inappropriate time to be getting wet, but my body reacts predictably when he calls me good girl again in Italian.

"What's going on?" I can finally ask since him giving me an answer will no longer slow us down.

"Zeus's informant contacted him. Two teams arrived yesterday, maybe earlier, from Russia. Their orders are to take me and Zeus out and to nab you."

"What do you mean nab me?" I brush my hair into a smooth, wet ponytail and hold it in place with the scrunchie. "Why?"

"Ivan."

Dropping the brush into my purse, I go hot and then cold, remembering what this Ivan wants to do with me.

Atlas calls his brother and puts him on speaker. "I'm heading to the mansion with Lucia."

"Do you think that's wise? One of the teams is targeting me and I'm here."

"They don't know we are aware of them. If it were me, I'd wait until you leave the estate. Easier to get to you. Our biggest point of vulnerability is when we arrive."

"There's no vantage point for a sniper. You made sure of that," Zeus says. "If they attack it will be at close range."

"It doesn't look like they had anyone on the club yet. We aren't being followed."

"Good. They got in yesterday. They may still be sourcing their weapons. Plenty of time for you to hunt."

Why does Atlas have to track these guys down? He's one of the targets, for goodness' sake.

Only I know. This is the way it is in the mafia. It's his job.

"I'm not going hunting until I know Lucia is in the saferoom where no one can get to her." It's the second time he's put that out there.

Warmth unfurls inside me. He's determined to keep me and the baby safe. After what he said in my apartment, I don't believe this is only because I'm pregnant either. I am his sun, the star around which his world turns.

His future.

"Of course not, brother. Your woman's safety comes first." There's a strange tone in Zeus's voice and I wonder what it means.

The SUV lurches to the right, goes up on a curb and back onto the street with a bone jolting thump. A rock hits the back window causing small cracks, but the window doesn't shatter.

Another rock hits and I realize they're not rocks. They are bullets.

"Down, Lucia," Atlas barks.

I tuck under the chest strap of the seatbelt and bend in half, my arms wrapped around my knees, my head resting sideways on them.

The car swerves right to left and then back again.

"We're taking fire," Atlas says to his brother, his voice filled with quiet rage.

"Orion and his team are heading your way."

Atlas climbs into the far backseat and I hear a soft whir, then the road noise gets louder. He's opened the back window somehow.

"Atlas, get away from the window," I yell, but I don't lift my head.

"Don't worry, Lucia, my X7 is designed for this."

For firefights? How dangerous is his life? Armored cars are not uncommon in our world, but SUVs tricked out to make shooting at pursuers possible? Not so much.

He shoots at whoever is pursuing us and then grunts. "One down, nine to go."

He starts whistling *Another One Bites the Dust* and despite the situation I smile.

"Are you whistling, boss?" Theo demands from the front.

Two more shots sound and then the cacophony of a crashing vehicle. The window whirs as it rises back into place and Atlas comes back over the seat.

He rubs my back. "You can sit up now, *ílios mou*."

I jerk upright and examine Atlas for any injuries. But there's nothing. "You're okay?" I ask.

"I am. Were you worried about me?" He sounds almost bemused. "No reason to be. I'm very good at what I do."

"Like gold medal good," Theo pipes up.

Great. The man I love is a gold medal killer. Better that than dead though.

And yes, I do love him. I knew before the whole protection money debacle, but have been trying to convince myself it was anything but love for the last week.

"I'm so glad for you. Everyone should have something they are good at," I say acerbically. "But don't scare me like that again. What if they had shot you through the open window?"

"Nah. The opening was too small and both of our vehicles were moving. Only a handful of shooters in the world could have made that shot."

"It's a good thing they weren't using armor piercing rounds," Theo adds. "The window would have shattered then."

I gasp.

Atlas barks something at Theo in Greek.

"Sorry," the other man says contritely. "I didn't mean to upset you, Lucia."

"Um, you didn't. I mean, if they had used armor piercing rounds, I would be more than upset. But Atlas is okay."

"You care," Atlas teases me.

I'm not reacting to that statement. At all. Of course I care. If I didn't, I wouldn't have been so devastated to learn he was using me.

In a blatant attempt to change the subject, I point out, "Your entire whistling repertoire is from a different century, or haven't you noticed that?"

"So? I like the songs. And they fit." He starts whistling "My Girl" again, but sings a single line, "I've got sunshine on a cloudy day," before he slips back into whistling.

I swipe at wet eyes. "Darn pregnancy hormones."

"If you say so."

I glare at Atlas. "I do."

"If you two are finished," Zeus says from the car speakers.

Oh, sheesh. We have been on speaker phone all this time.

"We need to check my SUV for trackers. Unless the bratva bastards are that good at tailing a car undetected, they found me with technology."

"I assume you didn't take time to check for a tracker before you left the club."

"No," Atlas bites out between gritted teeth. Oh, he's angry with himself for not doing it.

"They shouldn't have been able to act that quickly," Zeus says, like he's giving his brother an out.

"They might be sourcing a specialty weapon, but they obviously brought guns with them. No reason to assume they didn't bring everything else they needed for their op."

"I'll reach out to my informant."

"I thought he only contacted you, that you didn't have a way to contact him," Atlas says.

"Sh...they called me with this intel instead of texting me," Zeus says. "They didn't block their number like usual."

"Helios needs to scrub the traffic cams," Atlas says.

Zeus grunts an assent. "I'll put him on it as soon as you all get here."

"Helios is your hacker?" I guess these Greek mafia men wear multiple hats in their organization. "He's really good at managing a club."

Atlas scans the empty streets around us. "Helios has tech geniuses on his crew. They run the online gambling operation and money laundering from that angle."

"And cover your asses with traffic cams in their off hours?" I tease.

"Pretty much."

Zeus grunts and Atlas frowns. "I'm not hiding shit from her."

"You got brotherly disapproval of oversharing with me from that grunt?" I ask, impressed.

"More like *anax* disapproval," Zeus says.

"Are you worried I'm going to take my newfound knowledge to the FEDs? Really?" Zeus misses my epic eyeroll because...phone and not video call.

But Atlas sees it and winks at me.

I grin back at him.

"The thought crossed my mind."

"Well uncross it. Or whatever. I'm no rat."

"Good to know."

"Will you be very upset with me if I shoot your brother?" I smile sweetly up at Atlas.

"I knew that look meant nothing good."

"You're so astute."

"You cannot threaten to shoot me." Zeus sounds ticked.

"I just did, so it looks like I can."

"Lucia," he barks.

Ooh, the *anax* is angry. Atlas doesn't look worried, but Theo is gripping the steering wheel tighter than he was when trying to avoid the Russians chasing us.

I sigh. "Fine. I won't threaten to shoot you anymore."

"Thank you."

Theo jerks and gives me a wide-eyed look in the rearview mirror.

"You're welcome. Don't call me a rat and we're good."

Zeus sighs. "You should not threaten your *anax* regardless."

I shrug. The obedient mafia princess has been squeezed right out of my DNA.

"Lucky for you all, this happened on this street." Portland is a population dense metropolitan and not many areas are like this one with no foot or car traffic.

Even luckier, Portland decided against using the gunshot recognition system that was hotly debated for several months. Unless a security guard for one of the warehouses calls in suspicious sounds, the cops won't be the wiser.

No doubt by the time another car drives down the deserted street, Atlas's people will have removed all evidence of the gun battle and car accident.

"Not luck. Planning," Zeus says. "We located our compound where we did for a reason."

"Because it is surrounded by mostly industrial buildings, or no buildings at all." East of the city, it is closer to the seedy bar we first saw the bratva soldiers in than to my club.

"You have a very mafia centric mindset." Atlas puts one hand on my thigh, but the other holds his gun ready and his eyes are fixed on the world outside the SUV.

"I guess. It was fun living like a normal person for a few years though." When I wasn't stressing over making a success of the club and keeping Lenny where he's happy.

Or worrying about if someone from my past would walk into the club once it became so popular with out-of-towners.

Okay, normal might be overstating the case.

CHAPTER 46

LUCIA

We reach the mansion without further incident. Rolling right through the gates open to let us in, Theo brings the SUV to a lurching halt in front of the house.

Neither he, nor Atlas, open their doors though.

Theo is watching something behind us. Atlas is casing the area with laser focus. I wait in silence.

"It's shut." Theo must mean the gate.

Atlas nods. Takes another look around the house and then opens his door. "Let's go."

He steps out and then puts his hand out to me.

I slide across the seat to take it. By the time I get out of the SUV, Theo and the rest of the crew are there, creating a protective barrier around me.

"I thought Zeus said there are no sniper vantage points," I say as I'm ushered inside.

"There aren't," Zeus himself affirms.

Bobby shuts the door behind us. "But the boss won't take any chances with you."

This over-the-top protectiveness is for me. I shudder to imagine what he'll be like once our baby is born. I'm thinking helicopter dad with an automatic rifle.

"I'll take Lucia to the saferoom," Zeus says. "Timio has some intel for you, Dimios."

Executioner. That's what that means. I do a quick internal check, but the reminder that Atlas is an assassin doesn't impact my feelings for him at all.

"He can tell me on the way to the saferoom." Atlas is serious about seeing me there with his own eyes before he's willing to go hunting.

"You don't trust me to see to her safety?" Zeus asks.

"If I had no other choice, you are one of a few I would trust. But I do have a choice and I will not leave *ílios mou's* safety to anyone else."

Zeus nods. "Protect your sun well, brother. Our souls are darker than Hades' Lair."

Tears prick my eyes. These pregnancy hormones really are a bitch. But Zeus sounds resigned to an immutable truth. Like Atlas did when we first met.

Atlas takes me by the hand and leads me down the hall toward Zeus's office, but we stop halfway there and he slides a picture upward and puts his hand on a scanner pad. The once seamless wall slides outward and the next scanner is for his eye.

He then tugs me forward. "Try not to blink so it can scan your eye for access, *agape mou.*"

Once the heavy door swings outward, he pulls it wide enough for me to step through the opening. Inside, is a smaller version of his suite upstairs without the kitchenette, though there is a microwave and a minifridge.

Gina is sitting on the small couch watching something on her phone. She looks up with a smile. "You hanging out with me while they get whatever sorted?"

I nod.

"Theo will be staying too," Atlas says from the open doorway.

"No." The word comes out louder than I intend. "You need him with you. We'll be fine here on our own."

Atlas shakes his head. "I am gold level good at what I do, remember? I don't need Theo with me, but I do need to know you are safe so I can concentrate on doing my job."

I can't help noticing he's a lot more circumspect about what that job is in front of the housekeeper. It surprises me, but I don't comment on it. If the brothers and cousins don't tell her all the details of their business, I'm not going to point that out.

Zeus would prefer *I* didn't know the nitty gritty details either. Too bad for him.

If Atlas and I have any chance at a future, it will not be with him treating me like a mushroom. Keeping me in the dark and smothering me with shit to cover what's really happening.

Atlas turns to go.

"Atlas!"

He stops and faces me. "I will be fine, *agape mou*."

"I know." He has to be. There is no other option. "When Tino left that night to go into work, he didn't kiss me goodbye."

Atlas's eyes flare with emotion. "You want me to kiss you?"

"Yes."

"I thought she hated his guts." Orion says from the hallway.

The snarky brother has joined them. Good. I want as many people watching Atlas's back as possible.

Atlas ignores his brother and cups my face with both hands. "Remember to eat something."

I nod.

He kisses me, his lips soft at first, but the kiss quickly turns possessive. I mold my lips to his, parting them in invitation. His tongue delves into my mouth, claiming and arousing. Proof of his constant desire for me, even when the world is burning around us.

No one rushes the kiss. Not even Orion.

When Atlas finally lifts his head, his blue gaze is dark with desire. "Do not leave this room until I come for you."

"Okay."

His face shifts into an emotionless mask and he turns away. A predator's energy emanates from him and it turns me on way more than it should. No matter what I tell myself, I have always sensed the danger in him. The darkness.

And I am in love with it as much as everything else about him.

The way he treats me like I'm the only person in the building even when the club is filled with gorgeous women on the make. The way he listens to me and values my opinion. The way he makes love to me like I am the only woman he will ever want.

The way he takes charge in the bedroom to take care of me, not keep me under his thumb.

An apex predator, Atlas doesn't need to treat me like I am less than to make himself more.

"Be careful," I call as he leaves.

He nods without looking back. I know why. It's as hard for him to leave me as it is for me to let him go.

But Atlas has a job to do.

He has to go hunting to protect his family, me and the baby included.

ATLAS

"We are staying at the house..." He names a surprisingly populated area, but it is in the Dobro Pozhalovat community.

Hiding in plain sight, this property is not on the list the *pakhan* gave us. Does that mean he hid it from us deliberately, or doesn't know about it? Both are equally likely scenarios.

Its location explains Dimitri naming the neighborhood in Moscow during interrogation. While there are many Baltic immigrants living in the area, the name for the community is Russian. *Welcome*.

No way do the inhabitants want to welcome the Golubev Bratva.

Pricking slightly deeper into my *guests* ballsac, I ask, "House number?"

He shakes his head and I drag my knife slowly down, making a clean cut right between his testicles. His scream tells me he's close to giving me what I want.

It's a myth that soldiers can be trained to withstand torture indefinitely. If the man has a certain personality type, he will die an excruciating death before giving up information he isn't supposed to. If he doesn't, he will break. And I am not just a gold medal assassin; my torture techniques do not fail.

I wipe my bloody knife on his cheek. "House number."

The words are a whisper, but I hear them. Helios is there and he sends the address to one of his tech geniuses for confirmation.

It takes fifteen minutes, during which the prisoner sobs and begs for death.

"Satellite images and traffic cams close to the address confirm the arrival of sixteen men the day before yesterday. There is no sign of Ivan. My guy is tracking two four man teams through traffic cams now for approximate locations."

"What about the other four men?" I took out three of the four men trying to kill me earlier.

My current 411 connection to the bratva is the one still living picked up by the clean up crew.

"What was your directive?" I ask the now weeping man.

"To kill the Rokos brothers."

All three of us? "Why?"

I can guess, but I prefer to know.

"In...our...way..." he gasps out.

"The *pakhan* agreed to a truce." Not that any of us trusted him.

"We take our orders from Ivan."

Now, that is interesting. Bratva and mafia have one thing in common. The second-in-command does not issue orders counter to the boss's. That is treason, a capital offense, regardless of what syndicate you are in.

"Does the *pakhan* know that Ivan sent you here?"

"Ivan said...was gift."

Ah, so the *pakhan* doesn't know. He is still responsible because it's his job to control his men.

"You came here to kill me and my brothers?" I toss my knife and catch it right in front of the Russian man's face.

Will he confirm Zeus's source's intel?

"After you are all dead, we take the woman."

"What woman?" I press harder.

"Owns a club."

My woman. The mother of my child.

"I will bathe in the blood of you and your comrades." Making no effort to move, I slit his throat.

Arterial spray splatters my face and clothes, the warm droplets anchor me to the present and *my* directive. To kill every one of these motherfuckers.

Helios's guy tracks one team to an unpopulated spot outside the city where they have been for the last hour. Getting the specialty weapon that they ordered?

The other team is on a major street near the mansion and I smile. Lucia and Gina are safe in the panic room and the compound is equipped to handle any attack short of one from a rocket launcher.

The bastards are making this too easy for me.

Currently in the onsite interrogation room in the basement of our mansion, I am ready for them.

We prefer to keep things to the warehouse, but that's not always possible. When we set up the compound, we designed this room for easy disposal and mop-up.

Barking orders to my crew, I jog to the armory and get my sniper rifle with a suppressor. It won't block the sound of the shot entirely, but it will be enough to make it unlikely anyone outside our compound will hear it.

There are no vantage points outside of the compound property where a sniper can create a nest and wait to take one of us out. We purchased and demolished the only two buildings that might have worked, with the added advantage of preventing any nearby neighbors moving in.

However, the top level of the mansion has several sniper nests in place that cover all approaches to the compound. Once we confirm the team's approach, I will get in place to take them out.

I prefer up close and personal kills, but with twelve more men to dispose of before *ílios mou* is safe, I need to keep things fast and efficient.

~ ~ ~

The head of the last man on the kill team explodes inside their vehicle when Helios's guy tells us that the last team and the one in the industrial district are both on the move. Because I do not know the nature of the weapon, or weapons, they have procured, I need to take them out before they come to the compound.

A rocket launcher is unlikely but not out of the realm of possibility.

They are heading toward the same area of the city. It could be the compound, or some other rendezvous point.

If I play this right, I can intercept the team from the industrial area first. Since I was eleven years old and made my first kill, I have always played it right.

This time is no exception.

I take out the tires of the SUV they are driving in from my sniper position. Then I wait for it to crash into a nearby building and pick off the two men who get out. The driver is still at the wheel, either knocked out or dead from the collision. The man in the front passenger seat shows more self-preservation, diving to the back.

Bobby moves in on the SUV and takes him out with a head shot through the back window while Michael secures the driver. Alive then.

The cleanup crew arrives with a tow truck. They're trained as well as any Formula One pit crew and have the SUV up on the tow truck bed in less than three minutes. They take the prisoner. He'll be waiting for me at the warehouse when I'm ready to interrogate him later.

I want confirmation that Ivan instigated this attempt to take me and my brothers out and to kidnap Lucia, more intel on the Golubev bratva in Russian and information on Ivan's routines and whereabouts.

My crew and I move on to intercept the last kill team. They are driving through more populated areas and we have to wait to make our move. It soon becomes obvious the rendezvous point is supposed to be the compound.

It's almost anticlimactic how easy these assholes are making this for me.

Not that I mind this time. Not when Lucia's safety is at risk as long as the bratva soldiers are at large in the city.

I challenge myself to take them alive, and succeed with all but one. He jumps from the sedan, brandishing an automatic rifle and starts spraying automatic fire immediately. I take him out with a shot to the head before joining my team to surround the car.

One of the other bratva tries to be a hero, but I take him down with a shot to the shoulder and knee. He won't die before I get the information I want, but he'll wish he did.

Once the threat is neutralized, I want to get Lucia out of the panic room, but I don't. I need confirmation the four teams are the only Golubev bratva in the city before she comes out.

If I wait to get the other intel I want, there's a good chance the injured man will die before he can give up what he knows.

~ ~ ~

It's the early hours of the morning when I finish. Blood covers my face, arms and clothes.

"Good work, brother," Zeus says. "Go. Take a shower. Get your woman. She refused to leave the saferoom when I let Gina out because she'd promised you she would stay until you came back."

That's Lucia. She makes a promise and she keeps it.

"She's too good for me."

"You think? You're one of the best men I know. Loyal. Strong. Honest."

"I'm an assassin. I have killed more men than any serial killer on death row."

"War has casualties."

"She lost her first husband to a syndicate war." I hate acknowledging Lucia once belonged to another man.

"She won't lose you."

"I hid who I am from her. What we are. It hurt her."

"You didn't mean to."

"Does it matter?"

Zeus sighs. "I don't know. Intention doesn't prevent outcome."

"No." I wipe the blood from my hands, but don't attempt to clean it off anywhere else. "I didn't want her to know about Dimios. When I told her about being an assassin, I didn't plan on giving her details."

"Did something about today change that?"

"Not today. Just thinking about what she said. I'm not hiding anything else about who I am."

"Are you prepared for her rejection if she can't accept what it means for you to be Dimios?"

"No." She's mine. Now and always. "But she deserves to know what she is allowing into her life."

"You are not a thing, but a man."

"Sometimes, I don't feel human."

"We all lost part of our humanity when Grandfather refused to negotiate your return."

"Not when we made our first kills?"

"No. For you, the first time they tortured you, they took away a little bit of what makes you human. For me and Orion, the day Constantin snuck us into his father's office to show us the videos of you being beaten peeled away part of ours."

"Lucia deserves a man with his humanity intact." But I am the man she gets.

"Your sun deserves the man she wants. If that is you, you will only hurt her if you try to protect her from yourself."

"When did you get so wise about women?"

Zeus shakes his head. "Go. Talk to her, but take a shower and change your clothes. You look like an extra from a horror movie."

Maybe that's exactly what Lucia needs to see. Me as I am, not how I wish I could be for her.

CHAPTER 47

LUCIA

At the sound of the saferoom's door opening, I leap from the bed and rush into the outer room. The low-level light reveals Theo standing near the small sofa.

He nods toward the front door. "Boss. She's sleeping in the bedroom."

"I'm right here." And I haven't been sleeping.

Gina left the panic room hours ago when Zeus came and told her she could, but I promised Atlas I wouldn't until he came for me. So, I stayed.

"Uh, boss, do you want to go take a shower? I'll bring Lucia up to your suite."

Something dark is speckled over Atlas's face and arms. The scent of old copper permeates the air.

"Are you hurt?" I rush over to him and start patting his body, looking for wounds.

"The only men hurt are the ones who wanted to kill me and my brothers and kidnap you." The way he says *kidnap you*, that's the part he holds against them the most.

Because I matter to him.

Atlas cups my shoulders. "You don't look like you were sleeping."

"I wasn't."

"Why not?"

"I didn't know where you were."

"Didn't Theo tell you my mission was a success?"

I nod. "But no one would tell me where you were. I didn't know if you were hurt. Theo said you weren't but..." I shrug.

"You didn't know if you could believe him."

Theo puts his hand up like he's going to touch me. Atlas growls and Theo's hand drops. "I wouldn't lie to you, Lucia."

"You would if Atlas told you to, or one of his brothers."

Theo has the grace to look chagrined. He knows I'm right.

"I didn't tell him to lie."

"You didn't tell him to answer my questions either."

"I was torturing the men I did not kill for information." Atlas holds his body tight, his expression stoic.

He didn't take time to wash up before coming to get me. Because he couldn't wait to see me? Or because he wanted me to see him fully for who he is? He's not hiding anything from me anymore.

This is him as much as the sexy man in a black leather jacket and jeans, or the ruthless enforcer in his custom-tailored designer suit. And he wants me to see, wants me to accept him for who he truly is.

No more secrets. No more hiding behind half-truths.

"Yes, I see the blood of our enemies on you. It doesn't scare me." I lay my hand over his heart. "The only thing that scares me is that you don't love me."

"Uh, that's my cue to leave. Good luck there, boss." Theo grabs something off the back of the sofa and leaves the panic room.

Atlas is staring at me like he's trying to see into my head. "Not love you?" he demands. "What the fuck do you think I have been saying?"

"You say I'm yours. That you will never let me go, which is pretty arrogant, you know?" My hand fists in his shirt.

It's damp. More blood.

"I don't feel arrogant." His arm comes around me, pressing me flush with his big, muscular body.

"You said that our baby makes us a family. Would you have let me go if I wasn't pregnant?" I need to know.

"I told you I wasn't going anywhere before we found out you are pregnant."

True. "You know what you haven't said a single word about?" I frown up at him. "Loving me."

I am deeply, irrevocably in love with my Greek mafia assassin but don't know if he feels the same. Yes, he's over-the-top protective, but is it about ownership or love?

"What do you think I'm saying when I call you *agape mou*?"

"You said it can mean darling as well as my love."

"And I told you I'd never called any other woman *agape mou*. Like I've never called another woman my sun or my lover. You're it for me, my one chance at happiness."

Dio mio. The things he says.

"Are you saying you love me?" I need it spelled out. My heart needs the words, not endearments.

"With everything left of my fractured soul." The emotion in his eyes defies me to disbelieve him.

"There's this quote," I say softly. "We are all broken and that is how the light gets in. I think it's Hemingway. Anyway, if I'm your light then the only way I get into your soul is if it is a little broken."

Pain fills Atlas's expression. "It's more than a little broken. It's shattered."

"Is it? Knowing you love me has brought the pieces of my broken heart back together. What does knowing I love you do for your soul?"

"You love me?"

"What do you think I have been saying?" I use his words back on him.

"Say it."

"I love you, Atlas. Dimios. Enforcer. All of you."

He shakes his head. "No. You cannot love me. Not after what I did to you."

"Did you have sex with me to get information out of me?" That's the idea that hurt the most.

"No. When I saw you, I wanted you like I have never wanted anyone or anything. Making love to you that night wasn't smart, but I couldn't help myself."

His words soothe the rough edges of the raw wound inside me.

"I should have left your club alone. It's my job to protect you and I cost you your dream."

"Nuovi Inizi is not my dream." It never was.

"But your little house." He shakes his head like he can't stand to think of it.

"I hope whoever buys it has the carpet in the primary bedroom cleaned. We left a stain from our lovemaking," I tease.

"That person should be you."

"No. You can't live in that house with me. I can't live there pregnant with your baby. It's not safe."

"I've turned your life upside down."

"Yes, you have, but love has a way of doing that. Didn't you know?"

"No. I have never been in love before."

"But you are now." I need to hear it again. It seems so impossible that Atlas loves me as deeply and irrevocably as I do him.

"I love you my beautiful sun. More than life. More than my family. More than the *Ádis Adelfótita*."

"Blasphemy." I'm teasing. A little. Part of me is deadly serious. "Nothing can come before your syndicate."

"Nothing can come before you."

Tears wash into my eyes. "You mean that."

"Yes."

"You said you would leave Portland and your brothers to be with me."

"Yes."

"But they are your family."

"You are my everything."

"You say stuff like that and it feels like there's a vice in my chest squeezing my heart."

"Good. If I have hold of your heart, I have hold of you."

"You know me so well."

"And you know me."

Done arguing truths my heart and my mind agree on, I nod. His kiss reforms my broken heart to an organ that beats only for him.

When he lifts his head, he frowns, swiping at my cheek with his thumb. "You're crying. And I got blood on you."

"Emotions can be messy. And I don't care."

"I should have showered before coming to you."

"No," I disagree vehemently. "You wanted me to see you as you are, to hide nothing from me. And I do."

"Yes."

"I'm glad. I love *you* Atlas. All of you." I'll say it as often as he needs me to.

"You deserve someone better, but I will never let you go." He squeezes me tight.

"If you try, I'll hunt you down and make you sorry."

"Would you?"

"Oh yes."

"If anyone could find me, it would be you."

I smile. He sees my stubbornness and my intelligence. Neither intimidates him. Because his strength of will easily matches mine. So does his smart brain.

I like it.

"How do you feel about sex in the shower?" My body is craving the kind of orgasms only he can give me.

But even more, I crave the closeness physical intimacy brings.

He doesn't answer, but he swings me up into his arms and jogs out of the room. My body on fire for his touch, I kiss along his neck and the underside of his jaw. I don't care about the blood.

I want him any way I can get him.

Reaching the bathroom in his suite, he sets me on my feet and turns on the water in the large shower enclosure. Watching each other, we both strip out of our clothes.

We don't even wait to wash before he's kissing me again, his tongue deep in my mouth, his hands roving over my naked body with purpose.

Atlas knows how to touch me to have me writhing against him. I rip my mouth from his. "I need you, Atlas, now."

He lifts me under my arms and slams me back against the wall of the shower. Spreading my legs, I wrap them around his hips, inviting him inside. Still tender from before, my pucker twinges.

But the small pain adds to the pleasure.

Lifting me so the head of his erection is pressing against the opening of my body, he surges upward, filling me with one powerful thrust.

My vaginal walls stretch and sting a little, but it feels good and I want this too much to stop and prepare my body more.

It's like he knows though, and he slows down, pulling out one slow centimeter at a time before sliding back in just as slowly. I try to shove downward, but his hold on my bottom is like steel and I'm not moving anywhere he doesn't want me to.

His kiss turns languid as well and the inferno inside me burns brighter and hotter than ever before.

"I need more." My words are both a demand and a plea. "Be gentle another time. Not now. Now, I need you to remind my body of our connection."

"I can do that without plowing you into the wall."

"Plow me. Please."

His laugh is evil. He knows how turned on I am. His huge, rock hard penis tells me he is as aroused as me. But he doesn't increase his pace.

Hot water falls around us, steam filling the large glass enclosure as Atlas takes me on a hellishly slow ride to heaven.

"Touch yourself," he demands, his voice dark and commanding.

Without thought, my hand slides between our bodies and my middle finger slips across my engorged nub. I keen, my head going side to side.

"It's too much."

"No." That's all he says. No.

And I believe him. Because he's right. It's not too much. It isn't enough. I circle my clit with my fingertip and then press against it, sliding my finger side to side and my climax storms over me.

I'm not moving my hand anymore, but Atlas is causing it to jostle against my bundle of nerves with his now hard and deep thrusts. Aftershocks roll through me and I cry out, over and over, the pleasure never fully abating.

Throwing his head back, he shouts while the heat of his semen pulses inside me causing another onslaught of ecstasy to wash over me.

I'm crying when we finish and he licks my tears away. Then he washes my body meticulous inch by meticulous inch. After washing my hair, he puts conditioner in it and then starts washing his own body.

I help him, making sure every droplet of blood is wiped away.

"Turn around," I tell him. "Let me get your back."

After kissing me, he does and I wash his back and buttocks before sliding my tongue and lips over every scar that has made him into the man he is today.

"Ilios mou," he grinds out. *"S'agapo."*

Pretty sure that means I love you in Greek. So I say the words back to him. Over and over against his marked skin.

He bends forward, his hands on the opposite wall, holding him up. I lean against him, pressing my breasts against his back, wrapping my arms around his torso.

We stay like that in tender silence for long seconds before he tugs me around so he can rinse the conditioner from my hair. Afterward, he turns off the water and we step out of the steamy cubicle to dry each other off.

We're careful with each other, like it's our first time.

In a way it is. It is the first time we make love that we both know we *are* making love.

He knows all my secrets and I know his. I will hold them in my heart for the rest of our lives.

[illegible] pressing his head to [illegible] shower [illegible] I [illegible]

[illegible] after washing [illegible]

[illegible] when he reaches [illegible]

[illegible]

[illegible]

[illegible]

"[illegible]," [illegible] "[illegible]"

After [illegible] I wash his back [illegible]

[illegible] him into the [illegible]

"Tomorrow," the gryphon [illegible]

[illegible] back to [illegible] his [illegible] skin.

He [illegible] his hands on the [illegible] lifting him up. I [illegible] him, pressing my [illegible] against his [illegible], wrapping my arms around his [illegible].

[illegible]

[illegible]

He knows all my secrets and I know his. I will hold them in my heart for the rest of our lives.

CHAPTER 48

LUCIA

I finish training Helios to take over Nuovi Inizi, but there's a subtle shift in things now. Atlas always stays close, but now he touches me constantly.

While Helios, and every other man in the Hades Brotherhood, keeps their distance. And woe betide anyone clumsy enough to bump into me.

Bobby grabs my arm. "Where do you want these crates?"

Before I can answer, Atlas is in front of me and the thunk of flesh hitting muscle sounds.

Expelling a harsh breath, Bobby doubles over.

"Atlas, you psycho. He was just asking me a question." I rush to help Bobby stand but he backs away from me with his hands up. "I'm fine."

His face is red and he's still breathing shallowly, trying to control the pain.

"You're not fine," I contradict and turn to glare at my boyfriend. "What is your problem?"

"He knows not to touch you. They all do."

"What if I was going to walk in front of a bus? Would you prefer he let me do it instead of grabbing me to save me?"

"You will never do something so stupid." Atlas's glower is sulfuric.

I roll my eyes. "Okay, fine. Bad example, but you know what I mean."

"If it is a matter of your safety, exceptions can be made."

"How are they supposed to know that?" I indicate the men milling around the bar where the staff is preparing for the night ahead.

There are always at least two other members of the Hades Brotherhood hanging around, sometimes more. It's for my security because they are there even when the club is closed.

I know it's about me because they follow me when I leave too. I might as well be royalty or something with my own security detail.

Tino was never this possessive, or protective. But then Tino was nothing like Atlas on so many levels.

"I don't like you punishing Bobby for trying to get my attention."

If anything, Atlas's frown gets more ferocious and it's directed toward the member of his crew.

"It's all good, Lucia. I won't forget again, boss."

I spin to face Bobby. "Don't let him off the hook like that. He should apologize."

Bobby's face contorts like he swallowed a lemon and he backs away quickly. "Yeah, no. The apology wasn't my idea, boss."

"Ask Helios where he wants the crates. He's in charge now, not me," I call as Bobby disappears down the hall toward the office and the back door to the club.

Atlas's hands land on my shoulders. "Is that what you really want?"

This again. "I don't want to talk about the club. Atlas, you can't threaten your men for trying to get my attention. It's not Bobby's fault my mind was elsewhere."

"Where was it?" Atlas turns me to face him, but doesn't let me go.

My hands automatically settle against his chest and I revel in the strength of his muscles and warmth of his body.

"Helios doesn't need any further training."

A tick develops in Atlas's jaw. "So? You promised Zeus thirty days."

"I'm not going anywhere, Atlas. I already told you that."

"You gave up your house and even though you have enough money to buy it outright now, you haven't talked to Elaine about renewing your offer."

"How do you know that?"

"I asked her."

Sighing, I rub my hands over his pectoral muscles. "That's a little invasive, don't you think?"

"No. You are mine."

"You say that a lot." Every time we make love and sometimes when we don't. Like now.

"Because it is true."

"I don't deny it."

"Orion thinks you want to keep a nest egg to fall back on. Is that it? I can buy the club for you, but you'll never be without resources. I'll make sure of that."

"That's a very generous offer, but I don't *want* the club. Opening Nuovi Inizi was the best way I could think of to make enough money to care for Lenny long term, but I never wanted to own a nightclub."

"You spent five years building the business. You want me to believe none of that matters?"

"No, of course not." I lean against him, inhaling his scent. Leather, bergamot and spice, but underneath it all, Atlas. My man. "I'm proud of what I did here, but that doesn't mean I want to keep doing it."

"Why not?"

"Why do you think?" I challenge back. He says he loves me. Does he know me?

Atlas pulls me closer to his body and rubs my back. "You don't like crowds. You won't miss working the floor."

"True." But that's not all.

"Managing the talent takes a lot of patience."

"It does."

"You put up with shit I wouldn't."

"Which is why Helios is running the club and not you."

A laugh rumbles deep in Atlas's chest, vibrating under my hands. He's not offended.

"I'm better at killing than cajoling." The words are filled with humor, but they are laced with a question.

One I am happy to answer. Again.

Tilting my head back, I smile up at him so he can see the acceptance in my gaze. "Yes, you are. Lucky for all of us, or that situation with the bratva kill teams would have gone very differently."

His kiss comes as no surprise and I let myself fall into it for long minutes, but then my stomach growls.

He moves his mouth from mine. "You need to eat."

"For a top assassin, you have a real mother hen complex."

"Eat some lunch and I'll show you my cock tendencies."

"That was bad, Atlas." But I laugh. I love his humor, especially since he doesn't reveal it very often.

Lunch is leftover pasta from last night. Atlas makes a salad while it's heating and I set the table.

"So, you don't want me to buy back Nuovi Inizi?"

I make a sound like a kettle letting off steam. "Seriously? How many times do I have to say it? I'm glad not to have the responsibility anymore. If I could have supported Lenny with a job as a bookkeeper, I would have."

We finish getting the food on the table in a companionable silence. Atlas isn't mad and if he finally hears me about the club, I'm not either.

"Are you interested in doing the books for us?" Atlas sounds intrigued by the possibility.

"That's something I've been meaning to talk to you about." Only, I don't want to get caught up in business with California's Hades Brotherhood. "By us, do you mean the Greek mafia here in Portland?"

"My wife doesn't work for the *Ádis Adelfótita*. You are family with as much of a stake in our success here in Portland as me, my brothers and my cousins."

"I am not your wife," I remind him with some bite. "We haven't discussed marriage."

"We did."

I roll my eyes. "That was a threat, not a proposal."

"I'm working on it."

"What's to work on?"

"I'll explain tonight."

He's going to propose tonight? And he's telling me about it? But then I did ask. Sort of.

"Yes, I would be interested in taking over the accounts for you and your brothers. I know a lot about laundering money."

"I thought you didn't want to work for criminals."

"Not as your patsy, but as a part of the family? That's different. I am not morally opposed to cooking the books, but I am categorically opposed to taking the fall for the organization."

"I will never let that happen." He looks dangerously angry at the idea.

"I believe you." Which is why I'm so intrigued by the idea of becoming their bookkeeper. "Talk to your brothers about me taking over the books."

"Don't you want to wait until after the baby is born?"

"No. I'd rather get stuck in now and get things running smoothly so that after the baby comes, I can cut my hours if I need to."

"You've thought about this."

"I have."

"And you want to be part of both sides of our business?"

"I do." I have no intention of existing on the periphery of Atlas's life. "You promised me I would always have a voice in your world. I'll hold you to that."

"There is no voice I would rather listen to."

"Not even your Godfather of the Night?" I tease.

"Not even my brothers."

And he puts his brothers over the head of the Hades Brotherhood. Atlas's priority is family over organization. That settles into my heart and fortifies my foundation for trust in this man.

Easier to believe I come first when he's already shown that, but also because his brothers come before the Hades Brotherhood.

I could argue they are one and the same, but Atlas and I both know that isn't exactly true.

[illegible] going to propose tonight. And he's still on my shoulder. But then I [illegible]

Yes, I was little [illegible] taking over the [illegible] for you and [illegible] [illegible] I know that doesn't [illegible]

[illegible]

[illegible] part of the [illegible]. I [illegible] the [illegible] [illegible] talking to [illegible] the organization.

[illegible] that happen? [illegible]

[illegible] When [illegible] I [illegible] of becoming [illegible] "Talk to [illegible] about [illegible] the boss."

"Don't you want to [illegible] probably [illegible]"

No. [illegible] the person [illegible] [illegible] [illegible] comes. I [illegible] [illegible]

[illegible] thought. [illegible]

[illegible]

[illegible] of the [illegible]

[illegible]

"You [illegible] I [illegible]" I'll [illegible]

[illegible]

[illegible] your [illegible] [illegible]

"Not [illegible]"

And [illegible] over [illegible]

[illegible] [illegible] [illegible] [illegible]

[illegible] before the [illegible]

[illegible] but [illegible] knows [illegible] the [illegible]

CHAPTER 49

LUCIA

Atlas hands me my coat. "Put this on."

"Where are we going?" I'm used to his abrupt ways.

Sometimes I push back to prove I can. Right now, I'm curious. Is this when he takes me somewhere romantic to propose?

"To the compound." He never calls it home anymore. He's even referred to the mansion as his brothers' house.

So, not someplace romantic, or I guess it could be. It depends on what is waiting for me in his suite. Crimson handcuffs? "Okay. I wouldn't mind eating Gina's food again for dinner. She's a great cook."

"Not as good as you," Atlas replies loyally.

Only, I'm pretty sure he means it, even though Gina prepares his favorite Greek dishes. She's offered to teach me and I'm looking forward to taking her up on it.

"You like my food because you know I make it with love." That is something my mom used to say.

She probably still does.

Atlas stops on the way to the backdoor, turns and pulls me in for a hard kiss.

When we get to the mansion, after taking off our coats, we head straight for the dining room. However, it isn't food spread out on the table. It's design plans for a house.

"What's this?"

"Our house."

What is he talking about? We don't have a house. "Did you ask me to move in together and I don't remember it?"

"No. We *are* moving in together, but you get final say on the details of the house."

"You know it doesn't work like that. You can't just tell me I'm moving in with you. It's not like showing up with extra clothes in a duffle and never leaving."

"I am aware."

"So?"

"What do you think of the plans for our house?"

"Seriously? That's how you're going to play this?" Though why I'm surprised, I don't know.

Irresistibly drawn to the design plans, I study them. The house is a lot like the one I planned to buy, only bigger. A lot bigger. It's one floor with four bedrooms, a giant kitchen with a sunroom breakfast nook, and formal living and dining rooms. Unlike the house I planned to buy, this one has a large family room too.

"It has the big windows you like, but these ones will be insulated with automatic blinds installed between the panes of glass."

"Where is it going to be built?"

"We'll expand our security wall to cover one of the properties we own to the east of the compound. It will give us enough distance for privacy without compromising security." He frowns. "We can't have a tree in the front yard because it poses too much of a security risk."

Flabbergasted at all the plans, I nod. "Is that a Wolf and Miele range in the kitchen?"

"Yes. Elaine said it was on your wish list."

"But totally out of my budget. Or at least it was." Sometimes, I have to remind myself that I have the money from the sale of the club and it's all mine.

It's not as much as I had to start the club, but it's plenty to do the things I want. Atlas is right. I could buy a small house and pay cash and still have enough left over to live on for quite a while.

He cups my nape. "Not out of *our* budget though."

I adore the way he can't keep his hands off me.

"You talked to Elaine," I say as his words click in my brain. "About what kind of house I wanted."

"She worked with me and the architect to design something that fulfilled all your dream elements and your absolute musts."

"The sunroom breakfast nook," I say.

He nods.

"Is there an herb garden in the back yard?"

"There will be. We'll have landscapers come in and create the front and back yard you want to raise our family."

"*Raise our family*. You're talking marriage again, but I can't help noticing, there has been no proposal." I step back and glare up at him, my arms crossed over my chest. "You are not dictating we get married, Atlas Rokos. You are going to ask like a normal person."

"But we are not normal," he points out.

"I don't care. In this, we are as normal as they get. I'm not getting marched down the aisle under duress and speaking vows I don't mean like with so many mafia marriages."

"Is that how you ended up married to Tino?"

"No. But it happened to my cousin. I wanted to marry Tino, but that was before."

"Before what?"

"Before I knew you existed in the world."

His face reflects his shock. "That is not what I expected you to say."

"The love I feel for you is intense and consuming, so much bigger than the crush I had on my first husband."

Love is not the sweet, gentle emotion I thought it was when I married Tino. It is powerful and sometimes dark, sometimes overwhelming. And always protective. At least that's how mine and Atlas's love is and that's the only love that matters to me.

He pulls a dark blue ring box with gold lettering in Greek from his pocket. I suck in suddenly desperately needed air. Opening the box, he holds it out to me.

The diamond is blindingly large.

Blinking away emotion filled tears, I say, "They'll be able to see that rock from space."

"As long as the men on planet Earth can see it and pay attention to what it means, no one has to die."

Of course, he goes there. "Maybe dial that back a notch. I'm pretty sure you don't need to kill someone for hitting on me."

"Agree to disagree."

I shake my head, my gaze locked on that ring. "You're so possessive."

"You are just realizing that?"

"No, but that ring." I shake my head. "It's huge. We could buy a house for what it cost you."

I'm a mafia princess. I know what a diamond of that quality costs.

He shrugs, not denying my claim and I groan. "How wealthy is your family?"

No wonder he is able to offer to buy the club back for me.

"Rich enough, but I'll use my own money to provide our home."

Oh, I hit a nerve with that. I didn't mean to though.

I hug Atlas. Hard. "The house is beautiful, and I love that you talked to Elaine about what I wanted. How long will it take to build?"

"It will be finished in four months."

"That soon?"

"Money talks, among other things."

"Tell me you didn't threaten to kill anyone."

"I didn't threaten to kill anyone." His face gives nothing away.

"Really?"

"The contractor has family that works for the Hades Brotherhood in California." Atlas takes the ring from the box and holds it between his thumb and forefinger, the diamond glittering under the light from the dining room chandelier. "So, you'll marry me."

I step back and look up into his face. "That wasn't a question."

His blue eyes narrow. "The nonvoluntary trip to Vegas is still an option."

"No. It isn't. Ask me, Atlas. You already know I love you."

Heat flares in his gaze and then he kisses me breathless. He never ignores when I say I love him. He treats the words as a gift every single time.

When I'm boneless against him, he says, "Marry me, Lucia. Be the light in my darkness for the rest of our lives."

"Yes," I sigh against his lips. "And you didn't have to kiss me into submission to get a yes out of me. Of course, I want to spend the rest of my life with you."

"Even though it means being part of a mafia again?"

"A mafia that is as much family as business. A mafia where I have a voice and a place." I smile. "Yes. Besides, I don't think I ever really left the mafia behind."

"That's good to hear." There's a quality to his tone that has me stepping back.

I scan his features. "What did you do?"

"Elaine said you were sad about losing your grandmother's pasta press. You had to leave it behind when you ran from Detroit."

"Technically, I ran from the Revello family cabin, but yes."

"You never told me that story."

"You don't like me talking about being married before."

He grunts.

"What does my grandmother's pasta press have to do with that look on your face?" And then it hits me. "You contacted my family to get it for me, but how did you know it wasn't at my house when it got blown up?"

"I contacted your mother to ask for help getting one like it to replace the one that got blown up, only to learn that you'd never taken it from your childhood home."

"There was already a pasta press in the kitchen when I moved into the Revello home." And Agustino Sr. said I didn't need to use an old relic when I had a brand new pasta press at my disposal.

For as hidebound to tradition as he was, he placed very little value on items passed from one generation to the next.

"You talked to *mamma*." Dazed, I stare up at him. "Did you talk to my father too?" What about Rocco? Do they all hate me for letting them believe I'm dead?

"You said you didn't want to withhold our baby from your family."

Yes, I said that, one night while he held me after we made love.

"It should have been my choice about when to contact them." If ever.

"They're flying in tomorrow."

"What?"

He winces. "You don't need to screech."

"I'm not screeching, I'm exercising my need to punch you with my voice."

"I'd rather take the hit."

"I would rather you had let me contact my family in my own time."

"Our baby would be starting school by the time you worked up the nerve. You were scared to tell them you're alive. So, I told them for you."

"How did that go for you?" I demand, but I really want to know. "Is my mother furious with me?"

"No. Both your parents are happy and relieved you are alive and your brother is too, though he's not as expressive about his emotions."

Pieces start to fall into place in the puzzle that is this man. "If they hadn't been happy, if they had been angry with me, would they be flying in tomorrow?"

"No."

Suddenly him going behind my back to contact my family makes sense. "You were protecting me."

He's trying to say it was about getting my pasta press, but it's really about him making sure no one hurts me. In any way. Not even my family.

"Would you have ever told me about it if they were angry with me?" I ask.

"Eventually, after I got them to see their error in being angry with you for being the amazing person you are."

The tears from earlier come back and this time I cannot blink them away. This man.

"I love you, Atlas."

"I love you, *ílios mou*."

"I know." There's no way to doubt him when he keeps showing me over and over again how important I am to him and how much he cares about my happiness.

EPILOGUE

Dímios in Russia

ATLAS

Ivan pulls an obviously drunk, or high, young woman into his penthouse apartment with him. It's her lucky night. She won't end up the recipient of his vicious bedroom games.

Dead men can't strangle women at the point of climax.

He doesn't notice me in the shadows near the window. Why would he? His attention is on the woman he is mauling. She's trying to push him away with uncoordinated movements.

Probably roofied.

The alarm starts to beep more insistently and he shoves her down on the couch before turning to disarm it. The woman throws her hand over her mouth and makes retching noises.

Ivan curses in Russian. "If you vomit on my furniture, you'll clean up your mess with your mouth."

Looking around wildly, she lurches to her feet.

"Find the toilet or pay the consequence." Ivan's voice is filled with anticipation.

He's played this game before. The thought of Lucia on the receiving end of his sadism makes rage erupt inside me.

The woman runs down the hall, the sound of her heels clicking on the marble floor joined by the splatter of vomit. She had no nope of finding the toilet before being sick and Ivan knew it.

What he doesn't know is that he's about to die.

Slipping up behind him on silent feet, I maneuver the garrot around him with quick movements. His laughter cuts off and turns into a gurgle as I pull the razor-sharp wire tight with the leather tethers.

A hard kick to the back of his knees sends him crashing downward. He tries to get his fingers between the wire and his neck, but it cuts right through skin and cartilage at the joints. He rears back, but has no leverage and I make sure he doesn't get his feet under him again.

All the while pulling that wire through his neck.

Blood sprays when his carotid artery is cut and seconds later, he goes limp. A few seconds after that, the blood stops pumping out of him.

He's dead and can't ever hurt another woman again. Lucia is safe. From him.

And I will continue to keep her safe from anyone and anything.

A woman's moans reminds me I'm not alone with the dead man. Not that my lizard brain ever forgot.

Dropping the body to the floor, I leave my garrot where it is, the leather tethers dangling down the back of Ivan's suit jacket. I sign my work into his cheek with the tip of my knife. δ for Dimios.

His Golubev brothers will know their *palach* killed the *vtoroy*.

Jumping lightly to my feet, I go in search of the woman Ivan was tormenting. She's sitting against the wall, tears streaming down her face.

When she looks up and sees me, she doesn't even flinch. She's too wasted.

"You are not safe here," I tell her in Russian.

She wipes at her face with the back of her hand. "I know."

In the past, I would have gotten her out of the apartment and left her to figure out what came next. But Lucia's face keeps superimposing itself over the younger woman's. I cannot leave this innocent for the bratva to punish for the justice I doled out.

"You need to leave St. Petersberg."

"I have nowhere to go."

Not good. Killing the *vtoroy* is sanctioned but that doesn't mean the *pakhan* won't look for someone to make an example of.

"What about your family?"

"I have none."

"Friends."

"If they could protect me from him and his brothers I would not be here." Her words are slurred, but their meaning is sound.

Maybe throwing up got some of whatever Ivan gave her out of her system.

"How do you feel about America?"

"It's not here."

"Does that mean you want to go?" She can fly back on the jet with me.

Getting her papers and a new identity will be child's play for Orion. With the large Baltic community in Portland, it's a good place for her to disappear.

"Yes."

Lucia will say that I should wait for the young woman to sober up so she can make an informed decision. I don't have time.

I text my brother.

Atlas: *I have a job for you. Be waiting at the tarmac when the jet lands.*

Taking time to clean the apartment of trace DNA from the woman, I leave her where she is until the last. Then I clean up around her and we go.

"Do you have things you need from your home?" I ask.

"Aren't you afraid of the bratva coming for you if we stay in the city?"

"No."

Ivan's attempt to have me and my brothers killed was a violation of the truce between us. Because my uncle was also a party to that truce, it was considered an act of war against the entire *Ádis Adelfótita*.

Dimitri is now enjoying my uncle's hospitality. The *pakhan* wants his son back and he does not want full out conflict with my uncle.

He offered Ivan's head as a peace offering. My uncle told him I planned to take it anyway and if the *pakhan* didn't want me to keep killing after the *vtoroy's* death, he had better offer something else to guarantee peace.

Whatever he offered satisfied the *Nonós tis Nýchtas* and my uncle told me to leave Russia after killing Ivan.

In the past, I might have argued, but I need to get back to my fiancée.

Such a beautiful word, but I like wife even better.

Getting her in touch with her mother should have waited though. The older woman immediately contacted my own mother and they are insisting on a huge Italian-Greek wedding with traditions from both sides being honored.

Lucia told them they have two months to plan the wedding. She refuses to waddle down the aisle heavily pregnant. Her words, not mine.

Determined mothers, with the force of two powerful syndicates behind them, could probably plan Armageddon in sixty days. The ostentatious Christmas wedding they have dreamed up is a piece of cake for them.

The woman packs quickly and efficiently and we are flying back to the U.S. before Ivan's cooling body is even found.

LUCIA

I wake up from a restless sleep to see Atlas undressing in the dim light spilling from the open bathroom doorway.

With each piece of clothing he drops to the floor, more of the assassin melts away to be replaced by the man that only I see when we are alone. Even around his brothers, there is something of Dímios in him.

It's why they hadn't heard him whistle since childhood.

He's whistling softly now. That must be what woke me. Or my body is so attuned to his presence that it pulled me out of sleep.

I sit up and smile at him. "When are you going to expand your repertoire to something from this century?"

The soft notes of "My Girl" accompany him across the room until he sings the last line in his panty melting baritone. Since I'm not wearing panties, my thighs get slick with my juices.

He puts one knee onto the bed. "Tell me what song you want me to whistle, and I'll learn it for you."

"I have something better for you to do with your mouth." I pull him down to me.

Delight shimmers to the depth of my soul as he blankets me with his heavy, muscled body and shows me he knows exactly what I'm talking about.

THE END

GREEK & ITALIAN GLOSSARY

GREEK

Ádis Adelfótita - Hades Brotherhood

anax - head (of the family)

dímios – executioner

(Atlas is called Dímios as a nickname by his mafia.)

eidikós - specialist (above foot soldier)

eromenis mou - my lover

gamó - fuck

ílios mou - my sun

kai - second in command

kalós sýntrofos - goodfellas (foot soldiers)

Nonós tis Nýchtas - Godfather of the Night

Hades Brotherhood Motto: *Dóste tous típota, allá párte tous ta pánta.* Give them nothing, but take from them everything.

Nemesis: Greek goddess of vengeance

ITALIAN

brava regazza – good girl

caspita – polite way to say holy shit

Che cosa? – What?

Dio mio- my god

Ho bisogno di te. – I need you.
Ho bisogno del tuo cazzo. – I need your cock.
per favore - please
porca miseria - damn it

ACKNOWLEDGEMENTS

I am grateful to the people who have helped this book become what it is. My husband, Tom, who not only supports me during the writing, but who reads the finished book and lets me see the story through a reader's eyes. Andie, my editor at Beyond the Proof. Her insights made Ruthless Enforcer more emotional and a stronger story. Two very special ARC readers who take the time to proofread after the copyedits are done before writing their reviews, Dee Dee & Haley. Any remaining typos or errors are my fault and mine alone. Thank you all! You are the very best!

ABOUT LUCY MONROE

With more than 10 million copies of her books in print worldwide, award winning and internationally bestselling author, Lucy Monroe, has published over 85 books and had her stories translated for sale all over the world. While her latest series is mafia romance, written as an indie author, all of Lucy's books are passionate, deeply emotional and adhere to the concept that love wins. Even if that victory isn't an easy one.

Want to talk about the characters, read snippets of Lucy's WIPs before anyone else, and chat with other readers who love Lucy's books? Join her FB Reader Group, Lucy Monroe's Book Nook.

Want to read more about Atlas and Lucia? Read their bonus scenes and be kept up to date on Lucy's books by signing up for her newsletter at https://www.lucymonroe.com/newsletter

FOLLOW LUCY ON SOCIAL MEDIA

BookBub: Lucy Monroe

goodreads: Lucy Monroe

Facebook: LucyMonroe.Romance

TikTok: lucymonroeauthor

Instagram: lucymonroeromance

Pinterest: lucymonroebooks

YouTube: @LucyMonroeBooks

Threads: lucymonroeromance

ALSO BY LUCY MONROE

Syndicate Rules

CONVENIENT MAFIA WIFE
URGENT VOWS
DEMANDING MOB BOSS
RUTHLESS ENFORCER

Mercenaries & Spies

READY, WILLING & AND ABLE

SATISFACTION GUARANTEED
DEAL WITH THIS
THE SPY WHO WANTS ME
WATCH OVER ME
CLOSE QUARTERS
HEAT SEEKER

CHANGE THE GAME
WIN THE GAME

Passionate Billionaires & Royalty

THE MAHARAJAH'S BILLIONAIRE HEIR
BLACKMAILED BY THE BILLIONAIRE
HER OFF LIMITS PRINCE
CINDERELLA'S JILTED BILLIONAIRE

HER GREEK BILLIONAIRE

THE REAL DEAL
WILD HEAT (Connected to Hot Alaska Nights - Not a Billionaire)
HOT ALASKA NIGHTS
3 Brides for 3 Bad Boys Trilogy
RAND, COLTON & CARTER

Harlequin Presents

THE GREEK TYCOON'S ULTIMATUM
THE ITALIAN'S SUITABLE WIFE
THE BILLIONAIRE'S PREGNANT MISTRESS
THE SHEIKH'S BARTERED BRIDE
THE GREEK'S INNOCENT VIRGIN
BLACKMAILED INTO MARRIAGE
THE GREEK'S CHRISTMAS BABY
WEDDING VOW OF REVENGE
THE PRINCE'S VIRGIN WIFE
HIS ROYAL LOVE-CHILD
THE SCORSOLINI MARRIAGE BARGAIN
THE PLAYBOY'S SEDUCTION
PREGNANCY OF PASSION
THE SICILIAN'S MARRIAGE ARRANGEMENT
BOUGHT: THE GREEK'S BRIDE
TAKEN: THE SPANIARD'S VIRGIN
HOT DESERT NIGHTS
THE RANCHER'S RULES
FORBIDDEN: THE BILLIONAIRE'S VIRGIN PRINCESS
HOUSEKEEPER TO THE MILLIONAIRE
HIRED: THE SHEIKH'S SECRETARY MISTRESS
VALENTINO'S LOVE-CHILD
THE LATIN LOVER 2-IN-1 HARLEQUIN PRESENTS

(WITH THE GREEK TYCOON'S INHERITED BRIDE)
THE SHY BRIDE
THE GREEK'S PREGNANT LOVER
FOR DUTY'S SAKE
HEART OF A DESERT WARRIOR
NOT JUST THE GREEK'S WIFE
SCORSOLINI BABY SCANDAL
ONE NIGHT HEIR
PRINCE OF SECRETS
MILLION DOLLAR CHRISTMAS PROPOSAL
SHEIKH'S SCANDAL
AN HEIRESS FOR HIS EMPIRE
A VIRGIN FOR HIS PRIZE
2017 CHRISTMAS CODA: The Greek Tycoons
KOSTA'S CONVENIENT BRIDE
THE SPANIARD'S PLEASURABLE VENGEANCE
AFTER THE BILLIONAIRE'S WEDDING VOWS
QUEEN BY ROYAL APPOINTMENT
HIS MAJESTY'S HIDDEN HEIR
THE COST OF THEIR ROYAL FLING

Anthologies & Novellas

SILVER BELLA
DELICIOUS: Moon Magnetism
by Lori Foster, et. al.
HE'S THE ONE: Seducing Tabby
by Linda Lael Miller, et. al.
THE POWER OF LOVE: No Angel
by Lori Foster, et. al.
BODYGUARDS IN BED:
Who's Been Sleeping in my Brother's Bed?
by Lucy Monroe et. al.

Historical Romance

ANNABELLE'S COURTSHIP
The Langley Family Trilogy
TOUCH ME, TEMPT ME & TAKE ME
MASQUERADE IN EGYPT

Paranormal Romance

Children of the Moon Novels
MOON AWAKENING
MOON CRAVING
MOON BURNING
DRAGON'S MOON
ENTHRALLED anthology: Ecstasy Under the Moon
WARRIOR'S MOON
VIKING'S MOON
DESERT MOON
HIGHLANDER'S MOON

Montana Wolves
COME MOONRISE
MONTANA MOON

Made in the USA
Monee, IL
21 November 2024

70770546R00233